LIFE IN THE OLD GIRLS YET

CELIA ANDERSON

Boldwood

First published in Great Britain in 2026 by Boldwood Books Ltd.

Copyright © Celia Anderson, 2026

Cover Design by Rachel Lawston

Cover Illustrations: Rachel Lawston

A CIP catalogue record for this book is available from the British Library.

Paperback ISBN 978-1-83617-165-2

Large Print ISBN 978-1-83617-166-9

Hardback ISBN 978-1-83617-164-5

Trade Paperback ISBN 978-1-80656-181-0

Ebook ISBN 978-1-83617-167-6

Kindle ISBN 978-1-83617-168-3

Audio CD ISBN 978-1-83617-159-1

MP3 CD ISBN 978-1-83617-160-7

Digital audio download ISBN 978-1-83617-162-1

This book is printed on certified sustainable paper. Boldwood Books is dedicated to putting sustainability at the heart of our business. For more information please visit https://www.boldwoodbooks.com/about-us/sustainability/

Boldwood Books Ltd, 23 Bowerdean Street, London, SW6 3TN

www.boldwoodbooks.com

For Jane and Tony Theakston, with grateful thanks and very much love

'Pray you now, forget and forgive.'

— WILLIAM SHAKESPEARE, *KING LEAR*

1

'Did you hear the latest? Venetia Prescott's coming back to Willowbrook after all this time. Who'd have thought we'd see any of that family again? Not me, that's for sure.'

Neither of Beryl's companions replied to her remark. Anthea was staring out of the taxi window, sucking on a humbug and wondering if her cleaner would have thought to put the heating on to welcome her back from her jaunt, and Winnie had dug out a bag of knitting and was frantically clicking away to finish a jumper for her smallest grandson's birthday. Beryl tried again.

'You *do* both remember her, don't you? Venetia Prescott? The kid from the family that lived next door to me? Called herself Vee. Skinny little thing with those big brown eyes and all that curly hair. An innocent kind of smile, like butter wouldn't melt in her mouth. Huh!'

The other two were looking more interested now. 'The Prescotts left in a bit of a hurry, didn't they? I never knew what really went on before they disappeared, did you?' said Winnie. 'Vee's dad was called Ivan.'

'Huh,' said Beryl.

'What's that supposed to mean?'

'Nothing, ignore me.'

'I always find that's the best option when you're being mysterious. You'll tell us what's on your mind eventually. Anyway, as I was saying, Ivan was a mate of my bloke. They used to play darts together at the pub. I heard he died a good few years back. I wonder if her mum Tallulah's still going strong? She was something of a firecracker back in the day, wasn't she? A real looker too. We were the only two exotic girls in the village, so we always stuck together.'

'Exotic? Oh, I get what you're saying. I thought you meant *erotic*,' said Anthea. 'Although...'

'Less of your cheek. You knew very well what I meant. Tallulah had a Spanish mother and an Italian father. I think it was that way round. I can't remember the exact details but they gave her some stunning looks. I wonder what happened to make them all do a flit like that? It was the talk of the village for a while.'

No comment came from Beryl. Winnie turned to stare at her. 'You know something about this, don't you, you minx? Come on, spill the beans. I suppose you were bound to hear all the gossip, living next door.'

Beryl shook her head. Her expression was bordering on smug, and Anthea was finally rattled enough to join in the conversation.

'That's typical of you, Beryl,' she said. 'Leading us on and then refusing to come up with the goods. Where's the fun in keeping shtum after so many years? Why are you hogging the secrets? And more to the point, what are they?'

The taxi turned left and made its way around the edge of the village green towards Beryl's terraced cottage and the driver pulled up outside. 'First of your three stops, ladies,' he said, over his shoulder. 'Whose house is this?'

'It's mine. My suitcase is the bright red one with the sparkly ribbon tied to it,' said Beryl. 'And the matching rucksack too, please. You take a leaf out of my book and try smartening up your luggage, Winnie. You've had that battered brown case for years.'

'Don't try and distract me. We'll talk about your new neighbour tomorrow when we have our film night at yours. Who's cooking? I'm guessing it's me again. Jerk chicken?' said Winnie.

The other two nodded enthusiastically and their driver got out to open the boot of the car. The three ladies surveyed the row of cottages. They were right outside Beryl's home, number five, which had a glossy scarlet door that was even brighter than Beryl's luggage. The lavish hanging basket that hung on a hook beside it had survived the heat of the summer thanks to regular watering and now, in early September, it was still sporting a flourishing ivy and some geraniums that matched the door.

To the left stood number six with its frontage painted a tasteful gunmetal grey, but the eyes of the group rested on the house on the other side of Beryl's. Number four Fiddler's Row was not living up to the standard of its neighbours. Faded green paint peeled from the door, and instead of the pristine white double glazing of Beryl's home, its window and door frames looked distinctly shabby. Weeds grew around the front step and through smeared panes of glass, elderly curtains could be seen sagging sadly. A wooden dragonfly with a broken wing hung lopsidedly from a nail underneath the tarnished number four and below them, the sign with the name of the house was almost too faded for the letters to be seen.

'Dragonfly Cottage,' read Anthea, with difficulty. 'What a shambles. It must be driving you bonkers, darling, seeing that mess every day when your place and Kate's the other side are so nice and neat.'

Beryl nodded, her grey curls trembling in her agitation. 'It really is beyond a joke now. There's been a whole stream of tenants in there ever since the Prescotts left and the place has just got worse and worse with each lot. Venetia's going to have her work cut out to get it back into a decent state. I've heard on the grapevine that it belongs to her now because your old pal Tallulah died a few months ago, Winnie. I thought I'd told you?'

'No, you definitely didn't mention it. I'd have remembered. At least, I think I would. We're all going a bit doolally these days when it comes to that kind of thing.'

'You speak for yourself,' said Anthea. 'Nothing doolally about me, thank you very much. I'm just as sharp as I ever was.'

Beryl shrugged. 'Must've slipped my mind. Oh, I think our driver's getting impatient, I'd better go. I'll chip in with my share for the taxi when you come round tomorrow evening, okay?'

Anthea and Winnie waved to Beryl, who had flatly refused any help getting her belongings inside. As the taxi moved away, she hefted her rucksack onto one shoulder and wheeled her case into the house, feeling the silence and slightly musty air close around her like a dark cloud. Beryl didn't usually mind living alone but after spending five action-packed days in the Majorcan sunshine with her two sidekicks, it was hard to come back down to earth. Her only sister had long-since settled far away from the sleepy village of Willowbrook, in Australia – how far away did she and her man need to get, for goodness' sake? Only Beryl's niece Sophie was still relatively handy, although the girl travelled around so much, it wasn't possible to see Sophie as much as her fond aunt would have liked.

Beryl's beloved husband had died some years ago and as for her only son... her mind shied away from the thought of Patrick.

She gave herself a little shake and thanked goodness for village life. Many of the locals and in particular Winnie and Anthea were Beryl's main source of entertainment and affection. The three of them were affectionately known in the village as the Saga Louts due to their penchant for a certain type of holiday and their shared love of Prosecco. Having good neighbours was very important to Beryl. The series of less than satisfactory tenants next door had been a thorn in her side for a very long time.

'Times are changing, and it's a good job too,' Beryl said to herself, as she filled the kettle for her first cup of tea. The weedy brews they'd been drinking on their mini-break weren't a patch on the real stuff. It was good to be home. She carried on with her monologue as she pottered around the kitchen. 'Young Venetia... who actually isn't young any more of course, she must be in her mid-fifties by now... she's bound to be a better option than the last crew who burnt a mattress in the garden and smoked those funny cigarettes day and night.'

Opening the fridge to find the carton of long-life milk she'd put in there to chill before setting off on her travels, Beryl decided a trip to the corner shop was in order. She'd need a few bits and bobs to tide her over before she asked Anthea to drive her to the big supermarket in Meadowthorpe. She shuddered when she remembered the last trip there, when Anthea had taken it into her head to go the wrong way round a mini roundabout at the entrance to the car park. The resulting chaos had quite put Beryl off the tea and cake she always treated Anthea to in the café afterwards. Maybe she'd start buying more of her shopping from Maryam and Rashid on the corner of Fiddler's Row. The extra cost would be a better option than being on tenterhooks for the entire journey there and back with her friend who still thought she had the driving skills of a souped-up Jeremy Clarkson.

Two mugs of tea later, Beryl was bustling down the road to the shop, an ancient wicker basket over one arm and her handbag over the other, in the style of the late queen. She hummed to herself as she walked, belatedly realising that the song was 'Agadoo', a tune which had been in her head ever since the balmy evening at the beach bar when she'd reminded Winnie, Anthea and all the other customers how to push a pineapple and shake a tree. Her hula-hula dance had been the envy of them all, she could tell. Youngsters these days had no idea how to party. That had been an excellent night but on the whole, it was good to be back home.

The shop bell clanged as she entered and the smiling lady behind the counter greeted her warmly. Yes, Willowbrook was the best place in the world to live, that was certain, Beryl reflected.

'Hello, Maryam,' Beryl said. 'I'm just going to grab a few essentials, the cupboard's bare after my holiday.'

'Oh, yes, I remembered you'd be home today. How was the trip? Did you dance until you dropped? I've heard hair-raising tales about what you ladies get up to when you go off on your travels.'

Beryl laughed. 'We did indeed, and I loved every minute but coming home to an empty fridge is always a bit depressing. I was wondering, do you think your lovely Rashid will deliver my shopping if I decide to place a bigger order from now on? I'd like to give you locals some extra business if I can.'

This was true enough, even if it was Anthea's driving that had nudged Beryl into making the change. The corner shop was well-stocked, and coming along the road for a good old natter was always a treat.

'Of course he will,' said Maryam. 'You can phone your list in if you like.'

'Even better, I can email it. I'm right up to date with the computer lark now, you know. Mind you, that won't stop me popping in every few days to check on new deliveries of the fresh stuff. I'd miss our chats if I didn't keep an eye on the shop. Nice sari, by the way,' Beryl said, looking the other woman up and down admiringly.

'A present from Rashid's sister,' said Maryam. 'Hot pink isn't really my colour, it's more a shade you or your glamorous friend Winnie could carry off, but I thought I'd branch out with something different, so as not to offend her. Any news?'

Beryl prided herself on keeping everyone up to date with local gossip, so she relayed her information about the return of Venetia Prescott. 'Of course, you won't know the family, being fairly new to Willowbrook, so it's as well to be aware of what's happening. She'll be living in what was her mother's house next door to me, so you'll probably see quite a lot of her.'

'That sad old place?' said Maryam, putting a hand to her mouth. 'The poor woman. She'll surely not move there in the state it's in, will she? Those last tenants weren't welcome at this shop. They ran up a bill before I could warn Rashid not to give them credit. He's too kind-hearted, that man of mine, and they fooled him with a proper sob story.'

'I know they did. Let's hope Venetia is a breath of fresh air,' said Beryl.

'You must remember her well. You've lived in the village for so many years, haven't you?'

'Yes, we've definitely got history. Ah, well, nice to see you, dear. I'm going to have a quick whizz round the shop to pick up some bits and bobs. I'll be sure to tell Venetia when I see her what a great little place you have here.'

Beryl's thoughts were troubled as, ten minutes later, she paid for her small basket of shopping and made her way back home. It was one thing talking about her prospective new neighbour but quite another preparing to actually meet her in the flesh after all this time. She only hoped that when Venetia Prescott finally decided to grace Fiddler's Row, they could somehow put the past behind them. Although she'd pretended to be keen to keep her own counsel earlier, Beryl had been longing to tell Winnie and Anthea what she was pretty sure really went on all those years ago. It wouldn't do to blab though. Some secrets were best kept under wraps. Definitely for now and possibly... forever.

2

Beryl would have been irritated to learn that she'd missed the start of the next part of the ongoing saga of Dragonfly Cottage because Venetia Prescott had arrived at number four Fiddler's Row a whole hour earlier and was now sitting cross-legged on the living room floor, wondering what the hell she was doing here.

If Beryl's house had felt musty on this rather chilly September afternoon, it was nothing to the damp, cloying atmosphere that hung around this cottage. There was a smell of stale cigarette smoke and something less tangible but equally nauseous that caught at Vee's throat and made her feel even gloomier than she had when she left her previous home. It was the scent of despair, she decided, glancing round at the few pieces of battered furniture and heaps of empty beer cans and wine bottles that had been left behind when the final tenants departed.

> I must be crazy to be thinking of living here, Cass. The last people must have been dancing and singing as they left, it looks as if they had the party of a lifetime before they went.

Vee had promised to update her younger sister Cassie about the house as soon as she landed in Willowbrook.

> The place is a disaster zone. I can't make it work for me here. I just can't.

But even as the ping of the sent message echoed around the largely empty space, Vee knew that her words were meaningless. She had to stay in Willowbrook because she'd completely run out of options. Her last relationship had been dead in the water for years, and when she'd told Nigel that she was going to take possession of the house left to herself and her sister Cassie by their mother, he'd not even bothered to raise any objections. Her little car was about the only thing Vee was missing from her former life. That decrepit green Mini had been with her through a lot of tough times. It felt like an old friend. She loved driving, but the car was showing definite signs of ageing, and she knew she wouldn't have been able to pay to get it through its next MOT, let alone afford petrol, so it had to go. The cottage was all she had left now.

Vee's sister, who had decamped to America some twenty-five years previously and now lived in Boston in a glorious clapboard house with her glamorous wife Marissa, wanted nothing to do with their legacy.

'It's all yours, honey,' Cassie had said, when Vee had tracked her down to the gym where a noisy personal trainer was impatient to move on with her sister's never-ending quest for absolute fitness. 'Go for it. Live the rural life again. Imagine you're back in the eighties. I hope you get on okay, but I'd rather eat my own arm, as our dear departed ma used to say. Ciao.'

With that, Cassie ended the call before Vee had even had chance to ask how Cassie and Marissa's son was doing at the moment. Finn was twenty now, a bright, genial boy, and news of his progress was always a joy. Vee made a point of marking his birthday and Christmas with as generous gifts as she could manage, and he never failed to thank her by email, but it would have been good to get some up-to-date family news today. She pulled a face at the phone. Cassie had no doubt gone back to the weights and treadmill with gusto. It was probably the last Vee would hear from her sister unless she made the effort to get back in touch herself.

It was getting harder and harder to keep the lines of communication open between them. As an exchange student, falling in love with Marissa and then much later marrying her high-powered American lawyer had changed Cassie's life in so many ways and if it wasn't for Vee's keen interest in Finn's life, she knew she'd have let things go even more. Cassie had only been seven years old to Vee's fifteen when the family had moved away from Willowbrook for a new life in Cardiff. Unlike Vee, her sister had left behind a few small friends but no significant ripples.

The eight-year age difference hadn't seemed so great in those days, but ever since Finn had come into all their lives, Vee had felt like an outsider. She loved her sister and would always want the best for her but the miles between them made a more comfortable sibling relationship tricky. FaceTime could only do so much in that respect.

Thoughts of the past made the present situation seem even more horrific. Vee pushed them away with her customary determination. It was time for a proper stocktake, and then she'd do what she always did in moments of crisis; make a to-do list. However, moving from room to room only served to send her deeper into the sense of foreboding she'd been fighting ever since she'd accepted that she would have to come back to Willowbrook.

Dragonfly Cottage, once a warm and welcoming family home, now had not held on to one single hint of its former cosiness.

Downstairs held a living room and a kitchen, with a single-storey utility room and draughty bathroom extension tacked on the end. The kitchen was possibly the unhealthiest place Vee had ever seen. Grease coated everything, an abandoned frying pan in the sink still held the remains of what must have been the tenants' last fry-up with half an ancient sausage clinging to the hot tap, and a dish that had once contained some sort of cereal was now full of cigarette ends, soggy with curdled milk. More empty cans had been abandoned under the table, spilling out their dregs across the tattered lino. The one window that should have given a pleasant view of the garden was streaked with years of grime. Fingerprints and other random smears decorated it on the inside and spiderwebs hung from every corner. It felt like the place where depressed flies came to die.

Vee pulled out her phone to call the letting agent, ready to blast him to high heaven for allowing the house get into this state, but the continuous engaged tone soon put paid to that idea. Her feet stuck to the floor as she made a quick exit. On leaving the kitchen and picking her way through the various discarded items of grubby clothing on the utility room floor, she found that the bathroom was also in a revolting state, but the two bigger upstairs rooms were, if anything, even more disgusting because they reminded her so strongly of how particular her mum had been about pretty bedlinen that always held the elusive scent of lavender. The bedroom that Vee's parents had shared held the remains of a broken bed. It was without a mattress but festooned with discarded clothing, including a red satin thong, a pair of tattered boxer shorts and a couple of threadbare towels. The carpet was so dotted with cigarette burns that Vee initially thought they were part of the pattern. The back bedroom had two badly stained single mattresses on the floor and the smell of stale urine was so intense that Vee gagged. Worse still, if that was possible, the tiny box room turned out to be the place where the last tenants had left parting gifts of bag after bag of dirty nappies, which were spilling out in gay abandon onto yet another moth-eaten carpet.

Vee stumbled downstairs, still feeling sick from the rotten stench of the upstairs rooms, and made her way to the garden, where the fresh air did a lot to settle her stomach but not much to raise her from the depths of gloom. So this was where the missing double mattress had ended up, and the effort to burn it had not been entirely successful. Rusting springs protruded from the blackened remains. Broken tricycles and other mangled items of play equipment were strewn amongst the long grass. The apple tree in the centre of the garden was a poignant reminder of the day her father had planted it, to celebrate Vee's tenth birthday. It was, of course, much bigger now, and the sight of it was somehow cheering. She headed for the tree and put her arms around it, taking some comfort from its steady support.

'My, how you've grown,' she said to it, echoing the words Aunt Yolanda had said to her, on each of Yolanda's extended visits from her home in France. Her mother's sister hadn't been in contact for some time now, which reminded Vee that she really should check up on her elderly relative. That formidable lady must be in her early eighties by now. Vee's mum, Tallulah, had reached eighty-five when she succumbed to pneumonia. Yolanda hadn't come to the funeral. She'd sent flowers and a card with an ornate cross and some very attractive angels on it, but had made the excuse that her lumbago was playing up and she couldn't travel so far.

Vee sighed. She'd known at the time that this wasn't true. Her aunt, although comfortably curvy and never built for speed, was still quite sprightly and wouldn't usually miss a funeral, with all the opportunities to gossip and gloat because she was the one still alive and kicking. Something had happened to cause a rift between Tallulah and her sister. They'd been close once, but Vee had never managed to get to the bottom of what had caused the split.

Sitting down on the grass, Vee began to make a list, if only in her head for now. Step one had to be to get someone to clear the place of all the debris, and then, only then could she begin the mammoth job of cleaning it. She leaned back against the tree trunk again and felt a little of her tension trickle away. She was fit, strong and only fifty-five when all was said and done. If this was going to be her new home, she must make the best of it. Sharing a home with Nigel had felt like a living death for a long time. An ageing rockstar who'd made his fortune in the eighties and lived on his considerable royalties ever since, Nigel's previous animal magnetism had long disappeared, along with his waistline and snake-hips. His blocked sinuses and clammy armpits had worsened as the years had gone by, especially when he'd decided that showering or bathing damaged the skin. The smell of unwashed male had permeated the flat almost as much as the various odours of despair in this cottage.

Vee watched as two dragonflies flitted by, circling each other in their age-old dance. Her mother had loved this time of year, when the warmth of the sun could usually still be felt on her bare arms and upturned face. The delicate insects with their translucent, rainbow-coloured wings often made a visit to the garden. Tallulah had watched them as the sun rose and when it began to go down. She'd bought the plaque and the wooden dragonfly, now much in need of repair, for the front door. It was a tiny home compared to Nigel's spacious flat on the outskirts of London but this place was Vee's, however unloved it was at the moment.

'I'm going to make you all better,' Vee said to the garden and the house, feeling faintly foolish when she spotted a figure in the next garden, peering over the fence.

'Oh, so you're back,' said the woman, when she noticed Vee staring. 'I wondered when you'd show up. Well, you've got your work cut out here, haven't you?'

Vee stood up and moved closer to the boundary, better to see the person spouting such obvious remarks. The gardens were separated by an overgrown hedge and a rickety fence which was almost as high as the neighbour, so she must be standing on something, unless she was enormously tall, thought Vee, with a smile. The woman was grey-haired with shrewd blue eyes that still sparked with curiosity and mischief, even though she must be almost old as Tallulah had been. She clung on to the top of the fence with both hands. Vee noticed that her nails were painted pillar-box red, and she was wearing a rather startling turquoise tracksuit. Clearly someone who didn't mind being noticed.

'Do I know you?' Vee asked, as politely as she could, given the tone of the other's comment.

The woman sniffed. 'You can't have forgotten me, surely? We lived next door to each other for years. I'm Beryl. And you're young Venetia, back from goodness knows where. I can't say I'm sorry to see the back of the shower that lived here last, although I know the reason you're here is that your dear mama has passed away.'

The memories came flooding back. Beryl Summerfield. Of course. She'd been out at work for a lot of the time when Vee had lived in the cottage.

'Yes, I've got you now. Didn't you work in Meadowthorpe at a...'

'...doctors' surgery. Yes, that's right. I ran the place, truth be told. And you were only a girl when you left, so we didn't know each other well. Why would we?'

The silence that followed felt somehow ominous. Vee rubbed her eyes. 'I can't remember much about that time. It was so long ago.' Her head was beginning to ache.

'Really?'

The word hung in the air as the two women eyed each other over the fence. Vee had the strangest feeling that Beryl was looking right into her soul.

'Anyway, I'm going to make this house as lovely as it used to be when we lived here before. I just need a bit of time,' said Vee, with a lot more confidence than she was feeling.

'That's good news. And the garden too? Will you be getting a few chickens again? I do love a fresh boiled egg with soldiers for my breakfast. Tallulah used to keep me going with them.'

Vee stared at her neighbour. How could she have forgotten such an important feature of the garden at Dragonfly Cottage? Mum had adored the hens. Each one had her own character, and Tallulah had greeted them all by name every morning. In the colder weather, she'd donned wellies and an old wax jacket over her pyjamas before she went outside to release them from the confines of the henhouse, but when it was warmer she'd be barefoot, drifting around in a flowing nightdress like a Victorian heroine and scattering their home-made feed around and chatting to them as if they were old friends, which of course they were.

'I always used to chuckle to myself when I heard your ma having her conversations with those chickens,' said Beryl. 'Do you remember how she called them after her favourite actresses from the *Carry On* films? There was Barbara Windsor, Hattie Jacques, Joan Sims, Fenella Fielding... and another one, I can't remember her name...'

'June Whitfield,' said Vee. 'Yes, I remember.' She peered down the garden. Behind an overgrown patch of shrubbery, she could just see the top of the old henhouse.

'It's falling to bits now,' said Beryl, following Vee's gaze. 'But you could do it up, no problem.'

Privately, Vee thought Beryl's confidence in her DIY abilities was misplaced but she wasn't going to admit that, and after all, why shouldn't she keep a few hens? Her new life was going to be very different from the London one. She imagined herself working from home but taking time out to talk to her chickens as she collected eggs in a basket, just like Mum used to do. It was an encouraging image, and went a little way towards blotting out the horrors of the cottage interior.

'And what is it that you do, Venetia?' Beryl asked. 'I don't suppose you have a job at the moment, what with moving house and everything. This village is very different from the big city, you know.'

Vee wanted to say, 'No kidding? I assumed it would be pretty much the same, apart from there being no Tube station at the end of the road and easy access to the Houses of Parliament and Harrods and so on,' but she bit her tongue and tried to smile. Her career as an actress was largely a thing of the past apart from the occasional small part in a radio play that her agent managed to secure, but she'd developed a lucrative sideline in voiceovers for adverts and narrating audiobooks. Now, however, she was miles and miles away from the recording studios where she'd done most of her work, with no transport and the nearest railway station a long bus journey away. There was no saying what would happen next.

'I'm between posts at the moment,' Vee said loftily, when Beryl was clearly still waiting for a reply. 'But even if I wasn't, there's no time for going out to work just now. I'll need every available hour in the day to make Dragonfly Cottage into a decent place to live.' She turned abruptly, and went back into the house, mumbling about being busy. The dragonflies had flown away now, and the afternoon had grown even chillier. There was much to do, but for the moment, Vee had absolutely no idea where to begin.

3

Rick Reynolds, local handyman and jack-of-all-trades, had been propping up the counter at the corner shop for the last ten minutes, telling himself that he wasn't killing time but was doing essential PR work for his one-man business. He'd been fighting a sense of doom for the last few weeks. Normally able to pick and choose when and where he worked, an unexpected lean patch had hit him hard. Any building and general repair work in the village had dried up lately. The younger families were only just getting back on track after the long school holidays and he supposed the older residents hadn't yet begun to discover the leaks and draughts that the colder autumn weather might soon bring.

Looking down at the pile of flyers he'd had printed in town, Rick tried hard to fight off the feeling of panic that came over him whenever his work diary was empty. He'd given quite a lot of the glossy leaflets out today and had a handful of tentative enquiries, but nothing was booked yet. The monthly maintenance that he paid to his ex-wife for their boys ever since she'd decamped with her new man to Munich was due soon and once that money was transferred, there would only be just enough left to pay his mortgage.

'Don't look so anxious,' said Maryam, handing him a mug of tea and beginning to tidy the counter. 'You were talking about renting out a room in your house the other day when you were in here, weren't you?'

'Yes, a long-term lodger would solve some of the problems, but it'd have to be the right person. Imagine if I got it wrong and landed myself with a fitness-freak who'd make me feel guilty for eating the odd pie and chips. I mean, I like to keep in shape myself, but some people take it to the extreme.'

Maryam laughed. 'I'm sure you'd choose wisely, and in the meantime we can find you a bit more of something to do in the shop. You've been brilliant since Rashid and I moved here. This place is looking much better already. And what about getting in touch with Nell and Barney to see if there's any more work going at Hollyhocks Cottage?'

'I don't think so. They'll give me a shout if they want anything else doing, surely?'

'Always worth an ask. You know Barney hates DIY and you did a great job there over the summer doing their place up and getting the annexe all ready for Frank to move into. Having his dad sleeping next door instead of across the landing has made Barney very happy. Frank too. He loves his privacy, doesn't he? Just give them a call.'

'It's okay, I don't want you all to think you're obliged to magic up jobs for me,' Rick said. 'I'll just have to be a bit more creative in putting the word about. I've finished all the work I needed to do on my own house and now I'm just rattling around the place on my own. I'm wishing I hadn't let Barney and Nell adopt my dog when I was so busy over the summer. Bathsheba was miserable being left alone all day when I was so busy. She didn't take to the run and kennel I made for her in the garden. I never had the time to walk her properly either. A big dog like a Borzoi needs a lot of exercise. I miss her.'

'I'm sure they wouldn't mind if you had her back,' said Maryam. 'But don't rush into anything, because hopefully you'll get more work soon and I know Bathsheba gets on well with Frank's dog. She's getting plenty of walks with Anton.'

Rick couldn't help smiling when he thought about Bathsheba's new friend. A strange mixture of breeds, the canine resident of Hollyhocks Cottage had an unusual feature; a toothy grin that had caused him to be named after a certain judge on *Strictly Come Dancing*.

'You're right. I'll try and be patient,' Rick said. 'It's not easy, though, I've never...'

He stopped talking abruptly as a bell jangled. The shop door opened wide, and a woman entered. She was tall, with lightly tanned olive skin and a short mop of dark hair which framed an elegant, high cheek-boned face. At the moment the face held an expression that Rick found hard to read, except that it definitely wasn't a happy one. Her eyes were brown and almond-shaped, fringed with long, sooty lashes, and her lips were painted a glossy red. She wasn't exactly pretty but there was something arresting about her. Something dramatic and vaguely unsettling.

The newcomer was wearing tight black jeans tucked into high-heeled ankle boots and the kind of long, swishy coat that Rick seemed to remember his ex, Stacey, describing when she was telling him what she wanted for Christmas one year, although even to his untrained eye, this one looked far from being brand new. Unfortunately, at the time he'd already splashed out on a fancy weekend in Skegness for the whole family and a new hoover to replace the one that had recently blown up. Stacey left soon after that. The rainy weekend hadn't been a success and she'd thrown the hoover at the wall as she departed.

'Hello there,' Maryam said, smiling. 'How can I help you? I don't think I've seen you in Willowbrook before. Aha, I've got it, you're...' She stopped and clicked her fingers, clearly trying to remember a name.

The woman smiled back, a little hesitantly. 'I've only just arrived here,' she said. 'I'm moving into Fiddler's Row. Number four,' she added, when Rick looked puzzled.

Light dawned. 'Oh, are you the new tenant?' Rick said, pulling himself together with difficulty. 'I know none of those houses are up for sale, but that makes sense. I guess... I mean, there's a lot to do there. The last people weren't very... they were a bit...'

'Tell me about it,' the woman said, pulling a face. 'The state of the place is a joke, except it's not in the least bit funny. I'm not a tenant, it's mine. I grew up there, and my mum left the cottage to me. I need to make a start somewhere but I'm not sure where.'

'I did wonder how anyone could live there as it stands. What will you do?' asked Maryam.

'Well, I need to eat tonight so I'm going to have to get milk and bread and a few other things. And wine. It'll have to be screw-top though. And plastic glasses and paper plates. Maybe some disposable cutlery. Oh, heavens, I need absolutely everything and that kitchen's a health hazard so it'll need to be a picnic in the garden anyway. I'm going to have to hurry up and find a B&B for a few nights while I start to get sorted. Why didn't I do this earlier? I must have been crazy, thinking I could stay in Dragonfly Cottage straight away. Is there anywhere in the village?'

Maryam and Rick regarded her with equal expressions of sympathy. Rick remembered starting pretty much from scratch in the months after Stacey left but at least he'd claimed some of their kitchen equipment and half the furniture for his tiny flat and had eventually managed to buy another house. It sounded as if this poor soul had nothing at all. Although the term *poor soul* didn't describe this woman one bit.

'You could stay at mine, babe,' he blurted out, and then closed his eyes in horror at what he'd just said. Not only had he invited her to live in his house, he'd called her 'babe', a name that some of the local women of his acquaintance had lately been trying to stop him from using.

The shocked burst of laughter that followed this bold invitation hit Rick with a bolt that rocked him. With his eyes still tightly closed, her looks didn't distract him, but the laugh took him straight back to a time when he was someone else entirely.

'You're Venetia Prescott,' Rick said. He opened his eyes at last and found her staring at him.

'Well, yes, I am, but I'm usually called Vee,' she said. 'Should I know you?'

Rick exchanged glances with Maryam, who, discreet as usual, had been busying herself with continuing to tidy the counter area. Her dark eyes were bright with interest, but her expression was determinedly neutral. Rick shook his head very slightly, hoping she'd get the message.

'I expect you bumped into each other at some point when you both lived here years ago,' Maryam said, taking the hint. 'And Rick isn't being presumptuous in offering you a home. He was only just telling me that he was thinking of advertising his spare room to see if he could find a lodger. I've a board over by the door where I pin up postcards about that kind of thing. He was about to put a notice there.'

'Oh, I see. I'm sorry I laughed, it was a surprise, that's all. I didn't assume you were propositioning me,' said Vee. 'I'm not that much of a catch. Middle-aged women tend to assume they're invisible unless proved otherwise.'

Looking more closely, Rick could see faint streaks of grey in Venetia's hair but there was no way this woman could ever be invisible. He opened his mouth to argue with her statement, but Maryam got in first. 'Tell me about it,' she said. 'If I wasn't dressed from head to foot in sparkly pink silk, I think I'd just blend into the wallpaper these days.'

Vee raised her eyebrows and smiled. 'I find that hard to believe. I can see that I'm a good bit older than you and anyway, you'd look amazing in whatever you chose to wear.' She turned to look at Rick properly. 'Anyway, if you're serious about letting me rent a room, I'd love to see it. I'd only need to stay while I make my place habitable. I don't know why I imagined I could just move in. In my head it was going to be like taking over an Airbnb that had been well cared for, but I'm going to need to gut the whole house.'

A flurry of customers made further conversation impossible for a while. Rick and Vee eyed each other somewhat warily as Maryam dealt with the queue. When the last of the people had left the shop, Rick said, 'Why don't you come back with me now and take a look at the room? Maryam can vouch for me, if you're worried about me being a bit dodgy.'

There was silence as Vee considered this suggestion. Then she smiled. 'You don't look like any kind of villain, to be fair. If you're sure that's not putting you out, it sounds like a very good plan. There's nothing in the kitchen fit to use.'

Vee paid for her purchases, saying that wherever she slept that night, she'd need them. Rick stood back to let her get on with her task, his mind reeling at what he'd done. It was one thing talking about getting a lodger but quite another to find one so quickly and for it to be none other than the notorious Venetia Prescott, who had caused such a stir before she left the village when she was in her teens and whose exit with her family was talked about for many months afterwards.

Maryam gave Rick a thoughtful look as he ushered Vee out of the shop. He expected that she must be wondering why, if he'd recognised the newcomer so easily, Vee seemed to have no clue as to who Rick was. This was no mystery to him. Back in 1985, when the Prescott family had left Willowbrook so suddenly, Rick hadn't looked anything like the man he was today. Now, his image was very different. Reinventing yourself took time and effort. Cut-off jeans, heavy work boots, a series of funky t-shirts and vests and a healthy outdoor tan were his trademark these days, along with the cropped hair, bleached by the local hairdresser every now and again to hide the greys, and just a touch of stubble. Rick was fit and strong, with a toned body and a friendly smile that showed off a dimple in one cheek.

He held the door open for Vee, and she thanked him graciously. On the pavement, she paused. 'I don't want to seem ungrateful, but can I say one thing?'

Rick nodded, alarmed, but she patted his arm.

'Never, ever call me *babe*,' she said. 'I'm Vee, and you're Rick. I'm not sure if I should recognise you from my dark and distant past but for now, that's all we need to know.'

Rick nodded and led her towards his van which was parked at the kerb a few metres away. He wasn't going to tell Vee that calling women *babe*, *sweetheart*, *doll* and a few other equally cringe-making names had been a part of his plan to morph into the character of a tough builder with a heart of gold. At the time, it had seemed like another layer of his disguise. Was disguise the right word? He'd certainly needed to make drastic changes in his life after Stacey left. If Vee had arrived in Willowbrook a few years earlier, there would have been a definite danger that she'd have known him immediately. He pushed the thought from his mind and opened the van door for her.

'Is your house far away?' Vee asked as they drove along Fiddler's Row, past the village green where an impromptu game of football was taking place.

'No, barely five minutes' drive. It's a semi-detached Victorian villa on the edge of Willowbrook,' he answered, as they took a turn that would lead them alongside the church and out towards one of the roads that led to Meadowthorpe town. 'It was a wreck when I bought it, or I'd never have afforded the place, but I've gradually done it up. I'm a builder and a general handyman,' he added, when she glanced across at him with interest.

Vee was staring out of the window again by the time the church came fully into view. Rick heard her sharp intake of breath. It came as no surprise. Some of his own memories probably mirrored hers far too closely for comfort. He glanced across at his passenger and saw that her hands were tightly clenched in her lap.

'So anyway,' he continued breezily. 'As I was saying, I can tackle most kinds of work. Plumbing, a bit of electrical, renovations. You name it, I'll take it on board.'

Even to himself, this sounded like a blatant sales pitch, knowing that Vee was in dire need of help in that area, but nothing ventured... Rick took a couple of left turns and pulled into the narrow drive next to his house and got out to open the door on the passenger side for Vee. He was relieved to see that she seemed to have recovered from her obvious tension by the church, and he quickly opened up so that he could usher her inside. Instead of going around to the back of the house and letting himself in through the kitchen door as usual, Rick had deliberately chosen to make this entrance Venetia's first impression of his home. It had been his pet project once the rest of the house was liveable. The hallway had polished terracotta tiles on the floor and the stairs with their ornate banisters that led up to the bedrooms were sanded and varnished with a vintage runner going up the middle. The lampshade that hung down was made of stained glass in rainbow colours and a large cheese plant with glossy leaves stood in one corner near a row of antique wrought-iron coat pegs.

'Oh, this is lovely,' Vee said. 'Did you do it all yourself?'

Rick nodded proudly. It had taken hours and hours of labour to reach this welcoming stage, but it had been worth every moment.

'I don't suppose... I mean, I expect you're booked up for weeks in advance... but if you could possibly find time to do some work for me, I'd be so, so grateful,' Vee said, turning shining eyes on him as she slipped off her coat and slung it over the newel post. 'It's so cosy in here, isn't it? I feel overdressed now but it's the first time I've felt warm all day.'

Rick's heart gave a lurch in his chest. He'd been desperate for a new source of income recently and here was an opportunity to not only charge some rent but to get weeks of work booked in. How could he refuse? But what if she recognised him? The past would be sure to get in the way at some point, even if his hair had been dark and greasy in those days and his body shape much rounder. Vacillating in the few seconds it took to answer, Rick took a decision that had the potential to rock his entire world.

'I think we can come to some arrangement,' he said, gesturing to the next floor of his house. 'Let me show you the room that's available and then I'll make us some coffee and we can make a plan.'

Rick followed Vee up the stairs, unable to even begin to admire her long legs in their tight jeans, being so preoccupied with his immediate future. The financial side of it was looking much more promising but what if Vee began to see past his carefully constructed smokescreen when she got to know him better? This was madness and could only end in disaster. Because the Rick who had been very much aware of Venetia Prescott back in 1985 was a very different character to the one that was currently offering her a safe place to stay and a way out of her tricky situation. And if she rumbled him, any friendly relationship would be totally out of the question. This whole thing could be a nightmare waiting to happen.

4

The room that Rick was displaying seemed like total salvation to Vee. She stood in the doorway as Rick ran through the amenities that could be provided if she gave the right answer.

'Okay, so I usually start work early when I have a job on, so you'd have the kitchen and bathroom to yourself as soon as I leave. I'm out most of the day as a rule and I cook in the evenings when I feel like it. Either that or I have a takeaway or go to the pub,' he added, with a burst of honesty.

'It's a lovely room. Have you always lived here on your own?' Vee asked, intrigued as to why this man had a whole house to himself.

'Yes, I bought it as a doer-upper after my wife... I mean my ex-wife left. I've tried to make it into a proper home. My boys used to come and stay sometimes, that's why there are two single beds. Stacey moved to Munich with her new man. Since then... well, circumstances have changed.'

Vee frowned. 'But what if your sons want to come and visit and I'm in their room? How's that going to work out?'

'They won't. At least, not anytime soon. My wife... ex... has given them a kind of life that's crammed with interesting activities. Seems like something's going on every day after school and weekends too these days.'

'That's a shame.'

'Tell me about it.' He closed his mouth like a trap.

Vee waited until the silence became uncomfortable. Rick had walked over to the window and was fiddling with the blind. His back was to her, and it looked forbidding. 'That's not fair,' she said. 'Do they want to come?'

'Are you always this nosy?'

The sharp retort made Vee blink. She cursed herself for the habit of speaking without engaging her brain. Her mother had told her time and time again to curb her tactless remarks. Would she never learn?

'I asked for that,' she said. 'You're right. It's none of my business.' She felt herself withdrawing into the shell she'd built over the years whenever life got challenging, or when her mother was being particularly frosty, which to be honest was quite often, latterly. There was no need for him to snap like that even if it had been a question too far, though.

Rick turned to face Vee. 'I'm sorry, the kids' visits are a bit of a sore point with me at the moment. I don't suppose you meant to pry,' he said, but the comment didn't sound very sincere.

'No, I didn't but I guess it was a rude thing to ask.' *And if I didn't need a refuge so badly, I'd walk out right now and tell you to stuff your kind offer,* Vee thought to herself. She bit back any further response and waited to see what he'd do next. In the meantime, she took a mental inventory of the room, as her host opened the blind and sunlight poured in, stripes of brilliance beaming through the slats. The weather was improving even if Rick's mood wasn't.

It was a large space, with a single bed on each side. Both had

brightly coloured duvet covers but most of the room was decorated in neutral shades of cream with just one feature wall
painted a deep peacock blue. The floorboards were sanded and
oiled. They glowed with care, golden and smooth. The rug
between the beds looked as if it would be soft and comfortable to
bare feet and the fitted wooden wardrobes echoed the colour of
the floor. The only other furniture was an old chest of drawers
that had been painted white. It was a very peaceful place. Vee
longed to have it for her own, even if only for a little while. The
contrast to what waited for her at Dragonfly Cottage was
daunting.

'So, do you want the room? Maybe it's not quite what you're
looking for.' Rick's words cut into Vee's troubled thoughts, and
she forced a smile. It was important to keep this touchy individual
on her side.

'Yes, please, very much. And... I wondered...'

He eyed her, clearly still firmly on his guard. 'You wondered
what?'

'You've said you can probably help me with getting the cottage
straight but there's so much work to be done and I don't know
where to start. Some I can tackle myself and I need to do that
because money's going to be tight, but I can afford to pay for the
harder jobs.'

'I'd have to charge you the going rate.'

This was beyond the pale and Vee drew herself up to her full
height, returning his glare measure for measure. The man was
insufferable. 'Of course I'm not asking for favours. I'd pay whatever you usually charge. On second thoughts, forget it. I'll find
somewhere else to stay and put a card on the board at the shop to
attract someone who actually wants the work.'

It was a stand-off. They faced each other across the room.
Vee's spirits were at an all-time low. How had she got herself into

this cleft stick? Okay, she'd asked an intrusive question but there was no need for Rick to react like that and now look where it had got her. She should learn to keep her mouth shut.

Rick folded his arms. 'You're a fiery one, aren't you?' he said, in what sounded like a very patronising tone. Vee didn't reply. 'Anyway, the room's yours if you want it,' he continued. 'And I *can* fit you in for the work on the cottage straight away, as it happens, so you're in luck.'

Am I really? thought Vee, but she took a deep breath and nodded. This was no time to make a stand. Desperate times called for desperate measures. 'Thank you,' she said. 'I'll walk round to Fiddler's Row and fetch what I need for now. Will you be in when I get back?'

'It's okay, I can drive you,' he said, his voice gruff. 'You'll struggle to carry everything.'

'I'll manage. See you later.'

Vee turned to leave, already regretting the spiky heels on her boots which had made her feel cool and powerful this morning but which she'd now happily swap for her old trainers. There were already blisters forming on both feet and the walk would definitely rub her toes raw.

'Look, I know we've got off to a bad start but that's no reason to cut your nose off to spite your face,' Rick said. 'Come on, we can go round and get your stuff, and I'll take a look at what needs doing at the same time. Let's go.'

Vee considered her other option. It wasn't tempting. 'Fine,' she said, and led the way down the stairs. 'Thank you,' she added, trying to sound magnanimous but only succeeding in verging on surly. She sighed. This landlord/tenant relationship looked as if it was going to be a rocky road, and now she'd gone and asked him to work for her too. Rick had seemed friendly to begin with in the shop.

What had happened to make him so prickly? It surely couldn't have just been her thoughtless question. She decided to make a big effort to start again with him. There was a lot at stake here.

'It's really weird being back in Willowbrook after so long,' she said, as they drove back towards Fiddler's Row. 'Everything looks the same, and yet...'

'And yet, you're so different,' he said, under his breath.

'What did you say?' Vee asked, not sure if she'd heard him right.

'Oh, just that you must find it so different after all these years. It's been a long time, you said. Anyway, here we are. Let's get on with the job in hand and then I'll give a quote. I can start work tomorrow if you like.'

Vee turned to look at Rick, but he was already climbing down from the van. She did the same and followed him to the front door, flinching all over again as she drew closer to the peeling paint and the broken dragonfly.

'Hmm, you're not wrong when you say there's a lot to do here,' Rick said, entering the narrow hallway and standing still to look around. The smell of damp, the curling, filthy carpet and the dangling strips of wallpaper were a dismal greeting. It all seemed worse than ever now Vee had been somewhere so much better, and her heart sank.

'Do you think you can make it liveable?'

Rick considered the question. 'I can make anywhere liveable,' he said eventually. 'The question is, do you really want to live here?'

'What do you mean by that?' Vee stared at him, instantly on edge. He blushed.

'Nothing... nothing at all. I guess I just wondered if it was going to be difficult coming back to a place where you'd lived a good few years ago. I expect you've got lots of happy memories though.'

Vee didn't respond. The question was way too complicated for a simple answer. Instead, she made her way further into the house that had been less of a safe refuge and more of a prison towards the end. It was time to move on, but it wasn't going to be easy.

5

Being inside Dragonfly Cottage for a second time wasn't quite as alarming as the first, especially as Rick immediately snapped into professional mode and produced a clipboard and pen. He went right through the house with Vee, making copious notes and coming up with various suggestions that would improve her living accommodation as well as get rid of the detritus of years of neglect.

'I don't want to put you on the spot, but exactly how much can you afford to spend here?' Rick asked, scribbling down the final in a list of figures and completing the sum that he'd clearly been working on in his head. He showed her the total, and she gasped.

'Not that much. Maybe... two thirds of it, at a push? Is there any way you can pare it back a bit more?'

'Well, I suppose there is, but to be brutally honest, the only way I can do a decent job for less and still make the place long-term liveable for you is if you do the decorating yourself as we go along.' Rick looked Vee up and down, and she guessed he was taking in the general appearance of someone who looked to be a stranger to hard work and practical tasks. 'Any chance of that?' he asked, raising his eyebrows in what he probably imagined was a humorous expression. It wasn't.

'I suppose you think because I look after my nails and wear make-up I don't know how to graft?' Vee said, through gritted teeth. She moved a bit closer to Rick, facing him squarely and narrowly resisting the temptation to poke him in the chest. 'Well, let me tell you, that's not the case. Definitely not. Here's a bit of backstory for you. I'm an actor by trade. I was in a touring company until the work dried up. I've done some modelling in my time, but I've also cleaned houses, waited tables, even done some gardening. I once laid a patio for a friend, and I can paint and decorate too. My most recent work was doing voiceovers and narrating audiobooks, but my dream is to work from home now I'm not handy for central London. Does that answer your question?'

Rick took a step backwards and almost fell over a heap of empty pizza boxes. 'You were an actress?' he said, after he'd regained his balance. 'I might have guessed... I mean if you've been on the stage, what are you doing back here in this backwater? Should I have heard of you?'

It was an effort, but Vee forced a laugh. Maybe she shouldn't have bitten his head off like that. 'I was an *actor*. And you're not likely to have seen my name in lights. I was touring in rep for some years. Small-town theatres and provincial halls, but since then I've had to find other ways to make a living.'

'And voiceovers? How can you do that from home?'

'Well, a few of the narrators I know managed to transform a room in their houses or a summerhouse into a small recording studio in the pandemic, when they couldn't go into work because of lockdown. I might do that... if I knew how to do the sound-proofing and set it all up.'

The concept of tackling this kind of task was daunting. Vee sighed. There was always YouTube. This scheme would have to be put on hold until the house was in a much better state though.

'And I want to rebuild the chicken house at the bottom of the garden and get some hens,' she added. Might as well get all the prospective jobs out there. At least this way Rick would see that she had plans and wasn't just some airhead who thought country living would be as easy as a picnic in the park.

Rick made another couple of notes in his book. He frowned. 'You don't want much, do you?' he said. 'I'm not sure you've really thought all this through. It's three builders you need, not one.'

'Look, let's make a deal,' Vee said. 'You do most of the donkey work and the skilled stuff and I'll muck in wherever I can. Where do we start?'

The sticky moment passed, and Vee breathed a sigh of relief. She mustn't antagonise the only person who was likely to help her. Rick looked around with an air of anticipation. It was as if he was looking forward to this, Vee thought incredulously. She half expected him to rub his hands together. It was a good job one of them was enthusiastic. The filth, the stench and the sense of desolation were making her feel nauseous again.

'We'll begin tomorrow by making as many trips to the tip as we need. Have you got something to wear that you don't mind getting dirty? If not, there's a spare boiler suit I can lend you. It's clean,' Rick added, when Vee didn't answer immediately.

'Oh, I'm sure it is, I was just doing a mental trawl of the clothes I brought with me and realising nothing would be much good,' she said hastily. 'Yes, that'd be useful. I did such a big clear-out when I moved here that I haven't much left.'

By the look on his face, Vee thought Rick was about to start asking her more about her previous life and there was no way she was getting into that discussion. 'If we've finished here, shall we

take my case and my bags back to yours?' she said. 'I've used up
enough of your time already.'

He nodded and began to head for the door with Vee's rucksack over one shoulder and her travel bag in the other hand. 'You
bring the wheelie case and lock up,' he said. 'I'll be glad to get
home, I'm starving. I'm planning on getting a pizza delivered
later, you can join me if you like. I mean, I'm not saying we should
always eat together, it's just that as it's your first night and
everything...'

His voice tailed away as Vee considered the suggestion. She
didn't want to get into the sort of arrangement where she'd be
obliged to schedule her meals around Rick, but she would need
to eat at some point and a takeaway pizza would be quick and
easy, especially as it seemed that he'd at least mastered his earlier
grumpiness... if only for now. 'Thanks, that's kind of you,' she
said, following him with her case and locking the door behind
them with relief.

Once her belongings had been delivered to Rick's house and
she'd unpacked, Venetia had an overwhelming urge to get out
into the fresh air for a while on her own. Rick was absorbed in
making a plan of the work he was going to do on the cottage and
there didn't seem to be anything useful she could contribute at
this point, so she swapped the sassy boots for trainers, excused
herself and set off towards the centre of the village.

As she walked, Vee had the strangest sensation of travelling
back in time, and it wasn't a happy experience. After ten minutes
of wandering through the rest of the estate where Rick lived,
passing rows of similar Victorian semis in varying states of repair,
she came to the village church. It was surrounded by an attrac-
tively rambling graveyard and fighting her first impulse to run in
the opposite direction, Vee turned to go in, making her way under
the arch of the ancient lychgate and along the cobbled path

towards the church entrance. The past came to meet her as she walked, and she steeled herself against the rush of memories. All these places had to be faced at some time and now was as good a time as any.

The peace of her surroundings enfolded Vee as she moved further into the churchyard and it gradually edged most of the unsettling thoughts out of her mind. She breathed deeply, appreciating the scent of newly mown grass. Not nearly so unkempt as the garden at Dragonfly Cottage, even so the graveyard also seemed to be a work in progress. An elderly man with cropped grey hair and a neatly trimmed moustache was finishing off the task of tidying the areas between the graves by chopping away at tufts of grass with a pair of shears. As she passed him, he stopped to greet her.

'Mornin', ducky,' he said. 'Welcome to St Stephen's Church. Are you a visitor to Willowbrook?'

'Not exactly,' Vee said. 'Well, no, not at all really. I'm living here now. I grew up in the village and I'm back. Dragonfly Cottage in Fiddler's Row was my old home... and it's my new one, for that matter.'

'Really?' said Sid. 'I must know you, in that case. Oh, hang on a minute... you're not... you can't be... surely?'

He paused, slid his spectacles to the end of his nose, and viewed Venetia over the top of them with keen interest. She waited, tension making her stomach churn.

'The eldest Prescott lass! You are, aren't you? I'd know those eyes anywhere. You have such a look of your grandma. She was a big friend of me and my missus, in fact I've only just been sprucing up her resting place.' He jerked his head towards a corner of the churchyard that was in the shade of a large yew tree. Its gracious branches spread over several headstones, neatly cared for but mostly bare. However, in front of the central one sat a stone jar containing a bunch of orange and crimson flowers.

'It *is* you, isn't it? Young Venetia? You probably don't remember me, I'm Sid Potter. We lived at the other end of Fiddler's Row when you were growing up. We did miss your gran when she passed away. She made the best cakes in the whole of the village, and she was kindness itself to my Jenny when our two were little. I still miss her, although a lot of water's flowed under the bridge since then. She was a good 'un, was Isabella.' He paused, then pulled out a large cotton handkerchief and blew his nose noisily.

Lost for words, Venetia gazed at Sid. When she'd been planning to return to Willowbrook, her mind had shied away from the past and she'd tried to focus on the problem in hand, which was coming to terms with the idea of living in her childhood home again. Now there was Beryl with her tight-lipped comments and this old gentleman with the benevolent expression, both taking Vee back to a time before the move when her turbulent teenage years had made family life very difficult. She tried to pull herself together, because Sid was still waiting for a response.

'You're right, I'm Venetia. Most people call me Vee these days though. I can't believe you recognised me after all this time. It's been over forty years.'

'Oh, there's no mistaking one of Isabella's brood. All with the same sparkling brown eyes. My wife used to say Bella's eyes had the colour and sheen of a newly picked horse chestnut.'

Vee wasn't too sure if she liked having her eyes compared to conkers, but she supposed it was meant as a compliment. She smiled. 'I'm guessing it was you that put the flowers on my gran's grave? That was so sweet of you.'

'Yes, dahlias out of my little garden. She always loved 'em. I live in the sheltered accommodation over the road from the church, now my Jenny's gone the way of your gran, but they let me have a patch of border to tend. It's enough. Shall we?' He indicated to the path that wound its way towards the yew tree.

Vee nodded. She wondered if instinct had made her take this detour against her better judgement as she'd headed for the village. It was a place she'd always intended to visit to lay flowers of her own, but over the years, the thought of coming back to visit Willowbrook had gradually slid further and further away from her mind. Now, as they approached the quiet corner of the churchyard, memories of the warm-hearted grandmother who, along with her aunt, had looked after her as a child while her mother and father were at work almost overwhelmed her. When they reached the plot, she bowed her head and let the tears come.

Sid stood silently beside her. After a few moments, when Vee's shoulders had stopped shaking, he dug in his pocket for a second freshly laundered handkerchief and passed it over. She took it gratefully and dried her eyes. The fabric smelt of the same old-fashioned washing powder favoured by her mother. She blinked hard and looked more carefully at her surroundings. The area around the grave was tidy and clean and unlike some of its neighbours, the stone was moss-free. It had clearly been recently scrubbed.

'Isabella Maria Martinez,' she read aloud, remembering that her beautiful grandma had been blessed with rather glamorous Spanish parents and had inherited her sultry good looks from them both. 'March 20th 1900–May 2nd 1985. Wife of the late Antonio, mother of Tallulah and Yolanda. Rest in peace, thou good and faithful servant.'

Sid automatically crossed himself and then grinned at Vee. 'Old habits die hard,' he said. 'I don't go to church so often now because I've grown lazy in the mornings since I've been on my own, and I'm not always washed and dressed in time for the ten o'clock service. The vicar's a bright spark though. I think you'd like her. Bright red spiky hair and studs all the way up her ears, but she's all right, is Bev. You'd enjoy her way of doing things, I reckon.'

Venetia doubted this very much. She'd not been into a church for many years. It was hard to sit still for so long, she found. Restless by nature, a whole hour of listening and trying to sing unfamiliar hymns wasn't her ideal way of spending a Sunday. Sid glanced at Vee sideways and then down at her left foot, which was tapping out a rhythm on the ground.

'You're a lot like your gran,' he said. 'She was never still for long. Always clicking her fingers and jiggling around. Jenny used to say to her, "Bella, for pity's sake, stop twitching, girl. You're making us all edgy." Mind you, I'd give a lot to be able to say it to her now.'

Vee made a big effort to stop tapping. It had been one of the things that Nigel had found so annoying about living with her, as he'd often pointed out when they were arguing. That, and her tendency to learn her lines out loud in her acting days, and her inability to face having sex with him when he hadn't washed for three days or more. In the end, there had been far more irritations than moments of affection. Leaving Nigel was the best move she'd made for ages, Vee told herself. For both their sakes.

'Let's sit down for a minute, Venetia,' said Sid. 'My legs ain't what they used to be.'

He led the way to a nearby bench and subsided onto it with a grunt. Vee joined him and they both leaned back, letting the September sunshine warm their upturned faces. The gentle aroma of mint and sage wafted around them. Vee looked to see where it was coming from and discovered that they were close to a perfectly tended grave that was surrounded by clumps of flourishing herbs sunk into the soil at its foot.

'That's my Jenny's resting place,' said Sid. 'She loved the scent of our herb garden. I have some thyme to plant next, and a tub of lavender. I like to sit here and have a chat with her. I... well, I don't want to upset you by mentioning it, but I did hear on the grapevine that your ma had died too, and your pa a lot longer ago. What happened to Ivan? He seemed such a lively chap. He was the life and soul of the party at the pub, always the first to stand his round.'

Vee winced. She'd not planned an answer to this question, and she wasn't in the least bit ready to discuss her dad's last years. The memories were still too raw. 'Oh, he... erm... he wasn't well for a long time before he died. It was very sad. I can't believe you already knew about Mum too.'

'News travels fast in a village. I was so sorry. It was sad news even though she was a good age. Where's she buried?'

'We decided against a grave in the end. Mum was cremated. My sister and her partner were over from America for the funeral, and they stayed until we could scatter the ashes. We argued about where to put them but in the end, Finn – that's my sister Cassie's son – he had a few suggestions.'

'I see. Nice that the next generation was involved too. It must have been a comfort to have the three of them with you.'

'Oh, my nephew wasn't able to come, unfortunately. He's an apprentice carpenter. He's learning how to make bespoke furniture, and my sister didn't want him to ask for time off when he's only just started work. They live in Boston, and Finn was lucky to get in at such a prestigious firm, apparently.'

Vee tried to make this sound quite normal but actually she'd been bitterly disappointed that Finn hadn't joined them. She'd been looking forward to seeing him and didn't think it was unreasonable for him to take a few days off for such an important occasion, but Cassie had been adamant that he shouldn't risk annoying his new employers.

'Ah well, at least the rest of you were there,' said Sid. 'Family's so important at times like this, isn't it?' He paused, then asked, 'So, where did you choose to take Tallulah?'

Vee could tell by Sid's tone that he wasn't impressed by the lack of proper resting place. She began to feel defensive. It had been hard enough to accept that her mum was no longer there to provide pithy advice and dispense her huge hugs, without someone with no right to judge trying to make her feel guilty for not having a grave to visit.

'We went to Whitby for the weekend, and then on the second day we drove inland until we found a secluded spot with a view for miles,' Vee added. 'Mum loved going there for some sea air. Chips on the beach and a paddle. But what she liked best was a picnic on the moors. No sand in your sandwiches, she used to say...'

Vee's voice tailed away. Sid shrugged. 'Well, if that's what you all wanted,' he said. 'I prefer to have somewhere to come and be close to my Jenny. I tell her my worries, that kind of thing.'

Vee had a vision of herself on the windswept Yorkshire moors shouting a random tirade of complaints about Nigel, her lack of acting roles, money worries and anxieties regarding the state of the cottage into the teeth of a north-westerly gale. She could see Sid's point, but it was far too late to change her mind now, and Tallulah always made it clear that she had no strong feelings about what should be done with her remains. She'd known she hadn't long left and had made Vee promise to make the funeral as low-cost as possible or even dispense with one altogether. That had been a step too far though.

'We didn't always have an easy relationship, but I miss my mum,' she said eventually. 'I did my best for her.'

At this, Sid's expression changed from one of vague disapproval to a much more sympathetic one. 'Of course you did,' he said. 'Ignore me, I'm just a traditionalist. You'll always remember your ma, wherever she is now, and your pa too. We keep our loved ones alive by thinking about them and being glad we knew them.'

Sid patted Vee's hand and stood up to leave, rubbing the small of his back and flexing his shoulders. 'I'm a creaky old bugger these days, if you'll pardon my French,' he said. 'At least your folks have been spared some of the indignities of old age.'

Vee couldn't help thinking that Tallulah would have rather been popping paracetamol for her aching joints than being swept away on a wild breeze, but she hadn't the heart to argue. She got up too and, on impulse, gave Sid a hug. He seemed startled but after a moment he responded warmly enough. His bristly chin rubbed against Vee's cheek briefly and then he let her go.

'I've held you up long enough,' he said. 'Where were you off to when I distracted you?'

'Just exploring. Revisiting a few old haunts,' Vee said. 'I'm moving back into Dragonfly Cottage just as soon as it's fit for habitation, but I expect you already know that too.'

As soon as the words were uttered, Vee realised how snappy they sounded and was about to apologise, but luckily Sid didn't seem in the least fazed.

'Ah, yes, I did hear Beryl was going to have a new neighbour, but not who it would be,' he said. 'Jungle drums, you know. I bet you'll uncover a lot of lovely memories today. Good luck, my dear. And always remember, you belong in Willowbrook much more than all those newcomers who keep turning up to buy our houses. This is your home again now.'

Vee couldn't think of a suitable reply to this well-meant remark. Good memories? Echoes from her past, certainly, but as

for lovely, not so much. Even so, she set off down the road to the
centre of the village with a new determination in her step. As Sid
said, this was going to be her home now. She would just have to
face her demons and get on with it. Enough years had passed by
for anyone who'd known her before to forget all about what
happened back in 1985.

But as it happened, Vee was quite, quite wrong.

6

Beryl took to her bed much earlier than usual that night with a hot water bottle and a good book but spent a restless few hours tossing and turning. These regular antidotes to wakefulness had completely failed her this time and she was unable to shake off the memories that were pouring into her mind like a river after a fierce rainstorm.

Contemplating a brandy to tip her over the edge into sleep, Beryl decided against it. That seemed a bit like desperate measures and smacked of being out of control. To be in charge of her own body was very important to her. She supposed that to an outsider she might look a bit giddy at times, with her love of Prosecco and dancing, but there were limits, she told herself.

After trying many times to get comfortable, she finally woke from a fitful doze at six o'clock and came downstairs in her dressing gown. It was a relief to have given up on sleep. She settled herself in her favourite chair and switched on the TV, choosing one of her favourite programmes about property renovation. Anything like that would usually help to soothe any anxieties. A large mug of tea and a couple of digestive biscuits should have settled her troublesome thoughts, but this tried and tested panacea didn't work its magic either. She got up to make more tea and turned off the excited chatter about removing walls and building extensions. It was distracting her from thinking, and today she needed to concentrate. On previous occasions, returning from a holiday with her two best friends had always been something of a letdown, but the arrival of the new neighbour had put all such gloom right out of her head. There was much to ponder on when she was back again in her chair.

'What's she doing coming back here after all these years?' Beryl muttered, aiming her question towards a photograph that stood in pride of place on the sideboard, a habit that had been growing ever since her husband had departed this life so many years ago. 'There was a very good reason why that family left Willowbrook, and it hasn't gone away. We know what it is, don't we, Eddie? And even though you're not around any more, there are some of us still living here that have long memories.'

Leaning back, Beryl wriggled her toes in the slippers which she'd left ready at the side of her bed last night. They were almost new; fake sheepskin, fleece-lined and trimmed with nylon fur. She picked up the second mug of strong tea laced with two sugars that she'd placed on a small table by her elbow and sighed with relief as her tired feet appreciated the welcome comfort of the slippers. As the sweetness and warmth of the hot tea permeated her body, Beryl made a huge effort to pinpoint why the fact that Venetia Prescott was about take up residence next door had rattled her so much.

It wasn't as if she'd known the girl particularly well when the Prescotts had been around, but Venetia's mother Tallulah had been a good friend, and Tallulah's sister Yolanda had been fun when she came to stay, which was often. Even so, the niggling feeing that she was missing something wouldn't go away. Of course, there were the disturbing rumours about Venetia that circulated just before the family from next door left, but Winnie and Anthea obviously knew nothing of those. Beryl, on the other hand, had been privy to rather more information about Vee's father, Ivan Prescott, which she'd vowed to herself never to pass on to a single soul in the village. What was even more unsettling was the gut feeling she'd always had that somehow her beloved son Patrick's deep unhappiness had been linked to Venetia and her little gang. But how? He'd never confided anything about his troubled state of mind to his parents. Beryl racked her brains. What was she not remembering? It might be something totally insignificant and nothing to do with the boy's misery at that time, but then again, it might not.

Beryl drained her mug and decided to do what she'd been putting off since she'd unpacked her suitcase and thrown a load of washing into the machine. She hauled herself to her feet with an involuntary groan – maybe joining that salsa class in Majorca had been a mistake – and went over to the bookshelf by the living room door. A recent cull of a lot of the older books had made the shelf look much tidier but Beryl hadn't been able to part with the albums, and she knew she never would. They dated right back to the early days of her marriage. The earlier photographs depicting Beryl as a baby had been appropriated by her sister when the family house was emptied, and she'd been glad to see the back of them at the time. With a small son to deal with and not much room to spare, number five Fiddler's Row had always been kept scrupulously tidy. That was no problem, the pictures she needed were right here in front of her.

Beryl made herself as ready for the experience as she possibly could. The photographs she was going to look at were those showing what she thought of as the golden years, when Eddie was bringing home a good wage and everything in the garden was rosy. She'd wanted more children after Patrick was born but it just hadn't happened. Their little boy was a joy to them both, and Beryl eventually resigned herself to the fact that Patrick was going to grow up without the gang of brothers and sisters she'd planned for him.

Homing in on the two decades that were at the forefront of her mind, Beryl reached for a large navy-blue album. She remembered sticking the photographs in this particular one herself, although Eddie had usually claimed that job. He loved cataloguing their life and writing amusing (or so he thought) captions, although in those days, he'd not exactly been a dab hand at photography. A lot of the pictures featured figures with various limbs or their heads missing, due to his impulsive habit of taking *point and press* snapshots. Others had the fuzzy image of a large thumb in the corner. Regardless of the lack of technical skill, the album now in Beryl's lap was a beautiful reminder of days gone by.

'Oh, Patrick,' she whispered, as she turned the pages, marvelling at the radiant smile and auburn curls of her first and only child. He'd been an adorable baby once he'd stopped being so red and dribbly, a chubby, loving toddler and a sturdy little boy with a fascination for finding out about rocks. His collection of stones had gradually taken over his bedroom and it was no surprise to Beryl and Eddie when eventually Patrick took off for university to study geology. It was earlier when he was at secondary school when things had started to go badly wrong in his life, and to be honest, Beryl had been glad to see him escape the confines of Willowbrook and get away from the school cohort that seemed to have been the catalyst for his anxiety.

Beryl closed the album and sat with it on her knee. She reached for the next one. This catalogued Patrick's teenage years up until he'd left home. As she turned the pages, Beryl felt her stomach clenching. The familiar trembly sensation was back. It happened whenever she pondered too deeply on her son's too-short life and how it ended. One picture stood out from the others. In it, Patrick stood on the edge of a group of his class-mates. Beryl remembered that this had been taken at a school camping trip to North Wales.

The date was under the photograph in her own neat writing:

19 August 1985

Patrick had an arm around the shoulders of a pretty girl with blonde curls. Venetia Prescott was standing on the other side of her. Aha. Venetia Prescott and Rhonda Clements. Both names triggered a whole lot more unwelcome memories. Patrick had been completely besotted with Rhonda for a while. When Beryl had been teasing Winnie and Anthea about her inside knowledge of past village affairs, she'd only been thinking of Venetia's involvement, but now... there was more, much more to think about.

Had she blanked some of it out? Had losing Patrick affected her mind in such a way that she couldn't handle all the memo-ries? Beryl knew about this sort of thing from her addiction to certain types of daytime TV, where digging into people's psyches was held up as entertainment. The thoughts crowding her mind were ones that she didn't usually allow in, but seeing Venetia yesterday had opened doors that should probably remain closed. The temptation to dig deeper was strong today. She shivered. There was nobody left to ask about those times. Then, an idea came to her right out of the blue. Someone who might know what really happened back then was Venetia's aunt, Yolanda, who had been staying in Willowbrook with her sister and family at the time of the summer camping trip to Wales. But Yolanda was far away now, living out her retirement in the small French town where she'd made her home many years ago. Beryl reached for her phone and pressed Winnie's number. The call was answered immediately.

'Hello, are you missing me already?' Winnie's voice was always reassuring and today it seemed especially warming.

'Ha! As if. No, I just wanted to ask you something.'

'You're seeing me later, couldn't it wait? I'm just preparing the chicken. My hands are all sticky.'

'This won't take long. A quick question, that's all. How much do you remember about the time when my Patrick...' Beryl swallowed hard and carried on. 'When my Patrick was at the secondary school in Meadowthorpe with Venetia from next door? I know your kids were younger and we didn't see much of each other around then. I was working full time at the surgery, and you had your hands full. You used to be looking after half the toddlers in the neighbourhood if I remember rightly.'

Winnie didn't answer for a moment. Then she cleared her throat. 'I haven't heard you mention your lovely boy for a long, long time,' she said. 'What's brought this on?'

'That's not important. What do you remember, Winnie?'

'I'm not sure what I'm meant to say to that,' Winnie said. 'You've already mentioned why we didn't live in each other's pockets then, like we do now. I didn't know Patrick very well. What I do recall is a handsome lad with a shock of ginger hair. He was...'

'He was what?' Beryl prompted. 'Go on.'

'Well, he was almost too good-looking to be true. Kind of... delicate, if you know what I mean. Fragile.'

'But you don't remember anything about the crowd he hung around with? Or tried to,' Beryl added bitterly.

'Sorry, no, I don't. As you said, we moved in different orbits at that time. Why are you asking? I'm guessing it's the new arrival next door that's set you off?'

'Ignore me, it was just a thought. I'll see you and Anthea later. Is she picking you up?' Beryl said, hoping to distract Winnie. Her ploy worked.

'Is she ever. That woman's driving gets worse every time I go out with her. I usually manage to make an excuse, but I need a lift to bring the food tonight. Wish me luck. Do you remember Jasper Carrott, the comedian? He did a great sketch about people's ridiculous car insurance claims.'

Beryl, mystified, said she didn't.

'Well, there was that one where he said something like, "The driver said the accident was caused by him waving to the man he ran into last week." Always made me giggle... until now.'

'You're not saying she's running people over? Please say she isn't.'

Winnie's hearty laugh made Beryl move the phone away from her ear for a moment. 'No, it's not quite that bad... yet... but last time she gave me a lift she nearly crashed into a tree while she was pointing to a bollard she'd backed into the day before. I'd ring for a taxi and arrange to call for her instead, but I suggested it recently and she hit the roof. We need to talk seriously to her about maybe giving up her car.'

'Good luck with that one,' said Beryl. 'It's about as likely as Anthea starting to wear jeans. Anyway, off you go and finish the chicken. Forget what I asked you. It's nothing. The Prosecco's in the fridge. We can share the holiday photos on our phones and plan the next jolly. Bye for now.'

Ending the call, Beryl sat back in her chair again and picked up the album. It fell open at the first picture of the small Patrick, taken when Beryl was still in hospital. She'd unwrapped him from his lacy shawl, but his wide-open mouth reminded her of just how loudly her boy was able to scream at that point in his life. A soft fuzz of ginger hair already indicated that he'd be a redhead like his father. Her mother-in-law, Glenys, had taken one look at him the day after this and said sadly, 'This baby looks like a potato. He's not been blessed with looks, has he?'

Beryl was mortified. She hadn't spoken to the woman for at least a week, and the comment still stung. Looking at the photo in question, she could see Eddie's mother's point. It wasn't Patrick's finest hour, but there was no need to mention it, was there? Grannies were meant to be doting. She'd made up for it later, but Beryl had never quite forgiven Glenys for the insult. Now, so many years later, she wished Glenys was here to talk to. Patrick's gran had still been around when he'd hit his worst patch. She'd be bound to remember the details of what went on at Mead-owthorpe Comprehensive after hours. School discos and luridly coloured alcopops had a lot to answer for. Patrick had often been to see his granny on the way home. It hurt her heart to think her son hadn't confided his troubles to his loving parents. Beryl put the book to one side and resolved to ask Venetia at the first opportunity if her aunt was able to chat on the phone. She'd say it was just for old times' sake. And it was. Sort of, anyway.

7

Rick unlocked his van and leaned on it. Venetia was still in the house, and if she didn't hurry up, half the day would be over before they'd even begun work. As he'd passed her bedroom door, Rick had heard muffled swearing, so he assumed she was fighting her way into the boiler suit he'd lent her. It was much too narrow for him since he'd been going to the gym and building up his muscles, but the legs were long, and he'd hoped it would fit his lodger.

Eventually, Vee emerged from the house, pink in the face but dressed for action in an orange jumpsuit and trainers.

'You didn't mention the million and one poppers on this thing,' she said. 'I thought I was going to have to shout for help. I've got into it, but I may never get out of it again.'

Rick grinned. 'I know what you mean,' he said. 'I bought six of them in a sale, hence the colour. It turned out they were all different sizes though. I'm not into looking like I've been Tangoed as a rule. In my defence, they were dirt cheap.'

'I can see why,' Vee said, pulling a face. 'But this is going to keep me from getting totally filthy so it's worth playing the part of a giant satsuma. Let's go.'

They got into the van and Rick tossed her a bright orange baseball cap. 'I bought these at the same time,' he said. 'Job lot, three for a tenner. It'll keep the cobwebs and dust out of your hair. I'll wear one too, then you won't feel such a prat.'

'That's a matter of opinion,' Vee said, but she put it on and peered at herself in the rear-view mirror. 'Lovely. Who wants to look cool anyway? It's so last season.'

They reached Dragonfly Cottage just as Beryl was emerging from her front door. She'd paused to chat with a woman who was standing outside the house on the other side of hers.

'Oh, you're back,' Beryl said, without enthusiasm. 'Well, good luck to you both. It's a job like those stables in the old myth. My teacher told us it at school when we were doing about the Ancient Greeks... I can't remember what they were called.'

'That's a bit harsh, Beryl,' said the lady standing beside her. 'It was the Augean Stables, and poor old Heracles had to clean out thirty years' worth of cattle dung. I'm sure this cottage isn't going to be that bad. I'm Kate, by the way. I hear we're going to be neighbours.'

'This is the amazing person who runs the café on Willow-brook Country Park. Best cakes and scones for miles around,' added Rick, tipping his orange baseball cap to Kate. 'You should get yourself over there for a visit sometime, Vee.'

'I think I might be doing my dung-shovelling challenge for a good long while yet, but I'll put it on my list of things to do when I get this place in a liveable state,' said Vee. She smiled at Kate. 'I don't usually look like an Oompa-Loompa. Nice to meet you. Rick's decided on our team colours today.'

They headed indoors, with Vee carrying bin bags, a broom and a shovel and Rick following on with a couple of cardboard boxes he'd fetched from the back of the van. He also had a transistor radio which he switched on as soon as they were in the living room.

'I work better with music on,' he said, as an old Queen hit blasted out of the tiny speaker. '"Another One Bites the Dust", how appropriate. Let's start in here.'

Vee looked around at the mess and her shoulders slumped. 'It's impossible,' she said. 'We need a skip, not bin bags.'

'And that's why meeting me was so lucky,' said Rick. 'I know a guy who drives a skip lorry. I gave him a call this morning and he agreed to drop us one off. Mate's rates, don't worry,' he cut in, before Vee could object. 'I know we said we'd do loads of tip trips but this way we'll save time, and I can get on with the real work much sooner, okay? You might want to add one of these to your fetching outfit. It'll block out a bit of the stink, at least. I had some left over from the Covid times.'

He rummaged in the pocket of his jeans and passed Vee a mask. She put it on and nodded her thanks. Both masked, they got stuck in immediately, falling into a sort of rhythm where they took turns to hold the plastic rubbish sacks while the other shovelled in anything lying on the floor. There was very little that was good enough for a charity shop but as they worked their way through the house, now and again Rick spotted a small piece of furniture that was salvageable and put it into the back of his van.

By lunchtime, both Rick and Venetia were flagging. They'd grown used to the smell, which thankfully lessened as the bags were filled, drunk all the bottled water that Rick had brought with them and breakfast seemed like a very long time in the past. Rick was about to suggest they might adjourn to go and find a roadside café somewhere that wouldn't mind them being so grubby and dishevelled, when a knock came at the front door.

'That might be Jed with the skip,' said Rick. 'I'll go.'

He was wrong. Standing outside on the path was Beryl and she was carrying a loaded tray. 'Here, take this off me before I drop it,' she said. 'I've already nearly gone arse over tit trying to get it this far.'

Rick wasted no time in relieving her of her burden. 'You are an angel,' he said. 'Come on in.'

Beryl followed him down the hall, looking around with interest. 'We did talk about the Labours of Heracles,' she said. 'But this is even worse than I imagined. It smells like something's died in here.'

'You'd be right there,' said Vee, straightening up from her shovelling and rubbing her back. 'We've found three dead birds and a couple of deceased rats so far. Is there a neighbourhood cat that likes to have somewhere to stash its victims? There was a window left open in the utility room.'

'That'll be Slasher,' said Beryl. 'He keeps the vermin down for us all. He's an enormous ginger tom. Lives at number two but has dinners wherever he can get them. Here, don't let the tea go cold, and I thought you might be ready for a snack.'

She whisked a tea towel decorated with royal wedding portraits off the tray that Rick was still holding and revealed two large mugs of tea, some sachets of sugar and a plate of hefty bacon sandwiches. 'You're not one of them *vegetarians*, are you?' she asked Vee, giving the word the same kind of connotation as if she'd said *axe murderers*.

Vee shook her head. 'Not me,' she said. 'Oh, this is really good of you, Beryl. We were just about to keel over from lack of food and hot drinks, weren't we, Rick?'

Beryl folded her arms and sniffed. 'I'm not going to be making a habit of waiting on you, so don't get any ideas. I just thought for today, you'd need a bit of sustenance. I'm off now. I've got the girls coming round later for film night and I'm still not straight after my holiday.'

'Girls?' said Vee, reaching for a mug of tea. 'Do you have grandchildren then?'

Beryl snorted. 'Not me. No, it's my gang. The Saga Louts, they call us, in the village. We like our holidays. Anyway, I'll see you around. You can bring the things back later.' This remark was directed at Rick, who had put the tray down on a somewhat cleaner part of the floor for want of a table.

He saw Beryl to the door. 'I'd hug you for doing this, but I don't think you'd thank me for transferring all my muck onto your dress,' he said as he held the door open.

'Absolutely correct, you disgusting man,' she said, but patted his arm affectionately before heading back into her own house with what looked like relief.

After this impromptu picnic, Vee and Rick got on with the job with renewed gusto. By the time Jed arrived with the skip, most of the rooms were clear of rubbish and the pile of bin bags on the front path and snaking their way all down the hall was in danger of collapsing under the strain. Jed, a burly individual with a Mediterranean tan and a beer belly that must have been the result of years of propping up a range of bars, had helped Rick to load the skip while Vee did a last trawl around the cottage to see if anything had been missed. The floors were swept, fresh air had been pouring in through all the open windows and the back door for hours, and it was possible to see that one day this would be a cosy, friendly place to live.

'I'll drop the rest of the stuff at the nearest charity shop tomorrow,' said Rick as they climbed wearily into the van. 'We've done plenty for today. Bagsy first shower.'

'Well, it's your house after all,' said Vee.

He glanced across at her as she leaned on the passenger window. Exhaustion screamed from every part of her body. The baseball cap had long been discarded, and her hair was wildly curly, but even in an orange boiler suit liberally streaked with dirt, Rick couldn't help noticing that this was a beautiful woman who didn't need fine clothes to be stunning. He forced himself to think about something else. The last thing he needed was to get ideas about his lodger. That would be a disaster.

'Shall we ring for a takeaway when we're clean?' he said. 'I told you that was what I was intending to do and I don't think either of us is going to feel like cooking up a storm tonight. Or... have you made other plans?'

Vee laughed. 'Well, I was going to get my best frock on, call for a cab and go out for some fine dining,' she said. 'But as you're asking, a pizza would be a good second best.'

They regrouped an hour later, both with hair still damp from the shower. Rick had changed into joggers and a sweatshirt and was padding around barefoot in the kitchen trying to find the paper leaflet that had been pushed through the door a few days before.

He turned as Vee came into the room, dressed in a floor-length silky caftan in shades of emerald green and gold. His mouth dropped open. 'Oh...' was all he managed to say.

'Too much for a night in?' she asked, doing a twirl. 'Sorry to outshine your evening gear, but I threw away all my tattiest sweatpants and t-shirts when I moved, and I haven't had chance to go shopping again. I can't afford posh clothes now, but this was left over from the theatre days.'

'It's... it's very pretty,' Rick said, swallowing hard. 'Hey, I found a menu. There's a new pizza place opened in Meadowthorpe, and they deliver out here. What do you fancy?'

'Anything and everything. I'm starving. And before you say

anything about paying, I'll get this. It's the least I can do after today. Let's get two small ones and share, with some dough balls and wedges and things? It's more fun than just choosing one each, unless you're a fussy eater.'

Rick reached for his phone and tapped in an order. A fussy eater he definitely was not. He got two bottles of beer out of the fridge, opened them both and passed one to Vee. She nodded her thanks and tilted the bottle to drink.

'Oh, my life, that's perfection,' she said. 'I can't believe how lucky I was to meet you at the shop and for you to let me have the room for now and then to take on the horrible job of making the cottage right again.'

Rick was just about to fall down the dangerous rabbit hole of saying how wonderful it was to have Vee here when he realised that she hadn't finished talking.

'When I came back to Willowbrook, I wasn't sure if I could get over the bad memories from when I was fifteen,' she said. 'You wouldn't believe the cruelty of some of the kids at the school where I went. There was one group... they called themselves the Vipers, although goodness knows why.'

'Really?' said Rick. His voice came out as a croak, but Vee didn't seem to notice.

'Yes, ridiculous name. There were three girls who nobody else wanted to hang out with, and two horrible sleazy boys, ditto. They used to roam around the village trying to look cool. I always thought they had something to do with...'

'With what?' prompted Rick, although the last thing he wanted was to hear the rest of the sentence.

'Oh, nothing. I just hope I never, ever meet them again. Hey, that was the doorbell. The food's here.'

She jumped to her feet and was at the front door in seconds, while Rick still sat at the kitchen table. He heard Vee chatting to the delivery man and put his head in his hands. How was he going to make sure that Vee never found out the identity of one of those unlikeable boys? He should have listened to his instincts when they met in the shop, but he'd fooled himself that the past wouldn't rear its ugly head if he played his cards right. It was going to be an uphill struggle from now on.

8

To Beryl's amazement, Winnie and Anthea turned up for film night in a taxi after all, and came staggering in under the weight of various pots and pans containing Caribbean food of the highest quality.

'What's all this, Anthea?' Beryl asked, exchanging glances with Winnie. 'Couldn't you get your car to start?'

Anthea drew herself up to her full height and fixed Beryl with a steely glare. 'There's nothing whatsoever wrong with my lovely motor, thank you very much,' she said. 'I just felt like having a glass or two of Prosecco tonight. It's no fun watching you pair drink your way through the whole lot while I'm stuck with apple juice, you know.'

Beryl refrained from commenting on this change of heart and concentrated on getting her guests organised. Winnie was soon in the kitchen assembling their feast while Anthea busied herself popping the first cork. 'Cheers, darlings,' she said, raising her champagne flute. 'Here's to many more holidays, although I'm not sure my hip's up to any more salsa for a while.'

'Get away,' snorted Winnie. 'You've got more go in you than the rest of us put together. I saw the way you looked at that DJ at the Bar Tropicana. Silver fox, or what?'

'He was a bit tasty,' said Beryl. 'Are you ready for husband number five, Anthea? Have you given up on Maurice already?'

Anthea took a large swig of Prosecco and topped up their glasses. 'It's very sad but I think he could be a total washout,' she said. 'We've had dinner together on a couple of nights, but both times he started yawning about nine o'clock, just as I was revving up for the evening. Last time he took me out I was in bed by 9.30 p.m. On my own,' she added sadly. 'Still, you never know. He's a sweet man and he might up his game yet.'

Winnie turned the heat down on her pans and they adjourned to Beryl's cosy living room. Two easy chairs and a sofa were positioned so that her large TV screen could be seen from anywhere in the room, each with access to an occasional table and a footstool. This, along with the many embroidered cushions, made the small room seem rather crowded, but Beryl had long ago decided to forego elegance in her home and go for comfort. The walls were hung with enlarged photographs of places she'd visited, both with the Saga Louts and previously with her husband Eddie. There was only one family photograph on show.

Winnie looked round the familiar room appreciatively. 'I always love looking at your gallery,' she said. 'It's like travelling back through time. We've had some fun, haven't we?'

'We certainly have,' said Anthea. 'And there's plenty more to come. I know it was a sad business for you two, being widowed like that, and for me with my last divorce, although to be fair, that wasn't so much sad as being given a *Get Out of Jail Free* card. Number four was a pain in the neck. Quite literally, actually. Conrad insisted on having the bedroom window wide open and it played havoc with my rheumatics. Remember him, Beryl?'

'Yes, I certainly do, Conrad wasn't your finest choice, was he? Mind you, they haven't all been bad. I quite liked Grenville until he took off with your gardener.'

'Who'd have thought Grenville batted for the other side? And Marcus was the best gardener you'd ever had so it was a double whammy. You do know how to pick them, Anthea,' said Winnie.

She pulled a face. 'This is exactly why I'm going to be less hasty in the future. I don't want to go through all that malarkey again unless it's worth it.'

'You're wise to be careful. What about Quentin who took all your best silk knickers with him when you threw him out? Although to be fair, Laurence was okay, apart from the rambling. He was never at home, was he? Lived for his treks across the countryside.'

Beryl laughed. 'I know, except that last time he rambled off and was never seen again.'

'But at least the final divorce meant we could team up and take our first trip together,' said Winnie. 'When you eventually threw Conrad out it was a relief to all of us. A weekend in Marbella we started with, didn't we, Beryl? Sun, sea, sangria...'

'We did indeed. I got sunstroke for the only time ever. Without Eddie there to nag me about sun cream, I took my eye off the ball. As for you, Winnie, I've never seen anyone be so keen to go on a banana boat.'

'And I only fell off once,' said Winnie, preening herself. 'I showed those youngsters a thing or two, didn't I, Beryl? You were hanging on for dear life.'

'Yes, it *was* two things you showed them, if I remember rightly. Your bikini top came right off. That lifeguard will probably never be the same again.' Beryl giggled and reached for the TV controls. 'What's it to be then? A bit more of lovely Hugh Grant? *Notting Hill*?'

The other two agreed, and for the next hour, peace reigned apart from the popping of another cork and somewhat bawdy asides about the marvellousness of Mr Grant's bottom. When a timer pinged in the kitchen, Beryl paused the action.

'Time to eat,' she said. 'Trays on knees, as usual? Then we can carry on with the action.'

Anthea and Winnie agreed readily and got to their feet to help with serving the food. Soon the three ladies were sitting with a padded tray on each lap and the delectable aroma of Winnie's legendary jerk chicken filling the room. For a while, eating took all their attention, but then Beryl put her fork down and paused the film again.

'I wanted to talk to you both about something,' she said. 'I need some advice. I'm... well, I'll be honest, I'm proper worried.'

'That sounds ominous, darling,' said Anthea. 'Have you been thinking inappropriate thoughts in church again?'

Beryl snorted. 'You know I only go to church if the Rev Bev has something interesting on, with cake afterwards. I miss her Happiness Gang meetings. We should arrange a get-together again soon. They gave us a lot to think about, did those get-togethers. But no, it's nothing to do with Bev. This is more serious.'

She had the full attention of the other two now, which was gratifying. 'Go on,' said Anthea. 'You can't stop there. Hang on, let me just top our glasses up again if it's going to be confession time.'

With this task completed, Anthea sat down again and she and Winnie waited for Beryl to continue.

'It's about *her-next-door*,' said Beryl, lowering her voice slightly as if Vee was hiding outside the window with her ear to the glass. She took a large gulp of her drink and burped in a ladylike manner. 'That Venetia Prescott's unsettled me, and that's the truth.'

'In what way? I sussed that you knew something about what happened when the Prescotts left Willowbrook in such a hurry. Come on, spill the beans,' said Winnie.

Beryl took a deep breath. 'I can't stop thinking about my Patrick,' she said, in a rush. 'I'm certain Venetia and her nasty little group had something to do with him being so unhappy. There was a big cover-up at the time. The vicar then was a nice chap, quite sexy in his way, but not very... forceful, shall we say. He turned a blind eye to the stuff those kids were getting up to in the churchyard on the nights when their parents thought they were at the youth club.'

'Oh!' Winnie's exclamation made Anthea jump so much she spilt some Prosecco on her dress. 'The fire! You're talking about when they set fire to the shed, aren't you?'

'Don't do that again, darling,' Anthea said, dabbing at the wet patch with a napkin. 'This is my new one. Can't go wrong with linen, I always say, but stains never look good. Carry on, Beryl. It's getting to be like an episode of *Grantchester*. I do love a handsome vicar and a bit of intrigue. What fire? What shed? I must have been on one of my extended adventures and missed it.'

'Our vicar wasn't quite as fanciable as those *Grantchester* ones on the TV, but I didn't hold that against him. He was just weak, I guess. He wanted the teenagers to like him, so they'd come to church. It didn't work. And the fire was what triggered all the other bad things. It was while you were living in Gibraltar with husband number two, Anthea. That's why you don't remember. Someone burnt down the shed where all the gardening equipment for the churchyard was stored.'

Winnie got up to clear away their plates. Her expression was thoughtful. 'It's all coming back to me now,' she said as she came back from the kitchen with a tray loaded with a dish of banana fritters, a carton of rum and raisin ice cream and three bowls. 'It was hushed up at the time. The vicar said he didn't want a fuss, and that the fire was probably caused by somebody flicking a stray cigarette end over the wall.'

Beryl shook her head. 'That was the party line,' she said. 'The head at the school where the kids all went didn't really want there to be a full investigation and the police couldn't do much if the vicar wasn't going to press charges if anyone was caught so it all went quiet. We all suspected that there was something he'd stored in the shed that he didn't want anyone to find out about. Whatever the reason for the cover-up, Patrick was never the same after that and the Prescotts left soon afterwards.'

Anthea was definitely interested now. 'So, tell us more,' she said. 'What do you think was going on in the churchyard after dark? What was your boy so upset about? Who do you think caused the fire?'

'And more to the point, why?' said Winnie. 'Was it just a prank that went wrong?'

'I thought it was, to begin with, but looking back, I'm not so sure. And then soon after that, there was the awful camping trip in Wales.' Beryl guessed by the look on her face that Anthea was going to ask for more details, so she pressed on quickly. 'At the time, Eddie and me were just intent on getting Patrick on an even keel again. He went off to university and we were so proud. We thought he'd put it all behind him. But then he...'

'The poor lad got sick, and it was all over very quickly,' finished Winnie, when she could see that Beryl was unable to say any more. There was a short silence while Beryl pulled herself together.

'Yes, and when Patrick died, the light went out of our world and we forgot all about everything else,' Beryl said huskily. 'And now... Venetia's back and I want to know exactly what happened around that time. I owe it to my son. I've got to put these thoughts to rest. I'm sure she was involved, and not in a good way. Ladies... I don't care what it takes, I mean to find out.'

and we forgot all about everything else. Perry and I finished. And we Vanessa, that's that I want to know. So do I – what happened about the things for 'Around Again' you're to get those back his for. Look, I'm sure she was invelled, promise you. Good way. Ladies too. You? what it takes, I need to find out.

9

After the evening with Rick, which involved a very decent curry and a trawl through his old vinyl collection, Vee struggled to get up the next morning. She lay in bed listening to the gushing of the shower backed up with a very passable rendition of 'Born to be Wild' and couldn't remember when she'd had such a good night's sleep.

Rick was obviously not averse to being clean. So far, he'd always smelt pleasantly of some sort of zingy shower gel and a delicate spritz of aftershave, which was a welcome contrast to Nigel. Her new landlord had also blitzed the kitchen before they went to bed and even remembered to put out the recycling for the next morning's collection. Vee knew she'd landed on her feet, but the thought of all the work that was going to need doing at Dragonfly Cottage was incredibly daunting.

Raising her arms in a big stretch, Vee yawned noisily and dragged herself out from under the duvet. A fresh boiler suit courtesy of Rick was waiting for her on the chair by the window, as orange as the previous one, and the filthy version was already whirling round in the washing machine along with Rick's clothes from the day before. The singing stopped abruptly, and Vee heard the bathroom door open, so she gave Rick a few minutes to get back to his room and then hurried to take her turn in the blissfully hot water of the power shower.

Less than an hour later they were back in the van, having eaten toast and marmalade at speed. 'We'll call at the big DIY place on the edge of Meadowthorpe first,' said Rick. 'I've made a list of the basics we need to start us off. You can borrow my decorating gear and my bucket and mop and so on to save a bit of cash. I loaded them into the van while you were getting ready. After that we'll make a very quick stop at a supermarket to grab something for lunch and then we'll do a drop off at the charity shop, okay?'

Vee flexed her aching shoulders and nodded gratefully. She knew she'd given Rick a highly inflated rundown of her physical prowess yesterday. It was a while since any of her gardening experiences and as for the patio-laying job, that had been a very small area and she'd been helped by Nigel when he was still trying to impress her. Now, stiffness was setting in, and she wasn't sure if she had the stamina for another full day of grafting in the cottage. But it had to be done, and there was no way she could afford to pay Rick to do the whole lot himself.

The DIY store was vast and full of items that Rick seemed to think were vital, but he was very restrained in the end and didn't overspend. Laden with paint and a variety of other commodities, they set off again, dropped the furniture at a local charity shop and were soon pulling up outside Dragonfly Cottage.

Vee glanced across at Rick as he killed the engine. 'Where do we start?' she asked wearily. 'I feel as if anything I do will be a drop in the ocean at the moment.'

'Well, we can't do a thing until all the stinking carpets and that horrible, cracked lino is history,' said Rick. 'And that's a mucky job. Are you up for it?'

She nodded and climbed out of the van, going to the back doors to help unload their purchases, but Rick held up a hand. 'Don't bring anything in yet, we need to clear the decks first. Jed's coming back with another skip after lunch, and he'll get rid of it all. Before you say anything, remember that he owes me a couple of favours. Let's get to it. All we'll want is my radio, toolbox, gloves and masks for the moment.'

Five minutes later, both Vee and Rick had baseball caps, thick gloves and masks on. The radio was playing hits from the eighties, which were already making Vee want to dance, tired as she was. She realised that without the music, her morale would be at rock bottom and blessed Rick's forethought in providing it.

'Come on, let's get stuck in,' said Rick. He began to pull up the hall carpet. 'You get the brush and dustpan and a bin bag, Vee. You can follow me round picking up any underlay and sweeping up the bits. It's so old it'll disintegrate as we go. Everything's full of dust.' He coughed and sneezed. 'Urgh, it's getting to me already.'

They worked together at the same steady pace as yesterday, sometimes singing along to the music, stopping for regular swigs from Rick's fresh supplies of bottled water and both having several bouts of tempestuous sneezing and coughing. Although Vee felt grubbier than she'd been in her entire life, there was something therapeutic about this total destruction of the remnants of the past. 'A clean sweep!' she shouted at one point and they both took these words up as a kind of battle cry, whenever they struggled with a particularly tough area.

Soon, rolls of chopped-up carpet and bags of debris were piled up in the hall, leaving just enough room to squeeze past when Jed rang the doorbell at two o'clock. Exhausted but jubilant, Vee let him in and between them they lugged all the rubbish they'd collected outside and flung it into the new skip.

'Cheers, mate,' Rick said, slapping his friend on the back just as he left. 'We couldn't have managed without you. Well, we could, I guess, but it would have been a right faff to keep driving to the tip.'

In the lull after Jed departed, Vee and Rick sank down onto the now-cleared living room floor. The windows were open to let in a warm breeze and the bad smell had almost gone. Outside, birds were singing, and sunbeams were lighting up the dust motes that danced in the air. Vee thought about washing the floor next but was so shattered that she couldn't bring herself to make another start.

'Hungry?' asked Rick. 'I'll get the picnic. Stay there, I'll be back soon.'

Vee couldn't have moved if she tried. She leaned back against the wall and viewed her property. It was a pleasing room now that everything that had been cluttering it was gone. A tiled fireplace with a hideous gas fire was on one wall. That was going to have to go. She didn't see any reason why the old grate and surround couldn't be ripped out and the chimney opened up. As a child, Vee had loved watching the flames flicker in the grate. Her parents were big fans of a roaring coal and log fire as soon as there was a chill in the air, and their daughters had both been trained from an early age to roll and twist newspaper tightly to make the 'paper sticks' her dad insisted on as firelighters.

Rick came back into the room carrying a supermarket bag. 'I've washed my hands. You'd better do the same before we eat. You're a health hazard at the moment,' he said, grinning down at Vee.

She rolled over onto her knees and got to her feet, groaning as she straightened up. 'This is saving us a whole lot of money in gym memberships,' she said. 'I must have used muscles that haven't been exercised for years.'

'But Venetia Prescott, you told me you were used to hard work,' said Rick. Vee turned to look at him and he gazed back innocently.

'I think we both know I was exaggerating,' she said, laughing. 'But I'm getting there. I'll do my bit. Teamwork, that's what this is. We're doing a great job. I feel as if I've known you for ages.'

Rick didn't answer, but a look of such sadness passed across his face that Vee hesitated. 'What's up?' she said. 'Did I say something wrong?'

He shook his head. 'No, no... it was just... oh, nothing. Go and get clean, I'm starving. It's warm enough to be in the garden now, see you there.'

They ate everything that was in the bag, sitting shoulder to shoulder on the steps leading to the rough expanse of lawn. Vee was relieved that Jed had come back into the house after finishing loading the skip and asked if there was anything else to go, as he had a bit of room left. Just in time, Rick had remembered the half-burnt mattress in the garden. While he and Jed were lugging it through the house, Vee collected as many other bits of old play equipment and broken garden furniture that she could find, and they'd flung those in on top of everything else. Now, the garden looked a lot less depressing, although it was very overgrown.

'You two are looking very comfy,' said a voice from over the fence.

Both craned their necks to see who had spoken, but the direction of the sound meant it could only be one person. 'Hang on, I'm coming over,' Beryl called. 'Give me a hand, Rick. It's easy to break bones when you get to my age, and you don't want that on your conscience for the sake of a piece of cake.'

Rick got to his feet and made for the part of the garden where the hedge met the decrepit fence. Sure enough, Beryl's head could be seen getting higher and higher.

'This is how I used to get over when I came to visit your mum,' she shouted to Vee. 'Only I was a good bit younger then and the hedge wasn't so high. Give us a hand, young man. I'm wobbling on these pesky steps.'

As Rick reached out to help, Beryl passed him a cake tin and slung one leg over the fence. He put the tin down quickly and caught her just as she teetered over towards him. Vee had jumped to her feet by this time, certain that this acrobatic elderly lady was going to plunge headfirst into her garden, but Rick lifted her up as if she was no heavier than a child and placed her gently on the grass.

'Phew, that was trickier than I expected,' Beryl said, tidying her hair. 'I'm glad I was wearing my oldest leggings. That fence hasn't had a rub down for years, and the hedge is a disgrace, I'm all mossy.'

She began to brush herself down and Vee helped by picking twigs of privet out of her jumper. 'I'm not sure that's the safest way for you to come and visit,' she began but Beryl quelled her with a look.

'I think I'll be the judge of that,' she said, with a sniff. 'Do you want a piece of my fruitcake, or what? It's said to be the best in Willowbrook. I won a rosette for it at the village show last summer.'

Rick gestured for Beryl to come and sit down on the steps. 'We can't offer you a chair at this point,' he said. 'But as for cake, it's yes from me.'

'Actually, I didn't just come to bring supplies,' Beryl said. 'I heard the music. Fancied a bit of a dance, I did. It took me right back. Me and your mum.' She pointed to Venetia. 'We used to dance on the grass when the mood took us. We cut the hedge right down in one place so we could hop over and see each other.'

'I don't remember that happening,' said Vee. 'Where was I?'

'I suppose it was when you'd be at school. We were nifty movers in those days. Turn the volume up, lad, and I'll show you a thing or two.'

Somewhat bemused, Rick did as he was told and the sound of Billy Ocean singing 'When the Going Gets Tough' filled the garden. Instantly, Beryl began to dance, first jigging from foot to foot and waggling her elbows in the style of the more senior wedding guests at the evening disco but then branching out into a kind of solo tango, up and down the lawn.

Vee and Rick looked on in amazement, mouths gaping. As the tempo speeded up, Beryl whooped as she headed back towards them, gave a skip and fell over a tussock of grass. Before she had chance to hit the floor, Rick leaped forward and caught her again, scooping her up in his arms.

'Ooh, Ricardo.' Beryl giggled. 'You're sooo strong. Good job you were there.'

Vee's heart was pounding. The sight of the elderly lady heading for what could have been a nasty fall had taken her right back to the final days with her mum, when Tallulah had fallen over more times than she was upright. Then the use of the different name caught at her attention. Ricardo? Why did that ring a bell?

'What did you just call him?' Vee asked, in case she'd misheard.

Rick put Beryl down and made a big performance of making sure she wasn't going to wobble. 'Oh, it's just a daft nickname she sometimes uses,' he said. 'Right, you're okay now, aren't you, Beryl? How about cutting that fruitcake? We really need an energy boost.'

Beryl gave him a sideways look but said no more, busying herself with opening the tin and bringing out a knife, three paper plates and a large cake, gilded with glacé cherries, walnuts and almonds that glistened under their sticky glaze of apricot jam.

Vee thought about pursuing her question, but the sight of the cake put that idea out of her head. She accepted a large slice, almost forgetting to say thank you in her eagerness to bite into it. Silence reigned apart from happy munching noises. Beryl looked to be enjoying her own creation as much as the other two were, but when they'd all finished, she collected their plates and said, 'It was funny, that song playing just at the right time.'

'Why was it funny?' Rick said, brushing the last crumbs from his boiler suit.

'Well, Tallulah did the exact opposite of *getting going* with life when things got tough. Instead of sticking around to sort out her problems here, she voted with her feet, didn't she, Venetia? She did a runner. Tallulah got going in quite the wrong way. Why was that? I always wondered. Your ma wasn't the kind of woman to quit, as a rule. Must've been something pretty drastic to make you all run away like that.'

Beryl pursed her lips and gave Vee the sort of look that made her feel she was back at school and had once again forgotten to give in her homework. It felt as if Beryl was blaming Vee in some way for what had happened back in 1985. Perhaps she was. Or did she know something else? Something that had been hidden for all these years. Maybe the secrets Vee was keeping weren't the same ones on Beryl's mind after all. Vee suddenly felt icy cold, even though the spring sunshine was warming the garden and making the daffodils that had survived the tangled mess of the border almost luminous in their golden glory. How to answer that question? She stalled, and Rick stepped in.

'I don't reckon Vee's up for talking about the past just now,' he said. 'Maybe another time, eh?' He gave Beryl his biggest smile. 'Now, what I'm wondering is, are we allowed more than one slice of cake?'

Distracted, Beryl began to fuss with the plates again, offering Vee more too, but the churning in Vee's insides made that seem like a very bad idea. She shook her head. Beryl eyed her suspiciously.

'Don't you like my fruitcake? Oh, I get it, you're on some sort of health kick, I suppose. Well, you'll be getting more than your five-a-day with this beauty, let me tell you. Sultanas, dates, cherries – you name it, it's in there. Come on, don't be shy.'

Vee wondered if it would be easier to give in now and risk being sick on Beryl's purple slip-on shoes, or try and brazen it out. The first piece, although as delicious as the very best Christmas pudding, lay heavily in her stomach and all this talk of her family's departure from Willowbrook was making her want to weep. It had been a tough time for them all even before events had escalated and triggered what amounted to a moonlight flit.

'Could we possibly have a piece each to save for later?' she asked. 'I can't resist your lovely cake, but I'm full now. We had a big lunch. Maybe it'll give us both an energy boost when we're flagging later? There's still a lot more to do before we go back to Rick's.'

Beryl considered this suggestion, and then agreed, cutting them each a slice and wrapping it in the greaseproof paper that had been underneath her cake. 'There you go,' she said. 'Now I must get back and do a few more jobs before I get ready for tonight. It's going to be a good one, I'm on a roll. Colonel Mustard with the dagger.' Beryl mimed stabbing someone, rather too realistically for Vee's liking.

'Tonight?' Was she missing something, Vee wondered? She

felt as if she'd dropped into a parallel universe. One that was strangely familiar but also very unpredictable.

'It's games night at the pub,' Rick said. 'We go every Thursday, don't we, Beryl? I play solo whist with three friends and the Saga Louts usually have a go at Cluedo, or Monopoly if they're feeling like being property magnates. You should come along.'

That wasn't how Vee had imagined her evening progressing. She'd had hopes of a hot, bubbly bath, some warm pyjamas and her fluffy dressing gown, and an early night with a sandwich to eat in bed while she read a thriller. She tried to find the right words to refuse gratefully, not wanting to offend the man who'd rescued her from sleeping on an ancient camp bed in a house that still smelt faintly of weed and other people's sweat. Luckily, Rick seemed to sense her discomfort before she had chance to reply.

'I can see you'd rather have some chill-out time later,' he said. 'There'll be plenty of opportunities for you to soak up local life at the pub in the future. You're here for good now, aren't you?'

Two words echoed around Vee's mind. *For good.* Was she? To make this new life work and to really love it, she was going to have to make a massive effort to face up to her past, and that was something that Vee had absolutely no idea how to do. Not a clue.

10

Beryl said her goodbyes, picked up her tin and returned home by the safer route. She would have rather scaled the fence again just to show those youngsters that she wasn't past it, but using the front door would avoid the danger of another tumble like the one that had landed her in hospital earlier in the year. She felt fully fit again now but it had to be admitted that she wasn't a spring chicken any more and old bones took longer to mend. Today's climb had definitely been a bit of bravado. She knew she'd been shamelessly showing off to Venetia, but the music had got into her soul as she stood in her garden taking the air and Beryl had decided to throw caution to the winds.

Caution. That had never been one of Beryl's favourite words. It belonged with *careful* and *sensible* and *prudent*. Her mother had been fond of words like these, but Beryl had never tried to conform to anyone else's rules unless it was the only option. It was a minor miracle that she'd managed to wangle an interview for the post of doctor's receptionist. She remembered giggling with Tallulah as she had tried on the borrowed skirt and jacket in serviceable gunmetal grey. It had been a perfect fit. Both women had been petite and slim, with small waists and dainty feet.

'I can't believe you own an outfit like this,' Beryl had said. 'It makes me look like a funeral director. When did you ever wear it?'

'Funnily enough, I bought it to go to Ivan's godfather's funeral,' Tallulah said. 'It was a really boring affair. Only one hymn, a very long eulogy and no booze afterwards. I haven't worn it since, needless to say. Mind you, with your pink shirt underneath, it does jazz the whole thing up a bit. And those are killer heels.'

Beryl did a twirl in front of the mirror. 'Do you think they'll employ me?' she said. 'I think I've got what it takes. I could scare away any troublesome patients, no problem. And not only that, I peeped through the hatch into the office last time I was in the surgery and if you ask me, they're in dire need of a good sort out.'

'That's your joker, so don't forget to play it at the interview,' said Tallulah. 'Your house is always tidy and neat. Not like mine. It looks like a tornado's hit it. I've only two kids, but Venetia and Cassie make enough mess for six. Now off you go and impress those doctors. You're going to be a brilliant receptionist.'

Tallulah had been right. Beryl *was* very good at her job, and she'd gradually adapted her work clothes so that she reminded everyone less of a funeral director and more of a very smart hotel manager. It had been a good time, and it only ended when Patrick fell ill. After his death, there hadn't seemed any point in going to work, even if she'd been able to. Crippling sadness had taken every bit of her energy. Eddie had been bringing enough money in for both of their basic needs and neither had the heart for frivolities. They'd clung together, seeing nobody else unless they had to. Gradually they had emerged from the worst of their grief, but then Eddie had succumbed to a rare form of cancer, eerily similar to the illness that had done for their poor Patrick.

It was odd, but instead of plunging Beryl back into her pit of melancholy, Eddie's death had the opposite effect. It was like an awakening. She missed him terribly, but nothing could have been worse than what happened to Patrick, so there was no choice but to pick herself up and carry on. And that was where the Saga Louts came in.

Thinking of her two best friends, Beryl realised she was going to have to hurry if she wanted to have time for a shower and a spruce up before games night at the pub. She rushed through her household tasks like a whirlwind, ending by mopping the kitchen floor and singing along to her favourite Michael Bublé CD. Beryl's energy levels were flagging now but she'd had the forethought to prepare a snack tray so that she didn't have to paddle across the wet floor. She took it upstairs to eat while she relaxed, propped up with a heap of pillows on her bed. Stilton cheese, crackers and a couple of tomatoes. Lovely.

Fortified, she swallowed the last mouthful, reached for her phone and called Winnie. 'Are you all ready for tonight?' she said, when her friend answered, sounding out of breath. 'I'm wondering whether to wear the peach dress with the peacock-feather pattern or my mauve with spots. What do you think?'

'Peach. The mauve one drains your colour, honey. Makes you look like you've been dug up. Excuse me panting, I was just bleaching the loo. Bending doesn't suit me these days. Too much padding in the way.'

Beryl couldn't decide whether to be offended or not. The mauve dress was her secret favourite. Still, she *had* asked. Best not to respond. 'Are you getting a lift with Anthea?' she said.

'Nah. She's still saying she doesn't want to be the only one on soft drinks. We're taking a taxi again tonight. See you there at 7 p.m.?'

'Okay. Frank's calling for me and we're walking across.'

Beryl ended the call and frowned. It wasn't like Anthea to avoid driving twice running. Was there some other reason? Their friend had had a health blip of her own fairly recently. Beryl had a sudden panicky feeling when she imagined what her life might be like without her two sidekicks. It didn't bear thinking about. Her relationship with Frank, who had moved to Willowbrook from Sheffield with his son and daughter-in-law, was still in its fledgling stages. He was a kind man, but their friendship didn't compare with the bond between the Saga Louts.

Stop being so depressing, she told herself sternly. *You're a lucky woman. You still have a fair bit of life left to live, with luck, and so have they. Go and have a shower and put your glad rags on. Tonight's going to be fun.*

Without further ado, Beryl hastened to get ready, and by the time Frank rang the doorbell, she was primped and prettified, dressed in the rather startling peach frock with matching lipstick and nail varnish. She opened the door with a flourish and Frank took a step back, pretending to swoon.

'Who are *you*, you dazzling creature, and what have you done with my friend Beryl?' he said.

Beryl rolled her eyes at him and led the way to the living room. 'Come in and wait for a minute, you sweet-talking devil. I just need to give my hair a quick spray,' she said.

This didn't take long, although there was a short delay to fetch Frank a glass of water when he had a coughing fit as a cloud of heavily scented hairspray hit the back of his throat. Soon, however, they were making their way down the path to the pub arm in arm, with Frank extolling the virtues of the willow trees flowing gracefully down into the brook that wound its way across the village green.

'Oh, Beryl, those trees are stunning,' he said. 'I didn't think I was going to like it here, but I can't imagine living in a city now.'

'You say that every time we walk over the green,' said Beryl. 'I hope you're not going to get boring on me.' But she couldn't help taking furtive sidelong glances at Frank as he strode along. When he'd arrived in Willowbrook not so long ago, he'd been something of a shambles, in Beryl's opinion. Recently widowed after a very difficult time when his beloved wife Lottie had suffered from gradually worsening dementia, Frank had looked dishevelled and mournful.

Now, the sadness was still there underneath, of course it was, but he'd definitely upped his game looks-wise, helped by his daughter-in-law Nell and encouraged by his attendance at the Reverend Bev's meetings that had explored what it meant to find true happiness and contentment. Now he was wearing what Beryl classed as a very natty sports jacket over an open-necked white shirt teamed with navy chinos. His shoes were well-polished, and his hair looked as if it had been recently trimmed. Even his bushy eyebrows were neat and tidy.

'You're looking very dapper, Frank,' Beryl said. 'You're not such a mess as you used to be.'

'Thank you, my dear. You say the nicest things,' he said, laughing. 'Yes, we both scrub up rather well, don't we? Shame to waste all this magnificence on a village pub. Shall we run away to Paris and dine by the Seine instead?'

Beryl watched a group of teenagers making their way through the trees and down to the bank of the brook where they were probably going to do all sorts of unmentionable things together. She felt an unaccustomed pang of envy for their carefree life. Frank's joking comment stirred something inside her and she turned to face him.

'And why not?' she said, giving him a wide smile. 'Why don't we do just that? Let's send a message to the others and pop back home for our passports. I'd only need a toothbrush and some clean knickers.'

Frank's jovial expression now changed to one that looked remarkably like fear. 'I was j... just kidding,' he stuttered, blushing to the roots of his wavy grey hair.

'I know you were. So was I,' said Beryl, giving his arm a squeeze and setting off down the path again, taking him along with her. 'But don't you ever get the urge to do something crazy for once? I like my life here, but now and again, I want to...'

She broke off, not actually sure what it was she *did* want to do. Going on holiday with her two friends was all well and good and had been perfectly fine for years, but they always did the same sort of thing. Package deals in hotel rooms with ground-floor access, without any steep hills around them and with entertainment suitable for holidaymakers who still loved to party but didn't want to be woken up at four in the morning by noisy revellers returning, vomiting into the flower beds and waste bins on their way back to base.

'Don't you ever feel as if life's passing you by?' Beryl asked as they reached the pub and paused by the door.

'I'm in my eighties. I think most of it already has,' he said, smiling down at her.

Beryl looked back up at him and her heart missed a beat. Why had she never noticed what beautiful blue eyes Frank had? They shone with kindness and good humour. There were many wrinkles and laughter lines around them but that only seemed to add to his charm.

'I reckon you're wrong,' said Beryl. 'It's my view that we've still got quite a bit of living to do, and I have a plan.'

'Why does that sentence fill me with terror?' Frank answered, but he was still smiling.

Beryl didn't reply. She stood back so that Frank could perform his usual gentlemanly act of opening the door for her and then led him towards the table in the corner where Anthea and Winnie were sitting. They waved, and Beryl waved back.

'Are these two lovely ladies part of your mysterious plan?' asked Frank, pulling a chair out for Beryl to sit on.

'Oh, yes, they certainly are,' she said. 'And so are you, Frank, my friend. So are you.'

11

Back at the house, Vee kicked off her trainers and headed for the stairs. Rick watched her go up with mixed feelings. The suggestion that she might want to come to the pub with him had been a spur-of-the-moment one. He was half-disappointed not to be able to introduce her to his friends but also somewhat relieved that they were going to have a break from each other. The last two days at Dragonfly Cottage and their evenings together had been intense.

It had been a long time since Rick had spent so much time alone with another person. His marriage break-up had left him vulnerable and reluctant to form close friendships with women, although he'd thought for a while that he and the Reverend Bev could have something going for them. She was a great character, and they'd seemed on the same wavelength, but it turned out that she was still emotionally bruised from a disastrous marriage of her own and wasn't anywhere near ready for another relationship. Neither was he, for that matter.

Rick was glad they'd found this out about each other before they got in any deeper. He was well aware that some people in the village saw him as a kind of lothario, footloose and fancy free and a bit too ready with the flirtatious chit-chat. This was very far from the truth, but he'd built up that image for himself, along with the blond hair, muscles and tan, so he couldn't complain. After the mutual non-starter with Bev, he'd been sure that he wasn't any readier than she was for a new relationship, but being in close proximity with beautiful Vee was making Rick unsettled and full of an uncomfortable longing to get to know her better.

He ambled into the kitchen and got himself a beer from the fridge, flipping the cap off and draining half of it in one go. It was thirsty work gutting a house and the weather had been getting gradually warmer all day. The early-evening sunshine was flooding the room with an almost ethereal glow, lighting up the jewel-coloured tiles that he'd lovingly installed around the work-tops and casting beams of sunlight across the floor. Reflecting idly on how long it would take to get to the stage of making a proper kitchen like this one in Dragonfly Cottage, Rick's thoughts swung back to Vee, and he sighed. Even though they'd got off to a bad start they were on an even keel now, but it was absolutely no good getting any kind of ideas about her. The past was there between them all the time, huge and daunting, even if she didn't yet realise it. She would though, and when Vee began to remember who Rick really was, their paths would be bound to diverge very quickly.

It had been a nasty moment when Beryl had called him Ricardo, which had been his nickname back then. Not many locals had known him as that, which was lucky. Ricardo had enjoyed graffiti and had become quite a dab hand with the spray can. What he'd seen as his physical deficiencies in those days – a tendency to spots, greasy dark hair, a lot of excess weight and painful shyness – had all seemed unimportant when he was creating his artwork around the more run-down areas of the nearby town of Meadowthorpe.

Rick's graffiti hadn't been of the traditional kind. He'd had no tag and no desire to put a name to his art, just an overwhelming urge to make his mark in as dramatic a way as possible. He'd focused on derelict buildings, creating wild landscapes at great speed in vibrant greens and blues. Rick worked alone, and even his closest friends didn't know how he spent his time after dark, through the small hours of the night. He'd never been caught, he was too savvy for that, but after a while the novelty had worn off, and that's when he'd joined the Vipers, a gang that changed his life in a very bad way.

The beer was soon finished, and Rick decided to have a quick shower and head to the pub. He could eat there and that would leave the coast clear for his lodger to have a long soak in the bath.

'Are you okay to get yourself something to eat, Vee?' Rick called, when he reached the top of the stairs. 'There's plenty of bread and you'll find everything else you need in the fridge if you're making a sandwich.'

He stepped back as Vee opened the door suddenly. She was wearing her dressing gown, and his feverish imagination told him she probably had nothing on underneath it. He wrenched his gaze away. 'I'm just going for a shower and then I'll be out of your way,' he mumbled.

'Don't be silly, it's your house. And yes, I'll have a cheese toastie after my bath. I'm too grubby to eat yet, but there's no rush.'

She retreated into her room and Rick swallowed hard. He was worse than a teenager, thinking steamy thoughts about the woman in the spare bedroom. Stripping off his dirty clothes in the bathroom, he made himself have a cold shower for at least two minutes before he turned the dial to warm. That should do it.

No more smutty thoughts. Tonight was for nice innocent card playing.

The volume of chatter seemed unusually loud to Rick as he entered the Fox and Fiddle half an hour later, after a brisk walk through the village and a jog across the green. He'd been ravenously hungry after his shower but determined not to start snacking before he left the house. The obvious ways he'd shifted the pounds when he'd taken stock of his life were exercise and less food. He'd enrolled in a gym, started running and totally reorganised his eating habits. It hadn't been easy, but Rick had always been up for a challenge. His skin improved gradually, the weight dropped off him and he'd treated himself to his new hair colour when he'd begun to feel better about himself.

'Over here, mate,' a voice called as Rick headed for the bar. He turned to see his friend Sam already settled at their favourite table near the biggest window overlooking the village green, where either side of a temporary net, a game of volleyball was already in progress.

'I'll get the drinks in,' called Rick. 'Are you eating here?'

Sam gave him a thumbs-up. 'I am, steak pie and chips ordered already. I've got a babysitter for Elsie tonight so I'm making the most of it. And another pint of Timothy Taylor's Landlord would be great. The first one hardly touched the sides.'

Rick ordered two beers and added a chicken salad for himself to his tab. He was well aware that over the last two days, his eating habits had reverted to those he'd slipped into after his divorce. The takeaway with Vee had been necessary after all their hard work. There was no point in stressing that he was going to put on weight again because he'd had plenty of exercise in the cottage, just as he had when doing his own house up, but it was time to get a grip.

'Right, are you ready to annihilate the opposition tonight,

partner?' said Sam as Rick set two pints down on the table and tried not to think about his rumbling stomach. The two of them had played solo whist together on several occasions since Ned, the landlord of the Fox and Fiddle, had introduced games night. They made a good-looking pair and always turned a few heads. Sam was as blond as Rick, but his hair was a naturally golden tumble of curls. Many of the women who frequented the pub had been impressed by his charm. Unfortunately for them, although Sam was a single parent, his dalliance with the female sex had been a brief blip in his teens. His priority was his young daughter, Elsie, but Sam's other passion was called Luka, and he was currently away at university.

'How's the love of your life these days?' Rick asked, taking a sip of his beer. 'Still living it large on the campus?'

Sam pulled a face. 'A bit too large, if you ask me,' he said sadly. 'Luka adores student life. He was meant to be coming home this weekend, but *something came up*. The mind boggles.'

'Try not to worry, it's you who's got his heart. He's just...'

'Young?' Sam said, forcing a smile for the girl who was delivering his pie. She gave him a broad wink, which he didn't even notice. Sam peered down at the plate as if he'd never seen food before. 'I'm even losing my appetite,' he whispered, so that the girl wouldn't overhear him as she walked away. 'I don't want this really.'

'Well, you'd better hurry up and change your mind or I'll eat it,' said Rick, looking enviously at the pile of crisp golden chips. 'I'm having a salad. Want to swap?'

Sam picked up his knife and fork and set to with more enthusiasm. 'I hate bloody salad,' he said. 'I'm always telling Elsie how good it is for her, but I don't really believe it. My mum used to make me have lettuce sandwiches for my school lunch. I've been scarred for life.'

'Just lettuce? Are you sure?'

'Well, she swears blind there were other things in there too, but I can't remember them. Oh, here's yours coming over. That's the one good thing about lettuce. You don't have to cook it, so it's quick.'

The girl was back. This time she aimed her wink at Rick, and he grinned back, glad he wasn't totally invisible next to the glorious beauty of Sam. They ate in silence as the jukebox pumped out tracks selected by three women who were clearly out to drink as much as possible before happy hour ended. When 'I Will Survive' came on, they all punched the air and danced.

'I reckon they're celebrating someone's divorce,' said Sam, laughing.

A pang of sadness hit Rick for a moment when he remembered the pain of his own marriage ending. He'd felt more like howling to the moon than dancing. Then it occurred to him that this wasn't how the memory affected him nowadays. He was settled in his new home and supporting his estranged sons as best he could at a distance, even though they were living in Germany. There was no need to look back over his shoulder any more. Unless... unless Vee's arrival meant he would have to do just that and delve a lot further into the past.

The two men carried on eating. Finally, both sat back and finished their beer.

'That was immense,' said Sam. 'I *was* hungry after all. How was yours?'

'It was great, actually. Oh, and here's her highness, the queen of Fiddler's Row.' Rick turned as the outer door swung open and Beryl sashayed in.

'I love Beryl. Are you being sarcastic?' asked Sam.

'No, not at all. So do I. It's just that she looks very regal tonight, and I kind of feel as if she has a lot of power in Willowbrook, don't you? Along with the other two, of course, but Beryl's in charge, even if they don't know it.'

Beryl and Frank made their way to the Saga Louts' usual table and then Frank went back to the bar to order drinks, just as two more customers entered the room.

'The full set,' said Sam. 'Here are our missing links.'

The two elderly men who had just walked in looked as dashing as Frank tonight. Sid Potter, who Rick had known since childhood, wore a hand-knitted fair isle sweater in gentle, muted shades over a navy shirt with smart jeans and Maurice Fortesque, another old friend, was his usual dapper self in a vintage smoking-jacket edged with gold braid, teamed with burgundy velvet trousers. They both ordered a large glass of red wine and brought their drinks over to Rick and Sam's table.

'Good grief, you two have put me and Rick to shame,' said Sam, pretending to swoon. 'I know Maurice always makes an effort, but even he's gone the extra mile tonight and I've never seen you looking so magnificent, Sid. What's brought this on?'

'Wait and see,' said Maurice, tapping the side of his nose mysteriously.

'Ready for us to wipe the floor with you?' asked Sid, setting his glass down and pulling up a chair.

'As if,' said Rick. 'We're on a winning streak since Ned got this new beer of the month in, remember? It makes our brain cells work twice as well.'

'Ha!' Sid took a sip of his wine and shook his head. 'You've no chance. Get the cowries out, Maurice. Let's get this show on the road. I've got the cards.'

The two packs were soon on the table along with the ornate wooden box that held Maurice's collection of tiny cowrie shells. When Ned had introduced games night, he'd laid down a couple of basic rules: no cheating and no gambling with money. Rick was disappointed to begin with. He'd had hopes of putting his giant whisky bottle that was almost full of coins to good use, but now he'd grown fond of the little shells, used as betting currency. They'd been in Maurice's family for years and he was the last man standing so he'd inherited them.

'And don't do your usual trick of picking out the shiniest ones for yourselves,' said Maurice, as Sam started to count the cowries out, fifty for each player to start with and five for the initial kitty.

Rick laughed. 'The grubbier ones don't seem worth as much somehow,' he said, helping his friend with the job. 'There you go, are we ready for off? Cut for dealer.'

The serious business of the evening began, as all around similar groups were setting out their stalls too. Beryl had fetched the box containing Cluedo before anyone else could snaffle it, and a group over at the far side of the room were already in their first argument as they played Monopoly. A game of Uno was absorbing a younger crowd who had separated into two tables and were making more noise than the rest of Ned's customers put together. Rick caught the landlord's eye as he pulled more pints for a group of newcomers. They gave each other a thumbs-up sign. Rick had been instrumental in publicising the games night, and both were delighted with its success.

'That was a daft mistake, partner,' said Sid, after he'd dealt again, and they'd started a second round. 'You must know I had no hearts left. It's not like you to mess up. What's the problem?'

'Everybody drops a clanger sometimes,' said Maurice. 'You need to wind your neck in.'

This was so unlike Maurice's usual genial approach to playing cards that Rick and Sam both stared. 'Are you okay, Maurice?' asked Sam, concern all over his face. 'Have you had a bad day, or something?'

'No, I haven't,' snapped Maurice. 'I'm just a bit preoccupied...

I... oh, I might as well tell you what's on my mind.' He lowered his voice, and the others leaned in to catch his next words. 'I've decided to ask Anthea to marry me. I've got a ring in my pocket.' He patted the side of his coat as his three companions' mouths dropped open in unison.

'Whaaat?' Rick couldn't hold the exclamation in, and several people turned to see what the fuss was about, including Beryl's team.

'Ssshh. Keep your voice down. I'm waiting for the right moment. I'm going to propose as soon as I get my courage up. And don't all look so horrified. She's a wonderful woman. Any man would be lucky to have her hand in marriage.'

There was a moment or two of silence, and then Sam said, 'But I think that's the whole point. Quite a few men already have. Had her hand in marriage, I mean.'

'Yes, he's right. You'd be... let's see...' Rick counted on his fingers. 'One, two, three, four... you'd be number five on her list of husbands, Maurice. Doesn't that bother you?'

Maurice thought about this briefly. Then he smiled. 'I think she's just never found the right person so far,' he said. 'Let me ask you something. What would you all be looking for in your ideal woman? Or man,' he added hastily when he saw Sam open his mouth to protest.

Sid smiled. 'That's easy. A companion for life. A happy smile and a hug to greet you when you come home. Someone who laughs at the same things. If they were a cracking cook too, that would be the icing on the cake. Literally. I could go on.'

'And you've had that already,' said Maurice. 'You're lucky. Would you do it again though?'

'I might. I just might. I miss it all, you know.'

Rick noticed that Sid's eyes automatically strayed to the table where Beryl and co were having a very loud discussion on one of the finer points of their game of Cluedo. Interesting. Was Sid about to make a play for Anthea too? Surely he wouldn't step on Maurice's toes. Or was he planning to home in on one of the other two ladies? Beryl was pink-cheeked, giggling at something that Frank had said, and then there was Winnie, magnificently arrayed in a brightly patterned red and blue gown with a matching head wrap. She was a glorious sight, and she was laughing too, her whole body shaking. He heard his own name and was jolted out of his musings.

'What about you, Rick? What's your ideal woman like?' Maurice said. 'And Sam? Or have you already found your perfect person?'

Sam shrugged. 'I thought I had, but Luka, gorgeous though he is, seems to be having a bit too much fun at uni. I'm trying to give him some space, but it's not easy. Rick? What do you have to say about this?'

Rick wasn't sure where to go with his answer. When his marriage had imploded, he'd been devastated, especially when his boys were taken away from him. He'd fought hard for access and won, to some extent, but visiting them and having them to stay was complicated. What if he had someone to share his life with? Would the partings each time be less painful? But you couldn't start a relationship just to use it like a sticking plaster on old wounds.

'Okay, I can see you're struggling. Forget the past for a moment. Imagine your dream partner,' Sam said, putting his cards face down on the table and leaning back in his chair.

This was even trickier. With the best will in the world, these words only conjured up a vision of one woman. Venetia Prescott. Close proximity to Vee over the last couple of days had definitely stirred up something deep in Rick, an undercurrent of heat that his almost-relationship with Rev Bev had never touched. But that scenario didn't involve forgetting the past. If ever there was to be anything between Rick and Vee, the past would be an all-too-vital part of it.

In the time it took Rick to think of a reply, Maurice had been getting more and more agitated. Finally, tired of waiting, he got to his feet and drank the remaining wine in his glass in one gulp.

'It's no good shilly-shallying. I'm going to ask her and I'm going to do it right now,' he declared, squaring his shoulders and turning to march across the short distance that separated their tables.

'Should we grab him?' murmured Sam. 'Or I could rugby tackle him to stop this happening?'

'No, you might break him,' said Sid. 'Hold your peace, lad. A man's gotta do what a man's gotta do, as they say in all the best films. We'll just need to be on hand to pick up the pieces if it all goes badly wrong. I'm not convinced he's doing the right thing, I'll tell you that for nothing.'

12

Beryl had been wondering when it would be best to share the details of her plan for a new kind of adventure when she looked up from the scrutiny of her Cluedo cards and saw Maurice get to his feet. He hesitated for a few seconds and then appeared to make up his mind about something. Turning towards their table, he marched smartly over to their group as if he was going to drop in for a chat and then just as abruptly veered away and headed for the cloakroom area at the back of the pub.

'Did you see that?' asked Winnie. 'I thought Maurice was going to come and tell us off for making too much noise, like he did last week. He looked very stern.'

Anthea raised her eyebrows. 'Just let him try, darling,' she said. 'We're no noisier than the rest of the people here. It's a free country.'

'Have you been out with him again this week?' Beryl said. 'Didn't you say he was taking you to the pictures?'

'No, I had to cancel because my boiler blew up, remember? He was quite miffed about it. Said he'd been planning a nice meal for us afterwards. We usually do a matinee so there's no danger of one of us dropping off to sleep partway through. He hasn't been in touch since.'

'Both of those guys are looking real smart tonight,' said Winnie. 'Maurice always makes the effort, but Sid's gone to town too this time. I wonder why he's decided to smarten himself up. You're looking very stylish as well, Frank, if you don't mind me saying. What is it with you men this evening? Are you all on the pull?'

Winnie laughed uproariously at her own question, but Frank didn't reply. He stood up to fetch more drinks but paused when he saw Maurice coming back. This time the other man didn't pass by their table but stopped right in front of Anthea.

'Hello there,' said Anthea. 'I wondered when you'd get around to noticing me tonight. Thought I'd done something to offend you.'

Just then, the jukebox finished playing the last track selected by the celebrating ladies and the sudden lack of background noise caused most of the games players to stop talking momentarily. Maurice cleared his throat.

'Anthea... erm... Anthea...' he said, his voice husky.

She looked up at him and smiled. 'That's me, darling. Is there a problem?'

'I hope not. I mean... the problem is, if there was one... is that I've waited so long.'

Everyone in the pub was obviously waiting too. Maurice had upped the volume this time and his words carried clearly right around the room.

'The thing is, Anthea, I want to ask you a very important question.'

There was a collective sharp intake of breath, and somebody called out, 'Go on, mate, spit it out.'

Maurice took hold of the back of Anthea's chair and lowered

himself carefully onto one knee. 'You're a fine woman, Anthea,' he said. 'I respect you and I... I love you dearly. Will you make me the happiest man alive and marry me?'

Still nobody spoke. The tension in the air was so strong that Beryl feared one of them was going to have a stroke. She fervently hoped it wasn't her. Anthea still hadn't replied, so Beryl gave her a nudge. 'Answer him. Go on,' she hissed.

Anthea looked down at Maurice as he knelt on the hard tiled floor. 'Get up while you can still move, you silly man. Your knees aren't as young as they were. Yes, of course I'll marry you. I thought you'd never ask.'

The pub erupted to wild cheers and Maurice hauled himself to his feet, helped by Sam and Rick who rushed across to give him a hand. Anthea stood up too and as soon as she could see that Maurice was stable on his feet, she opened her arms and they embraced, holding each other close for so long that wolf whistles and cries of 'get a room' replaced the cheering.

Beryl swallowed hard, blinking to stop her tears falling. How romantic was that? She looked across at Frank and saw that he was similarly moved, pulling out a handkerchief and wiping his eyes. Fancy Anthea saying *yes* to Maurice. Beryl had assumed after their recent talk that four marriages would have been enough for her friend but here she was, obviously up for another try.

'Congratulations,' she said loudly, joining everyone else in a round of applause. Even Ned was whooping from behind the bar.

'Fizz on the house for the happy couple,' he called to his staff, who busied themselves assembling a tray with glasses and popping the cork on a bottle of Prosecco.

'You'd have thought he'd have managed a bottle of proper champagne for an occasion like this,' said Frank under his breath to Beryl. 'Never mind, we can have our own party with them another time, and it'll be Veuve Clicquot for that one. There's a lot to be said for second-chance romances.'

'Or fifth-chance,' said Beryl, with a grin, but Frank wasn't smiling. He looked as if he was about to say something, but the arrival of the Prosecco distracted him, nestling in a silver ice bucket, an extra touch from Ned who was smiling at them all benevolently from the other side of the bar.

Maurice and Anthea were now accepting congratulations from all and sundry, even people they had never met before. Beryl thought she had never seen her friend so relaxed and happy. With the best will in the world, you couldn't describe Anthea as chilled. She was a tad haughty at times, with a tendency to look down on lesser mortals, but her generosity knew no bounds and Beryl hoped to goodness that this marriage would bring Anthea the happiness she'd been searching for. So many failed attempts at finding the right partner would have soured most people but Anthea was made of sterner stuff. She was still brave enough to have another go.

When the hubbub had died down and they were all seated again, with Maurice having abandoned his game of cards to sit by his beloved, Beryl leaned over to Anthea and whispered, 'Good for you, girl. No looking back, onwards and upwards now.'

Anthea smiled at Beryl and reached out to give her friend's hand a squeeze. '*The past is another country,* don't they say? I'm all for living life in the present moment, aren't you?'

Beryl wanted to say yes to the last question, she really did, but the more she thought about it, the more the past was looming much too large in her life since Venetia Prescott had returned to Willowbrook. If only she could be like Anthea and shrug off everything that had gone before. Beryl had a feeling that even if she wanted to seize the day and forget it all, the trigger of her new neighbour rejoining the village community was going to make that task absolutely impossible.

13

Vee stretched out in the bath and twiddled the tap with her toes to let in more hot water. Her skin was already starting to turn prune-like, and pangs of hunger were making thoughts of toasted cheese sandwiches very tempting, but the water was blissfully hot, and Rick's bubble bath was one of those muscle-relaxing ones that smelt of eucalyptus. This experience was too good to cut short.

She half-closed her eyes and let her mind drift to a time in the past when she'd enjoyed this kind of luxury. It had been a while ago because one awful day, Nigel, in the earlier years when cleanliness had still been important to him, had decided to surprise her with a brand-new wet room. He'd waited until Vee had gone away for the weekend with some work friends, got someone in to rip out the lovely old claw-footed bath that she'd adored and replaced it with a state-of-the-art power shower with a rainfall feature and room for two people inside.

When Vee returned home, he'd unveiled his reconstruction with such pride that for a few minutes she was speechless.

'But I loved having a bath,' she'd said eventually. 'Why didn't you ask me first?'

Nigel's face fell and his bottom lip stuck out. He soon became a giant toddler if anyone dared to disagree with one of his ideas, able to sulk for several days or sometimes weeks if he was crossed.

'I thought you'd like it,' he said. 'And anyway, this is my flat, in case you'd forgotten. If I want to make improvements to increase its value, you should be pleased, not stand there looking like I've done something bad. What's wrong with you?'

Vee had swallowed her first comment, which would have been, 'Nothing's wrong with me, you great baboon, I thought we were partners, and I pay my way, you know I do, have done for years.' Instead, she forced a smile and tried to admire the smooth grey tiles and matching towels. The whole room was completely bland. He'd got rid of all her leafy plants and quirky vintage bathroom accessories. Even the vintage basket chair with the squishy, embroidered cushions had gone. This had been the best room in the flat, in Vee's opinion, and now it was ruined.

Looking back, now Vee was able to view her last relationship more dispassionately, the bathroom debacle was the beginning of the end. Long soaks in the bath had been Vee's escape from the real world and without them, she felt lost and tetchy. Nigel hadn't understood, and ironically, it hadn't been many weeks afterwards when his personal hygiene gradually hit an all-time low, so the high-tech shower had never been properly appreciated.

Vee pulled the plug when the water was once again growing chilly and dried herself, putting on her comfiest pyjamas and her fluffy dressing gown, then padded downstairs barefoot and made herself familiar with the idiosyncrasies of a strange kitchen, ending up with a mug of instant hot chocolate and a plate heaped with toasties oozing melted cheese. She drew the curtains, settled herself on the sofa in the living room and switched on the television, scrolling through the programmes on offer as she ate her snack.

At last, after many forays into murder mysteries, thrillers and grim documentaries, Vee decided to play it safe and go for a series she'd watched before. However, it wasn't long before she realised her mistake. The last time she'd seen this particular programme had been some years previously, when she and Nigel were still reasonably happy. Now, seeing the relationship in question gradually disintegrate before her eyes, Vee experienced a sense of déjà vu. The couple in the story were almost carbon copies of Nigel and herself. Their relentless misunderstanding of each other's feelings was painful. Worse still, the issue that was driving them apart was something from the woman's past that had reared its ugly head and refused to go away.

Vee put down her mug and paused the action, frowning as she at last faced up to thinking about possibly the most significant part of her own history. These were the memories that she'd been avoiding ever since she left Willowbrook. The ones that sometimes kept her awake long into the small hours of the night with their unspecific niggles. They were cloudy memories, lost in the fog of anxiety that had surrounded her family's sudden departure from the supposedly idyllic village life of her childhood.

The room was quiet now, and Vee glanced around, taking in the ambience that Rick had created for himself. The furnishings were simple, consisting of a large and comfortable sofa, several bookcases, a beautiful oak coffee table and the enormous TV in the corner. It was a good place to ponder, but try as she might, Vee couldn't bring to mind any firm details of what had happened in those long-ago days. A few names floated around in her brain and also one or two vague recollections of the fun she'd had growing up here, but something was getting in the way of total recall. There must be some way of breaking through whatever barrier was holding her back.

Vee stood up and began to pace up and down the living room, finally ending up facing the largest bookshelf. It was lined with all kinds of books in every shade of the rainbow. Some were clearly from Rick's early years, brightly coloured, battered and much loved. Others were leather-bound copies of the classics, equally well-used. There were glossy non-fiction books and a whole shelf of thrillers with covers in black or muted colours. But on the very bottom shelf, Vee hit pay dirt. Here she found a whole row of photograph albums propping each other up, their plastic bindings dusty from lack of use.

'Wow,' she breathed as she ran a finger along the edges of the albums. 'You are one organised bloke, Rick.'

Each volume was labelled with its own dates. Was it overstepping the mark as a lodger if she leafed through some of them? Vee knew she'd hate anyone looking at her own rudimentary collection of old photos but the more she peered at the dates, the harder it became to resist them. At last, she reached for the one labelled '1984'. She couldn't bring herself to take it back to her chair to look at in comfort. That seemed even worse than having a quick, casual peek by the shelf, so she sank to the floor and opened the book, holding her breath as she turned the pages.

The two large photographs on the first page were a surprise, because they were pictures of the school Vee had attended. Why would anyone want to remember that place? It had been built in the late sixties and never been properly modernised, merely had bits added on when the volume of pupils grew too great to fit inside. It consisted of a square, rather bleak-looking group of buildings surrounded by concrete play areas and car parks. In the distance could be seen the playing field which had been the scene of some of least professional games of football and hockey known to mankind.

Vee soon saw that Rick was one of those people who liked to caption his pictures. Underneath these two photos were printed the words:

They say heaven is a place on earth... but in that case, so might hell be.

Vee shuddered and almost closed the book. It had been a loveless experience, being at that school. Some teachers had been better than others, but the general atmosphere was one of barely suppressed frustration. Small fights often broke out at lunchtimes and the midday supervisors always seemed to be out of range at these moments, usually smoking behind the bike sheds. There had been several teenage pregnancies while Vee was there, and the girls concerned had left under a cloud, never to return. Rick must have been there at the same time as she was. Why didn't she remember him? A blond, good-looking boy like him would surely have stuck in her memory. She braced herself and turned to the next part of the album, stomach in knots.

There in front of her on the following pages lay many snapshots, some clear, some blurry. They were neatly laid out, and each one had its own tiny label. Long-forgotten names floated before Vee's eyes. Rick must have an amazing memory to be able to recall all these schoolmates along with their nicknames. Mackie Pearson, Dino Butler, Shazzie Smith and Rhonda Clements...

Rhonda Clements. Vee paused in her perusal, feeling cold fingers of dread running up her spine. Rhonda had never allowed anyone to shorten her name or give her a new ridiculous one instead. She had been a fearsome character, cooler than cool, deferred to wherever she went. For a while, she and Venetia had been friends, or what passed for friends in the gang that hung around with Rhonda. Vee had been so eager to fit in that she'd turned a blind eye to a lot of the things that went on around them at that time. To fall out with Rhonda would have been the biggest mistake of her young life, so she made sure she was always on the right side of her. It wasn't easy. Rhonda had very little in the way of scruples and she wasn't averse to treading on everyone who got in her way.

Vee turned another page. This time she was confronted by a few of the kids she thought of as the rival gang. They'd been a sorry lot. In Rhonda's words, *a right bunch of tossers and losers*. She supposed that in any peer group there would be those who fell into Rhonda's very own set of categories. The teachers' pets and swots. The geeks and nerds. The cool kids. The tossers and losers. The bullies. The victims.

The last category stuck in her mind as Vee thought back to the painful early days at high school when she had been one of the victims. Tallulah's mixed Spanish and Italian background and her father's rather brooding good looks had provided Vee with the dark hair and soulful eyes that she hadn't appreciated in her teens but it had also been something that was seized upon by the bullies. She had been relieved when for some unknown reason Rhonda had adopted her into the cool kids' gang, which effectively stopped all the bullying but had its own price to pay. A high price, as it turned out.

Now, unable to stop looking, Vee scrutinised some of the group that had irritated Rhonda so much. There were three of them in this particular snapshot; two girls and a boy. Both girls had long, straight hair, looped behind their ears. One had particularly large ears, which the style emphasised. The other had pink-rimmed glasses. The boy was dark-haired and skinny. His expression was one of abject misery. He had a bad case of acne, in fact all of them were plagued with spots, as Vee now remembered. She looked at the label beneath the clearest of the photographs.

Ginny Burton (GeeBee), Sharon Smith (Shazzie) and Brad Potter (Petrol Head or BP).

Vee carried on flipping through the pages. There were no photos of Rick himself that she could find. The album wasn't just full of Vee's year group and others in years above and below. The last few plastic-covered pages had newspaper cuttings tucked inside them instead. They all involved the local police's search for a graffiti artist who was making themselves increasingly unpopular with the townspeople of nearby Meadowthorpe. There were close-ups of some of the artwork, and Vee couldn't hold back a gasp of admiration. They were stunning. Swirling images that reminded her of a rough sea, of dramatic waterfalls, of rivers in full spate. The final page brought sudden tears to her eyes. It was a short notice cut from *The Meadowthorpe Recorder*, describing the death of Sharon Eva Smith, aged twenty-seven, former resident of Willowbrook and by then residing in Manchester. She didn't appear to have been married, and no family members were mentioned. There had been a post-mortem, but no suspicious circumstances had been found. Shazzie Smith, she of the owl-like glasses and terrible stutter, was no more.

Vee closed the book carefully and placed it back on the shelf. She retreated to her previous seat and tucked her legs up beneath her, reaching for the fleecy blanket that was folded over one arm of the sofa. Wrapped in its warmth, she contemplated all that she'd just seen. To think of Shazzie, dead at such a young age with apparently nobody to mourn her and no explanation given, was heartbreaking. Vee was aware that even if she hadn't been directly unkind to the girl herself, she hadn't made any effort to prevent Rhonda from teasing her unmercifully whenever their paths crossed.

Had Rhonda been equally mean to all the people she classed as losers? Yes, she had. There was no avoiding that, and if Rick had been at school at the same time as Vee, he must remember what Rhonda had been like too, even if he'd been in a different year group. She wondered why he hadn't made himself known to her when they first met. Surely that was unnatural. It would have been normal to say something like, 'Hey, we go back a long way. I was at your school, but we didn't...'

Didn't what? Didn't hang around in the same crowd? Maybe Rick remembered her family leaving, and the events leading up to it. The uncomfortable feeling was growing and there was nobody else to ask about what really happened around the time that the Prescotts left Willowbrook. Vee honestly couldn't recall anything but the most basic of facts. Maybe she'd blocked it all out. In that case, there must be something really bad lurking in her subconscious. This growing sense of unease and unexplained guilt was making her edgier by the minute. To ask Rick to talk about the past might wreck their working relationship and Vee so badly needed both a safe space to live in for now and someone to make her own house ready for the future.

Reaching for her phone, Vee clicked on Facebook and stared at her list of friends. Rhonda must have some kind of social media presence, she was far too egotistical to be anonymous in this world of Instagram, TikTok and so on. She tried a Facebook search first, with no joy. Then she moved to Instagram and suddenly, there was her quarry. Rhonda Clements-Barrymore. So she'd married at some point. Rhonda's profile picture showed a glamorous woman who was holding back the years very successfully, unless she'd used a whole lot of filters. Ash-blonde hair in a classy bob, vermillion lips and eyes that stared straight out of the photo with a challenge in them, or so it seemed to Vee. Her hand shook. She hesitated for seconds before she pressed *follow*. Then she pressed the message button and typed:

> Hi, it's Venetia Prescott here, remember me? Would be great to have a catch-up sometime, now I'm back in Willowbrook and I can see from your profile that you're still living somewhere nearby.

The words were on their way through the ether before Vee had given herself the chance to change her mind. It was done.

Faintly horrified at what she might have set in motion, Vee headed for the kitchen and opened the fridge. There was a bottle of gin in there and one of tonic. Mentally apologising to Rick for pinching his booze, Vee found some ice cubes in the freezer, sliced a lemon from the fruit bowl on the worktop – might as well do this thing properly – and poured herself a very large G&T. If Rhonda got in touch with her, there was at least a chance of getting straight in her mind what had closed her memories off so effectively. Knowing must be better than guessing. That way madness lies, she told herself, taking a large swig of her drink. Her eyes watered at the strength of it, so she took another slurp and added more tonic. Then, turning her back on the cosy living room, she took herself to bed.

14

Back at the Fox and Fiddle, the celebrations were still bubbling. Rick had bought another bottle of Prosecco and delivered it to the happy couple before reorganising himself and Sam into a game of Scrabble. Maurice was beyond any sort of sensible conversation, now happily clutching Anthea's hand and staring into her eyes, while Sid had joined their table and was busy pouring drinks for everyone in the group, paying special attention to Winnie.

'Is it just me or do you feel a bit out of it tonight?' Sam asked, setting up the Scrabble board and passing Rick one of the little racks for his tiles.

Rick shrugged. 'Yeah, I know what you mean. It's nice to see the oldies all getting on so well but it does make me wonder what I'm doing with my life.'

'Have you ever tried online dating?' Sam was occupied with setting out the letters and didn't look at Rick. 'I was about to do that when I realised Luka was interested. I wasn't sure if I should go for it, with him being younger than me, but I couldn't resist him. How about you?'

'I can definitely resist Luka,' said Rick, grinning at his friend. 'Oh, I see what you mean. No, I haven't tried it. I'd be terrified, to be honest.'

'Why? You're a great-looking bloke. They'd be queueing up to meet you.'

Rick wasn't so sure. If he was such a good catch, why had Stacey left him high and dry? Her new man hadn't been tall, dark and handsome and he'd seemed incredibly dull to Rick but even so, she'd left without a backward glance. That relationship had since imploded but Stacey still hadn't made a move to return to England, even though for a while Rick wished she would. Now he was reconciled to his life as a single man and had long ago realised that he didn't want her back, but even so, it would've been nice to know she regretted her rash decision to go to Germany and set up home in Munich with the boys, even if only a little bit. His sons were now fully bilingual and loved their school. They'd made lots of friends, which was excellent, but Rick still hurt inside when he remembered tucking them up in bed and reading them his childhood stories, revisiting Paddington Bear and Thomas the Tank Engine and doing all the voices, just like his own father had done for him.

'Online dating definitely isn't for me,' Rick said, as they began to play. 'I like my independence these days.'

'Oh, come on, mate. You're not telling me that if the right woman came along, you wouldn't pull out all the stops to get her to go on a date?' Sam put down a row of tiles and punched the air. 'I've still got the knack. That's fifty-one scored for me. Write it on the list.'

Rick did as he was told, hoping that Sam would drop the subject now. The phrase *the right woman* was making him melancholy. It wasn't as if he believed in such a person. He'd thought his marriage was forever and look what happened there. Even so, a vision of Venetia, barefoot and clad only in her fluffy dressing gown, popped into his tired mind. He wondered what she was doing now. She'd probably have had her toasties and be snuggling on the sofa in front of the television, or maybe she was exhausted by the work on the house and had got into bed to read and then to cuddle down to sleep.

'How are you getting on with your lodger?' asked Sam, as if he'd read Rick's thoughts. 'It must be strange having someone in the house after you've become used to living on your own. I'd be lost if I didn't have Elsie to keep me company. She's only eight but she's such good fun to have around.'

Rick considered this question as he made his next move, causing Sam to mutter when he topped the last score. 'I suppose I *have* got used to being alone,' he said. 'But I think it's going to be fine having Vee around for a while, and she really didn't have anywhere else to go.'

'Must've been strange for her coming back to Willowbrook after so long,' said Sam. 'You went to school around here, didn't you? I'm surprised you don't remember each other. Or... do you?'

The question hung in the air. Rick didn't answer for a few moments, pretending to be absorbed in planning his next move. When Sam had played his tiles, he placed his own word down as he said, 'It's a long time ago, you know. Vee left when she was only fifteen.'

'But I'm still in touch with some of my own mates from when I was a kid,' said Sam. 'And I haven't forgotten the others. It's an important time in your life, puberty, isn't it? I was totally confused by it all; taken in by a girl when all I really wanted was to hang out with the boys and have my first proper kiss with one of them. Tough times. I can't believe you don't remember something about Vee. She must have been pretty unmemorable.'

That wasn't a word that Rick would use to describe Venetia

Prescott. The very opposite was true. He thought back to the time that was meant to be the best years of your life. What a joke. He'd never been so miserable, even when Stacey left him. The final camping trip was the worst part of it all. The previous ones had been only for weekends and much closer to home. They'd had such high hopes of the week-long school visit to North Wales, he and his sad little gang talked about it for weeks, taking in ten pounds at a time to the geography teacher and having it marked down on little cards the man kept in his desk. None of the four had parents who were well off enough to pay for the whole trip in one go. Shazzie was in foster care, Ginny was one of five with a single mum on benefits and Brad lived in a council care home with a group of other displaced teenagers. Rick's dad had been made redundant about that time and money had been tight, but all of the Vipers, as they called themselves so misleadingly, were desperate to get away and have seven nights of fun and freedom in the mountains of Wales.

'Talk to me, Rick,' said Sam, putting down the Scrabble tiles he'd been about to play. 'You look... I don't know... kind of grim.'

Grim. Yes, that was a good word to describe the hideous memories from that fateful trip. Rick wondered how best to explain why he was struggling with recalling his first experience of camping.

'We went on a school holiday,' he said, and then stopped.

Sam waited. 'And?' he prompted eventually, when no more information was forthcoming.

Rick heaved a sigh. 'And... well, for a start, it rained every bloody day. Then there was the fact that my three friends and me had a couple of ancient tents we'd borrowed that leaked, as it turned out, and our sleeping bags got soaked on day one.'

'Oh. Yes, that does sound bad. Is there more?'

There was more. A lot more. Rick chose his words carefully.

In the end, there wasn't a nice way to put it. 'There was a boy that nobody liked and everyone teased him unmercifully. To be fair, he was a bit of a drip. Not only that, he'd always gone out of his way to snitch on people whenever he could. It was kind of a hobby with him to get everyone into trouble.'

'Hmm,' said Sam. 'Still, being teased is horrible.'

'I know. We were mean. He'd never slept away from home before that week, and we found out that he'd been too scared to leave the tent to go to the loo in the night, so he'd wet himself. We never let him forget it. He cried a lot.'

'Go on. That's not all of it, is it?'

'No. The boy was Patrick Summerfield.'

'But isn't that…?'

'Yes. Beryl's son, who died later, when he was at uni. How did you know his name?'

'I heard Kate and Milo talking about him once when I was working in the café. So sad.'

'Yes, and I've never stopped feeling guilty about how we were then. Anyway, a girl named Rhonda was the instigator of the teasing. We were all secretly terrified of her and her gang. She organised a practical joke. She drew a big picture of a baby doll with a nappy on and hung it outside Patrick's tent. He got hysterical and…'

Sam waited. Rick took a large swig of his beer and tried to control the storm of emotion that was breaking in his heart. What a shit he'd been when he was a teenager. So proud of his graffiti but unable to share his work with anyone in case he got into trouble, and desperate to fit in with the cool kids.

'Anyway, the upshot was that Patrick jumped in the lake the next evening while we were all supposed to be on a night walk. He slipped away while the teachers weren't looking and the only reason he didn't drown was that my friend Shazzie caught sight of him leaving the group and followed him without telling us. She was a great swimmer, she'd done life-saving lessons, and so on. Shazzie went in after him and saved his life.'

'Jeez! That must have been a huge scandal! Did the teachers get the sack?'

Rick shook his head. 'It was all hushed up. Patrick didn't want anyone to know he'd tried to top himself and Shazzie was scared that if it all came out, her foster family would disown her.'

'But why would they? She behaved like a hero, surely?'

'I know, but she was neurotic about rocking the boat. She loved being with that family. It was the first time she'd stayed anywhere for more than a few months. She was... difficult.'

Rick thought back to that dark, wet night. It had seemed crazy to go on a torch-lit walk in the rain, but the teachers had insisted because they said it would be character-building. With hindsight, Rick suspected that this was also due to the fact that they had no contingency plan for such awful weather and they were too far from a town to do anything else. Half the torch batteries had failed which was why nobody had noticed Patrick slipping away on his own. Everyone except Shazzie had been too busy fussing with spare batteries to be bothered about what he was up to. They'd all been stumbling around in the dark and the teachers had been more worried about the swearing that was going on than doing their customary head counts.

By the time Patrick and Shazzie's absence had been discovered and everyone was running around in a panic, the two were on their way back to join the group, both soaking wet and shivering so much that the whole lot of them had to go back to the campsite and have hot chocolate while the teachers tried to get to the bottom of what had happened. Shazzie and Patrick had been in for a big telling off for being out on their own but Patrick had told the teachers that Rhonda and her gang had dared him to try out the stepping stones at the edge of the lake. He said he'd decided to do it and fallen in accidentally.

'The true story never came out,' Rick told Sam, who was still gazing at him in disbelief. 'I guess these days it couldn't happen, with all the safeguarding checks and so on – there should have been more staff there and a walk like that would never go ahead on such a filthy night. Patrick didn't want his parents to know what he'd tried to do, Shazzie felt the same about her foster family and the teachers... well, they were obviously scared shit-less that they'd be suspended. Brad and me only knew about it because Shazzie was one of our best friends. We kept shtum for her sake.'

'And what happened to Patrick afterwards? Did he get over that bloody awful trip?'

'Well, that wasn't the only bad thing that happened on the camping holiday... but I don't want to talk about the rest. It's all water under the bridge now.'

Rick looked at the floor. He couldn't bear to meet Sam's eyes. The shame was still there. It hadn't faded at all over the years. 'And no, Patrick never really got over it. He was even more of a loner after that. He's... he's dead now, as you know.'

Tears pricked Rick's eyelids, and he sniffed hard. Patrick hadn't really had much of a life.

'He didn't try to kill himself again though, did he?' Sam's voice brought Rick back to the present.

'Not that I know of. He got sick while he was at uni. It was nothing to do with him being...'

'Suicidal?' Sam filled in the missing words and there was no mistaking the disapproval in his tone.

'I don't think he was suicidal by then,' said Rick, hoping against hope that this was true. 'I'm not even sure he meant to go through with it the first time. He loved his university course, by all accounts. It was just bad luck that he got so ill. And, Sam...'

'Yes?'

'Beryl knows nothing about what happened on the camping trip. So please, please don't let on. I don't think she could handle it.'

Sam didn't reply. His face said it all.

'Are you okay with that? To keep it to yourself? I shouldn't have told you, but you did ask.'

Sam shrugged. Rick guessed that would just have to do.

15

The next morning, both Vee and Rick avoided mentioning how they'd spent the previous evening. Vee thought Rick was unusually quiet over breakfast and she was still feeling guilty for delving into his photograph albums, so it was a relief to get the table cleared and clamber back into the van for the day's work.

'I've packed us up enough food for the day,' Rick said. 'We can't keep hoping Beryl will turn up with cake and it's going to cost us a fortune if we do a supermarket sweep every day for lunch. I hope you like tuna and mayo? I should have asked first but it was either that or cheese and I know you had toasties last night.'

Vee said she liked most things, although she did draw the line at squid, and Rick promised never to give her squid sandwiches. She asked him to make sure he added extra to her rent bill to cover food, and he agreed. It was a stilted conversation and neither of them smiled. After that, the rest of the short journey passed in silence.

When they reached Dragonfly Cottage, Vee helped Rick to unload the van and decided that she really needed to focus on one room this time because there was a distinct danger of getting overwhelmed by the volume of work to do.

'Can I leave you to it downstairs and start decorating the main bedroom?' she asked Rick. 'I think we did enough prep in there yesterday for me to give it one more clean and then give all the walls a coat of white emulsion.'

'But I thought you wanted the floor sanding?' said Rick. 'That's a big job and you shouldn't start painting until I've done it. And anyway, don't you want a colour? It's going to be a bit bland if you do the whole room in white. I'm happy to take you back to the DIY place later.'

'No, I just want a peaceful, fresh look in there. I sleep better with white walls and ceiling around me,' said Vee. 'I can gradually get pictures to put up and a rug from a charity shop, maybe. So long as the floor's clean, it can wait.'

Rick's look said he would much rather get a few colour blocks and feature walls into this sad little cottage, but he left Vee to her own devices after helping her to carry everything she needed upstairs and move the bed base to the centre of the floor. Vee heard the sound of the radio as Rick began his day's work with a complete scrubbing down of the kitchen. She opened the door a crack so that she could enjoy the *Grease* medley pounding up the stairs and then looked around the almost empty room, trying to imagine what it would look like simply furnished. The one good thing about this house reconstruction was that the walls had never been papered so there was no messy stripping to do. Vee's parents had favoured plain plaster which was given a regular coat of magnolia gloss emulsion by her dad. Bland, but easy.

Luckily, none of the tenants seemed to have had grand designs when it came to decorating so the paintwork and walls were just in need of a lot of refreshing. Vee opened the window wide, taking a moment to look across the road outside her house and view the village green in the morning sunshine. One of the council employees, dressed in a high-vis vest and combats, was already making tracks across part of it astride a giant sit-on mower, but Vee noticed that a large part was being left to grow and was peppered with wildflowers. The scent of new-mown grass reached her, and she was immediately catapulted back to her childhood, when playing on the green had been part of everyday life unless the weather was so rainy that she and Cassie were grounded.

On those days, they'd made dens under the table and played with their doll's house and other toys with as many of their friends as they could invite in. The age gap hadn't really bothered them when they were younger. Tallulah had been very sociable, and had never minded a crowd, particularly on wet days, so each had their own classmates round to join them. Their mum's view was that the guests were amusing her children and all she needed to do was provide drinks, snacks and an indoor picnic when the hunger pangs became too much. It was only in her final years that Vee's mum had become trickier to deal with. Bad health and pain had made her crotchety and critical of everything Vee did, which, looking back, was understandable. Hard work at the time though.

Vee turned away from the window but left it open to flood the room with a cleansing, energising breeze. Soon, not a single vestige of the many tenants would remain, and her home would be truly her own. She filled her bucket from the bath tap and, armed with soapy water, she began to give the room an extra scrub, reflecting that it might not be nearly so easy to slot back into village life as it was to get rid of years of neglect. To fit in properly she was going to need to make her peace with the past. She quickly checked her phone but there was still nothing interesting to see. Maybe Rhonda hadn't seen the message yet. Or perhaps she was as reluctant as Vee had previously been to look back at those turbulent times. It was only now that Vee was starting to feel ready. Rhonda had never been one for empathy. She might have changed over the years, of course, but perhaps she was still the stubborn, unkind girl who had ruled the roost at their school for so long.

When she'd given the walls and ceiling a thorough brush down and the bedroom floor was as clean as it could possibly be, Vee set to with the paint and roller. Rick had provided dust sheets for the floor, and they were soon liberally spattered with white matt emulsion, because what Vee lacked in expertise she made up for in speed. She was thankful for the baseball cap that protected her hair from drips and for today's clean boiler suit which now felt like an old friend. What would her mother think if she could see her now? Tallulah had always been very image-conscious and would have probably been horrified that her daughter now looked like a giant, white-spotted orange.

'Sorry, Mum,' Vee said aloud. 'Needs must. You'd be pleased with the effect when I'm done, I know you would.'

'Did you say something?' Rick's voice called from the landing. He opened the door cautiously to check if Vee was anywhere near it and then made his way in.

'I was... erm... talking to my mum,' Vee said, blushing.

'Right.' He looked disconcerted for a moment but was distracted by the brilliance of the new paint. 'Wow, you've made great progress in here. Why don't we have a coffee in the garden while you let this coat dry? You can see what I've been doing in the kitchen. I have chocolate biscuits,' he added.

Vee needed no second bidding. She washed her hands in the bathroom and then joined Rick, who was already spooning coffee into mugs. The kitchen was gleaming. Rick had made good use of the heavy-duty sprays and the bleach he'd bought. The tiled floor and the units now looked quite presentable and the tiles on the splash back were shining too.

'This is amazing,' Vee said, wanting to cry at the transformation. 'I don't need a whole new kitchen after all. I know the units are a bit tatty but they're sound enough, aren't they?'

Rick handed her a steaming mug of coffee. 'I hoped you'd say that. Some women would insist on ripping everything out and starting from scratch but if you can wait a while, it'll save you loads of money because we can shop around and get discounted stuff later.'

Vee was about to reply when the sight of him stopped her in her tracks. Rick was wearing the same kind of boiler suit as she had on herself but for some reason, the one he had donned today was a size or two larger than usual and billowed around him. He also had the matching cap with the peak turned backwards, and his face was smeared with dust and cobwebs. He looked... different... vaguely familiar. Something tugged uncomfortably at Vee's memory.

'I... you...' Vee began and then stopped.

Rick paused in the act of taking a swig of coffee and turned away, but the damage had been done.

'Ricardo... Beryl called you Ricardo, didn't she? Why didn't I realise? I must be going daft. I know you, Rick. You were one of the Vipers, along with Shazzie, Ginny and Brad. You were on that... that trip...'

The ground seemed to shift beneath her feet and Vee's body swayed. She felt Rick's strong arms go round her as he gently guided her outside and lowered her onto the step.

'Put your head between your knees,' he said gruffly. 'You'll be okay in a minute. Take some deep breaths.'

Bemused and nauseous, Vee did as she was told, and gradually the world returned to normal. She opened her eyes and blinked. The garden stretched out in front of her, looking just as unkempt as before, but she hardly registered what she was looking at.

'Why did you suddenly recognise me?' asked Rick, avoiding Vee's eyes as he stood surveying the same view. 'I looked totally different in those days.'

'I suppose it was because your hair's covered up... or it was...' she said, because Rick had now removed the cap, and his short blond hair was visible again. 'And you're wearing a much bigger boiler suit that makes you look...'

'Fat?' Rick finished the sentence for Vee when she stalled, trying to think of a more tactful way to put it.

'Not fat, just kind of wider. And your face is spattered with dirt. I mean, not that you were dirty in those days...'

'But I was spotty,' he said, trying to smile. 'I hated almost everything about myself back then. The only thing that kept me going was my artwork. The graffiti.'

'Oh!' Realisation of how the newspaper extracts related to the man now standing beside her caused Vee to pause for thought. Then she remembered the other cutting.

'And your friends... what happened to them?' she said.

Rick stared at Vee. 'Why are you asking me that?' he asked, narrowing his eyes. 'Have you been snooping while I was out? You have, haven't you?' He slapped his forehead. 'The photo albums. Of course. I should have hidden them.'

'Well, you didn't!' Vee snapped, stung by the accusation that she'd done something shady. 'Bookshelves are fair game, surely? Everyone likes to look at a person's books. It says a lot about their character. It's what I always do when I visit someone new.'

'What, rootle through their private possessions?' Rick's tone was as loud as hers, and much harsher than usual. Vee, still feeling shaky, jumped to her own defence.

'I didn't rootle. They were there, for anyone to see. And I don't know why you're being so weird about the albums. Unless you've got something to hide?'

There was a silence. Rick put his coffee mug down on the ground and turned to face Vee. Still furious at his accusations, she wasn't expecting the sudden surge of pure lust that hit her as she looked into those blue, blue eyes. No, no, no. This couldn't happen. Rick was her landlord, at least for now, and their joint past was now rearing its ugly head. What did he know about fifteen-year-old Vee? And what was he hiding about himself?

16

On the other side of the hedge, hidden by the overgrown privet, Beryl stood stock-still. She'd been pegging her washing out when she realised her neighbour was in the adjoining garden. Just as she was about to call over to Vee and Rick to see if they fancied another slice of fruitcake, she heard voices being raised. Never one to avoid a good chance to eavesdrop, because unless people were obviously whispering, what you naturally overheard was free information in Beryl's opinion, she froze where she was standing and leaned a little closer to the hedge.

As the conversation developed, getting louder by the minute, Beryl's mouth dropped open. She listened until Rick and Vee stopped shouting at each other. Had they gone inside? She risked a peek through the only small gap in the hedge she could find. Vee was sitting on the concrete step staring up at Rick, who had folded his arms and was looking back down at her. Intrigued, Beryl leaned closer. Still the other two didn't speak. She waited.

After what seemed like half an hour but was actually only five minutes, she heard Vee say more quietly, 'I don't want to talk about this here. We've got work to do. Can we just get on with what we were doing and discuss this later? I'm expecting a message from someone who might be able to help me with getting back my memories of what happened before I left the village.'

'You're kidding me. You're not saying you've forgotten all that?'

'That's exactly what I'm saying, and it's no joke. I want to get a complete picture of the time just before I left so I can put it all to bed. It's been bugging me for years.'

'Who are you trying to contact?'

Beryl could hear the apprehension in Rick's voice even from over the hedge. Vee took a while to answer, but then she said, 'Rhonda Clements.'

This was a shock. Beryl hadn't heard that name for a long time and had hoped never to hear it again. She'd never liked the girl but her suspicions about Rhonda were many. Her parents had been loaded, even by the standards of the other well-heeled families who lived down by the river in the big houses. Fancy calling your daughter after an old Beach Boys' hit. That was the nouveau riche for you.

Beryl remembered being at a school function with the girl's parents, and Rhonda's father, smoking a fat cigar at the time, puffing smoke into Beryl's face and telling a bawdy story about his daughter's conception at a party when he and his then girl-friend had sneaked away to a deserted bedroom and consummated their relationship while the song played downstairs.

Even now, the scene haunted Beryl. The lyrics of 'Help Me, Rhonda' started to sing themselves in her mind and she knew that they'd be an earworm for the rest of the day. It was ironic really. There were very few people who would be able to drum up any help from Rhonda Clements. She had always been as hard as nails.

Rick cleared his throat. 'Yes, you're probably right. Let's wait till we're back at home. There's a lot to say and I think we both need some breathing space first.'

Damn. How disappointing. Beryl willed Vee to change her mind and decide not to postpone their argument but instead she answered more quietly, 'That seems like the best thing.'

'Well, I'm going to start on the living room in that case. I'll be in there if you want to carry this on after all but otherwise, we'll talk later. I'm afraid though that you're going to be gutted if you think anyone can fill in all the blanks for you. It's a long time ago, and I don't think there's a person alive who can do that.'

Beryl heard them go inside and ground her dentures in frustration, then remembered that the dentist had warned her not to do that after she broke the last set. She left her empty washing basket by the line and went indoors. The first thing she did was to pick up the phone and call Winnie. Her friend answered on the second ring.

'Have you rung up to talk about last night?' Winnie said. 'How about that for a turn-up for the books? Our Anthea getting married again. Some folks never learn, do they? Mind you, I wish her well, you know I do, but five times? She's a glutton for punishment.'

Throughout this tirade, Beryl had been trying to butt in, and when Winnie drew breath, she seized her opportunity. 'I *was* going to call you to have a natter about that, but something else has come up. We need to talk. Do you think Anthea might be free for coffee at the country park café for lunch? She could still be with her beloved, I suppose. I wonder if she took him back to her place when we left the pub. She was very cagey about what their plans were.'

'If she did, I hope the poor chap survived the night,' said Winnie with a chuckle. 'I have a feeling there's a lot of pent-up passion in our old friend.'

'Oh, me too,' said Beryl. 'He's going to need a lot of stamina and some extra vitamins, I reckon. I'll ring her and see. Will you meet me at the café anyway? I've got one or two things to say to you both. It's the day Milo usually makes his lemon drizzle cake, and I never like to miss that.'

Beryl set off upstairs to get ready once Winnie had agreed on a time for their rendezvous and she'd managed to contact Anthea, who also said she'd be there. She changed into a scarlet dress, feeling that this might be an occasion to celebrate if she played her cards right, and added a slick of lipstick and her favourite scarf, patterned with poppies. Then she set off for Willowbrook Country Park and the Golden Brown café run by her friend and next-door neighbour from number six, Kate.

It took Beryl half an hour to potter across the green and wind her way around the lake past the rows of memorial benches with their brass plaques. She was soon out of breath and was tempted to have a sit down and a rest on one of them but anticipation about what she was about to do spurred her on. Her previous plan had been a vague one but now it was all becoming clear, and she knew without a doubt what she wanted to suggest for the Saga Louts' next adventure. All she had to do was be convincing enough. It was time for some action.

17

The area around the café was unexpectedly busy when Beryl arrived, and she remembered that today had been scheduled for the farmers' market. She checked her watch and found that she was early. Knowing that Winnie probably wouldn't be on time because she'd said she was going to get a bus from the retirement complex where she now lived, and they were notoriously unreliable from outside the crescent of bungalows, Beryl decided to have a quick look at the market stalls.

The main point of interest for most of the older residents of Willowbrook was always the stall selling jams and pickles. Winnie and Beryl had for years made their own preserves, each priding themselves on being the best at creating their signature recipes. Beryl loved to make traditional jams such as strawberry or raspberry, plus lemon curd and the odd wildcard of her own invention such as greengage and rhubarb, and Winnie preferred to cook up spicier relishes that would complement her Caribbean dishes, so they never clashed when they entered local competitions and shows with their wares. Even so, many of the senior villagers liked to check that the market stall wasn't selling

anything better than the creations they could produce themselves, and to stand and comment loudly on the standard of
goods on sale.

The stallholder in charge of preserves today saw Beryl coming
and nudged her partner, rolling her eyes and muttering, 'Here we
go. Brace yourself.' However, Beryl, preoccupied with her own
affairs, didn't stay long at the glowing display of jams, jellies and
pickles on show. She merely picked up one or two jars, sniffed at
the prices and made her way to the café.

'We got away lightly this time,' said the other woman behind
the stall. 'I was expecting a lecture on basic food hygiene and the
use of pectin, but she seems a bit distracted. I hope she's okay.'

'Don't worry about Beryl,' said her friend. 'She's got that look
on her face. I know it well.'

'What do you mean?'

'She's got a bee in her bonnet. Look over there. It's already
nearly lunchtime and she's heading for the café. I can see her
buddies going in too. She has bigger fish to fry, I reckon. I'd love
to be a fly on the wall.'

Beryl greeted Anthea and Winnie with a nod – they'd never
gone in for this modern habit of exchanging hugs and kisses
every five minutes when they'd only seen each other the day
before and anyway, it was a surefire way of spreading germs. The
three sat down at their usual table which Winnie had phoned
ahead to reserve, just in case some pretentious newcomer
decided to muscle in on their spot. Beryl looked around with
approval. It was the first time they'd been in since Kate's latest
upgrade of the decorative features. The new tablecloths were
patterned with autumn leaves and blackberries and each table
had its own small pot of crimson chrysanthemums in the centre.
A much bigger terracotta pot of the same flowers but in a vibrant

rusty red stood on a wooden stool in one corner of the café. The whole effect was warm and friendly.

'Do you like the seasonal look, ladies?' called the woman standing behind the counter. She beamed at them when they chorused their approval.

'You've really got a flair for design, Kate,' said Winnie. 'I feel as if I've accidentally dressed to blend in.' She gestured to her own flowing robe and head wrap which were decorated with burnt orange and chocolate-brown ferns.

'You'll never do that,' said Kate, laughing. 'Look at you all. None of you are wallflowers. Beryl's colours are always stunning and you're so elegant, Anthea. The linen look is very Judi Dench, and you've gone for more subtle shades of green and mushroom this morning. It was as if you all knew you were going to be asked to do me a huge favour. Can I get Milo to take some photos of the three of you for my next publicity leaflet? Would you mind?'

The Saga Louts looked immensely gratified as Kate called her partner and he came in holding a very fancy digital camera. Milo was tall and broad shouldered. His short, dark hair was peppered with grey which in Beryl's opinion added a lot to his charm and his kind eyes twinkled when he saw them.

'Good heavens, I didn't realise this was a proper photoshoot,' he said. 'Kate asked me earlier if I'd take some shots of the café's new autumn look, but I didn't know we had glamorous models on tap. No, don't move, I'll take the pictures just where you are.'

He clicked away merrily while Kate made coffee. 'It's on the house this time,' she said. 'These photos are going to look great in my leaflet and on the posters. I'm guessing you wouldn't say no to a slice of Milo's lemon drizzle cake, if it's not too near lunchtime?'

Soon, the excitement was over, and the three ladies settled down with their coffee and cake. 'Well now, Anthea,' said Winnie.

'Last night was a bit of an eye-opener, wasn't it? Did you have any idea that was going to happen, you dark horse?'

'Not a clue, darling, and if I had known in advance I'd have probably decided to say no. Maurice has seemed a bit lacklustre lately, as I told you, but when I looked into those twinkling eyes and saw the longing look on his face, I couldn't turn the poor chap down. One more marriage can't hurt, I thought. Nothing ventured, nothing gained. And when I took him home with me later, I found out there was nothing lacklustre or *poor chap* about him in that department, after all.'

She fanned her face with a menu and chuckled at the expressions on her friends' faces, which were a mixture of surprise and envy.

'Too much information,' they chorused, but Kate, overhearing, began to applaud.

'You're not telling me you and Maurice have finally got it together?' she said.

Anthea said they had indeed, and Kate called Milo back in to tell him the news. Soon Beryl's mission to talk to her cronies about future plans had been derailed as a couple more regular customers came in and were told Anthea's news and then Maurice himself turned up, to be greeted by a rousing round of applause.

'I wasn't expecting a reception committee,' he said, coming over to kiss his intended on both cheeks. 'But this is very gratifying. Can I join you? How about I treat us all to lunch as a celebration of this wonderful lady agreeing to make me the happiest man alive?'

This idea went down very well, and it wasn't long before Maurice had pulled up a chair. Four soups of the day were chosen because Kate's chicken and leek broth was everyone's favourite and also the scent of freshly baked bread rolls was too tantalising to resist.

'Now then,' said Beryl at last. 'There's something I want to talk to you all about. Let me outline my latest holiday scheme before we all get distracted by food.'

The others leaned forward slightly. Beryl was well known for her imaginative suggestions, and they were all in the mood for something new. It was as if Anthea and Maurice's news had energised them all. Even Anthea's usual cool demeanour had been exchanged for one of barely suppressed glee.

'Go on then,' she said. 'Don't keep us in suspense.'

'It's a bit more ambitious than our usual trips and it's going to include more people than just us three,' said Beryl.

'Oh, hurrah,' said Maurice. 'Does that mean I can come too? I've always wanted to join a Saga Louts jolly.'

'Certainly, you can come,' said Beryl. 'That's all part of my plan. Also, we'll ask Sid and Frank. The younger element, if they agree to it, will be my new neighbour, Venetia, and of course, the lovely Rick. That will make a total of eight, a perfect number for a road trip, in my opinion.'

Silence followed this astonishing announcement. Beryl could see by the looks on their faces that she'd shocked them into speechlessness, something that rarely happened.

'I think you'd better carry on,' said Winnie. 'We're going to need a lot more details. A heck of a lot.'

18

Beryl's summons came as a complete surprise to Vee, when Rick showed her the text message he'd just received.

'She wants us to go round to her house tonight for "drinks and nibbles",' he said, the puzzled look on his face mirroring Vee's own. 'What's all that about, do you think? I know Beryl loves a good gathering, but this is out of the blue, and I had the impression she wasn't that keen on you, to be quite honest.'

'Well, thanks for the vote of confidence,' said Vee. 'The feeling's mutual. The thought of spending an evening with her isn't filling me with joy. You go. I'll have another night in.'

Rick fixed her with a steely look. Vee could see that he was imagining her *rootling* through his possessions again and a pang of guilt hit her, even though she felt in her heart that she hadn't done anything wrong. At least they were speaking to each other though, which was an improvement after the icy stand-off between them since their earlier argument.

'I don't think you've properly got the measure of Beryl yet,' Rick said. 'In Willowbrook, when you get an invitation from her, you tend not to say you're busy. We should both go. It'll be… interesting.'

Vee pulled a face. 'Interesting? Like a trip to a zoo and a walk through its collection of tarantulas?'

'Oh, come on, Vee. Beryl's not that bad, and she did bring us some great snacks. Maybe tonight you can start again with her. You're going to be neighbours. You should try to understand what makes her tick. She's a generous woman with a heart of gold.'

Vee considered her options. The thought of making Rick even crosser with her wasn't appealing and neither was the prospect of getting even more on the wrong side of Beryl. These people were going to be in her life for the foreseeable future. She really should make the effort to get along better with them both.

'Okay, you win,' she said. 'How about we call it quits here in a couple of hours, go back to yours and have showers and I'll make my favourite pasta dish? If we're going out for drinks, we don't want to end up flat on our backs because we haven't eaten beforehand.'

There was a pause as Rick considered this suggestion, and Vee regretted the wording of it. The thought of having Rick flat on his back with her had brought on an attack of the shivers, which was most unwelcome. She breathed deeply and tried not to look at him.

'That sounds good,' he said eventually. 'And… I guess I should say sorry about being so touchy earlier. I know you weren't prying and you're right. Anything out on show in someone's house is free to be looked at.'

'I'm sorry too,' said Vee, thankful that they appeared to be getting over the sticky patch. 'I should have asked first. Anyway, let's forget it and hope tonight's not too dull.'

'No visit to Beryl's is ever dull,' said Rick, grinning. 'She'll give us Prosecco and to go with it, hot sausage rolls, fresh from the oven. Winnie's bound to be there, and she brings the spicy bits and bobs. Anthea usually provides olives and posh crisps.'

'Is it a party then? I thought it would just be us. That does sound more fun.'

'Definitely not just us but not exactly a party. Maurice is bound to be there – he asked Anthea to marry him in the pub last night and she said yes. In fact, I bet this do is to celebrate their engagement. We should get them a card and maybe a bottle of fizz.'

To her surprise, Vee found herself actually starting to look forward to this impromptu event. She mentally ran through what she might wear. So many of her old clothes had gone to the charity shop when she moved but she'd kept a few favourite dresses that would go well with her ankle boots. A rush of excitement made her wriggle with delight at the thought of having something to smarten herself up for, after the long hours cleaning and decorating over the last days. She noticed Rick looking at her more closely.

'What's up? Have I got paint on my nose, or something?' she asked.

'No... I was just thinking... you looked happy,' he said.

'And I don't usually?'

'Not very, no. I guess you've been under a lot of pressure lately, one way and another. A night out will do you good, even if it's only at a fuddle next door.'

'A fuddle?' That word was unfamiliar to Vee and she raised her eyebrows. Rick smiled.

'A bit of a do. A get-together. A shindig. Call it what you like. Not quite as big as a party, but something fun and cosy. Let's do it.'

'Yes,' Vee agreed. 'It sounds great. I'm going to crack on with painting the ceiling and then we'll go and get our glad rags on. Turn the radio up, I need a bit of inspiration.'

Several hours later, Rick and Vee were standing in his hallway ready to leave for Beryl's fuddle. Vee had been pleased with how her pasta dish had gone down. She'd rustled up a simple sauce of tinned tomatoes, onions, garlic and dried herbs. Rick had been very appreciative and even had seconds. They had eaten before they took turns to shower, deciding that it was safer that way, so that they didn't arrive at Beryl's liberally spattered with tomato sauce.

Vee had overcome a wave of tiredness and rummaged in her belongings until she found a dress that reached almost to her ankles and showed just the slightest hint of cleavage. She'd teamed it with trainers, when she remembered that they were going to be walking to Beryl's house. The sassy ankle boots would have to wait for another night. Her newly washed hair had now dried naturally in curls that fell in just the right way around her face, for once. A touch of mascara and a generous application of scarlet lipstick had given Vee a final lift, and by the time she'd slipped on her denim jacket and gone to meet Rick downstairs, she felt as good as she was ever likely to feel after such an intensive couple of days' work.

The look on Rick's face when he watched her come down the stairs made the effort of getting ready instead of climbing into the comfortable bed all worthwhile. He didn't say anything for a few moments, but then just murmured, 'Wow.'

Vee smiled at him, taking in his faded jeans and white linen shirt, sleeves rolled up to reveal tanned forearms. He was wearing baseball boots with stars on the sides, and he grabbed an ancient leather jacket from a hook on the wall to complete the look as he turned to open the front door.

'This was my dad's biker jacket,' he said, when Vee automatically reached out to stroke the sleeve. 'I know a lot of people don't approve of leather and I wouldn't go out and buy one of these nowadays, but I think it's okay if it can be classed as vintage, don't you? It reminds me of him. He used to let me sit on his bike and pretend to ride it when I was little.'

Vee nodded, with a sudden vision of a small, excited little boy in her head, bouncing on the seat of something like an elderly Harley Davidson, maybe. 'Good memories come in all sorts of places,' she said. 'I'm finding a lot of mine in Dragonfly Cottage now it's getting clean and bright again.'

They set off through the village towards Fiddler's Row, with Rick carrying the bag containing a bottle of champagne and a congratulations card that they'd picked up on the way home earlier. As they passed the church, Rick raised his hand to a figure standing in the doorway. 'Hi, Bev,' he called, and the woman approached them, smiling. She was wearing denim dungarees over a red shirt complete with built-in dog collar. Her short, spiky hair was almost the same shade of red, and her many piercings glinted in the early-evening sunshine.

'This is Venetia Prescott,' said Rick. 'And, Vee, this is our Rev Bev. She's been the driving force in bringing people together in Willowbrook since she arrived.'

'He's good at laying on the praise,' said the vicar, shaking Vee by the hand. 'I haven't done much. They're a friendly bunch.'

'Bev's way too modest,' said Rick. 'What about all your groups? The Happiness Gang was the best one yet. We must be due a reunion sometime soon.'

'That sounds intriguing,' said Vee. 'What did your gang do?'

'We talked about what happiness is and if it's possible to go looking for it,' said Bev. 'In a nutshell, it boiled down to us all finding things that had made us feel good over the years and real-ising that just... you know... a kind of peaceful contentment was as good as a burst of sheer happiness now and again. Will I see you both on Sunday in church?' she added hopefully.

'I haven't been inside a church for years,' Vee said, wondering if Rick was secretly hoping to make her see the light.

'We might be there,' said Rick. 'I know I've missed a few services lately, but I love a good sing. If you promise me great hymns, I could be persuaded to drag Vee along with me. We're busy blitzing her cottage though. It's next door to Beryl's, and that's where we're off to now.'

They said goodbye to Bev, and upped their speed when Rick realised they were going to be late. 'She always says the time her fuddles kick off isn't set in stone,' said Rick, striding out more energetically. 'But I never like to risk it.'

Beryl's front door was already standing open when they arrived, and she welcomed them in warmly. 'The others are all here,' she said. 'I was hoping you'd come soon. The sausage rolls are just out of the oven, and they're always nicer eaten fresh.'

Vee followed Beryl into the small living room which was bursting at the seams with people. She felt a wave of panic when she saw that they all looked to be around Beryl's age so they might know her and remember her history, but then she spotted Sid Potter. He gave her a friendly wave and an encouraging smile, which was heartening.

'Right, everyone, this is Venetia Prescott from next door, if you don't already know her,' said Beryl. 'She likes to be called Vee these days, apparently, but I knew her as Venetia as a child. She left here when she was a teenager, so you won't all remember her.'

Vee looked around and smiled in what she hoped was a confident way. She could feel her knees shaking but then became aware of Rick moving up behind her more closely. He was barely touching her, but she sensed that he was trying to give her some kind of support. She began to relax. This was going to be fine. It wasn't a crowd, just six elderly people who all had friendly faces and were clutching champagne flutes.

'Have a drink, you two,' said Sid, as Beryl bustled off to the kitchen to sort out food. 'I reckon I should probably introduce everybody seeing as our hostess has gone missing.' He poured Rick and Vee a glass of Prosecco each and handed them over.

'I've already made Vee's acquaintance again after a long time,' Sid continued. 'We met in the churchyard. This is Winnie.' He indicated the voluptuous lady on his right who was dressed in a long robe of fuchsia cotton with a candy-striped head wrap. 'And this is the third of our lovely Saga Louts, Anthea.'

Winnie beamed at Vee and Anthea stepped forward. 'Hello, darling. Welcome back to Willowbrook,' she said. 'I didn't meet you when you were here before because there were a few periods where I lived elsewhere.'

'With one of her many husbands,' said the dapper man with a neat grey beard who was standing beside Anthea. 'I'm Maurice. I'm lucky enough to be engaged to this gorgeous woman. Husband number five-to-be, waiting in the wings.'

The others all laughed, and the warmth of their obvious friendship gave Vee the feeling of being part of something joyous. The third man was on his feet now too.

'My name's Frank,' he said. 'I'm a relative newcomer to the village. I moved here from Sheffield with my son and daughter-in-law, and I have to say I didn't want to come, initially. We live just around the corner, and it's turned out to be one of the best things we ever did.'

'So now you know us all, Vee,' said Winnie. 'Tuck into some snacks, both of you, keep topping up your glasses and we'll get around to the main business of the evening when we're fully fuelled up.'

'Oh, so there *is* an ulterior motive for this,' said Rick. 'I thought we might be celebrating the happy couple.' He handed over the champagne and card to Maurice and Anthea and they exclaimed with delight.

'It's not an engagement party as such,' said Beryl, coming in from the kitchen with a loaded tray. 'We *are* celebrating these two brave souls and their news but there's something else I want to run past you all. Anthea, Maurice and Winnie already know what it is, but I'll keep the rest of you in suspense for just a little bit longer. I'm hoping by the end of tonight, I'll have full agreement to set my latest plan into motion.'

19

When there was nothing left of the sausage rolls but flakes of golden pastry and every plate of Winnie's tongue-tingling snacks was empty, Beryl cleared the decks and asked Sid to refill everyone's glasses.

'It's time for the main business of the evening to commence,' she said, in her best WI meeting voice.

The others in the room fell gratifyingly silent in seconds. Beryl signalled for them all to sit down and settled herself in the highest chair. It was tapestry-covered with wooden arms and always made her feel slightly regal. She looked round at her assembled guests. Frank, Sid, Rick and Venetia wore confused expressions, but the other two Saga Louts and Maurice were gazing back at her with shining eyes. Winnie gave Beryl a thumbs-up sign.

'I've a proposal to put to you,' Beryl said.

'I thought Maurice already had the proposal covered,' said Sid, grinning at his old friend.

'Not that kind. This one is about an adventure. As most of you know, Anthea, Winnie and I love to go travelling but we usually either travel by train or plane and we've done so many city breaks and short package holidays to the seaside all over the place that I thought it was time to try something different. We were going to do a Yorkshire Dales trip last time, but it was cancelled so we swapped it for Majorca and going abroad again has given me itchy feet.'

She paused for a moment and Frank said, 'Go on, spit it out. I don't see what that has to do with us though.'

Beryl smiled. 'I'm hoping it has everything to do with you. I want us to go on a road trip together. Anthea, Maurice and Winnie have already said they're up for it. We'll just need a minibus and a couple of drivers. Last time we did this, when we were the Happiness Gang, Rick sorted all that out and drove us beautifully.'

Rick nodded. 'Yes, I did, and it was great. Are you telling me you want me to take you all to Norfolk again?'

'Not exactly. Let's go a step further this time. I'd like us to go to France.'

'But... I'm in the middle of helping Vee to sort her house out,' said Rick. 'I can't just take off to France at a moment's notice. What's brought this on?'

Beryl glanced across at Venetia, who wasn't looking at all impressed. 'It doesn't have to be immediately,' she said. 'And we'd want another driver, for a start, because Anthea...'

Her voice tailed off and Anthea pulled a face. 'Okay, okay – I know you all think I'm past my sell-by date for driving on the wrong side of the road,' she said. 'Do you have a driving licence, Venetia?'

Vee sat up straighter. 'Yes, I have, as a matter of fact. I haven't got a car any more though. Do you mean you want me to come with you? Most of you hardly know me.'

'Well, I for one think it's a superb idea,' said Frank. 'I haven't been anywhere exciting for ages. What about you, Sid?'

The other man was now sitting on the edge of his seat. He clapped his hands. 'I'm in,' he said. 'A road trip to the Continent sounds like a great jaunt. Anywhere in particular in France? Jenny and I loved Brittany and it's very easy to get to.'

'Hang on a minute,' said Rick, holding up a hand. 'I've already said I'm busy. We've got a lot of work to do before Vee can move into her house. I've promised her I'll make Dragonfly Cottage habitable as soon as I can.'

'How long do you think that'll take you?' Beryl asked. 'A week? A fortnight?'

Rick sighed. 'We could probably get the main jobs done in a couple of weeks as Vee's helping me, but I don't understand why you want to go to France. Couldn't you just plan a trip to Cornwall or somewhere even closer?'

Winnie shook her head. 'There are various places we'd like to visit as we drive through France. Sid would probably enjoy stopping off in Brittany, by the sound of it. Anthea loves La Rochelle. I visited Bordeaux with my man years ago and I'd like to have a wander around there again. Revisit old haunts.'

'And then there's St Emilion,' said Beryl. 'Some of my Eddie's favourite wine came from there. He was very partial to a glass or two of the red stuff.'

Vee gasped. 'But that's not far from where my Aunt Yolanda lives,' she said.

'You're quite right,' agreed Beryl. 'I expect you haven't seen her for a long time, and neither have I. You'd have a lot to talk about, I'm thinking. We're old mates, me and Tallulah's sister Yolanda. She stayed at Dragonfly Cottage with you all quite often back in the day, didn't she?'

Vee didn't reply. Beryl decided not to push the subject. From what she'd overheard in the garden, Yolanda, a very lively character who'd never married and had travelled the world even more than the Saga Louts, would be just the person to fill her in on a few of the details about the time when the family did their disappearing act and what made them leave so suddenly. Beryl had her own suspicions. It surely couldn't only have been the lure of a new job for Vee's father or the fact that Venetia was proving to be something of a loose cannon.

'What do you say, folks?' she said. 'Shall we make a plan? How about we give ourselves three weeks to get ready? Is it doable? Does everyone have a current passport?'

They all said they had, but Vee was still frowning. 'Are you sure you want me to come with you?' she asked. 'I've got to admit I'm pretty skint right now. How much will it cost?'

'Oh, don't worry about that, darling,' said Anthea. 'We'll split the cost for the minibus and the ferry, and we can stay in nice but cheap places as we go. *Auberges* and the like. Roadside motels, you know the kind of thing. You look as if you need a holiday and so does our Rick. Call it an investment for your mental health. Are we all up for it?'

Silence fell again and then a babble of voices said that yes, they were. Even Venetia sounded convinced, thought Beryl. She rubbed her hands together. It was time to make a proper plan. This trip was really going to happen.

20

The next fortnight passed by in a blur of activity. Rick put all his efforts into getting as much work done as possible on Dragonfly Cottage and Vee tried hard to match him for energy. They ate together most evenings and went to their separate beds early, although Vee sometimes woke in the night with feverish images in her head of Rick lying naked under the covers on the other side of her wall.

Vee was furious with herself for having these half-awake thoughts. She hadn't forgotten the feelings of unjustified shame after the incident with the photo albums and the last thing she needed was to let herself have a ridiculous crush on someone with so much emotional baggage of his own. On top of that was the inkling that Rick knew way too much about the murkier part of her past, but they seemed to have reached some kind of unspoken agreement to leave the memories where they were for now. The house project must come first. When Vee was safely installed in her own home, maybe she would have the courage to ask Rick straight out to tell her exactly what he remembered from that time in their lives. Or maybe she wouldn't.

Bit by bit, Dragonfly Cottage was coming together, and Vee was incredibly touched to see how hard Rick was prepared to work, even though she could tell that, like herself, he was getting more and more exhausted. When they'd reached the point where all the main rooms were clean and decorated, Rick called a brief halt.

It was now the start of October, and the warmth of the Indian summer that had been coming and going as they worked was back in force, although the mornings tended to be chilly. The leaves were glowing with autumn colour and Willowbrook Country Park with its ancient oaks and huge variety of other trees was looking at its best. Vee had always preferred spring and early summer when it came to choosing a favourite time of year because the popular love of the *season of mists and mellow fruitful-ness* reminded her way too much of the days after the time when her teenage world had fallen apart. Nineteen eighty-five had contained the worst autumn of her life, and even now, she found it hard to cope with the changing leaves and the chill in the morning air.

Vee came downstairs on 1 October, yawning widely and stretching her arms above her head as she sat down at the kitchen table.

'What's the plan for today?' she asked wearily, reaching for the coffee pot that Rick had filled up a few moments ago and pouring them both a mug of the fragrant liquid. 'I really need this,' she said, taking a sip. 'It feels as if we've been working on the house forever, doesn't it?'

'I wanted to talk to you about that,' said Rick. He looked down at her, and she gazed back, rubbing her eyes. 'I can't do any more until the varnish is properly dry on the living room floor and you shouldn't try another coat of gloss on the upstairs doors without letting the last lot set completely,' he said. 'I vote we have a day off today. Where shall we go? How about we visit the mattress shop first and you can choose the one you want for the main bedroom? We could also call into the place next door to it, where you can get bedding. It's not too pricey. All you'll need then is a window blind or some curtains or maybe both and your bedroom'll be ready.'

Vee looked up at him suspiciously. 'Is this all heading towards getting rid of me?' she said. 'I can move out as soon as we get this part done.'

'Oh, no,' Rick said hastily. 'The house isn't ready yet. I've got to rub down the kitchen units and give them a quick coat of paint if you're still agreeing to wait until the January sales or later for a new one?'

'Is it worth doing that if you're going to rip them out?'

'Yes. You need to feel comfortable with all the rooms. It won't take long. And the bathroom suite's being delivered in a couple of days. I'm going to have to leave you without any washing facilities while I fit that. You're welcome to stay here until your place is properly ready.'

Vee smiled at him. 'In that case, let's have a day off,' she said. 'We deserve it.'

* * *

Once they'd completed all the shopping tasks to Vee's satisfaction, they climbed back into the van and turned to face each other. It was now mid-morning, and the sun was breaking through what had been an unusually heavy morning mist. Vee had been about to ask Rick where he'd like to go next when her phone pinged.

'I'll just check this message in case it's Beryl about the road trip,' said Vee. 'She's texting me several times a day at the moment with different questions. I still can't believe she asked me along, although it's obvious that knowing she'd be getting an extra driver is mainly why she invited me.'

Vee dug out the phone from her pocket. 'It's an Instagram message,' she said. 'Rick, it's from Rhonda. I thought she was never going to answer.'

'What does she say?' asked Rick, his face falling. Vee bit her lip. This wasn't how she'd seen the day panning out. Rick had been looking more relaxed since they'd decided to play truant from the house. Now, he was visibly tense, his face pale under the tan. In Vee's opinion, anything from Rhonda was bound to put a dampener on their day, and just when they'd been getting on so well, too. The only way they'd managed to put what Vee privately thought of as *photogate* behind them was by never mentioning it. Now everything could be going to change, and not for the better.

'Hang on, I'll read it out to you,' Vee said. 'Uh oh, she wants to meet up with me. I thought we might just exchange a few texts, or something.' She cleared her throat.

> Hi Sweetie. Good to hear from you after all this time.

Vee rolled her eyes at Rick. 'Sweetie? She never called anyone that in the old days and I really can't see why she'd be pleased to hear from me. Anyway, listen to the rest.'

> Sorry for the delay in replying. I've been away on an extended Caribbean cruise. It's our third trip this year and my darling hubby always bans my phone when we're away so I'm a bit out of touch. Did you want to meet up? I guess we have loads to talk about?

'Urgh. I hate the word *hubby*,' said Vee. 'And an *extended*

Caribbean cruise too. Typical of Rhonda to marry someone who can afford that kind of stuff. What shall I say?'

Rick shrugged. 'You'd better say yes, I suppose. You're not going to be happy until you've dug deeper into the past. I can't help thinking it's a mistake though.'

Vee ignored the warning and typed a quick question regarding where she could find Rhonda, and more importantly, when. The answer came back immediately.

> By chance, I'm free all day today, which as you can imagine, doesn't often happen! Why don't you come to me? I'm assuming you're still in Willowbrook, but you can get here by car in half an hour. Come now! Can't wait for a good catch-up.

What followed was an address in a part of the county that Vee recognised as the nearest thing they had to a stockbroker belt. She read the new message out to Rick and raised her eyebrows.

'You're going to have to do it,' he said. 'You won't settle until you've seen her, will you? Rhonda's really hit the big time if she lives out there. I did some work for a friend of a friend in that neck of the woods and the houses around and about his were selling for upwards of two million.' He glanced at Vee who was gazing back in what she hoped was an appealing manner.

'Oh, okay. I'll drive you,' Rick said, heaving a sigh. 'Might as well get it over with, I suppose, and taking a taxi out there would cost you a fortune.'

Vee flashed him a grateful smile and sent back a reply saying they were on their way. She didn't explain who she was arriving with. Let that be a surprise. Rick started the engine and drove in silence, out of Meadowthorpe and into the surrounding country-side. The mood in the van was tense.

'Are you worried about meeting Rhonda again?' Vee asked,

although the answer was obvious in the set of Rick's jaw and the fact that he was tapping his fingers on the wheel whenever there was even the slightest hold-up.

'Nah. She's just a jumped-up social climber,' he said. 'She was nothing then and she's irrelevant now. I'm just fed up because she's ruined our one day off. We don't need to stay at hers long though, do we? We're heading in the direction of the coast now. There might still be time to go and see the sea.'

The idea of a trip to the seaside was tempting, but Vee couldn't ignore the churning feeling in her stomach. She half-wished she'd never tried to get in touch with Rhonda, but they'd come this far, and Rick was right. There would be no way of parking the niggling unease until Vee had faced her past and unravelled the tangle of memories that haunted her. They weren't even whole memories really, just snippets, hauntingly vague.

As they drew nearer to the address Rhonda had given Vee, the houses became more and more opulent, surrounded by well-manicured lawns. Finally, they drew up at number twelve, Woodland Row, which was at the end of a leafy cul-de-sac. Unlike Vee's own house in Fiddler's Row, the word was deceptive because the houses down this lane were so far apart from each other that they could hardly have been thought of as part of the same development. Number twelve, The Laurels, was the largest and had a garden full of mature trees and shrubs, with a drive that wound its way up to a gravel sweep and a flight of stone steps. At the top of the steps was an enormous front door, standing open. It was painted a glossy black with flourishing olive trees in terracotta pots on either side of it.

Vee and Rick were speechless for a few moments after he turned off the engine. They opened their doors and began to clamber out. Before they could think of any exclamations that would match the grandeur of this residence, a woman came out onto the top step. She was slim, very blonde and from her viewpoint by the van, Vee could see that she was dressed in a jumpsuit of the softest cornflour-blue silk that clung to her figure in all the right places and was open far enough at the front for a magnificent cleavage to be on view.

'Sweetie,' she called, gliding down the steps. 'It *is* you. I saw the van coming up the drive...' she turned up her nose very slightly '...and I actually thought it was the gardener. Glad you managed to get a lift anyway.'

Rhonda came forward to greet Vee, completely ignoring Rick. She grabbed her by the shoulders and air-kissed her on both cheeks with an extra third kiss for luck. Vee tried to smile, but the sight of the other woman's wide blue eyes and bouncing curls was taking her right back to a place she'd tried not to visit for many years.

'Hi, Rhonda,' she said. 'This is my friend Rick. I expect you remember him from our schooldays. Probably as Ricardo though?'

There was an icy silence and then Rhonda moved over to stand in front of Rick. She peered at him. 'I didn't expect to see *you* again,' she said. 'What are you doing here?'

Rick pulled himself up to his full height and stared down at Rhonda. 'I'm here because Vee asked me to come,' he said. 'Long time, no see. You haven't changed much but I guess *I* have, if you didn't recognise me.'

'You most certainly have. You weren't nearly so easy on the eye in those days, Ricardo... or Rick, I should say.' Rhonda was clearly beginning to appreciate Rick's finer points the more she took in the muscular frame, outdoor tan and short hair, as blond as her own. She gave him a brilliant smile and turned to head back into the house.

'Follow me, both of you. I arranged for some champagne to be put on ice ready for your arrival, sweetie,' she said over her shoulder to Vee. 'But this is a double celebration, isn't it? Two throwbacks for the price of one, you might say.'

'I'm driving,' said Rick tersely. 'And we won't be staying long. We're on our way to the coast for an afternoon out.'

'How super. I'm tempted to hitch a lift and join you, but I try to keep out of direct sunlight these days. So ageing,' said Rhonda, glancing at Vee's healthy complexion as she ushered them into a spacious hall where a wide staircase curved up to a gallery that reached all around the upper level. An enormous crystal chandelier hung in the centre. Vee couldn't decide if it was pretentious or stunning. Rhonda caught her looking up at it.

'Oh, I can guess what you're thinking, sweetie. A bit over the top, I know, but my hubby...' Vee winced but Rhonda was in full flow and didn't notice. 'He *adores* that kind of thing and I have to let my gorgeous Hubs have his way sometimes to keep the peace, if you get my meaning? Come into my parlour, said the... something or other... I can never remember all that stuff we had to learn at school, can you? Waste of time, most of it.'

Vee had the strong feeling that if she was to meet 'Hubs', she would need to offer him all her sympathy. The idea of spending your life with this brittle creature was toe-curlingly awful even at this short reacquaintance and she could tell by Rick's face that he was thinking the same. They trailed after Rhonda into the 'parlour' which was roughly the size of a ballroom. The chairs and sofas, which all looked brand new, were ranged around the room like guests at a party who didn't really want to speak to each other. The pale cream carpet was thick and soft under their feet, and Vee belatedly wondered if they should have taken their shoes off, but Rhonda hadn't removed her own high-heeled stilettos, so she guessed if you were as rich as this, you probably didn't worry about a few marks on the carpet.

'Have a seat, guys,' said Rhonda, gesturing to a little group of satin-striped chairs near the French windows. 'I'll just ring for the champers. I've asked them to do a few smoked salmon blinis and so on, in case you were peckish. I never eat at this time of day, just a kale smoothie when I wake up and then I fast until dinner, but not everyone has the same strict regime.'

She reached for an ancient bell pull that hung on the wall nearby and gave it an impatient tug. Within seconds, a girl in a white apron had bustled in with a silver salver of canapés which she placed on the coffee table. She then scuttled away and returned with a champagne bucket full of ice. An expensive-looking bottle could be seen sticking out of the top. Another, older woman brought up the rear with another tray of champagne glasses and napkins. Vee exchanged looks with Rick. She could see that he was having a similar response to hers at all this opulence. Top-class fizz, elegant snacks at the drop of a hat, staff on call to serve them at a moment's notice, grand surroundings... it was mind-boggling.

'Get that bubbly open, Sandra,' said Rhonda. 'And make it snappy. We haven't seen each other for donkey's years. This is a celebration.'

Soon, the three were alone again. Vee and Rhonda were clutching flutes of chilled fizz, but Rick had his arms firmly folded and a stern expression on his face.

'I don't know why you're being so prudish, Ricardo,' said Rhonda, giving Rick a flirtatious smile. 'My Bernie always says a little bit of a tipple helps him to concentrate on his driving. Mind you, we've had a chauffeur ever since he—' She stopped talking abruptly, reached for the tray of blinis and held it out.

'Here, have one of these. At least you can eat something,' she said to Rick. 'Or are you against caviar and smoked salmon at this time of day too? You look as if you can take care of yourself.'

Rick said he had nothing against eating at any time of day. He and Vee both took a napkin and a couple of the delicious-looking canapés. It had been a long time since breakfast, after all. Rhonda topped up Vee's champagne and sat back in her chair. Vee noticed that she'd barely touched her own drink.

'So, let's have a good old catch-up,' Rhonda said, slipping off her shoes and wiggling her toes. The nails were varnished a deep burgundy, and her feet were slim and dainty. Vee suddenly felt like a baby elephant, clumsy and out of place. Rhonda had always made her unhappy in her own skin, she remembered.

'Fill me in on what you've been doing with your life, Vee,' she continued. 'I'm guessing Ricardo has been busy doing something *manly*. You don't get abs like that in an office.' She giggled and batted her eyelashes at him.

Vee stared. So some women actually did do that eyelash thing. She'd only ever read about it in a romantic story. 'I haven't come for a gossip, Rhonda.' She put down her glass. 'I wanted to ask you... if you...' The words caught in her throat and she shot an agonised glance to Rick, who thankfully took pity on her, although he didn't look happy about it.

'Vee wants to ask you about the summer that ended around the time when she left Willowbrook,' he said. 'She's having trouble recalling the details about what went on just before her family moved away. It's been troubling her. Can you help her out?'

Rhonda sat up straighter in her chair and stopped wiggling her toes. 'Seriously?' she said. 'How can you have forgotten anything about that time? It was like living in a soap opera for a while, and we were all the stars of it. You in particular, Vee. That camping trip...'

'*I* was a star?' repeated Vee. 'What do you mean? I know it all ended badly. I wasn't that much involved though... was I?'

'Is this some kind of trick?' Rhonda started to laugh, then changed her mind.

Vee reached for her glass again and took a swig of champagne to steady her nerves. 'I don't know what's happened to me, but I must have somehow blanked out the memories. I remember you being horrible to Patrick. You were nasty to most people, come to think of it, but especially to him.'

'I was a bit of a tease, I'll give you that, but he needed to grow a pair. I was doing him a favour. You can't go through life being scared of your own shadow.'

'And he didn't, did he?' said Rick. 'He died, the poor sod.'

'You're surely not blaming me for that, are you? Oh, come on, Ricardo. He was a drip. He might have been trying to do himself in when he jumped into the fishing lake, but that wasn't because of me. Your mate Shazzie pulled him out. Oh, yes, I know all about what happened that night and the one after, so don't pretend you've forgotten your part in it, Venetia Oh-So-Perfect Prescott. You can't have. If you really need your memory jogged, don't ask me. Try asking your aunt.'

There was a stunned silence. Vee could tell Rick was as surprised as she was by this new twist. 'Aunt Yolanda? What do you mean by that?' she asked. 'I don't know what you're talking about. *Yolanda* was there? That's insane.'

'The reason you can't remember what went on is because you were so drunk. Absolutely legless. One of the teachers phoned your mum and dad to come and fetch you back but they were away somewhere, so your lovely Aunty Yolanda came instead. You were puking your guts up by then.'

'But... but...'

'Oh, yes, you weren't so perfect as you liked to make out, were you? And as for what happened to get you in that state or where you got the booze, I have absolutely no idea but when she finally got you to stop throwing up and took you away, you were screaming, "I never meant any harm!" over and over again.'

Rick opened his mouth to say something, but the sound of a loud male voice bellowing Rhonda's name made them all swing around to face the parlour door.

'Oh, shit. Bernie's back,' said Rhonda, jumping to her feet. 'He's early. That's never a good sign. Look, you'd better go. I don't know anything else about the stupid camping trip and Hubs doesn't like unexpected visitors. Go, quickly. He's gone upstairs to look for me. I'll tell him the van belongs to a man looking at the drains. They've been very smelly lately.'

As she spoke, Rhonda was ushering Vee and Rick towards a different door, which led to a side passage. Before either of them could protest, even if they'd wanted to, they were outside and hurrying around the corner of the house.

'Don't bother to get in touch again, Vee,' hissed Rhonda, already turning away. 'I don't know anything else, and I'm not going to talk about old times again. Let it go. Move on.'

Her voice faded away as she padded barefoot back towards the side door.

'Come on, let's get out of here,' said Rick, taking Vee by the arm. 'We're not wanted in Princess Rhonda's palace, and it sounds as if meeting lovely hubby might be a very bad idea.'

Vee let him lead her towards the van. She couldn't have spoken if she'd tried.

21

Rick drove away from Rhonda's house without a backward glance. In the passenger seat beside him, Vee sat huddled against the window, her arms wrapped around herself. He thought she might be crying but she wasn't making a sound.

'Are you okay?' he asked unnecessarily, because she so obviously wasn't. Vee didn't answer.

'Look, I'm going to shelve the seaside trip for a little while and take you somewhere different,' Rick said. 'We need hot coffee and a team talk.'

There was still no response, so he took the next turnoff, where a large, colourful sign told him that a garden centre was not far away. Within five minutes he was pulling into a large car park. He got out of the van and came round to open the door for his silent passenger.

'Come on, Vee,' he said. 'I remember going to this place before when Stacey... well, anyway, that's not important, they do great cake, nearly as good as Beryl's. We need sustenance and we need it now.'

She blinked as if waking up from a long sleep but undid her

seatbelt and swung her legs round. Rick thought she looked as if she'd forgotten how to move properly, so he held out his arms and when she made no protest, he lifted her down from her seat. They stood together beside the van, half-hidden from the view of anyone passing through the car park and on impulse, Rick tightened his arms around her. Vee stiffened for a moment but then leaned into the hug and started to cry. Great, heaving sobs racked her body and her tears were hot and wet on Rick's t-shirt.

'I'm s... s... sorry,' she gulped, when the storm of weeping had subsided a little. 'I never usually cry. It was just... just... so awful and I don't know what she meant. I still can't remember anything about... being drunk? What the hell did I do back then?'

Vee reached back into the van for her bag and rummaged for a tissue. Rick left her to her mopping-up and went to lock up. When Vee had made herself as presentable as possible after such an emotional moment, he took her gently by the hand and led her towards the garden centre's café which was mercifully not too busy. He settled Vee at a table as far away as possible from the few other customers and went to place his order.

By the time Rick was back, carrying a tray loaded with black coffee and large slices of chocolate cake, Vee was almost her usual self. She smiled up at him, still pink with embarrassment after her outburst. 'I'm sorry...' she began again but Rick shook his head at her as he deposited the coffee and cake on the table.

'Stop right there,' he said. 'You've absolutely nothing to apologise for. Just seeing that poisonous woman would be enough to make anybody howl, and that was a very tricky conversation. It's probably a good thing to get a meeting with her out of the way though.'

'Yes, we'll never have to see her again, will we?'

The use of the word *we* gave Rick a strange sensation in the pit of his stomach. He realised with a shock that he'd also been feeling very much as if he and Venetia were a team, working on the house, eating together in the evenings, watching TV sometimes and laughing at old comedy shows. Now, it seemed that she had the same image of the two of them. Was he overthinking this, just from one small word? He'd been so angry with Vee when she'd looked through his photographs, but he'd soon calmed down, uncomfortably aware that he'd only snapped at her because that part of his life was somewhere he never revisited if he could help it, either in pictures or in his memory.

'No, we definitely won't have to see Rhonda's smug face again or hear her blather on about her lovely hubby,' he said. 'Now get stuck into your cake, drink your coffee and we won't mention that woman again until you're ready. Maybe we can talk about all this later if you want to, but if you don't, that's fine by me. Today's for having fun.'

Rick and Vee ate, listening to the chatter of a group of cyclists who'd also called in to refuel. The men were on the far side of the room, but their voices boomed out as they planned their next pitstop and discussed the huge distance they'd covered already that day.

'Thank goodness you're not like those blokes,' said Vee, brushing cake crumbs from her sweater before peeling it off and tying it loosely around her neck.

'Why's that?' Rick asked. 'They look perfectly happy to me.'

'Yes, *they're* happy, but all that Lycra and those bulging thigh muscles turn my stomach.' Vee shuddered. 'Think of their poor partners... if they have any.' She looked across at them doubtfully. 'Those guys will be out all day and come back sweaty and knackered. All they'll want to talk about will be how fit they are, and they'll have to have long, hot showers and be fed low-fat dinners. They probably eat a lot of lettuce and drink protein shakes.'

Rick was still mystified. He couldn't see why all this was

annoying Vee so much. 'And your point is?' he said, finishing his coffee.

'I just think that the people they're going home to, whoever they are, deserve better. Being a live-in partner is hard work sometimes. Being self-centred about your hobbies, or your working life too for that matter, can be destructive.'

'Are you speaking from bitter experience?'

The question hung in the air. Vee stood up and grabbed her handbag. 'Oh, ignore me, I'm just being scratchy for no reason. They're just a gang of blokes enjoying a bike ride. Let's get going or the day will be over,' she said, not meeting his eyes. 'Thank you for the cake and coffee. You were right, it was essential. Where are we heading next? Do you still want to go to the seaside?'

Rick needed no further bidding. Soon, they were on their way. The van ate up the miles as they sang along to the radio, although Rick quickly changed channels when a string of old Beach Boys hits included 'Help Me, Rhonda'. They bypassed King's Lynn and Rick branched off, taking several winding roads that took them through pretty countryside.

'Are we nearly there yet?' asked Vee, grinning as Rick rolled his eyes at her. She was looking much better now, exclaiming every so often at a wooded lane or a wide-open meadow.

'We are, as it happens,' he said. 'I bet you've never been to this spot before. It's a closely guarded secret, just a tiny beach with a café. It's mostly only used by locals, but my gran had a cottage not far from here and we used to come and stay as often as we could when I was small. You can only get there on foot, there's no parking. We'll need to walk for ten minutes or so, but we've been sitting still for ages, so I guess that's fine?'

'Oh, yes,' said Vee, clapping her hands. 'I can't wait. I haven't seen the sea for a couple of years at least. The last time my ex, Nigel, and I had a holiday it rained all the time, and he had a cold, so he spent every day sneezing and grumbling. He'd taken his bike with him on top of the car, but he didn't use it in the end, and that made him even crosser. I love the Yorkshire coast but even I'd had enough by the time we got home. We never went away again. Not together, anyway,' she added.

'You mean you went on holiday on your own after that?'

She laughed rather bitterly. 'No, Nigel did. He discovered golfing trips. He went to the Algarve, and Majorca and mainland Spain. There was a vague suggestion of me going with him, but the golfing wives only liked shopping, and I was skint.'

'Sounds a bit depressing,' said Rick, holding back from the observation he'd have liked to make. What kind of a man wouldn't want to take his partner on holiday where *she* wanted to go too?

'No, it was fine, to be honest. I had the house to myself, I could eat when it suited me, only cook if I felt like it and read in the small hours if I couldn't sleep. Bliss.'

Rick once again forbore to comment. He took a side road and saw the familiar landmarks that always lifted his spirits. An ancient farmhouse with moss on the tiled roof, a rickety barn, a huge oak tree with a rope swing dangling from one of the bigger branches and an area of scrubland where an elderly Land Rover sat rusting in the October sunshine.

'Here we are,' he said. 'This is as far as I can drive. I love this place. Hope you do too. Are you hungry?'

Vee said she was, even though the cake had been substantial. 'The sea air always gets your appetite going, doesn't it?' she said happily. 'I should have brought a towel so we can paddle.'

Rick went around to the back of the van and opened the door. 'Listen, you're with the man who loves to get his feet wet,' he said. 'I've got beach towels, emergency biscuits just in case the café's shut and a bottle of water. All a bit last minute, my gran would have had a flask of tea and some chocolate too, but this'll do for today.'

He hefted a rucksack onto his shoulder, locked the van and began to lead the way to a gap in the fence where marram grass pushed its way through the wooden slats. The sound of the seagulls wheeling and crying above them made Vee's eyes sparkle as they navigated the rutty lane that promised to lead to the shore. Occasionally, parts of it were boarded, but the planks were so old and wonky that it was safer to avoid treading on them and walk on the grass.

'Here we are,' said Rick, hearing the excitement in his own voice as they broached the last rise. 'This is the hamlet of Lower Niddling. Great name, isn't it?' And there was the beach stretching down to the sea, pebble in places, narrow and secluded, absolutely perfect in Rick's eyes.

'Oh...' breathed Vee. She stood still, hands clasped in front of her, eyes wide with delight. 'This is... beautiful.'

Rick heaved a sigh of relief. He'd been pretty sure she would love Lower Niddling cove but even so, his heart leapt at the sight of Vee's joy as she wandered down towards the shoreline. He turned to the right to see if the café was open and was glad to see that there was a chalkboard propped up outside. The delicious aromas of roast chicken and garlic mingled and drifted across on the breeze and his stomach rumbled.

'Let's go and eat before they run out of all the best things,' he said. 'They only serve food until the main dishes have gone. After that it'll be bottled water and chocolate digestives for us.'

They covered the short distance to the wooden building very quickly. It looked as if it had grown out of the dunes, with its weathered clapboards and decking. As Rick led the way inside, a voice called, 'Well, bugger me, look what the cat's dragged in.'

'Hello, Maddie,' he said. 'Long time, no see.'

It was a tradition between them to exchange as many clichés and sayings as possible. Rick opened his mouth to speak again, but she beat him to it.

'Close the door behind you,' she said. 'Were you born in a barn?'

He didn't answer, waiting hopefully for what he knew would follow.

'What's the matter? Cat got your tongue?' She came forward and enveloped Rick in a huge embrace. Maddie must be around sixty-five, he calculated, and she was more attractive than ever with her wild auburn curls and ample figure. The red of her hair must be enhanced these days, surely, but Rick couldn't imagine Maddie with grey hair.

'This is my friend Vee,' Rick said, turning round to introduce her. 'We're only here for a little while and we're ravenous. What've you got?'

Maddie looked at them both with her head on one side, then smiled broadly. 'It's roast chicken in baguettes with my home-made garlic mayo today. Bit of salad to pretty it up. Take it or leave it. Beggars can't be choosers,' she added, with triumph.

Rick was so hungry he couldn't think of a single trite phrase to throw back at his old sparring partner. He held out the nearest chair to Vee and sank down himself at one of the only two tables. A girl he'd never seen before brought them a jug of water and two glasses. Rick felt any residual tension draining away as he looked around the tiny room where he'd eaten so many simple, lovely meals. It had been a difficult day, but they were here, in this comforting oasis of calm. Classical music played quietly in the background. Rick looked across at Vee.

'Shall we put off any talking until later?' he said.

'Good idea,' Vee answered. 'But we should have a regroup of ideas soon. I've been thinking. Beryl's scheme for taking us to

France looks kind of fishy now. How did she know I'd need to see my aunt? I haven't thought about Yolanda for years until Beryl mentioned her the other day. There's something funny about this, and when we get back, I'm going to find out exactly what's going on.'

22

Beryl sat at her kitchen table with a map of France spread out in front of her. She had Frank at one side writing in a notebook, Sid directly in her eyeline and Winnie sitting on the other side pouring them all mugs of tea from Beryl's biggest teapot. It was bright red with a knitted cosy, and the mugs matched. A piping hot cup of tea always made the day go with a swing, thought Beryl, and if it was accompanied by a custard cream or two, life couldn't get much better.

'So we're settled on the route, are we?' asked Frank, picking the book up as he prepared to share his notes with them.

'Go on, read it out to us,' said Sid. 'It's going to be a grand trip.'

Frank stood up to make the most of his moment, smoothing down his pullover. He took a sip of tea. 'I'll just wet my whistle,' he said. 'Right, here goes. I've done bullet points. I do like a bullet point, don't you?'

'Get on with it, Frank,' said Beryl. 'You're making a right meal of this. I mean, I do appreciate you all coming round to help but we still have to arrange a meeting with the other four and we need to make sure we know what we're telling them.'

'Do you think they mind us doing the preliminary plan?' Sid asked. 'I'd hate to tread on anyone's toes.'

'There's no point in us all chipping in at this stage or we'll end up having a road trip that goes on for a month instead of a fortnight,' Beryl said firmly. 'Rick's had a look at his diary and he says he can manage two weeks at a push, but he's got another job on after that and he'll be finishing off Venetia's house in between times.'

'I wish it could be a month. That would be fine with me, Beryl,' said Sid. 'The longer we're away the better, as far as I'm concerned. I love a good adventure. Haven't jetted off anywhere since I lost Jenny, in fact the last time would have been before she took ill. All this has made me realise how much I've missed our holidays.'

'Yes, but the young 'uns have work to do,' said Beryl. 'They're not footloose and fancy free like us. Now, Frank, go for it before I lose the will to live.'

Frank cleared his throat importantly. 'Right, here's the plan so far. You'll have to imagine the bullet points as I read. I've added extra information and tips.'

'Oh, good heavens, it's going to be like one of those interminable parish council meetings,' Winnie muttered to Beryl but luckily she was sitting on Frank's deaf side. He launched into his list.

'There's no need to take notes, if you were thinking of it,' he said. 'I'll make everyone a printout of their own when we've all agreed on this itinerary... so here goes... We leave Willowbrook on 2 October at 6 a.m. precisely; drive down to Dover, with Venetia at the wheel. Ferry from Dover to Calais, approx. ninety minutes. We'll have a snack on board unless anyone has the collywobbles. Remember seasickness tablets if you know that's a likelihood. Note: Apologies to Sid. We have ditched the Brittany starting point because of Anthea's tendency to be nauseous on long ferry journeys.'

'No problem,' said Sid. 'It was just an idea, I'm happy to go wherever the rest of you want to be.'

Frank nodded and carried on.

'Arrive in Calais. Drive down through France to Rouen, Rick at the wheel. After this the two of 'em can sort out their own driving rota. Arrive approximately 4 p.m. local time. Dinner and a night in a motel. To be arranged later, as with all the overnight accommodation. October 3rd: Rouen to La Rochelle. Approx. five hours' journey. Suggest we stay for three nights because plenty to do there. October 6th: La Rochelle to Bordeaux. Approx. two hours. Another three-night stay. October 9th: Bordeaux to Lot-et-Garonne and the village where Yolanda lives. Approx. two hours. I'll add its name later, because we might not be able to get accommodation there if it's a very small place. I haven't added dates for coming home because we'll need to see how long Venetia wants to stay with her aunt, but we'll travel back to Dover over two days if our drivers are agreeable, stopping in Chartres overnight en route and avoiding too many toll roads which will keep the overall costs down.'

Frank sat down and Beryl, Sid and Winnie gave him a spontaneous round of applause.

'It all sounds grand,' said Sid, his face flushed with excitement. 'I can't wait.'

'Right,' said Beryl. 'I'll need to round the others up for a full team meeting. Are you lot still free tonight? We can go to the pub this time, if you like. Seven o'clock?'

The others all thought this was a good idea, so Beryl sent texts to Rick, Vee, Maurice and Anthea. The latter two replied immediately. Beryl suspected they were together and grinned to herself. Anthea was really getting into the swing of this new engagement.

Beryl hoped the relationship would fare better than the last ones. There was nothing from Vee or Rick as yet, so the group decided to adjourn to the nearby annexe where Frank lived alongside his son Barney and daughter-in-law Nell.

'Our Nell was making chocolate chip cookies this morning. I smelt them as I passed by their kitchen on my way here,' he said. 'Let's go and see if she's got a few to spare.'

Sid stood up, ready to lead the way. 'And as soon as we hear from the youngsters, we can get at least a couple of those overnight stays booked. I'll be happier when I know where I'll be laying my head at night.'

They set off along the lane and round the corner to Frank's home, chatting as they went about what they'd need to pack, or more importantly what they might need to leave out to save space in the minibus. Beryl brought up the rear, delighted that her travelling companions seemed so enthusiastic about what had felt at the start to be something of a wacky suggestion.

All she needed to do now was to contact Yolanda, check she'd be around at the right time and prepare her for the onslaught. Beryl was usually supremely confident of her welcome when she visited friends. This time she wasn't so sure. It had been a long time since Yolanda had left Britain to settle in France and Beryl was aware that Vee and her aunt hadn't been in touch very often during the intervening years. Maybe it was just a case of distance emphasising the old saying 'out of sight, out of mind', but the more she pondered on this interesting subject, the more Beryl wondered if there might be more to the situation than met the eye. She only hoped that Yolanda would be pleased to see Vee and her entourage. If not, it would make for a very sticky end to their new adventure.

23

Vee and Rick polished off their lunch in record time and decided the moment had come to get their toes wet. Vee left Rick to say a fond goodbye to Maddie and went to stand outside the beach shack, drinking in the sound of the waves lapping against the shore and the seabirds calling to each other. The breeze was cool and fresh on her face, and she stooped to pick up a tiny cockleshell, slipping it into her pocket as a memento of this day of mixed feelings. Vee heard Rick call, 'See you later, alligator,' followed by Maddie's reply of, 'In a while, crocodile,' and she smiled. It must be lovely to have childhood and ongoing memories of a friendship like this one, one so strong and affectionate that it could be picked up at a moment's notice even after a long gap.

Leaving Willowbrook seemed to have fractured Vee's life to such an extent that the only people she remembered clearly were the ones like Rhonda who left a bad taste in her mouth. There must have been less traumatic friends, but much of anything to do with Vee's school life that came before their departure from the village was lost in the mists of time. She gave herself a mental shake. She was starting to catch Rick's habit of thinking in clichés today.

Maddie and Rick were still exchanging familiar phrases, but it sounded as if they had almost run out of steam. 'See ya,' shouted Rick as he left the café.

'Wouldn't wanna be ya,' replied Maddie, and they both laughed uproariously.

'Okay, race you to the sea,' Rick said as he approached Vee, and without further ado, he dumped his bag of towels on the sand and set off at a gallop.

'Hey, that's cheating, you had a head start!' she yelled, and took off after the departing figure, catching up with him before he reached the waves.

They screeched to a halt just in time to avoid splashing straight into the water, and Rick turned to face Vee. 'We'll call that a dead heat,' he said. 'Come on, we'd better roll our jeans up. We don't want damp ankles all day.'

Soon they were tentatively stepping forwards, a few sharp pebbles causing them to wince. Vee wobbled sightly and Rick reached for her hand. They inched along until it was clear that if they waded in any deeper, the water would reach their rolled-up jeans.

'This is bliss,' said Vee, breathing in the salty air. 'I don't know why I didn't do it more often when I still had my Mini. There was no need for me to wait for Nigel to come with me. I could have had lots of days like this, just enjoying the fresh air and sunshine.'

They paddled back out again after a while and wandered up the beach. Vee wondered if Rick had forgotten he was still holding her hand. She decided not to mention it because the feel of his warm palm and his fingers entwined with hers was both comforting and strangely exciting. When they reached the discarded bag, Rick handed Vee a towel to dry her toes and spread the other one on the ground.

'A day like today calls for chocolate digestives,' he said.

They were already halfway down the packet and sharing the bottle of water when both their phones pinged.

'Shall we ignore them?' Rick said. 'What could be more important than sitting on a lovely beach with my favourite... biscuits?' he added hastily as Vee turned to look at him.

But Vee had never been able to leave a message unread for long. She took her phone out of her pocket and clicked on the latest text. 'It's Beryl,' she said. 'She wants us to meet them all at the Fox and Fiddle tonight at seven o'clock. Final planning for the trip. Is that okay with you?'

Rick pulled a face. 'I'd been thinking that we might call for fish and chips and then have a night in front of the TV,' he said. 'But I've never yet managed to ignore a summons from Beryl, and we do need to talk about the details, especially as we're the drivers. Tell her we'll be there. We can go in early and eat at the pub if you like?'

They began to pack away their few belongings. Vee was torn between disappointment that the lovely outing was over and an odd feeling of contentment that Rick had been automatically including her in his plans for the evening, as was usual these days. The thought of moving into the almost-complete Dragonfly Cottage was exciting but she would miss the easy co-existence they'd gradually developed. In between now and then, there was this unexpected bonus of a holiday but with the spectre of what might end up being an uncomfortable reunion with her aunt. Yolanda had always been somewhat unpredictable. She was a law unto herself and the prospect of meeting her again was unnerving. Not only might she hold the key to what really went on at the camping trip, there was still the unresolved question of why Yolanda had so effectively distanced herself from her family.

The drive home was punctuated by a couple of hold-ups, and Vee and Rick barely had time for a quick change of clothes before they set off on foot to the pub. The weather had grown cooler as they walked, dark clouds scudded across the sky and a smatter of raindrops made them both up their speed. Rick had lent Vee his spare waterproof jacket, so both were warmly wrapped up, but she felt chilled and mildly grumpy when they reached the warmth of the Fox and Fiddle.

'I'm having fish and chips, because I half-promised it for us before we knew we couldn't stay at home for the night,' Rick said. 'How about you? Glass of red?'

Vee agreed to both suggestions and went to find them a table. The bar was fairly quiet so early in the evening, but when she sat down, Vee noticed that a man and a small girl had just come in and were talking to Rick. He turned and pointed to Vee and after a few moments all three came over.

'Vee, this is my friend Sam and his daughter, Elsie,' said Rick, pulling up an extra chair. 'They've ordered food too, so we decided to eat together.'

The girl peered at Vee with interest and sat down next to her. 'I've heard all about you,' she said, beaming up at Vee, sliding her arms out of her bright yellow waterproof coat. 'You're going to live next door to Beryl and next-door-but-one to my friend Kate. I have sleepovers at her house sometimes. She's got a purple sofa.'

Vee digested this random snippet and wondered what the correct response was. She didn't have much experience of children. This one looked to be around seven or eight years old, at a guess. She had curly auburn hair held back by a sparkly headband and she was dressed in leopard-print leggings and a baggy hoodie.

'Erm... I don't even have a sofa yet,' she said. 'I don't know what colour mine will be.'

'Maybe you should have a nice red one,' Elsie suggested. 'A bright sofa cheers up a room, you know.'

This strangely adult comment seemed to put an end to the subject and Elsie began to rummage in her backpack. She brought out a sketchbook and pencil case and set out her stall.

'What are you going to draw?' asked Vee, as Elsie bent over her book.

'You,' came back the brief answer, as, tongue protruding slightly between her teeth, the girl began to sketch an outline of an elongated body.

Now the younger member of the party was occupied, Vee had time to look at Elsie's dad. He was young-ish, maybe not more than mid-twenties, and slender with long blond curls tied back in a ponytail. At first glance he seemed to be having a cheerful conversation with Rick, but as she listened, Vee got a totally different picture.

'No, I'm okay, honestly, mate,' Sam was saying. 'You win some, you lose some. I've been expecting this. Luka was bound to want to be free before long. I'm surprised we lasted until now, if I'm honest.'

The two men noticed that Vee had tuned in to what they were saying and paused, as if trying to decide how to explain all this to a stranger. She smiled at Sam, hoping to give him the message that she was friendly, and saw that although he was smiling back, his eyes were red-rimmed and the hand that reached for his beer was shaking slightly.

Rick lowered his voice, glancing at Elsie as she sketched. 'Sam's had bad news today... erm... I guess there's no easy way of putting it, his relationship's over. He's...'

'He's upset,' chimed in Elsie, not looking up from her sketch-book. 'Luka's a knob-head.'

'Elsie!' Sam said. 'That's not a nice thing to say.'

'Well, he is. He's made you sad. He's a knob-head and I hate him.' With that, she handed over her drawing to Vee, who took it, glad of the distraction.

'Oh, wow, Elsie, this is really good,' she said in surprise. The sketch showed a tall, smiling woman with a pompom of hair and very big eyes. She was wearing slim-fitting trousers, trainers and a baggy striped shirt. The detail was impressive even though there was something of the marshmallow about Vee's face and her feet looked like canoes.

'I know it's good,' said Elsie. 'Art's my best subject. I don't like maths or writing much. I wish we could draw all day.'

'That's exactly how I felt when I was at school,' said Vee. An instant flashback made her blink. She saw herself sitting cross-legged in a field while the other children ran around doing various athletic activities. It had been a glorious summer and a sprained ankle from a cartwheel that went badly wrong had meant that Vee was able to sit on the sidelines during all sports lessons for a magical week or two. She'd been allowed to take her jotter and pencil case outside with her and had loved these moments of pure pleasure.

'Did you? Do you still like drawing?' Elsie asked, eyes wide with interest.

'I... don't know. I haven't done any for ages.'

'Why not?'

It was a natural enough question, but Vee couldn't think of an answer. Eventually she said, 'I suppose I've just been busy.'

This was met with a look of incredulity. 'How can you be too busy to do art?' said Elsie. 'It's just the best thing ever. You should start again right after you get home tonight. Have you got any felt-tips?'

Vee shook her head, realising that the last time she'd had any art supplies, Nigel had slung them out, thinking (or so he claimed) that they were rubbish.

'You'd better get some then.'

Elsie turned over the page in her sketchpad and began a new drawing. This time she was looking at a plant in an alcove nearby and soon had the basic shape outlined. Vee's fingers itched to have a try herself. Should she get kitted out with a whole new set of paints and so on? There wasn't much money to spare at the moment, so it would be an extravagance. Then she saw the happy concentration on Elsie's face and changed her mind. It was years since she'd had a hobby. Maybe she could get herself a drawing book and a basic set of pencils. It would be a great opportunity to restart what had been her favourite way to spend any spare time.

The food arrived at this point and all four turned all their attention to the best fish and chips Vee had ever tasted. The batter was crisp, and the thick-cut chips were perfectly cooked, golden brown and lightly sprinkled with sea salt. Mushy peas and tomato ketchup came with this feast. For a while nobody spoke.

'That was awesome,' said Elsie at last. 'Are we having pudding?'

The two men said they were much too full, so Vee took Elsie to the bar to order them both a knickerbocker glory.

'You're pretty, and you're nice too,' said Elsie, looking up at Vee and slipping a hand into hers.

Vee felt a lump in her throat. Motherhood had passed her by somehow, except for that one chance. The chance she'd let go. Dragging her thoughts away from the subject she never let into her mind if she could help it, Vee grinned. 'I bet you say that to everyone who buys you a pudding,' she said.

'No, I don't,' said Elsie, seriously. 'Only the really cool ones. Are you staying here now?'

'In Willowbrook? Yes, I am. My cottage is nearly ready.'

'Can I come and visit you when you move in?' asked Elsie. 'I know where it is.'

'That would be lovely,' said Vee, immensely flattered.

'We can do drawing together. I'll show you how to do a tree. My dad taught me. I haven't got a mum. Well, I have, but she doesn't visit much.'

This was getting heavy. Vee wasn't sure what the right way to answer this would be. Her inexperience with children, something that had never worried her, suddenly seemed like a huge gap in her life. Elsie wasn't waiting for a response though.

'I thought my daddy might marry Luka. Boys can marry boys, you know. But Luka's turned out to be a—'

'Yes, I got the message,' said Vee, laughing. 'Oh, well, you and your dad get on well, don't you? It's good that he has you to keep him company.'

'That's what I told him. Hey, here's our pudding. Wow!'

The towering layers of ice cream, fruit and various other delicious ingredients piled into tall glasses were a timely distraction, and Vee carried them back to their table. She breathed a sigh of relief. That was one way to pause a tricky conversation. By the time she and Elsie had finished, scraping out the last melted drops with their long spoons in a race to reach the bottom, the holiday team were arriving.

First came Beryl and Frank who busied themselves pulling two tables together in the quietest corner of the room and setting out eight chairs around them. They were followed by Anthea and Maurice, graciously accepting congratulations from a few customers who hadn't seen them since the night of Maurice's romantic proposal. Finally, Sid appeared escorting Winnie, resplendent in a flowing robe of magenta and sky blue.

'I love Winnie,' said Elsie. 'When I'm bigger I'm going to have clothes just like hers, only mine will be in animal print. Look at her hoopy earrings,' she added. 'I might get some of those too. What's going on?'

Rick explained about the planning meeting and he and Vee joined the others. Before long, Frank was in position at the head of the table with his notebook at the ready, and the rest of the party were silent, faces turned towards him. When he'd finished reading out his list, Beryl stood up. 'I'd like to say a big thank you to Frank for organising us so well,' she said. There was a chorus of *hear hears*. Frank nodded graciously.

'I enjoyed it,' he said. 'And now we must decide loosely where our accommodation will be. I vote we split the bookings between a few of us with iPhones. How about you find us somewhere in Rouen, Vee? You take La Rochelle, Rick. Maurice has already told me he and Anthea are happy to sort out a place in Bordeaux but we can do that when we're on the way. It's not a busy time of year. I've made a list of possibles for each of you, it's just a case of making the calls or online bookings. We don't have to do them all in advance, because our plans might change.'

'Yep. On the case, whenever you give me the nod,' said Rick.

'We'll look up some possible options later, at home,' said Maurice. 'I can't concentrate in here and Anthea's the whizz on the computer.'

'Good man. Beryl wants to ring your aunt next, Vee, to let her know we're on the way and find out more about the village where she lives,' said Frank. 'It may well be too small for us to find a hotel there. Unless you'd rather do it yourself, of course. She *is* your relation, after all,' he added, as an afterthought.

Now it was becoming all too real. Vee felt her stomach give an uncomfortable leap as she imagined what her aunt might say when confronted with the idea of eight visitors, one of whom was the niece she'd been avoiding for quite some time.

'No, it's fine. I'm sure Yolanda will love hearing from Beryl,' she said. She watched Beryl tap in the number she'd given her earlier and held her breath. Hearing one side of a conversation was never satisfactory but she would just have to do her best to follow it. The thought of making this call herself was nerve-racking and she was very glad Beryl had taken the initiative. She heard the deep, distinctive tones of Yolanda's voice after several rings, just when Vee had begun to think she might have changed her number. But no, although it seemed it was just an answer-phone message. Beryl left a brief message of her own and ended the call.

'Never mind, I expect she'll ring me back soon,' she said. 'I suppose it was too much to hope for that she'd be able to talk to me at the drop of a hat.'

Relieved and disappointed at the same time, Vee sat back in her chair. She felt as if she'd dodged a bullet but told herself she was being ridiculous. After all, where was the harm in visiting one of your family? Yolanda would be happy to see her. Wouldn't she?

24

The morning of the trip came round quickly, but to Beryl's dismay, she still hadn't heard from Yolanda. She'd left several more messages on the answerphone, trying to convince herself that Yolanda was merely busy, and not ignoring her on purpose. Finally, just as she was eating a very early breakfast at half past five, after a quick wash and brush up, her mobile rang. Yolanda's number was displayed on the screen. Thank goodness.

'Hello?' she said, taking a gulp of tea to get rid of the toast crumbs.

'Beryl, it's me,' said the booming voice. 'I've just picked up all your voicemails. What on earth is going on? What's bringing you and my niece to France after all this time?'

Typical Yolanda, thought Beryl, cutting straight to the chase. No *'Hello, old friend, good to hear from you, how have you been?'* And what was she doing out of bed at such a silly time? Then she remembered that France was an hour ahead of the UK, but even so...

'You're up early,' she said. 'I'm glad I've got hold of you at last. I was beginning to think you were avoiding me.'

'Phone broke, pesky thing,' Yolanda said. 'Had to wait for a new one to be delivered. Idiots sent it to the wrong village. Anyway, I'm here now, and I'm always an early riser, aren't you? Shame to waste the best part of the day snoring your head off.'

Beryl had never been particularly keen on early mornings but forbore to comment. Time was ticking away and Vee and Rick would soon be here to collect her. 'We're having a bit of a road trip,' she explained. 'There are eight of us and we're calling at several different places in France. You're the last stop-off on the list. We're going no further south. Venetia's back in Willow-brook to live in her mum's house and she's keen to catch up with you.'

Keen was pushing it somewhat, thought Beryl. Vee had shown absolutely no excitement at the prospect of a meeting with her aunt. Rather the opposite in fact, but there was no need for Yolanda to know that.

'Oh, I see,' said Yolanda. There was silence for a moment or two. 'And where were you thinking of staying? I've no spare bedroom, you know, and by the sound of it you're travelling with a whole coach party. I can't accommodate any of you. I live very simply here.'

'If you give me the name of your village, I can try and find a hotel and—'

Beryl's explanation was interrupted by a snort from Yolanda. 'Hotel? You'll be lucky! What sort of place do you imagine this is? We're not grand enough for hotels in Brugnac d'Agenais. The best you'll get is bed and breakfast and there's only one house where that might be possible. When are you leaving?'

'In ten minutes,' said Beryl, trying to keep her voice even. 'And I've been wanting to get this sorted out before now, of course I have, but without speaking to you, I had no idea what to book.'

'Right. Well, I can't say I'm delighted at the idea of seeing

Venetia, but I can give you the number of the Pension Simone, if
you like. She might fit you in as it's out of season.'

Beryl reached for a pen and soon had all the relevant details
down. Her years as a doctor's receptionist had trained her well
and she wasted no further time in chit-chat, because she could
hear the sound of the minibus pulling up outside. 'I'll call you
when we're nearly there. Bye, Yolanda.'

The relief at getting the final piece of the puzzle almost in
place carried Beryl through the next tedious twenty minutes of
collecting the others and getting them and their luggage stowed
in the minibus to everyone's satisfaction. Soon they were on their
way as the darkness lightened and the sky changed from inky
black to pearly grey.

'It's going to be a nice day later,' said Sid. 'I caught the news
before we left. How's everyone feeling today? All ready for our
adventure *en Francais*?'

There was a chorus of agreement, and as Beryl looked around
the minibus, she could see that although some of her travelling
companions looked a little blearier than others, they were all
smiling. 'Dover, here we come,' she said, feeling Frank take her
hand in his much larger one. She wasn't sure how she felt about
this unaccustomed show of affection, but it felt kind of... cosy.

They had one brief pitstop at a service station for toilets when
Maurice's agonised expression told Vee it was necessary, but
made the ferry port in plenty of time and rolled onto the boat in
great spirits.

'We are sailing, we are sailing,' trilled Winnie, and the others
all joined in, although Frank could be heard to mutter that they
weren't actually moving yet and it might be better to wait for this
song until the shores of Britain were well behind them. The
voyage passed peacefully, with all but Anthea managing a hearty
breakfast in the cafeteria. An hour and a half later those of the

party with traditional watches were adjusting them to French time, an hour further on.

'Over to you, Rick,' said Vee, as they made their way to the lower deck to collect the minibus. 'I haven't driven on the right for a long time, but I'll do the next leg after Rouen, no problem. I'll have a go on the quieter roads later.'

Once they had escaped Calais, only getting lost three times, the open road beckoned and the minibus picked up speed with a whoop of relief from Rick.

'This is it, folks, the start of our French holiday,' he said. 'I was a bit dubious when it was suggested but now I can't wait to see all the places on the list.'

The minibus ate up the miles quickly and the party arrived in Rouen just after 4 p.m., local time. Everyone was ready to stretch their legs, and Rick found their motel easily, so once he'd parked up and the overnight luggage had been dropped off, they all set off for a wander.

'I thought I'd want a nap after that early start, but it seems a waste of time to sleep when there's so much to see,' said Winnie, linking arms with Sid, who looked surprised but gratified. 'Let's have a coffee stop first.'

'Or a beer?' said Sid hopefully. 'I've been learning a bit of the lingo so I can order a round. I hope nobody wants a cocktail, I haven't got round to those yet.'

They set off at a cracking pace, but Rick soon realised that they were all flagging and murmured to Vee that they'd need to slow things down if their older friends were going to be able to keep their energy levels going for two weeks. The medieval streets were fascinating and led them towards the magnificent Notre-Dame cathedral, but they'd all need a break before tackling any sightseeing.

'Let's find a bar,' he said, steering the others towards a café with a shady awning. 'Go for it, Sid. Let's see what you can do. Mine's a beer.'

Sid took everyone's orders, and they sat down to wait for service. When the young man came out to greet them, he reeled off his list with pride but was met with a bemused expression.

'Could you just run that past me again?' said their waiter, in perfect English. Sid sighed.

Their drinks arrived, regardless of the language hiccup, and Rick called for a toast. 'To our first continental road trip,' he said, raising his glass. Most of the others echoed the words but Vee looked puzzled. 'The first road trip anywhere, surely?' she said.

'Oh, no, don't you remember we mentioned that we had one before, in England?' said Beryl. 'It was when we formed the Happiness Gang with the Rev Bev. We went to Norfolk. It was a grand day out. All of us were there, and Kate, and Frank's daughter-in-law Nell and the Hendersons – they're an old couple who live down by the river, very posh.'

'It *was* fun, wasn't it?' said Winnie. 'We should make it a regular thing.'

Personally, Rick wasn't sure if his nerves would stand doing this kind of trip very often. The promise of seeing a few of the sights of France was keeping him going but he was beginning to feel very sleepy as he drank his beer in the warm sunshine, and going anywhere with this particular collection of people was a bit like herding sheep.

'Right, time to have a look at the cathedral,' said Frank. 'Drink up, we need to get moving.'

There were a few groans but soon they were all heading for the main entrance, gazing up at the huge splendour of the ancient building. Inside, the atmosphere and the splendour of the place silenced even the chattiest members of the party. Wordlessly, they separated to view it, although Rick noticed that the couples stuck together. Beryl and Frank set off in one direction, with Winnie and Sid heading straight for one of the places where they could light candles. Anthea and Maurice found seats and sat down, to drink in the beauty of the place in comfort.

'They're all okay,' said Rick to Vee. 'I feel a bit like a teacher on a school trip, don't you?'

She laughed. 'Yes, I keep wanting to do a head count to check we haven't lost any of them. I hadn't realised what a responsibility it would be, but they're all having a great time, so it's worth it. I just hope nobody has a funny turn or falls over.'

'Let's not worry about that,' said Rick. 'At least we're in this together. We can cope.'

Vee smiled at him and his heart did an uncomfortable flip. It was that word. *Together.* He was beginning to get used to Vee being around permanently, and that was dangerous. It was a mistake to rely on anyone. Experience of marriage had taught him that, if nothing else.

'Let's have a look around,' he said. 'Do you want an official guided tour?'

'No, we can just do our own thing,' Vee answered. 'Come on, I want to light a candle for my mum.'

Rick followed her down the main aisle, still unsettled by the rush of warmth that had overwhelmed him for a moment. They were friends, and that was the way it should stay. Vee still had issues with her past and he certainly wasn't in the market for a new relationship. Best to squash these strange, unpredictable moments of longing that were creeping up on him. They were going to get him nowhere.

When everyone had reached sightseeing overload, Rick and Vee shepherded their tired flock back towards the accommodation, giving them all half an hour to freshen up before it was time to eat. They all reappeared looking a lot more lively. The three older ladies had donned colourful dresses and applied bright lipstick, while the men hadn't changed their clothes but had clearly had a wash and brush up. A cloud of mingled aftershave fragrances hung over Sid and Maurice, while Frank smelt strongly of Coal Tar soap and Euthymol toothpaste, evocative scents that brought back memories of Rick's grandfather.

* * *

Dinner in a little bistro next door to the motel was an exuberant affair. All were in good spirits, but they resisted ordering more than a couple of carafes of wine because Beryl warned them that tomorrow was going to bring another early start.

'Not the crack of dawn again though, darling,' said Anthea. 'This is a holiday, after all.'

'No, but we're heading south for La Rochelle straight after breakfast,' said Rick. 'Next stop, the seaside and some very swanky boats. We'll choose the yacht we'll buy when we win the lottery. Now, off to bed if you've all finished. We all need our beauty sleep.'

'You speak for yourself,' said Anthea, but they trooped out of the bistro obediently enough.

'Day one of our school trip competed,' whispered Vee, bringing up the rear with Rick, and they high-fived each other.

'Let's hope the rest of the holiday goes as smoothly,' he answered. 'If this was a real school party, we'd be going round checking their rooms after lights out to make sure they're all in the right places. I might be getting the wrong idea here, but I have a feeling that some of them might not be.'

Vee giggled. 'Well, they're all grown-ups, aren't they? So long as none of them have a lovers' tiff, we'll be fine.'

Rick hadn't thought of this possible scenario. Taking six of the older generation away with three potential couples included was obviously a more complicated situation than he'd bargained for. He really hoped there wouldn't be any ructions between his fellow travellers. Being confined to a minibus with a crew of warring pensioners was definitely not his idea of a fun holiday.

25

Beryl was definitely getting into the swing of this holiday lark by the time they reached La Rochelle the next day. They were all looking a bit jaded though, so she suggested an early dinner after they'd explored the area around their hotel and by nine o'clock the entire party were tucked up in bed. Even Vee and Rick, whom Beryl had assumed would want to go out and find some action later, had said they were ready to sleep.

It was fascinating to watch the chemistry developing between the two younger members of the party, Beryl thought to herself as she dressed the next morning. They'd obviously struck sparks off each other when her new neighbour first arrived in Willowbrook but now Vee and Rick had fallen into an easy kind of camaraderie, teasing each other and the rest of the party and making sure that everyone was safe and well. It was almost as if they were the parents of a crowd of rather unpredictable children, which felt like the case a lot of the time. Beryl considered herself to be easily the most flexible one of the party. The rest of them weren't always easy to manage, mainly because they tended to want to take off in every possible direction wherever they landed.

'Let's go and look at the boats this morning,' she said, after their usual breakfast of powerfully strong coffee, freshly baked croissants, crusty bread and apricot jam was finished with.

'But there's such a lot to see here,' said Anthea. 'Maurice wants to visit the Old Town and maybe the Museum d'Histoire Naturelle de la Rochelle.'

Beryl bridled slightly as Anthea showed off her French accent. She sniffed. There was no need for that. Beryl herself had learned most of her own inflections from an old sitcom and the *Pink Panther* films. They could all talk like the cast of *'Allo 'Allo* if they wanted to.

'There are some other interesting museums too,' said Sid. 'I like a bit of history, I do.'

Rick sighed. 'How are we going to please everyone today? If you all go off separately, we might never find you again.'

'We're grown-ups, Rick,' Frank said. 'I'm sure we'll be fine. You don't have to watch over us all the time.'

That decided, the group set off in pairs, arranging to meet for dinner later. Winnie and Sid looked to be getting on particularly well and had taken to walking everywhere arm in arm, which was unexpected, to say the least, as Beryl pointed out to Frank as they headed for the harbour. 'Winnie's not one for much in the way of... you know... physical contact,' she told Frank. 'I mean, with her late husband, yes, of course, that was an exuberant marriage, if you get what I'm implying.'

She paused, noticing that Frank was blushing. Bless the man. 'As I was saying,' she continued. 'Our Winnie isn't much of a hugger as a rule, but she's really taken to Sid lately, hasn't she?'

Frank looked down at Beryl. 'And what about you?' he said quietly.

'What *about* me?' she replied, busy swapping her usual spectacles for sunglasses and pulling on a sun hat.

'Are you a hugger? I sometimes feel as if it's been years since I was held in someone's arms, don't you?'

Beryl bit her lip. This conversation was getting out of hand, but the poor man sounded troubled, so she was reluctant to brush the question off. 'I do sometimes get that feeling,' she said. 'It's been a long time since my Eddie died, and you lost your lovely wife to dementia, didn't you? That must have been hard.'

'It certainly was. The last months were especially difficult. I found myself longing for the old affectionate Lottie. She didn't seem to like me or even know me at all towards the end.'

They were sailing into deep waters now. Beryl decided to fall back on her usual remedy for stress, although she was more accustomed to relying on a nice cup of tea. Any hot drink should do the trick though. She pointed to a pavement café nearby. 'It's almost coffee time,' she said. 'And what do you say to a brandy to go with it? I think we both need perking up, don't you?'

Frank agreed enthusiastically and soon they were sitting in the shade of a beautiful plane tree alternately drinking café cremes and sipping a cognac apiece.

'I have an idea,' said Beryl, when they eventually stood up to leave. She had to admit she might be a little squiffy, being unused to strong drink so early in the day, but it was a lovely, fuzzy feeling.

'Do tell,' said Frank, rummaging in his wallet and leaving some notes on the table weighed down by his empty glass. 'That should be plenty. I always like to give a decent tip, don't you?'

The last remark consolidated the vague thoughts whizzing around Beryl's head. Frank was kind-hearted, well-organised and in need of somebody to care properly about him. He smelt incredibly clean too, which wasn't the case with all men, as she well knew. She led him away from the table and into a nearby side street, where the traffic noise died away and they were alone.

'What I'm going to suggest might sound a bit odd,' Beryl said, feeling as fluttery as a teenager on her first date. 'But how about we be each other's hugging partners?'

She hiccupped and put a hand over her mouth. That wasn't going to help the atmosphere she hoped to create between them.

'I'm not sure I understand what you mean,' said Frank, but he inched closer as he spoke.

'Yes, you do. I think we both need some human warmth. A cuddle is one of life's great pleasures. How about we do that for each other, as and when we need it? No ties, of course. We don't need to be a couple...'

'Don't we?'

Beryl looked up into Frank's face and his kind eyes gazed back. The wrinkles around them were a testament to years and years of smiling and she had the strangest feeling of coming home.

'Erm... I...'

'Beryl, can I say something important?' Frank asked, placing his hands on her shoulders. Still nobody had disturbed the peace of their shady side street and after a glance around, she nodded.

'I've been getting very attached to you, Beryl,' Frank said. 'It seems to have crept up on me. You keep an eye on all your friends and always make them welcome in your house, and you never look on the black side of life like so many people do these days. Doom and gloom isn't in your nature, is it?'

'No, I suppose not,' Beryl answered, wondering where this was heading. Frank was making her sound like some sort of saint, and she knew full well she wasn't. It was unexpectedly lovely to be appreciated like this though. She smiled at him encouragingly, hoping for more. He wasn't slow to oblige.

'I guess what I'm trying to say in this clumsy way, because I'm not used to courtship...'

Frank paused, and Beryl's heart, which had been beating faster than usual, began to really pound. Courtship? It was a beautiful if old-fashioned word, and one she hadn't heard for a very long time. Her vision blurred slightly. She fervently hoped she wasn't going to keel over on him, here in a strange town. A brief panic about what a French hospital might be like flitted through her mind, but he was speaking again, and she tried hard to focus on his face. Deep breaths, that was the thing, wasn't it?

'I wonder if you might consider... I mean...' At this point, Frank very creakily lowered himself to one knee, reminding Beryl of all those splendid footballers who made this gesture as a mark of respect in times of trouble. She looked down at him as he steadied himself against the wall of the house where they were standing.

'Beryl, will you do me the honour of becoming my wife?' he asked, rather breathlessly. 'We could hug as much as we like if we lived in the same place, and I could take care of you for a change, instead of you always looking after everyone else. What do you say?'

There was a pause as Beryl's world flipped over even more. Then she beamed at him. Dear Frank. Marrying again had never been on her agenda. Life with Eddie had been everything she'd ever wanted and being without him had been very hard to bear, but... perhaps it was time?

Frank was looking extremely anxious now, and Beryl could tell by his agonised expression that his knees were giving him pain. Poor soul, going to all this effort just to ask a simple question.

'Get up, you daft thing,' she said affectionately, giving Frank her hand to help him to his feet. 'This isn't how I expected the holiday to go, not one bit, but yes, I will marry you. I reckon we'll make a great team, you and me, and the hugging will be a bonus too.'

'In that case, we'd better start practising right now,' Frank said, hauling himself to his feet, aided by Beryl's hand and the wall. He opened his arms to her, and she moved closer, feeling the strength of his embrace and the warmth of his body against hers.

'I love you, Beryl,' Frank said huskily. 'I should have said that first of all instead of giving you all that waffle.'

'I know you do. And I love you too,' said Beryl, suddenly wanting to cry. It was so wonderful to feel like this again after so long. She had a momentary pang that the others would think the two of them were ridiculous but then remembered that Anthea and Maurice were in exactly the same position.

'We're a right romantic lot, aren't we, us oldies?' she said, looking up at Frank. 'All we need now is for Winnie and Sid to get it together.'

Frank laughed. 'I can't see that happening. I think they're just good friends, as the saying goes. Sid's a confirmed bachelor nowadays. He misses his wife but he's not about to jump in again. And you said yourself that Winnie isn't very tactile, as it were. No, I think two brand-new couples is enough for now, don't you?'

Beryl drew away from Frank, conscious that a group of people was approaching. She heard their chatter and laughter getting closer. 'Come on, let's go and see some very grand boats and maybe toast ourselves with a glass of wine with our lunch.'

'We'll do better than that, my pet. It's champagne today for us. Nothing but the best for my fiancée,' Frank said, holding out his arm for Beryl to take.

They strolled towards the harbour, dodging the crowds and taking a diverse route that meandered through ancient streets. Beryl couldn't remember when she'd been so contented.

Shocked, stunned, a bit aghast at herself for accepting Frank's proposal so readily when she'd always told herself that she was her 'own woman', but very happy all the same. She squeezed Frank's arm, and the answering pressure told her that he felt the same.

'Do you know what? I'm already quite tired of travelling around,' said Beryl. 'I wonder what the others would say if I suggested cutting out Bordeaux and heading straight for Yolanda's village. Maurice still hasn't booked anywhere there. He and Anthea can't agree on a hotel. It'd be more peaceful further south, and we could settle into some nice accommodation for a few days instead of always being on the move.'

'I don't mind what we do, so long as I'm with you,' said Frank. 'But wasn't it your idea to go to as many places as possible? Won't you be disappointed?'

'No, not at all. We can always call in at Bordeaux on the way home if everyone wants to,' said Beryl. 'I think we need time to sit back and watch the world go by. Find a café with a bar where we can relax, go for walks to explore, eat lovely food and have time for some proper afternoon naps. I booked the pension that Yolanda suggested so I'd only need to phone and ask if we can arrive early. Shall we see what the others say?'

'Absolutely,' said Frank. 'And it'll give you and me time to get to know each other better, won't it? Let's not tell the others our news just yet. I want us to have at least a day or two when it's our secret. Do you mind?'

Beryl didn't reply because they'd reached the sparkling waters of the harbour and the sight of all the yachts and pleasure boats took her breath away, but later as they walked back, she began to have misgivings. Frank seemed to think she was perfection itself. How was he going to react when he *did* get to know her better and discovered what emotions simmered under the surface? Beryl was well aware that although time might have been expected to do its job of healing, she'd never stopped being a boiling mass of resentment that her only child had died and she was still trying to find out what had actually happened to upset him so much all those years ago. Surely Frank would think that she should have left her resentment behind a long time since. But that was impossible. There had to be answers, and Beryl was now more determined than ever to find them.

26

Beryl's suggested change of plan went down surprisingly well with the rest of the party. The older members in particular were all exhausted by the time they met for dinner and were more than ready to opt for a peaceful few days. It was a matter of moments for her to ring the owner of Pension Simone and change their arrangement, and a quick call to Yolanda followed.

Vee had very mixed feelings about all this. On the one hand, she was also feeling tired. The long, gruelling hours that she and Rick had been putting in on the house renovation were catching up with her and she'd seen Rick stifling yawns too, even as she was driving them down to Dover. But then there was the looming prospect of seeing her aunt. She'd managed to put this out of her head for most of the time since they'd set off, concentrating on the fun of new scenery and amenable company. Now it was getting far too real.

'Well, that's settled, we'll head south tomorrow morning,' said Rick, as they finished a leisurely dinner. Beryl's suggestion had sparked a mood of relaxation in everyone, and when the last of the wine had been drunk, they all headed for their beds quite happily.

The next day, a new sense of excitement altered the atmosphere in the minibus as Rick started the engine.

'Lot-et-Garonne, here we come!' shouted Sid as they wove their way through the already busy streets and out towards the road that would take them south and east. 'What kind of place is this village? I hope there's a good bakery. I'm addicted to those pain au chocolat things now. I'm still going to need my fix.'

'I'm sure there will be,' said Beryl. 'And hopefully a lovely bustling market in the square... if there *is* a square in Brugnac d'Agenais, of course.'

They all fell silent, thinking about their destination. Vee's reservations about her own welcome grew bigger with every mile they travelled and by the time they'd reached the quieter roads, some hours and a couple of comfort stops later, her stomach was in knots.

'This is beautiful countryside, darling,' said Anthea to Vee. 'It's so rolling and green. Your aunt's chosen well. I wouldn't mind living here. What do you say, Maurice? Shall we sell up and buy a rambling old chateau? They might do a TV programme about us. I've always fancied being the mistress of a magnificent estate in the country.'

She laughed when she saw the look on Maurice's face. 'I'm joking, don't look so panic-stricken. I know you'll never leave Willowbrook. I don't think any of us would.'

Vee noticed that Beryl and Frank had chosen the back seats of the bus and were whispering to each other. 'What's going on with you two?' she said. 'You're looking really furtive. Have you been up to mischief? Did you rob a bank in La Rochelle?'

'N... nothing,' stuttered Frank. 'We were... ah... talking about...'

'...Talking about whether we should have bought a gift to take for Yolanda,' finished Beryl. Her cheeks were very pink, and she didn't meet Vee's eyes.

'Oh dear, we ought to have thought of that sooner,' said Winnie. 'Can we stop somewhere, Rick? What about a nice bunch of flowers?'

Rick muttered something under his breath. He was yawning now and tapping his fingers on the wheel. Vee could sense the tension mounting inside the minibus. It was as if her own jittery feelings had spread themselves amongst everyone else. She supposed it wasn't surprising because the closeness that was developing between the eight of them was more noticeable with every mile they travelled and every meal they ate together.

Luckily, at this point they entered a small town, and Winnie spotted a stall selling flowers and plants by the roadside. 'Look! Can you stop, Rick?' she said. 'I think we'd be okay to pull up for five minutes. I'll go in.'

Rick screeched to a halt behind a delivery van and sat back in his seat. He stretched both arms above his head. 'Go for it, Winnie,' he said. 'But don't be long. I don't know what the parking rules are in France. We don't want to be landed with a massive fine.'

Winnie scrambled out of the bus with a groan as her stiff legs met the concrete, followed by Sid and Beryl, who couldn't resist being in on the action. They were soon back with a magnificent chrysanthemum plant covered in yellow flowers. Vee gasped. 'Oh, no, I should have warned you. We can't take that. Chrysanths are the plants they put on graves over here. They're used especially around All Saints' Day but nobody gives them as gifts. Yolanda would be really offended.'

Winnie sighed. 'We'll just have to find a nice grave to put it on when we get there, in that case. Back inside, gang.'

Eventually, the three returned with two large bunches of assorted flowers in different colours. 'We have no idea what she likes so we hedged our bets, and we bought one for the lady who owns the pension too so she doesn't feel left out,' said Beryl. 'Drive on, Rick. We're on the last lap now.'

The final part of their journey took them through more gently hilly countryside, ever greener and more verdant. Every now and again the road passed alongside or through the middle of woods of graceful birch trees, tall and slender. The warm breeze coming through the open windows was energising, and everyone began to perk up. In some places row upon row of twisted vines marched across the fields and further on they were replaced by small fruit trees.

'Plums,' said Frank. 'I've been reading up about the area. This is the prune capital of Europe, you know.'

'My mother would have approved of this place,' said Sid, pulling a face. 'She was always feeding us prunes. She was obsessed with our bowels. She used to say—'

'I think that's quite enough of that,' said Beryl. 'We don't need to know more. How much further, Rick?'

'Ten minutes at the most,' he said. 'Are you going to ring Yolanda to warn her we're nearly at her village?'

Beryl made the call and disconnected. 'Yolanda's going to meet us in the marketplace to show us where to park,' she said. 'Apparently there's nowhere closer to our accommodation. We can have a coffee or a beer in the bar there before we unload, if you like?'

This suggestion met with cheers of approval and soon Rick was slowing down to make his way into the little village. All around were old stone houses, some shuttered as if already preparing for the winter. There was a post office and a *boucherie* near the square and above the roofs of the houses could just be seen the towers of what looked like a small chateau. The autumn sunshine was still plenty warm enough for them to sit outside, and the tables set outside the café in the market square seemed an ideal spot to bask and take in the ambience of Brugnac d'Agenais. There was no sign of Yolanda.

'This place is gorgeous,' breathed Anthea. 'I can see why your aunt chose to stay put when she got here, darling. Why have you never visited her before? I'd have been down here like a shot.'

Vee shrugged. It was hard to explain the restraints that had held her back for all this time, and even now she was very unsure of what her welcome would be like. Rick parked the van in the shade of what looked like an uninhabited house and got out, coming round to the back to help everyone climb down. They were all somewhat creaky after their journey but once their legs had got going again, they began to look around with interest.

'Shall we sit down and order a beer? Maybe we should call Yolanda again?' said Frank. 'We could be in the wrong place.'

Just as Vee was about to snap that there couldn't be more than one marketplace in a village this size, a small, round figure came bustling out of an alleyway and headed their way, calling, 'Coooeeee!'

'Is this your Aunty Yolanda, Vee?' asked Maurice, somewhat unnecessarily as by this time the woman was nearly with them and was beaming widely. Her grey hair was wild, and she was wearing a faded garment that was a cross between a caftan and an overall. On her feet were ancient wellington boots of the green variety favoured by the hunting set.

'Sorry I'm late,' she said, breathlessly. 'I was about to leave the house when one of my chickens came into the kitchen and I noticed she was limping. It was Bella,' she added. 'She's an old girl now, and I wanted to make sure she wasn't in pain before I came to meet you. Anyway, she rallied and here I am now.'

She came to a standstill in front of Vee, and they eyed each other warily. Yolanda's smile faltered slightly but she held out both hands to her niece. 'Venetia,' was all she said.

Vee took her aunt's hands in both of hers. She couldn't speak for a moment. Memories came flooding back of this warm, friendly lady who had been such an important part of her childhood. Yolanda was the one who'd taught Vee to make iced lemon biscuits and bonfire toffee. She had helped Vee with her homework, especially when she'd struggled to learn her spellings. It was only when Vee reached her teens that the two of them had clashed, sometimes spectacularly.

'It's... it's good to see you,' Vee managed to say, before tears spilled down her cheeks. Yolanda reached out and pulled her niece close. Vee was a lot taller than the older woman and her chin rested comfortably on the top of Yolanda's head as they clung together. She inhaled a fragrance that was so familiar that she wondered how she'd gone so long without seeing this dear person. It was a mixture of vanilla and garlic, with a hint of herbs fresh from the garden. Yolanda had always loved to cook. Something had gone badly wrong between them over the years and it was high time they fixed it.

'Let's get you organised,' said Yolanda, letting Vee go and beaming round at the others. 'We can do introductions later. Beryl and Winnie are old friends of mine, I'm not sure about the rest of you though. Once I moved over here, I was only in Willowbrook for visits so we might not have met.'

'Would I be able to drive to the place we're staying and drop off the luggage to save them all carrying their stuff?' asked Rick. 'I can come straight back here and park. We were going to have a drink, but I think we'd be better to get ourselves sorted first.'

'Of course, just follow along behind us in the van and I'll escort the rest of you to Pension Simone. I think you're going to be very comfortable.' Yolanda set off, and the rest of the party tried to match her pace. She certainly wasn't hanging around.

'Is she training for a marathon or summat?' Frank muttered to Sid as they turned a corner. Sid didn't answer. He'd stopped to offer an arm to Winnie who definitely wasn't built for speed.

'Come on, ducky,' he said to her. 'Hang on to me and I'll get you there.'

'This place had better be worth the hike,' said Winnie. 'My feet are killing me and I'm dying to spend a penny.'

Luckily, after only a few more metres, Yolanda came to a halt outside a three-storey, traditionally built house. Its shutters were open and outside the front door sat a large tabby cat.

'Hello, Chantelle,' said Yolanda to the cat. 'These are your new visitors. If you're nice to them, they might sneak you a prawn or two at dinner time. I hope you all like seafood? Simone's cooking her famous paella tonight and she doesn't care for picky eaters.'

'Are you saying we don't get a choice of menu?' asked Anthea, pursing her lips.

'Oh, yes, you get a choice. Eat it or don't eat it,' said Yolanda, laughing merrily as she pushed open the heavy wooden door.

27

The door creaked alarmingly but swung on its hinges to reveal a long, tiled hallway. The back door was also wide open, revealing a stone-flagged patio, and at the other end Vee glimpsed a sunlit garden with – blissful sight – a swimming pool at its centre. Thank goodness she'd put her swimsuit in at the last minute. She wondered if the others had too. Their holiday had never been intended to be a beach, swim and sunbathe trip. Around the pool, metal folding chairs were grouped cosily, as if they were having a conversation.

'This looks great,' she said to Yolanda, who had given a shout to whoever was inside and now paused to make sure all her charges were safely through the door. Rick was indoors too by this time and echoed her opinion. 'Terrific,' he said, grinning at Vee and giving her a thumbs-up sign.

'It's the only place that was likely to have enough rooms for you all,' said her aunt. 'You're fortunate that you decided to come out of season. Simone gets very busy through the summer. Ah, here she is.'

Yolanda herself was well-rounded but the lady that emerged

from the kitchen was even more ample, both in height and girth. Vee looked on admiringly as the two women kissed each other on both cheeks. Their hostess was magnificent. Vee had expected someone older, but Simone might have been any age from mid-forties to sixty. She had a sort of timeless beauty and opulence, with her cloud of long chestnut hair loosely tied back by a brilliant blue scarf which perfectly matched her eyes. Her feet were bare apart from a few toe-rings, and her skin was burnished to a healthy bronze. She wore a flowing sleeveless dress in shades of turquoise and green and a quantity of elaborate gold jewellery topped by dangling earrings. Her cleavage was also spectacular, and Vee stifled a giggle as she saw the effect this vision was having on the males in the group, who were goggling at their hostess open-mouthed.

'So here you are,' said Simone, smiling around at them. 'This is such a treat for me. I love to practise my English. Let us get your bags inside and we can get you settled.'

Without further ado, Rick unloaded the luggage and between them they carried it inside. Yolanda and Simone were presented with their flowers and both looked suitably gratified. It had been a good idea of Winnie's, thought Vee with relief. The hall felt cool after the warmth of the street and she began to think longingly of a cold drink.

'I don't often say this to my guests, but *you* can park around the back if you like, *cheri*,' said Simone, smiling so widely at Rick that a gold tooth flashed somewhere in her upper jaw. 'Drive a few doors along the road and down the lane on your left; you'll see a yard with a red baker's van in it. You'll be fine there. Hang on, it'll be easier if I show you.'

As she said this, Simone came closer to Rick and took him by the arm, ushering him outside, presumably so that she could point him in the right direction to take. Vee felt a prickle of unease. Surely the woman didn't need to hold on to Rick quite so tightly. The front door was ajar, and instead of opening it fully Simone made a big performance of squeezing past Rick to get through first. He looked bemused, blinking as they emerged into the sunlight. Vee could hear a trilling laugh even as they moved further away from the door. She shivered.

'Not cold, are you?' said Yolanda, fixing her niece with a beady stare. 'Simone's very friendly, she'll look after you all well.'

'I'm sure she will,' said Vee, trying to tell herself that it was nothing to her if Rick wanted to gaze at the splendid bosoms of the lady of the house. He was a free man. He could do exactly as he liked.

The two were soon back, although Rick looked rather flushed and came to stand next to Vee as if in need of protection, so she began to relax. The woman was just exuberant, that was all, and Vee was tired. They collected their bags and cases, with Rick carrying as much as he possibly could and Vee helping with the rest. Soon, almost everyone was installed in a room with an en suite. Some had views over the quiet street and the rest looked out on the sheltered garden with its azure pool and pots of bright geraniums. Chantelle was curled up on a lounger in the sunshine, washing her whiskers. It was an idyllic scene.

'This is going to be heaven,' said Beryl, as she looked around her spacious room with its heavy oak furniture and enormous bed. 'But Rick doesn't have a place to sleep yet, does he? Where's he going to go, Simone?'

Simone smiled. 'Oh, don't worry about your driver. I've had to put you in the annexe down by the pool, Rick. I only have seven guest rooms in the house but I'm sure you'll be very cosy there. I'm still living upstairs in the flat over the annexe at the moment after the influx of summer visitors so you can call me if you need anything. I never sleep well, so don't worry about waking me.'

Rick's eyes met Vee's, but then he turned and smiled back at Simone. 'Yes, I'll be fine wherever you want me... I mean...' He gulped and stopped talking, pushing his hands into the pockets of his jeans.

Beryl suggested that they all adjourn to their rooms to unpack and freshen up, which Vee read as *have a bit of a nap*. The others agreed with alacrity, except for Rick who was immediately spirited away by Simone to help her with the preparation of the paella.

'I do so hate cleaning mussels,' she said. 'You don't mind, do you? I miss having a strong man about the place to help around the house and I bet you're a great cook too, aren't you?'

Beryl gave a subtle wink in Vee's direction but didn't comment as Rick was ushered away. Yolanda was still waiting on the landing, watching the others depart to their various rooms. She didn't seem keen to go anywhere. Vee yawned. It would be good to have a base for this last part of the holiday, and she was ready for a space of her own too but although their aim had been to see more of France than this, Vee's focus had always been to see Yolanda, and now the time had come. She was torn between the urge to get the inevitable chat over with and a feeling of dread in the pit of her stomach when she tried to imagine where such a conversation would lead.

'Would you like to come back with me for coffee, or do you need a lie down?' Yolanda asked her, in the tones of someone who considered having a lie down during the day to be a gross admission of defeat.

Vee sighed. 'Just give me five minutes to unpack a few things and I'll be with you,' she said. 'Will Simone mind if you wait for me in the garden?'

'Oh, *she's* too preoccupied with her new kitchen hand to mind what the rest of us are getting up to,' said Yolanda, grinning. 'Your friend will need to watch his step, or he'll be stuck in her web. Catching younger men is something of a hobby for that one.'

The image of Simone as a giant, man-eating spider wasn't a comfortable one, and Vee shuddered. 'Do you seriously think she's interested in him?' she asked, trying to look unconcerned. 'I mean, Rick has a lot of emotional baggage. I'd hate to see him being used.'

Yolanda shrugged. 'Only time will tell,' she said. 'I'll see you by the pool. Don't be long though. I need to get back to feed the girls.'

'You've got friends staying?'

'My *hens*,' said Yolanda, turning to go downstairs. 'Hurry up, do. They don't like waiting.'

Vee did as she was told, and was outside in less than ten minutes, feeling a lot better for having washed her face, changed into shorts and a sleeveless top and added a slick of lipstick. She'd swapped her trainers for sandals and felt more ready to face this next part of the day now she was properly in holiday mode. The autumnal temperature here was definitely higher than it had been at their last stop and she could smell the thyme and other herbs that grew in tubs near to the kitchen door. The fragrance of late climbing roses mingled with the sweet scent of honeysuckle. It was like being transported to a kinder, less frantic climate.

'This is a lovely spot,' Vee said to Yolanda as the older woman stood up, ready to be off.

'It's the best place in the world. I'll never leave it. Come on, let's get going. I must say you look a bit brighter now. Endlessly driving around always makes me feel like a limp rag so I don't do it any more. When my last car died, I parked it around the back of my house and now I use it to store food for the girls. I much prefer having an extra shed to beetling around these lanes trying not to run over grumpy French farmers brandishing guns.'

Yolanda was talking as she walked, carrying her bunch of flowers under her arm as she led the way out of a back entrance from Simone's garden into a narrow tree-lined lane. Vee saw Rick's van as they passed a yard on the right and briefly wondered how he was faring in the kitchen, but Yolanda was still in full flow, and it wasn't easy to keep up with her and listen at the same time.

'Here we are,' she was saying as they skirted a row of tumble-down outbuildings and emerged into a secluded kitchen garden, sheltered by a stone wall and a rampant shrubbery. 'I bought this place for a song, years ago,' she said as they headed for a rather ramshackle cottage at the end of the path. 'The owner died, and his kids didn't want the bother of it. Excuse the mess.'

Yolanda opened the back door, and Vee followed her aunt into a small kitchen, complete with range and stone sink. At first glance it looked as if nothing had changed in there since the year dot but then she noticed the gingham curtains at the window. The blue and white of their check was echoed in the pottery that lined the wooden dresser that filled one wall. The scrubbed pine table in the centre of the room could hardly be seen for piles of books, papers and the general paraphernalia of someone who lived alone and had no desire to tidy up just for the sake of it.

'It's a tiny house but it's big enough for me and the girls,' said Yolanda. As she spoke, a loud clucking could be heard, and in through the open door came five beautiful hens in assorted colours and with a wide variety of plumage. Most were handsome and healthy-looking but one looked as if she'd been in a battle. They all made for Yolanda and began to fluff up their feathers.

'We'll not be able to chat until I've dealt with these ladies,' said Yolanda, looking down at her brood fondly. 'There are another three waiting outside, I'll be bound. Here we have Bella, Esmerelda, Lucy, Camilla and Felicity. Bella's not been very well, as you can probably see. Why don't you put the kettle on and make us a pot of coffee while I sort out their teatime? And you can dig out a vase for those flowers from the dresser.'

Vee experienced a sharp pang of nostalgia, remembering how her mum had loved the hens that had scratched around happily in their back garden when she was a child. Feeding them each day had been one of Vee's jobs, and she'd been proud of being given the responsibility of collecting eggs too. She gazed dreamily at the hens, wondering again if it would be possible to reinstate the chicken coop behind Dragonfly Cottage.

'Coffee?' her aunt repeated, giving Vee a nudge.

Before Vee could ask any useful questions, such as 'Where will I find everything else?', Yolanda was off, with her five charges following close behind making happy noises. Vee looked around, wondering if she was going to have to tackle the range, but it was stone cold. With relief, she spied a reasonably modern electric kettle and the cupboard above it revealed mugs and a tin of ground coffee beside a battered stainless-steel cafetiere. While she waited for the water to boil, Vee located a substantial stone vase and quickly arranged the flowers. Soon the fragrant scent of coffee brewing brought Yolanda back inside, sniffing appreciatively.

'Good girl. Let's take it outside. I think there are some biscuits somewhere. Oh, no, I gave them to the birds because they were stale. Never mind. I'll just check on Ferdinand first.'

'Another hen?' asked Vee, but Yolanda shook her head.

'Tree frog,' she said succinctly, as if this explained everything.

Sure enough, nestling in a plastic sandwich box on a shelf of the dresser, Vee saw a tiny green frog, blinking up at Yolanda.

28

Vee was starting to feel as if she'd slipped into a different world, like Alice falling down the rabbit hole to Wonderland. Would a white rabbit appear next? She waited for her aunt to explain this extra member of her family, hoping the idea of keeping a frog in your kitchen might make more sense then.

'I adopted Ferdinand last year,' Yolanda said. 'He looked very sick, so I caught a few tiny flies for him, and he recovered very nicely. It's perfect in the warm weather because there are plenty of insects for him to find but during the summer I have to swat any stray flies and pop them in a box in the freezer so he has a supply to keep him going through the winter.'

Vee tried to think of a suitable response to this information, but nothing came to mind. Yolanda was already making her way into the garden, so she followed her outside. They settled themselves on rickety garden chairs by a table mosaicked in a myriad of small chips of coloured tiles. The pattern was of a sunburst and the whole effect was stunning.

'I did this myself,' said Yolanda proudly, gesturing to the tabletop. 'Simone admired it so much that I had to do one for her and since then her guests have often ordered them from me. It's a nice earner. Every little helps to keep the wolf from the door, you know.'

'Erm... yes, it must do,' said Vee. She'd been wondering how her aunt managed for money, and this must only be a small part of how she paid for this idyllic lifestyle.

'I cycle round the villages whenever there's a house clearance or similar and I buy up old tiles,' said Yolanda. 'The people here save them for me too, and bits of pottery and so on. Ferdinand likes to come with me in my bike basket. He travels in his sandwich box. I've customised the lid so he can breathe, obviously. It'd be cruel otherwise.'

In Vee's opinion there was nothing obvious about travelling around France with a frog in a box, but she was starting to realise that her aunt was a person full of surprises. She supposed Yolanda had always had her quirky side, but to be fair, when Vee was growing up, anyone over thirty had seemed a law unto themselves, quite out of her orbit. She was reflecting on this when Yolanda said, 'So what's the real reason you wanted to see me? Not just for old time's sake, I'm assuming.'

Vee took a sip of her coffee, which was hot, strong and very good indeed. It gave her the confidence to make a start. 'There are two reasons. The first is that I've been trying to remember more details about the weeks leading up to when our family left Willowbrook,' she said.

'Why?'

The bald question stalled Vee, and she took a moment to form her thoughts into order. 'Because... there's a blank in my mind around that time and I've always had a feeling that I've forgotten something significant. Something very bad, that had to do with that final school camping trip,' she added, watching her aunt's face closely.

Yolanda didn't answer for a while. She stared into the distance, as if she was attempting to conjure up the past from the trees that surrounded her garden. Then she stirred herself.

'You're thinking of Patrick Summerfield, aren't you?' she said. 'Beryl's boy.'

Just the sound of his name was enough to make Vee flinch. She put down her coffee cup. 'Yes,' she whispered, hands now clenched in her lap. She could feel her nails biting into the soft palms. 'Tell me what happened, if you know. All of it. Please,' she added as an afterthought when Yolanda's expression grew even grimmer.

'You really don't remember?'

Vee shook her head. 'I know you fetched me back from the campsite and I was in bed for a few days. I was pretty sick, wasn't I?'

'You were very poorly. We were seriously worried about you. A fever is always scary, and you were rambling – burbling about being sorry and wishing you were dead. We called the doctor, but he couldn't find anything wrong with you, apart from a dose of summer flu. He said you were probably run-down and you just needed to rest. Of course, it didn't help that everybody thought you were just plain drunk.'

'You mean I wasn't drunk?'

'Oh, you were, most definitely. I suspected that Patrick had stolen some brandy out of his mum's cocktail cabinet. Beryl has never been short of a bottle or two of her favourite tipple.'

Vee rubbed her eyes. A sudden flashback had transported her to the times when she and Rhonda had met up with a few others in the churchyard and passed around various dregs in bottles filched from their parents' stocks. She'd never had anything of her own to contribute because Tallulah wasn't keen on having strong drink in the house. Some of them had smuggled in their booze offerings to the campsite, she now remembered. Vodka had been popular because if you ate enough mints, the teachers couldn't smell it very easily, but Vee hadn't liked the taste of that, so Patrick had made a point of sharing his brandy with her. She'd thought he was being kind for once.

'Do you have any idea what I was sorry about?' Vee said, going back to the part of Yolanda's tale that seemed most significant but already dreading the answer.

Yolanda sighed. 'I think you've worked it out by now, surely? Patrick was a troubled soul by that time. He was a fairly happy little boy, as I recall, but when he reached his teens, something happened to him. I suspected he'd fallen in with a bad crowd and drugs were involved but when I tried to warn Beryl, she completely flew off the handle and said her lad would never meddle with anything illegal. Anyway, whatever the reason, he became withdrawn and started to act very oddly. You must remember that Patrick had a massive crush on you all that summer?'

Long-buried memories stirred in Vee's mind. She shivered. 'I... yes, I think I knew that.'

'Knew it? Of course you did. Everyone who had anything to do with either of you was aware of it. Patrick used to follow you everywhere. You were kind to him to begin with, but he was always a bit of a joke to you and after a while you lost patience with him mooning around. He still wouldn't leave you alone, even when you grew stroppy with him, and boy, you knew how to be stroppy in those days. Is that why you were sorry? Then you all went off on that camping trip. It was just after the incident in the churchyard. You can't have forgotten that?'

'No. I remember the fire, of course I do.'

'They never did get to the bottom of who started the blaze that destroyed the shed, but Patrick was involved somehow, I'm certain of it.' Yolanda folded her arms and stared at the table. She was miles away.

Vee waited. She didn't want to hear the rest but now they'd come this far, there was no going back. The gentle clucking of the hens as they pottered around the garden scratching at patches of bare soil and fluffing up their feathers would have been soothing if she hadn't felt so wound up. Yolanda refilled Vee's cup and took a big gulp of her own coffee.

'You'll probably call me a busybody but after the camping trip I made it my business to find out exactly what went on there. Your mum was preoccupied with... well, you don't need me to tell you what was bothering her, do you? She hated the thought of leaving Willowbrook and she'd gone into a kind of downward spiral. She was depressed and anxious and she wasn't paying much attention to what either you or your sister were up to.'

There was another pause, longer this time. 'Go on. I'm listening,' said Vee.

'He assaulted you, Venetia.'

The words were out and there was no going back now. Vee swallowed hard.

'You're saying... Patrick raped me?'

'Well, technically, no. He tried to, there's no doubt about that, but it was a cold night and he didn't manage to get through all the layers of clothes you were wearing. You fought him off as best you could, my dear, but you didn't tell anyone what had happened. I always thought you must have blamed yourself for some reason, which was crazy, of course, but there's no other explanation for why you didn't report him to your teachers.'

'I didn't tell them because I didn't remember anything about it after I got better.'

Vee took a few deep breaths. It was all coming back, bit by hideous bit. The chilly night with rain pouring down yet again, the way she'd turned on the white-faced boy in front of her, yelling at him for... for what? Yes, that was it. She'd caught sight of Patrick hiding behind her tent, soaking wet but still intent on spying on her, as he had been doing for weeks. As if it wasn't enough that he'd ended the previous evening by falling... or jumping... into the nearby lake. Nobody had seemed to know what really happened. And here he was once more. Did he not mind being freezing cold and completely drenched yet again?

Seeing Patrick lurking around and still watching her, after all she'd said to him, had pushed Vee's patience – never her strong point – to its limits. Before the trip, she had pretended for a while not to notice his crush in the hope that he would get bored and find someone else to obsess about, but eventually she'd rounded on him and told him in no uncertain terms to leave her alone. That should have been the end of the whole sorry business, but Patrick had completely ignored her harsh words. It was as if she'd never uttered them. Seeing him lurking out there, dripping with rainwater, Vee lost her temper in a big way, and desperate to rid herself of Patrick's attentions once and for all, went in with all guns blazing in the hope of stopping the relentless, tiresome pursuit. It had only taken moments for him to flip and to start to tear at her clothing.

'He was suddenly so powerful,' she murmured, as flashbacks of that awful night shot sharp pains into her brain. 'I think he wanted to show me that he was a real man after all. I never saw him as a danger before that. Annoying, so very annoying, but there was never any harm in him until then.'

'That's what most people thought. That he was tedious and needy but not a bad soul.'

'Exactly.'

Yolanda looked as if she was about to say more but then changed her mind. Vee carried on when the pause became uncomfortable. She was shaking now. It was all flooding back, moment by painful moment.

'We'd already had the brandy earlier. I was feeling wobbly and not very well by then too. Patrick was stronger than he looked. He got me by the shoulders and wouldn't let me go. Then he tried to get my coat off me. I'd been sneezing and coughing all day, and I couldn't get warm, so I was wearing two jumpers under my coat plus a scarf and hat. I bit him and kicked him, Yolanda, but it wasn't until he heard someone coming towards us that he stopped and ran away. I can't remember what happened next... my stomach heaved, and I think I was sick then. I must have blacked out.'

Her aunt moved her chair closer and took both Vee's hands in hers, as she had when they'd met earlier. The warmth was soothing, and gradually Vee began to stop shaking. They sat together like this for what seemed like a long time but could only have been five minutes. Then Yolanda sat up straighter.

'I sussed there'd been something dodgy going on when I picked you up, but I couldn't hang about for long because I needed to get you home. You were in a bad way. They'd rung me to tell me you were too ill to stay at the campsite and your mum and dad weren't due back for another couple of nights, so I just got in the car and came to get you.'

'That part's still a complete blank.'

'I'm not surprised. The teachers were all set to call an ambulance, but I decided that your own bed and me there to look after you would be better. Your mum used to get flu really badly when she was younger and all she ever needed was rest and lots of fluids.'

Vee wrapped her arms around herself. The kindness of her aunt had never been in doubt, but why had she kept away from Vee for so long if she cared enough to nurse her back to health so tenderly? Yolanda was still talking, and Vee tried to focus. This was important and she mustn't miss anything.

'The teachers were more than happy for me to take responsibility,' said Yolanda. 'They looked shell-shocked. Everyone was frozen and some of the girls – and a couple of boys too – were wailing. But later, I did some digging.'

'And?' The one word was all Vee could manage. Her throat was dry, and her heart was pounding. *Please let it not have been Rick who saw what happened*, was all she could think. *If it was, and he didn't help me, I don't know how I'll cope.*

'I had a friend who fostered teenagers at the time. Her name was Anneka, and I remembered she was looking after a girl who'd been on that same trip. They called her Shazzie. I don't know what her proper name was. I pretended to bump into the girl accidentally when she was on her way home from school soon afterwards. I told her I was your aunt and that you'd mentioned her name. We started talking. I think she was glad to blurt it all out to a grown-up, to be honest, but she made me promise not to tell anyone.'

'Tell anyone what?' Still Vee felt as if she didn't have words to say much more than this. Her mind felt numb. More splintered fragments of the heaving emotions of that night were coming back to her now, in shocking waves. How had she buried them for so long?

'Shazzie was the one who saw Patrick attacking you. He dropped you and ran away when he realised that he'd been rumbled. She could hear someone else approaching who she assumed would be bound to look after you, so she ran after him. She was livid, and she wanted to warn him off ever trying anything like that again. She'd already fished him out of the lake the evening before, and she was heartily sick of his antics.'

At last, the mist that had been dogging Vee's memories for so long was clearing. With a jolt, she knew who it was that had appeared as Shazzie left, chasing Patrick towards the lake and shouting at him to come back. She remembered as clearly as if it had only happened yesterday. It had been Rhonda. She was the one who'd turned up and found Vee lying on the ground in a pool of mud, sobbing uncontrollably and already in the throes of the virus that had felled her. Shivering and shaking, she'd felt sicker than she ever had in her life. Since that day, Vee had experienced odd times when she'd been unwell, even had Covid twice, but nothing had brought her down in the same way as that illness had done. Rhonda had done what Rhonda did best. She'd laughed, and shifted the blame, telling Vee she'd brought all this on herself.

'You should have stopped him in his tracks much sooner,' Rhonda said. 'This is what you get for leading guys on and then not coming up with the goods. Right, on your feet, let's get you to where the teachers are hanging out. Much use they are, but I don't know what else to do with you.'

'I know who it was now,' Vee said. 'I mean, the one who found me. But there must have been another person nearby because Rhonda shouted to them to go after Patrick and stop him pulling another stunt like the previous night's lake fiasco or we'd all end up being interrogated. Whoever was there didn't do it, though, or if they did, I was too far out of it to notice. It's all a muddle after that. The problem is, I've got an awful feeling that there's someone else who still very much wants to know the details of that night.'

Yolanda nodded sadly. 'Beryl,' she said.

'I'm going to have to go back to join the others for dinner now,' said Vee, glancing at her watch, although she couldn't imagine being able to eat anything, the way her stomach was still churning.

'Yes, Simone likes to serve drinks half an hour before the evening meal,' agreed Yolanda. 'She asked me if I wanted to come too but I think I'll give it a miss. I'm vegan now, which isn't easy in rural France, I can tell you. Look, we'll talk again tomorrow, shall we? Try and decide how we can avoid letting Beryl know all this when she asks. I think you've had more than enough for one day.'

Vee thought so too. She hugged her aunt and set off down the lane back to Pension Simone. It wasn't until she was almost there that she realised she'd completely forgotten the other part of her mission. She hadn't even mentioned the fact that she wanted to discover why Yolanda had distanced herself so firmly for years. That would have to wait until tomorrow now. The prospect wasn't enticing.

29

Beryl unpacked her belongings and had a quick shower before sitting down for a moment to get her breath back. A fleeting worry crossed her mind about how the news of the engagement would be received when she and Frank arrived back in Willowbrook. What would Nell and Barney think? Would the other villagers say she was too old to find love again? Beryl gave herself a shake. She'd never bothered much about other people's opinions, and she wasn't going to start now.

Changing into one of her less crumpled summer dresses, Beryl lay down on the bed for what her mother used to call *a little toes-up*. Then, completely refreshed and starting to notice pangs of hunger, she brushed her hair, added copious amounts of hairspray, put on a layer of her brightest lipstick and hunted around for her sandals. Even after her more casual holidays with Anthea and Winnie, it still seemed wonderfully decadent to be going to dinner without any tights on. This was the life. Mother wouldn't have approved at all, which made the idea even more appealing.

Downstairs, most of the others were already assembled

around the pool, sipping long, cool glasses of some sort of delicately pink drink, each with a strawberry floating in it.

'Champagne cocktails for your first night here,' called Simone, holding out a brimming glass to Beryl. 'I always add a tot of cognac to liven them up.'

'Liven *us* up, more like. You'll have us squiffy, drinking on an empty stomach,' said Sid, winking at Winnie, who smiled back, raising her glass to Beryl.

'Where are Anthea and Venetia?' asked Beryl, doing a quick head count as she sipped her cocktail. It was delicious, and she had to restrain herself from downing it in two gulps.

'Anthea's still beautifying,' said Maurice. 'I told her it was merely gilding the lily in my opinion, but she just rolled her eyes and called me a flatterer. I meant it though. She's a lovely woman. I'm a very lucky man.'

Beryl didn't think this gushing comment worth responding to. She was very fond of Anthea but to be husband number five and stick at it would take more than a bit of luck. 'And Vee?' she said. 'She should be having a drink with us. Has she fallen asleep?'

'I'm here,' said a voice behind Beryl, and Vee appeared from round the back of the property. Beryl noticed immediately that Vee was wearing shorts. The very idea! She sniffed.

'Aren't you dressing for dinner?' Beryl asked, pursing her lips. '*We've* all made the effort.'

They both looked around at the rest of the party. Winnie had on one of her trademark long robes in purple and fuchsia with a matching head wrap. Maurice, Sid and Frank were in their smartest trousers teamed with short-sleeved shirts and Rick was resplendent in black chinos and a striped linen shirt with a black waistcoat over it.

'Oh, I didn't realise we were pulling out all the stops tonight, with just having dinner here,' said Vee, clearly not hearing Simone approaching from the kitchen.

'So, you do not consider my cooking worthy of dressing up for?' their hostess asked, her French accent more marked as her eyes flashed fire.

'I... I... yes, of course,' stammered Vee. 'I went out in a hurry to see my aunt and didn't think I'd be this long. I'll pop up and change.'

'Don't bother,' said Simone. 'The paella is almost ready to serve, and I hate keeping my guests waiting for food. Ah, here's the other lady and doesn't she look *magnifique*.'

Anthea had certainly got the memo that Vee had missed, thought Beryl, gazing at her friend admiringly. The usual artfully draped linen layers had been eschewed tonight in favour of a simple black dress accessorised with an assortment of silver and amber chunky jewellery. Around Anthea's shoulders was draped a flimsy chiffon wrap that sparkled with gold lights as she walked. She was wearing peep-toed kitten heels and, like Beryl, had gone for the bare-legged look, but unlike Beryl, had taken the trouble to used tinted make-up to give the effect of a gentle tan. She'd also painted her toenails in pearly pink.

'You look splendid, my darling,' said Maurice, jumping to his feet.

'A credit to my little residence,' agreed Simone, handing a glass to Anthea and then another to Vee, with a less favourable glance.

'A toast to travelling,' said Sid, now also standing and raising his glass. 'A big thank you to Vee and Rick for getting us here, and to our beautiful hostess, Simone. I'm so glad we decided to have an extra couple of days in this lovely place.'

There was a chorus of agreement as they all raised their own glasses. Beryl could see that Vee was uncomfortable. She kept smoothing down her shorts and tugging her top straight, like a little girl getting ready for a telling off from her teacher. Beryl's heart went out to her. It was an easy mistake to make, after all. She went over to stand beside Vee.

'You look perfectly lovely, dear,' she whispered. 'Very summery.'

Vee shot her a surprised look and Beryl realised that she hadn't shown her much spontaneous kindness so far, apart from providing the odd tray of food or cup of tea. Perhaps it was time to start appreciating her neighbour. They were going to have to rub along together in Fiddler's Row, no matter what history there was between them.

'Take no notice of that one,' Beryl murmured. 'All tits and no taste, if you ask me.'

Vee had been swallowing a mouthful of her cocktail when Beryl spoke and now began to choke, coughing and spluttering until tears ran down her face. Rick handed her a bottle of water and started to pat her on the back and Winnie passed over a small packet of tissues, while Simone gave Vee a withering look and set off back to the kitchen.

'You'd better all get yourselves seated at the table,' she said. 'I'm ready to serve and I don't like my food to go cold.'

They did as they were told, shuffling around until everyone had a chair under the big umbrellas at the long poolside table. Vee had recovered now but seemed very glad to hide her shorts-clad legs under the table. Beryl sat down next to her, and they exchanged a grin.

'I went to see Yolanda and I didn't realise...' Vee began.

'I know, it's fine. Take no notice of that one,' Beryl said quietly, patting Vee's arm. 'Let's concentrate on eating her fishy stuff. Personally, I'd rather have a nice piece of cod, but *when in Rome*, as they say.'

Simone served up her paella with panache, and Beryl had to admit to herself that it did look very impressive. There were prawns, large and luscious, mussels peeping out of their shells, chunks of something that might be squid, she guessed, and all manner of other kinds of seafood, plus chicken and what looked like slivers of chorizo all nestling on a bed of perfectly cooked yellowy-orange rice. Give the woman her due, she could cook.

Their hostess was generous with the wine too, and carafe after carafe appeared before the last was even empty. Beryl could see that Winnie's eyes were beginning to glaze over and she was leaning towards Sid as if she might fall asleep on his shoulder, whereas Sid and Maurice were getting more verbose by the minute. Vee had hardly touched her wine. She hadn't eaten much either and although Rick had seemed to thoroughly enjoy his paella, he hadn't refilled his glass as often as the others. As for Anthea, she looked as cool and elegant as ever, sipping slowly and eating daintily. Beryl herself had stopped drinking after three glasses, changing over to water. She had no desire to make a fool of herself.

They were just stacking their paella plates tidily, ready to ferry the crockery indoors when Simone emerged from the kitchen bearing two more carafes of wine. Seeing her, Sid leapt to his feet so suddenly that his chair toppled over.

'A toast to our wonderful hostess,' he cried. 'Simone, come over here and let us raise our glasses to you. That was a splendid meal!'

Clearly overwhelmed with gratitude, Sid raised his glass so high that he overbalanced and staggered backwards, falling over his chair which still lay on the ground. For a couple of seconds, he teetered on the edge of the pool and then before anyone could cry out a warning, let alone reach him, he plunged straight into the deep end, hurling his wine glass into the air. It landed in the pool with a splash, just after Sid hit the water.

'Oh, dear Lord!' shouted Winnie, as they all stood up and moved together, a wave of anxious bodies hurrying across the short distance to the water. 'He can't swim, the daft bugger.'

By now Sid had come up for air and was opening his mouth to yell. His eyes were panic-stricken. Rick fell to his knees, reaching out to Sid, and their hands were almost touching. 'Nearly got him,' said Rick, leaning further. 'He's okay. If someone will just hang on to my belt, I can...'

'I never allow real glass at the poolside,' said Simone, glaring at Sid. 'My guests should have the common sense to use plastic tumblers if they're going to fall in. Can somebody please fish the man out? And his glass,' she added.

Beryl was about to remonstrate that she didn't suppose Sid had meant to keel over into the pool when the ample figure of Winnie hurtled past them all. She kicked off her gold sandals and flung herself into the water. 'I've got you, Sid, you silly sod. You're safe,' she spluttered, treading water and grabbing him by the collar of his now sodden shirt.

Sid gasped and coughed as Winnie towed him to the side, and Rick and Frank hauled him out, taking an armpit each and very nearly joining him in the water in the process. Soon Sid was lying on the tiles looking extremely sheepish, with water flowing from his clothes. His hair was plastered to his head, revealing a large bald patch, and his trousers had ridden up at the ankles, showing a pair of very flashy red socks.

'I'm so sorry, Simone,' he managed to wheeze. 'I got a bit...'

'Drunk?' suggested Beryl under her breath but Vee nudged her, and she closed her mouth with a snap. What a start to their visit here. She was just glad Yolanda hadn't witnessed the embarrassing spectacle.

By now, Rick had found a large net that Simone kept by the pool, possibly for such disasters, and was fishing out Sid's floating wine glass.

'No harm done, fortunately,' said Simone, graciously. 'I must admit to always getting a little overexcited when I visit a new place, myself. Take yourself into the poolside changing room over there for a shower.' She gestured expansively. 'And perhaps one of your kind friends will fetch a towel and some spare clothes.'

'I'll go,' said Rick, setting off at a trot into the house. 'Beryl, could you find something for Winnie to change into?'

'You should both go and get in that hot shower, before you catch your death,' said Beryl, doing as Rick suggested and heading for Winnie's room.

'They're hardly likely to do that on a warm night like this,' said Frank. 'But the ladies are right. Off you go, chaps. No harm done.'

Sid and Winnie sloshed their way around the pool and disappeared into a room under the eaves on the far side. The remaining members of the party looked at each other, at a loss for what to do next. There was a long pause as they waited for Rick and Beryl to return.

'Dessert,' called Simone, now back in the kitchen. 'Who's for a slice of my pudding?'

'Now *that's* a leading question,' Beryl said to Rick as they emerged from the house.

Rick shushed her with a finger to his lips. 'Behave, Beryl,' he said quietly. He raised his voice. 'What's your pudding, Simone?' he called.

'Paris Brest,' she replied.

That did it. Beryl started to chuckle, and seeing her becoming almost helpless with mirth, the others joined in, one by one.

'Why are you all laughing?' Simone said, coming outside with a magnificent choux pastry dessert on a plate. 'This is my signature dish. It's famous throughout France. Delicious rings of light pastry filled with cream and praline. Oh, I see.' Light dawned as she glanced down at her own mountainous cleavage, only just covered by the plunging neckline of her dress. 'It's not that kind of breast. You British are so literal.'

Winnie was waiting outside the shower room and gratefully took the bundle of clothes that Beryl handed over. 'I fetched you a clean robe and so on and I went in to help Rick get something for Sid because I could hear him opening and shutting drawers as if he couldn't find anything. Typical man,' Beryl said. 'I just brought Sid's towelling dressing gown and slippers in the end. We won't mind if he doesn't get properly dressed, will we?'

The others all shook their heads and Beryl continued. 'You wouldn't believe the state of his underwear. You single men are awful... he needs someone to revamp his style.'

Wordlessly, the others watched as Winnie headed into the shower room. They heard her call, 'Only me, no need to cover up.' The shower stopped running and silence fell.

Beryl was the first to rally. 'Well, this Brest thing looks scrumptious,' she said. 'After all that excitement, I'm quite peckish again. Let's get stuck in.'

Simone served generous portions to them all, being careful to leave enough for Winnie and Sid. 'They're being a very long time in there, aren't they?' she said, casting a suspicious glance over towards the changing room. Just as she spoke, the two in question emerged. Beryl grinned to herself as she saw that Sid was being very careful to walk on the side away from the water. She also noticed something else. Winnie and Sid were holding hands.

30

After their journey, the large meal and the excitement of Sid's poolside dive, everyone was ready for an early night. Vee didn't think she'd sleep at all, preoccupied as she was with all that she'd discussed with Yolanda and knowing there was another difficult conversation to come, but the vast bed and soft feather pillows were so comfortable that exhaustion overcame her very quickly.

She woke the next morning feeling much more positive. That is, until she wandered over to the window to fling back the shutters and feast on the view of early-morning sunshine over the sparkling blue water of the pool. The sight of Simone and Rick emerging from the back of the garden near to where the gite could be found filled her with a sudden rage, especially as Rick was wearing swimming shorts and Simone had covered her costume with a very glamorous silky robe.

As Vee watched, they both dropped their towels on loungers by the pool and Simone slid the robe from her suntanned shoulders, revealing a swimsuit that covered very little. Her generous curves were gloriously on show now, and Vee saw that Rick couldn't help giving them a glance before he climbed down into the water, with an involuntary yelp.

'Chilly, isn't it, *cheri*?' Simone's voice carried clearly. 'It'll warm up later, but this is my favourite time of day to swim. Race you. Last one to do ten lengths is a... I don't know the English word for it.'

'Sissy? Wimp?' suggested Rick, already halfway down the pool.

With a whoop, Simone plunged into the water, causing a major ripple effect and setting off with a dashing crawl to catch him up. Vee seethed quietly. Rick could easily have messaged her to see if she'd like to join them. He was obviously having far too much fun to think of such a thing. She ground her teeth until she realised that she was giving herself jaw ache and headed for the shower instead.

As the blissfully warm water flowed over her, Vee tried hard to analyse her bitter feelings. She and Rick were friends, that was all. What was it to her if he wanted to frolic in the pool with their hostess, who obviously appreciated his charms? It was up to him what he did with his free time. But the thought of the two of them being closeted together in the gite made Vee feel like the odd one out on the playground at school, or the last to be picked for the netball team. It would have been just as logical for her to be in the annexe rather than Rick as one of the two younger members of the group. Simone had chosen her housemate on purpose. She wanted him for herself.

Shrugging off these unwelcome thoughts as best she could, Vee finished her shower and dressed in shorts and a vest top with a baggy denim shirt over the top. The warm breeze coming through the open window told her that it was going to be another lovely day, even though they were now into the time of year when back in Willowbrook, she'd have been pulling on a sweater and jeans.

Half an hour later, the group were once again gathered under the parasols by the pool ready for breakfast. Vee noticed that Sid had made sure to be sitting at the farthest point from the water's edge and Winnie was cosied up next to him. The two of them were talking in low voices as the chatter of Beryl and Frank dominated the conversation. Beryl wanted to go for a walk to explore the village, and she was asking Simone for guidance.

'What I *will* do, although it's not my custom, you understand,' said Simone, placing a large dish of croissants and pains au chocolat on the table between the butter and various preserves and adding two golden-brown baguettes to a bread basket that had been laid out ready. 'What I *will* do is come with you, Beryl, and anyone else who would like to join us. I can introduce you to the people who run our excellent Café Associatif and you can enjoy a cup of the best coffee in Brugnac d'Agenais. Apart from mine, of course. I have already invited Rick for a tour of my home village. He said he would be delighted.'

Simone shot what looked suspiciously like a triumphant glance at Vee and went inside to fetch the coffee and also the pot of tea insisted on by Sid. Rick avoided looking at Vee, reaching for a croissant without commenting.

Just as she was about to say that she would like to come along for the walk, Vee's phone pinged with a message from Yolanda.

> We have a lot more to say to each other, I think.
> Come over to my house as soon as you have
> eaten.

It wasn't an invitation. More of a summons, Vee thought. Reluctant to leave Rick to the tender mercies of their hostess, she knew she must talk to her aunt again, and it would be better to get it over with now rather than have it hanging over her head. She texted back a brief *okay* and got on with her breakfast. To deal with emotional upheavals on an empty stomach would probably be a mistake, although she still didn't have much of an appetite.

Vee was ready to leave for Yolanda's house long before the rest of the party were mustered. Sun hats needed to be fetched, sun cream applied, which seemed ridiculous in October, but it was already warming up even in the shade, and cardigans 'just in case' had to be found by Beryl and Winnie. Vee said goodbye to them all, apart from Rick who had gone back to the gite without so much as a word. She set off for Yolanda's place via the gate by the annexe but there was no sign of him. Okay, if that was how Rick wanted to be, two could play at that game. The lack of contact stung, but Vee was determined not to chase after him. Let Rick have a wonderful time trailing round after Simone. He'd soon realise how irritating the woman was. Wouldn't he?

Yolanda was waiting outside in her garden, once again sitting at the mosaicked table with yet more coffee in front of her. Vee felt as if she was on a permanent caffeine high already, but any crutch was better than none, so she accepted a cup and sat down.

'You're looking very serious again today,' said her aunt. 'I have a feeling we're going to be heading into uncharted waters. Are you ready?'

Vee frowned. 'I suppose I am,' she said. 'I have to ask you this, I can't put it off any longer. Why have you kept away from me for so long?'

There. The question she'd been so wary of asking and yet so keen to have answered was out at last. Yolanda didn't say anything for a few moments. Then she sighed. 'It's complicated, and I'm not proud of this,' she said. 'But I... strongly disapproved of some-thing you did in the past. I can see now, with hindsight, that it wasn't my place to pass judgement on you. What business was it of mine to be so high-handed in my views? Nevertheless, it has driven a wedge between us.'

Vee stared at her aunt. This was like teetering on the brink of a vast precipice. She had to ask for more information but to hear the answer was going to open up a Pandora's box that had been firmly closed and locked for many years.

'Tell me what you mean,' she said, her voice cracking as she got the words out.

'I'm sure you've worked that out by now, unless you're much less intuitive than I give you credit for,' said Yolanda. 'I've gone over and over it all in my mind, and I still don't have the answer. You gave your baby away, Venetia. Your own flesh and blood. How could you bear to do such a thing?'

Yolanda's words shot through Vee like a lightning bolt. She thought about getting up and leaving, running away from the thoughts that were racing through her brain, but she'd come this far. There was no going back now. It was time to face Yolanda's question, one that had haunted her for a very long time without the need for anyone to ask it out loud. All around her, the sunlit garden glowed with autumn beauty. The chickens clucked around the bushes, contentedly scratching the soil just in case of a stray worm. Yolanda waited, her eyes half-closed against the glare.

'I didn't realise you knew about all that,' Vee said, eventually. 'It was meant to be a secret. Did my mum tell you?'

'Not intentionally,' said Yolanda. 'It was one night after you were in bed. I overheard Tallulah talking to your dad. They'd just come back from Boston. I'd been house-sitting for a while, and I was beginning to think it was time for me to go home. I went downstairs to have a word about arrangements for leaving, and I couldn't help hearing what they were talking about. They were discussing you and your sister. Cassie was very much on their minds, for obvious reasons, but they were even more worried about you.'

'Did they know you'd heard?'

'Yes, because I was so shocked I gasped out loud. Your mum flung the living room door open and there they were, both staring at me.' Yolanda reached for Vee's hand. 'Why don't you tell me your version of the story? I'm a good listener and I promise not to speak until you've finished, if that helps. I'll try really hard not to be judgemental, but I've kept my own feelings about this bottled up for too long already.'

Vee wondered where to begin. Did it start when she was just thirty-five years old, childless and depressed? Or did the roots of what happened go back to a much earlier time?

'How long have you got?' she asked.

Yolanda smiled rather sadly. 'I'm all yours for as long as it takes, my love.'

The old endearment that her aunt had often used when Vee was a small child touched her to the core and she had to work hard not to break down, but there was an explanation to be given, and they both needed it to be said. Vee took a deep breath and tried to get her whirling thoughts in order. To make this manageably short and concise would take some doing. She began to speak, quietly at first and then gaining in momentum as the old story took on a pace of its own.

'When Cassie was twenty-eight, after she'd put up with awful gynaecological problems since her early teens, she discovered she'd never be able to have children. This coincided with her moving in with Marissa, who as you know, lived in Boston and was making a big name for herself as a hot-shot lawyer. Marissa is quite a bit older than Cassie and she'd suffered all her adult life with endometriosis. They were both desperate for a baby, but Marissa thought it was highly unlikely that she could get pregnant, and also she was terrified of the idea of childbirth. Her own mother had died when she was born.'

Vee paused and drained her coffee. Its kick gave her the boost she needed to continue.

'I was visiting them in the States at the time to be present at their civil partnership. I had just lost my job and broken up with my long-term boyfriend. My thirty-fourth birthday had been spent alone, walking for miles to try and shake off the feeling of gloom. It was a bad time for me. We talked and talked over the time I was there and to cut a very long story short, I offered to have a baby for them. I was feeling useless. My life felt pointless and the idea that I could give them so much happiness was enticing. They didn't feel able to trust an unfamiliar surrogate but in this way, their child would have similar genes to Cassie too. They had a good friend who was prepared to be the sperm donor, and they organised everything very quickly.'

There was another long pause as Vee battled with the flood of emotions that digging up the past was triggering. Yolanda's expression was unreadable, but she was still holding her niece's hand. It was immensely comforting. Vee pressed on.

'The two of them had gone into the idea of surrogacy quite thoroughly already and they already knew about checking for ovulation and planning optimum windows for conception, and that kind of thing, which were still a mystery to me. As luck would have it, I got pregnant the very first time we tried. I couldn't believe it. The whole thing had seemed like a fantastic dream but suddenly it was real, and I was terrified and excited all at the same time. I had to go home after another fortnight, but by then we'd completely planned out the next nine months. I was living in the Midlands, and I landed a temporary job in a garden centre to begin with, but I was so sick in the early days that I had to keep missing my morning shifts, and so Cassie and Marissa funded me until I was okay to work again.'

Vee's chest was tight, and her palms were sweating now. This was even harder than she'd expected but it had to be done. The memories of those mornings when she'd not even been able to keep water down were sharp and painful. She'd been so worried that it meant that the baby wouldn't be healthy, but gradually she'd read up on all her symptoms and become calmer and less inclined to panic at the least little twinge. She forced herself to keep talking.

'I told Mum and Dad that I was pregnant when I couldn't put it off any longer. I was afraid they wouldn't approve because Mum in particular was very religious and she'd always seemed against any sort of intervention when it came to childbirth. I shouldn't have doubted them, as it happened. When my parents knew I was having the baby for my sister they were supportive, although concerned about how it would affect me mentally because they knew how low I'd been after the break-up. They decided to come to America with me when I was seven and a half months pregnant, and we all stayed with Cassie and Marissa until after the baby was born.'

'Finn,' said Yolanda, who had held her tongue until now. 'Your son. Call him by his name.'

Now the tears began to flow, and Vee didn't try to stop them. 'He was beautiful. He still is. He only knows me as his aunt, of course. The man who fathered Finn isn't on the scene now, he moved away and said he didn't want to be involved in any way.'

'What I don't understand is not only why but how they've managed to keep the truth from him for all this time. It would have been a given that one of them, if not both, isn't his natural mother, but hasn't Finn ever seen his birth certificate?'

'Marissa and Cassie have a lot of friends who are same-sex couples and it's not at all unusual for them to have adopted children or to have surrogate babies. Finn knows he's adopted but as far as he's concerned his father was an anonymous sperm donor and his birth mother was a surrogate that they engaged privately. His birth certificate is the adoptive one.'

'But, Venetia, don't you long to see your son? How can you stand not to be closer to him, even as an aunt?'

Vee's hackles were rising now. It was too much. Yolanda had no right to question her decision made in all good faith so long ago. 'I've visited them all in Boston twice in the last twenty years,' she snapped. 'I don't want to muddy the waters. He belongs to Cassie and Marissa. They send me photos every now and again. Finn's making his own life.'

'I know that,' said Yolanda. 'Cassie's in touch with me too, and so is the boy. I'm his great-aunt, after all.' She paused and bit her lip before carrying on. 'You really need to see him face to face and explain what happened back then. It's not right that he's nearly twenty-one and you still haven't talked to him about his birth. It's time, Venetia. It's way past time, in my opinion.'

Vee glared at her aunt. 'That wasn't part of the deal,' she said. 'Finn doesn't need to know who I really am. It's better this way. Cassie and Marissa are his parents now. Even if I did decide to do what you say and bring it all out into the open, it's not something you can do on FaceTime. Anyway, I'm not going to tell him. He doesn't have to know the truth. He's so far away.'

Yolanda shifted in her chair. 'Or is he?' she said.

'What are you getting at?'

Her aunt had the grace to look shamefaced as she blurted out,

'I hazarded a guess that this was one of the things you wanted to talk to me about before you arrived. I've already messaged Finn to say that you're here with me and that we're going to be discussing his history. I've told the boy who his mother is, Venetia. Somebody had to do it. He knows the whole story now and he wants to see you. Finn's coming to England.'

Rick was finding this day extremely trying and it was still only half past ten. The Willowbrook party, minus Vee, had assembled outside the front door of Pension Simone and had been waiting for their hostess for ten minutes when she finally emerged, wearing a wide-brimmed sun hat, sparkly flip-flops and a dress that was even lower-cut than the one she'd worn to serve breakfast.

'*Bien*, you're all here,' Simone said, nodding happily. 'Do you have cameras? Ah, you are so modern, you have your telephones at the ready. Then off we go.'

She seized Rick by the hand and forged her way to the front of the group, turning to lead them along the road and towards the main part of the village.

'Mind you don't get lost, Rick,' called Beryl, cackling. 'Maybe we should all hold hands in pairs too, like on a school trip.'

'Good idea. I'll be in charge of counting heads,' said Sid. 'Has everyone been to the toilet before we really get going?'

'Oh, now you mention it,' said Maurice. 'I could do with a quick pee. Hang on, Simone. I'll just nip back inside.'

Simone threw Maurice a filthy look as he tapped the four-digit code into the pad by the front door and disappeared into the gloom of the hall. 'We shall never get anywhere at this rate,' she muttered.

Rick tried to discreetly detach his hand from her grasp, but Simone merely held on tighter while Beryl made a big show of taking Frank by the hand too and falling into line behind their leaders. Winnie and Sid did the same, giggling quietly. When Maurice returned, slightly dishevelled from rushing, Anthea held out a hand to him too, bracelets jingling, her perfectly manicured nails glistening in the sunshine.

Simone didn't seem to know what to make of this show of uniformity, but she rallied quickly and marched off down the road, towing Rick along beside her. By now, Winnie and Sid's muffled laughter had transmitted itself to the others and they were struggling to contain their splutters. They followed Rick and Simone, but at a short distance so their hostess appeared not to notice that her party were being disrespectful. Simone had no trouble in keeping up a constant flow of conversation as she walked. It took a huge effort not to switch off and think about what was going on at this very moment between Vee and Yolanda.

Rick was very much afraid that if he didn't listen, Simone would rumble him and ask searching questions later, but his anxiety seemed to grow with every step he took. Usually a past master of keeping his memories in separate locked boxes deep inside his brain, it was quite possible that Yolanda had at least one of his keys. She was a mystery to him. What did Vee's aunt remember of the summer of 1985? He'd hoped the past was dead and buried, but now there was a very real danger that some things better left unsaid might be about to be dragged out of cold storage and given a very unwelcome airing.

'Come along, everyone, keep up,' Simone said, upping her

speed. 'To my left you can see the old post office, and beside it, the school. Not many children live in our village nowadays, but I believe Madame Beaumont runs a tight ship.'

'She's not the only one,' murmured Frank. 'Or do I mean *a tight grip*?'

This sally set Beryl off again, and by the time they reached the square, she was having to wipe her eyes. Luckily, Simone was now fully occupied in greeting a dapper little gentleman with a fine moustache and bushy grey eyebrows that seemed to have a life of their own. She kissed him soundly on both cheeks and then once again, nearly toppling him. He righted himself and turned to face the group.

'This is our mayor, Monsieur Pierre Phillipe,' Simone said, patting the man on the arm fondly. 'He's in charge of the Café Associatif. It's a great place for us to meet and we are very grateful to him.'

The man said something in rapid French and shrugged his shoulders. Simone nodded. 'Pierre says that most of the hard work has been done by Yolanda. He apologises for his lack of the English language, but he wishes to welcome you to Brugnac d'Agenais.'

The mayor gave a graceful bow to the group and, taken by surprise, they bowed back with varying degrees of success. Rick looked along the row of bobbing heads and a lump came into his throat. They were all precious to him now, like an extended family. He hadn't intended that to happen. He'd known them for some time, some more recently and some, like Beryl, for years. Through his business, Rick made plenty of contacts but getting attached to them had never been part of his plan. These were emotional connections he didn't want or need.

Simone broke into Rick's troubled thoughts, gesturing to the tables set out invitingly under a large striped awning. 'Have a seat, everyone. We will have coffee before we set off on our walk, yes?' She followed Pierre into the interior of the building and Rick was free at last.

'Do you know what she's talking about, with all this Café Associatif business?' Frank asked Rick. 'Is it some kind of joint effort in the village?'

'Yes, run by the community for the community,' said Rick, feeling that he had already heard more than enough about the place on their brief journey to be able to explain its purpose to the others. 'It's not just a café, it's the hub of the village. They organise events such as musical evenings where anyone can come to play their instruments and sing. It's ukulele night in three days. Simone's hoping we'll all come along.'

Rick thought privately that he would rather be at the pension with a good book and a glass of wine rather than having to sit through an interminable concert which would in all likelihood be torturous. However, he was surprised to find that the others were positively thrilled by this prospect.

'Oh, I do love a ukulele band,' said Sid. 'My ma had a whole heap of George Formby's records, and I knew all the words by the time I was five years old, so they told me.'

Frank was in full agreement. He began to warble in a pleasing baritone about leaning on a lamppost at the corner of the street and Maurice and Beryl joined in, with Winnie playing an imaginary banjo. Only Anthea looked horrified. She exchanged glances with Rick, and her look said, '*Oh no, I don't think so, do you?*'

Simone reappeared at this point and soon made it clear that she hadn't finished being their tourist information guide. She raised her voice to make sure everyone could hear. 'Tonight is an evening of singing. A local choir will entertain us and we will be able to join in at certain points. How about that?'

Rick shook his head at her briefly, casting around desperately for a reason why he wouldn't be able to be at this exciting event. For one thing, Simone's attentions were getting a tad too familiar now. Rick had been vaguely amused at her obvious flirtatiousness to begin with but after this morning, when she'd appeared at his bedroom door scantily clad, offering to help him find his swimming trunks, he'd had quite enough. The other reason, apart from baulking at the idea of an evening full of French songs, was, of course, that it was probably the only opportunity he'd have to catch Vee alone later. She'd looked so anxious at breakfast time when she thought nobody was watching her, but her phone had beeped, and she'd made herself scarce before Rick had had a chance to speak to her.

Coffee was served as they all sat down, and Rick wondered how any of them were ever going to sleep again with all this extra caffeine whizzing around their bodies. He sipped slowly, watching the world go by, or the small portion of it that passed through the marketplace of this pretty little village.

'Could you see yourself relocating to somewhere like this, Rick?' asked Simone as she joined them. 'It is a very good life, you know.'

She put a hand on Rick's knee, and he heard Winnie and Sid stifle a titter.

'Rick's a vital part of our own village, Simone,' Beryl said firmly, and there was a chorus of agreement.

'We wouldn't be able to manage with our resident handyman,' said Anthea. 'We know we can call on Rick for any task, no matter whether it's big or small.'

'That's quite true,' Frank said, reaching over to clasp Rick by the shoulder, almost causing him to spill his coffee. 'This man renovated the house I live in now and he made a sterling job of it. If it wasn't for Rick, I'd still be holed up in my son and daughter-in-law's spare bedroom instead of having the privacy of my own lovely annexe.'

'Rick's not just a driver for road trips, Simone,' said Winnie. 'We rely on him for all sorts of things.'

'And not only that, he's our very good friend,' finished Sid, raising his coffee cup in another of his toasts, which this time was taking place a mercifully long way from the swimming pool.

Rick was so touched by all these plaudits that he couldn't speak. He smiled at them all and gently removed Simone's hand from his knee.

'Well, I can see that there's no point in me trying to entice this lovely man over the Channel permanently,' she said, rather snappily. 'When you've all finished, we'd better get on our way, or we won't be back here at the café for lunch. I've taken the liberty of booking you a large table. I only cater for breakfast and dinner, as I'm sure you're aware.'

Simone finished her coffee and got to her feet, fixing them all with a look that said she wasn't prepared to wait. There was a short delay while everyone except Rick visited the cloakroom inside the building. Simone inched closer to Rick again.

'It must be tiresome for you to spend so much time with the older generation,' she said. 'But there are lots of other options. You only have to say the word.'

'Thank you, but I enjoy their company. They're a great bunch of people. I've been meaning to say that your English is excellent,' said Rick, with a swift change of subject. 'How did you become so fluent?'

Simone preened herself and smiled. The convoluted explanation for her astounding proficiency lasted all the way through the village with frequent stops while she pointed out places of interest and historical features. By the time they'd made a loop and arrived back at the café, Rick was heartily sick of hearing about Simone's various extended visits to the United Kingdom over the years, and how she had amazed and impressed all her hosts overseas.

'Well, thank you very much for the tour. I expect you've got plenty to do back at your place, so we'll see you later for dinner?' Beryl said, as she sank down at one of the tables again.

'Yes indeed, I must dash, as you would say. The devil makes work for idle hands. I love the English idiom,' said Simone, waving a hand as she sauntered back towards her home.

'I thought she'd never go,' whispered Beryl to Rick.

'I know, a little bit of her goes a long way,' said Frank, over-hearing the heartfelt remark. 'Mind you, she makes a superb paella, I'll say that for her. I wonder what she'll give us tonight.'

'She's making coq au vin,' said Sid. 'I asked. It's a sort of chicken stew,' he added helpfully.

They sat in silence for a while, drinking in the peace of the marketplace. Only a couple of other customers were waiting to order, both elderly gentlemen, and they looked as if they had all day, settling back in their seats, battered straw hats half covering their faces. The village drowsed in the sunshine, and Rick thought how perfect this would all be if only Vee was with them. He was just about to get out his phone and text to tell her where they were so that she could meet the gang for lunch when she heard Beryl shout, 'Oi! Over here, Venetia.'

Rick looked up and saw Vee walking down the street towards them. Storming down it would be more accurate, he reflected as Vee kicked a stone that had the temerity to get in her way and came to a halt right in front of him.

'I need to go home,' she said, eyes blazing. 'And I need to go now.'

33

'Home, as in back to Simone's place?' said Rick, with a horrible feeling in his stomach that this wasn't what Vee meant at all.

'No, home as in Willowbrook. I've got to get back. Something's come up.'

Beryl stood up and came over to where Vee was standing. She looked up at the younger woman. 'What's upset you?' she asked. 'It's that Yolanda, isn't it? She always stirred things up when she visited your mum and dad. What's she been saying?'

'It doesn't matter what she's said, I must go now. How can I get back?' Vee turned to Rick. 'If you drive me to the nearest airport, I can get a flight today, I expect. I'd better go and pack.'

Rick stood up too. 'Look, I can understand you want to act fast for some reason but let's talk about this,' he said as gently as he could. 'Come back to the pension with me and you can maybe fill me in on what's bothering you?'

After an initial protest, Vee reluctantly agreed to go with Rick. By now the rest of the party were looking anxious, but a girl with a notepad coming to take orders distracted them enough for Rick and Vee to escape. They hurried back down the street. As they passed the bakery, Rick could see that it was about to close for lunch, so he told Vee to wait and rushed in, just in time to buy a box of delicious-looking cakes.

Vee was pacing up and down outside the shop and raised her eyebrows at him as he came back out. 'It's no good looking at me like that,' he said. 'We're missing lunch, and I can't listen on an empty stomach.'

They reached base and Rick tapped the code into the keypad. The heavy door swung open with a creak, and he peered inside. Would Simone be hovering? The last thing they needed were questions about why they weren't having lunch in the café, but the house was mercifully quiet.

'She must still be out, or having a siesta,' Vee said. 'Let's go up to my room before she comes back.'

They tiptoed up the stairs. Rick's mind was in turmoil. He couldn't imagine what Yolanda could have said that was serious enough to provoke this dramatic reaction. Once safely in her bedroom with the door closed, Vee flopped down on the bed and leaned against the pillows. She closed her eyes. Rick thought it seemed a bit formal to sit on one of the easy chairs at the far side of the room, so he perched on the end of the bed, as far away as possible from Vee.

'Come on then, what's up?' he said, when she still hadn't spoken after a couple of minutes. 'It must be something pretty drastic to make you want to leave here.'

She still didn't answer so Rick undid the string on the box of cakes and held it out. 'Open your eyes and eat something, Vee,' he said. 'Nothing ever seems as bad after a chocolate éclair, that's my motto.'

At last Vee stirred. She sat up and made herself more upright on the pillows. 'Did you say *chocolate éclair*?' she asked hopefully, peering into the box. 'I'm starving. Being angry always makes me hungry.'

They ate in silence. Rick proffered the box again and they both took a meringue. 'That's better,' said Vee. 'Thank you for getting those. I was beginning to think I was losing my marbles but the sugar rush has helped.'

'Are you ready to tell me what's got you in this state?'

Vee licked her fingers to get rid of the last of the sugar. 'Yes, if you don't mind me wittering at you for ages. It'd be good to get it off my chest.'

Rick stood up. 'Let's go and sit over there,' he said, pointing to the chairs. 'I'd rather be comfortable if this is going to take a while. There's no rush. The others won't be back for a long time yet and I can't hear Simone crashing about. So, go for it.'

They settled themselves in the easy chairs which both had a beautiful view of the sparkling pool. The garden looked tempting, but Rick didn't want to risk suggesting they went outside. This seemed as if it was going to be a very private conversation.

'I'll make it as short as possible,' said Vee. 'This part of my story really starts about twenty years after my family left Willowbrook. I was in my mid-thirties and I felt as if my life was over. I know that sounds dramatic, but I'm trying to be honest.'

Rick nodded but said nothing. Vee's face was pale now and she was twisting her hands together.

'It was a while since I'd finished a run of minor acting roles, and I had a call from my agent who seemed to think I was washed up. Nothing else was forthcoming. The next day, my then-boyfriend told me he'd been sleeping with our divorced next-door neighbour, Cleo, who was in her late forties. We'd been together for ten years at that time and I thought the sun shone out of his backside. He'd been babysitting for Cleo rather a lot.

We had never wanted children, or so I thought. Anyway, he moved in with her and her four kids. I was devastated.'

'That's awful,' said Rick, longing to give her a hug but not wanting to stop the flow. 'Carry on.'

'Around that time, my younger sister Cassie, who lives in America – well, in Boston to be precise – was on the point of going into a civil partnership with her long-time girlfriend, Marissa. In a nutshell, I went over there to be with them on the big day and decided to stay on for a holiday. While I was there, it came out that they were desperate for a baby, but neither could carry one. I had a *what the hell* moment and offered to be their surrogate.'

'Bloody hell, Vee,' said Rick. 'That's a heck of a favour, even for a sister.'

'I know. I won't go into the details but a friend of theirs offered to be the donor and I got pregnant straight away. He's out of the picture now, by the way, but my son...'

Vee choked over the last two words and her eyes filled with tears. Rick reached out and took her hand. Her fingers linked with his and she sniffed hard.

'I don't usually call him that,' she said. 'He knows he's adopted but not who his birth mother is. Until now, that is. As far as he was concerned, I'm his aunt. He's almost twenty-one.'

Vee reached into her back pocket for her phone and scrolled through a few pictures. She held it out to Rick. 'This is the latest one they sent me of Finn,' she said, leaning back in her chair and watching him carefully as he took the phone from her and looked down at it. He saw a laughing young man, with short dark hair and brown skin. He was wearing running clothes and looked as if he was pausing to share a joke with whoever was taking the picture, but probably about to take off at a gallop.

'Finn's father was originally from Mauritius,' Vee said. 'He went back there soon after Finn was conceived. He was never going to be part of Finn's life, that was part of the deal. He was just a very kind person who wanted to help his friends. I've seen Finn a few times, but I don't know him well. That was also part of the deal. Cassie and Marissa have always said they would tell Finn the truth about his history one day, when he was older, but I think they're afraid.'

'Afraid he'll want to get to know you as his mother rather than his aunt?'

'Yes. And now, thanks to Yolanda and her meddling, that's exactly what's about to happen.'

Rick stared at Vee. Her eyes were blazing now, and she was sitting forward in her chair. 'Go on. Tell me what happened this morning,' he said.

Vee took a deep breath. 'It turns out that Yolanda knew about this all along. She disapproved strongly of me having a baby that I wasn't going to look after and nurture myself and also of the fact that they have never told Finn I'm his mother. Her view is that all children ought to be given the opportunity to be brought up by their natural parents unless there's a very good reason why that can't or shouldn't happen. I don't know why her feelings are so extreme. I felt that to have Cassie and Marissa as parents would be perfect for Finn. They're such warm, lovely people. It wasn't easy, Rick. I didn't do it lightly, but he's had a great life so far in Boston. He's fit and healthy and he's made my sister and my sister-in-law so very happy. He doesn't need yet another mum.'

'You don't have to justify yourself to me,' said Rick, soothingly. 'I think it was an amazing thing to do. But what has Yolanda done?'

'Apparently she's been in touch with Finn all along, and when she heard that I was coming to visit, she decided to pre-empt discussing the situation with me and go ahead and tell Finn about the story of his birth. Not only that, but she said he ought to come to England to see me as soon as possible.'

Rick found himself speechless. He tried hard to think of something useful to say but his mind was full of the outrageous liberty this elderly lady had taken, even if she'd meant well by it.

'And, Rick, he's coming over. Finn's actually going to be in Willowbrook next week. He knows all about me. My sister's furious. I had a call from her just before I left Yolanda's. She seems to be blaming me for stirring things up by coming here. I want to go home. I can't see Yolanda any more, I can't bear to be near her.'

Vee stood up abruptly and pushed open the long windows, letting in a warm breeze. For a terrifying moment, Rick thought she was about to jump out. He jumped to his feet but instead of moving closer to the window, she turned to look at him.

'You can see why I need to leave, can't you?' she asked. 'I can't settle here with all this going on, and I have to go and get ready for him arriving.'

Down below them on the patio, Rick could hear the rest of the party arriving back from lunch. They were laughing at Sid, who was still singing about leaning on a lamppost. Simone must have been in the kitchen, because she called out, 'It sounds as if you have all had a very jolly lunch.'

'Oh, yes, it was delicious, darling,' Anthea answered. 'We liked it so much in your little café that we've booked a table for tomorrow and the next day too, to make sure we don't miss out.'

'I'm going to have a dip in the pool now,' said Winnie. 'I'm going to try and teach Sid the basics of breaststroke, in case he decides to pull another stunt like the last one.'

Rick put his hands on Vee's shoulders, and she looked up at him. 'I can't let you go home on your own when you're this upset. And can you bear to tear this lot away from their holiday before

they're ready?' he said. 'Also, you'll miss the delightful prospect of
the ukulele band.'

Vee gazed at him in amazement and then laughed. Rick began
to relax at last. She still had her sense of humour, thank
goodness.

'You can hear how much fun they're having,' he said, pressing
home his point. 'Another three days won't make a difference,
surely. Your house can be made visitor ready as soon as we get
back. I'll help. And you'll have to talk to Yolanda sometime.'

'Oh, will I?' said Vee, through gritted teeth.

'Yes, and it'll be much worse if you leave it like this, with both
of you convinced you're right. If you run away now, the gap will be
so wide that you probably won't see her again. She is in her eighties, Vee. Think about it.'

Throwing caution to the winds, Rick pulled Vee close and slid
his arms around her. She stiffened, but then relaxed against him,
burying her head in his shoulder and starting to sob. He could
feel her whole body shaking as she let out years of pent-up
tension and grief. This was getting to be a habit, he thought
ruefully. Her arms went round his waist as if of their own accord
and she clung to him. After a while, the shuddering sobs lessened
and Vee let go of Rick, disentangling herself from his embrace.

She disappeared into the bathroom, and he heard water
splashing into the sink as she washed her face. When she came
out again, there was colour in her cheeks, and she was trying to
smile.

'I don't like admitting it, but you're right,' she said. 'I don't
really want to travel back on my own. I can't make them go home
early when they're having such a good time and I will have to see
Yolanda again before we leave. There have been too many secrets
in the past. At least now everything's out in the open. But... oh,
Rick, how am I going to face my son? I've never tried to play a

bigger part in his life other than as a distant aunt. I was afraid of getting too close to him because it didn't seem right to build a stronger bond when I'd made the decision to give him to my sister. He must think I didn't care about him now he knows the truth about his birth.'

'Well, this is your chance to show him just how much you *did* care,' said Rick. 'You gave Finn the chance of a different kind of life with two people who must love him very much. That's a fantastic thing to do. He'll understand, I'm sure of it.'

Vee took a long, shuddering breath. She was still hiccupping slightly even though the storm of crying had abated. 'I hope you're right. And as I said, it'll be good to have no secrets any more.'

Rick didn't answer. He was happy beyond measure that he'd been able to comfort her, but the last statement had been like a punch in the stomach. Yolanda had held on to her information for years before deciding to share it but there was still one more secret from his own and Vee's past that she was bound to know. The question was, how long would it be before the temptation to share it became too much for her?

34

The next three days passed much too quickly for Beryl's liking. She could easily have stayed another week if she'd had the choice, partly due to her affection for the village and the pension and also, if she was honest, because going home would mean telling everyone the news about her engagement.

Beryl wasn't in the least ashamed of her decision to marry Frank but the thought of people congratulating her in public and then privately having a good laugh at two people of their age getting together was making her edgy. She tried hard to reassure herself that Anthea, Maurice and Frank didn't seem to have any problem with all this, but the vaguely uncomfortable feeling refused to go away.

It was strange that Yolanda didn't come to see the group after that first welcome, but Simone more than made up for it. She organised a trip to a local vineyard one day and a chateau the next, which kept everyone amused. However, on the third day, Beryl knew that she needed to find Yolanda. Never a day had gone by since Patrick's death without her thinking of him, and there were still unanswered questions about his life in Willowbrook as a teenager. In Beryl's opinion, Yolanda was the only possible person who might be able to answer them.

The other problem was Vee. Ever since she'd made that startling demand for them all to go home early, there had been a distinct lack of communication between Vee and the rest of them. She'd grudgingly agreed to come on the trips with the others after expressing a preference to stay behind at the pension by herself. Rick hadn't let her get away with that one, thought Beryl approvingly. He'd insisted Vee shouldn't opt out of Simone's entertainment, and to give the girl her due she'd thrown herself into the visits fairly enthusiastically once they were underway.

The subject of why Vee had suddenly wanted to go home was skirted around, with the only rather vague explanation being that she'd had a message that a family visit was on the cards, and she needed to get her house ready. Beryl had been suspicious of that one right from the start. As far as she was aware, the house next door to hers was as ready as it would ever be. Who could the mysterious visitor or visitors be? There was clearly more to this than met the eye.

'What is everyone planning for the last full day of your little holiday?' Simone asked as she provided fresh croissants and bread that morning. 'I suggest another gentle walk around the village, lunch at the café and then a long siesta. Remember that tonight is the ukulele festival evening in the square. It's organised by your aunt, Venetia, so it will be excellent. I know how much you all enjoyed the singing.'

A chorus of approval met this reminder. 'I'm going to have another swimming lesson with Winnie before we go for a walk,' said Sid. 'I nearly managed a width yesterday.'

'You're doing splendidly,' said Winnie, squeezing his hand.

Beryl looked over her sunglasses at Winnie. She was getting very touchy-feely these days. 'Are you up for a walk with me,

Frank?' she asked. Frank said he'd be delighted to accompany her. 'And what about the rest of you?' Beryl added.

Rick said that he'd promised Simone to do a few odd jobs around the house before they left so he'd better get on with that. 'Want to help me, Vee?' he asked.

Vee opened her mouth to reply but Simone got in first. 'Oh, I'm sure we can manage perfectly well, *cherie*,' she said sweetly. 'You enjoy your relaxation. Maybe you'll be wanting to go and say goodbye to your aunt?'

There was no answer to this from Vee. Anthea suggested that they should invite Yolanda for lunch with them, but Vee said that she expected her aunt would be busy getting everything ready for the evening's entertainment. They carried on with their breakfast, and Beryl thanked whatever guardian angel was looking after her for making sure her false teeth had withstood the efforts of biting into the crusty baguettes every day. It would be back to soft brown bread when she got home, but for now, this was heaven. She took another dollop of apricot jam and beamed round at everyone.

'This road trip has been my best excursion ever,' she said, through a mouthful of bread. 'And that's saying something, because we've been on a fair few trips together, haven't we, ladies?'

The other two Saga Louts nodded their agreement, both too busy munching on pains au chocolat to answer.

Frank cleared his throat and stood up. 'I have something to ask you three,' he said to Beryl. 'Well, we all have. Us blokes, I mean.'

'Go on then,' said Beryl, intrigued. 'Let's have it.'

'I... we... were wondering if you would consider extending the Saga Louts trio to include three more, plus Rick and Vee, of course, if they're up for it. We've been thinking that we make such a good team that it's a shame not to keep it going. For holidays and such, I mean. We wouldn't try and muscle in on your regular film nights and so on.'

'No, you'd better not do that,' chipped in Anthea, frowning at him. 'Our film nights are sacred.'

'But for jaunts around the country and abroad, wouldn't it be good to have some extra company? We'd assist with carrying bags and ordering taxis and... and so on... wouldn't we?' Frank's voice petered out and he glanced at Maurice and Sid for support, but they were both looking down at their plates.

'We don't actually need any help,' said Winnie. 'We've coped perfectly well for this long.'

Beryl regarded her two friends thoughtfully. There was doubt on their faces, but the men were looking so downcast by now that she felt she had to take pity on them. 'We could give it a try when we plan the next city break. Barcelona, didn't we suggest?' she said to Anthea and Winnie. 'On the understanding that if it doesn't work out, we're not obliged to do it again?'

The other ladies looked at each other and then back to Beryl. 'I'm happy with that,' said Winnie. 'Anthea?'

'So long as I still get the window seat on the plane, I'm in,' said Anthea, grinning at Maurice. 'And no single beds if we're sharing.'

Maurice was very pink in the face by this time, but he led the whoops of delight from the men. 'What about Rick and Vee?' he said, when the excitement had died down a little. 'Do you fancy another jolly with us oldies or does that fill you with a deep sense of dread?'

Rick smiled at Vee. 'Depending on work commitments, I'm up for any kind of holiday with you lot, although I need to keep some time free in case I get a chance to visit my sons in Germany. It's... not easy with all their new commitments,' he said. 'Also, I think Vee might need a bit of settling-in time getting used to her new home before she takes any more trips?'

Beryl winced. It wasn't right for him to answer for Vee, surely, but she was looking at him with more gratitude than annoyance. 'Maybe the one after,' she said. 'Providing you don't strangle each other in Barcelona. It's lovely of you to ask though.'

With breakfast cleared away, everyone began to prepare for a more relaxing day. Beryl took Frank to one side. 'I *will* be going for a walk later,' she said. 'That much is true. But there's something I need to do first. How about you wait for me here and I'll be back as soon as I can?'

Frank looked mystified but he agreed readily enough. 'I've got a very good thriller on the go,' he said. 'I'll find a comfortable spot in the sun and be ready whenever you are.' He bent to kiss her cheek. Beryl thought, not for the first time, what a very kind man he was and how glad she was that she was going to be marrying him. *That was definitely one of my better decisions*, she told herself with a smile, and it was nobody's business but theirs. Time to stop wondering how the news would be received and begin to revel in the joy of being treasured again. Beryl went up to her room to tidy up and collect her sun hat, then quickly took the stairs down to the hallway and out of the front door before anyone could spot her and ask where she was going or offer to join her.

Out in the street, Beryl heaved a sigh of relief. She loved her friends, but this was one mission she needed to take alone. Then it occurred to her that she'd forgotten to ask Vee where Yolanda lived. To go back inside would probably involve answering questions as to why she wanted to know this, so she decided to take matters into her own hands. She headed for the square and found the café already open for business and the young waiter wiping tables ready for the morning coffee rush, if you could call it that in such a peaceful village.

'*Bonjour*,' she said to him, with as much confidence as she could muster, trying to dredge up a bit of creaky schoolgirl French. '*Ou est Madame Yolanda, mon amie?*'

He looked at her in bewilderment for a moment but then his expression cleared. '*Ah, oui. Madame Yolanda. Elle est...*'

After this came a long description in rapid French which involved many gestures towards the other end of the village. Sensing Beryl's confusion, he seized her by the arm and began to tow her up the street, talking all the time. When they reached the bend in the road, he paused and said very slowly, as if to a small child, '*A droit, et encore a droit.*'

Very pleased with himself, he performed a few more dramatic pointing actions and waved Beryl on her way with a merry '*bon chance*' as he left her.

Beryl called out her thanks and carried on walking until she met an opening between the houses heading right. She sincerely hoped that was what he'd meant as she picked her way over the grassy humps in the middle of the narrow lane. When she saw another turning and spied a tiny cottage under a sheltering bower of trees, she had a hunch she'd found the right place. Sure enough, at a table outside the door sat Yolanda with a large bowl and a chopping board in front of her. She was concentrating hard on her task which, Beryl realised as she approached, was the cutting up of a very large amount of apples. Hearing the snap of a twig underfoot as Beryl came closer, Yolanda looked up.

'Oh, hello, Beryl,' she said. 'I wondered when you'd turn up. I've been expecting you.'

'You sound like a Bond villain,' said Beryl, somewhat nettled at this lukewarm welcome. 'Shouldn't you have a cat on your knee?'

Yolanda gave a bark of laughter. 'My cat's out doing what she's meant to do; catching rats,' she said. 'Come and sit down. I'd make coffee but I need to get these done. I'm making a load of apple tarts for tonight and I'm behind with my jobs.'

'Want a hand?' Beryl said. It might be easier to broach the subject on her mind if they were both busy doing something mundane as they talked.

Yolanda got to her feet without another word and made her way inside, stumbling slightly on the uneven flagstones. Beryl thought it looked as if Yolanda's sandals were on their last legs and was thankful for her own sensible shoes, bought especially for walking and well broken in before they'd started their holiday.

The other woman was soon back, carrying an extra board and a sharp knife. She pulled out the only other chair for Beryl, who sat down and prepared to make herself useful. 'I'll peel and you chop,' Yolanda said. They worked in silence for a few minutes. It was very peaceful in the garden. The sound of the bees humming away as they flitted from flower to flower was timeless, and Beryl's mind wandered back to her childhood when she'd often sat in a cottage garden very like this one, giving her grandmother a hand to prepare fruit and vegetables.

'So, I expect you'll be wanting to dig up the past?' said Yolanda, still peeling apples neatly and placing them in a bowl of water between them, ready for Beryl to do her bit. 'There's been quite a bit of that in the last couple of days. I must say it's about time.'

'I suppose it is,' said Beryl. 'And you know all about burying your painful memories, don't you?'

'What's that supposed to mean?'

Beryl shrugged. 'Maybe that's a conversation for another time.

I've got more pressing things to discuss with you today. Although now I'm here, I hardly know where to begin.'

Yolanda smiled, although there was an underlying hint of sadness there. 'Start with what's in your heart,' she said.

The years rolled away as Beryl let her mind wander to the painful days when she'd realised that her beautiful son was gradually slipping away from her. Patrick had always been so sunshiny as a little boy, but his teen years seemed to bring him nothing but trouble. The culmination of all the stress had been during that fateful summer of 1985, when he'd tried so hard to be one of the cool gang, but had only succeeded in isolating himself even more.

'I guess what I want to know is whether your niece... whether Venetia had anything to do with the way my Patrick suffered at school,' Beryl said, getting the words out with difficulty.

'Have you asked her that question?' Yolanda's voice was stern now. Beryl pulled a face and shook her head.

'Is there any point? She's bound to deny all knowledge of what went on.'

'You mean with the fire in the churchyard and what happened afterwards?'

Beryl bit her lip. The night of the fire held one of her worst memories of that summer. Patrick had come home smelling of ash and cinders, tearing through the house and straight into the bathroom. She'd heard the bathwater running but had not understood at the time. When the police came calling the next morning, Patrick had been in bed with what he'd said was a bad migraine. He'd always suffered from these so Beryl had no compunction in telling the two officers that he was too ill to be disturbed. To her everlasting shame, she'd lied for Patrick, saying he'd been at home with her all the previous evening, as he wasn't well.

She took a deep breath and relayed this information to Yolanda, then braced herself for a scalding response. Instead, she was met with what felt like a sympathetic silence. Taking courage, Beryl carried on.

'I've always wondered if he set the fire himself,' she said. 'I thought it was probably a dare. And I decided that the classmates who dared him to do it were most likely to be that Rhonda' – she spat the name out with venom – 'and... Venetia. Patrick was always trying to impress those two. I think they made him very unhappy with their teasing. It was the start of his... mental health issues.'

Beryl had never used those terms in relation to her son before this, even in her head. She raised her eyes to meet Yolanda's gaze. There was a short silence. Then Yolanda cleared her throat. 'I think we both know that's not the case,' she said gently.

35

By the time evening came and a very fine cassoulet had been eaten, accompanied by the usual copious amounts of wine, everyone was in the mood for a party. Simone beamed round at her guests. They'd all made a special effort with their remaining clean clothes and looked very smart.

'We'll go along to the square in ten minutes,' she said. 'You don't want to miss the start of the performance.'

'What are these musical events like? Tell us honestly, darling,' said Anthea. 'Will it be embarrassingly awful even for the strange ones of this party who say they love a bit of ukulele music?'

Simone drew herself up to her full height. 'Awful? Why would it be anything but *magnifique*?' she said. 'People come from miles around to enjoy our music. We are famous in the region and beyond.'

Anthea had the grace to look mortified, which was never her default mode, thought Vee, exchanging glances with Rick. He widened his eyes at her and she grinned. 'I'm really looking forward to it,' he said. 'Come on, let's help Simone to finish clearing the table and we can get going.'

By the time the group reached the market square, the regular tables were all full and several men were putting out extra chairs. Yolanda was everywhere, it seemed, organising the seating, keeping an eye on the food preparation and making sure the musicians, who were tuning up, all had drinks in front of them. Vee decided to keep out of her aunt's way for now, but was well aware that at some point in the evening she'd need to make her peace with Yolanda. Since her outburst of white-hot fury of the other day, she'd had plenty of time to think. She was by no means settled in her mind about Finn's forthcoming visit but she was beginning to see that her aunt had a point, even if she still thought the interference was way out of order.

A burst of clapping heralded the mayor getting to his feet and making what sounded like a fulsome introduction to the musicians, and without further ado, they swung into their first piece. It was a toe-tapping number which the locals appeared to know well, and soon a few dancers were on their feet, resulting in another round of applause from the audience.

'I reckon most of them have been pre-loading, like us with all that wine,' said Rick. Vee noticed that he'd switched to water now, as he'd promised to take the first stint of driving on their homeward journey the following day. There were a lot of miles to cover, so they'd decided to make an overnight stop in Chartres, after which Vee would take over for the next part. The thought of getting home to Dragonfly Cottage was heartwarming but the prospect of what was to come next overshadowed this feeling. She reached for her wine glass and took a hefty sip, just as Yolanda tapped her on the shoulder, causing Vee to splutter.

'Choke up, chicken,' said Yolanda, patting Vee on the back and taking her back in time to a scary experience at one of her mother's birthday picnics when, desperate to eat more cake than her sister, Vee had got a glacé cherry stuck in her throat and

Yolanda had needed to step in to dislodge it. A slap on the back had done the trick and the cuddle afterwards had made Vee realise how much she loved her aunt.

'Thanks,' Vee gasped, reaching for Rick's water glass and taking a large gulp. 'You made me jump.'

'Sorry. I wanted to grab a quick word while the musicians are doing their thing,' said Yolanda. 'When they take a break I'll be busy again and by the time this is done, I'll be on my knees. Come with me.'

It was an order rather than a request. Vee followed the older lady to a bench under a tree, far enough away from the action for them to be able to hear themselves think. They sat down together, and Yolanda turned to her niece.

'I want to say how sorry I am for muscling in on your life,' she said. Vee opened her mouth to speak but Yolanda raised a hand. 'No, let me finish. I need you to understand what made me act in what must seem a very high-handed way.'

Yolanda paused for breath and instinctively Vee reached out and took her by the hand. The warmth of their entwined fingers was another blast from the past. They'd often walked hand in hand when her aunt had taken her to school on one of her many extended visits to Willowbrook.

'It's like this,' Yolanda said. 'When I was fifteen, I had a baby boy.'

There was a shocked silence as Vee digested this news. Before she could say anything, her aunt was speaking again.

'Mine and your mum's parents were very strict, but I think if I'd made more of an effort, I could have persuaded them to let me keep my son. As it was, I didn't want to be a mother. My much older boyfriend wasn't interested in me any more. I was desolate. I just wanted the whole affair to be over. The baby was adopted and I have never seen him since. I assume he didn't want to meet me because I know it's possible to trace your birth parents these days. I'd come to terms with that. Or I thought I had, until you had your baby.'

Vee squeezed her aunt's hand and tried to think what to say. Eventually she managed to croak, 'So that's why you're so keen for Finn to know I'm his mum? Although as far as I'm concerned, Cassie and Marissa are the only ones with the right to be called that.'

'Yes, that's why I stepped in, feet first,' said Yolanda with a wry smile. 'Vee, I'm so very sorry for what I did, in telling Finn the truth. I was wrong to meddle in your life, but I still think good will come of it. I hope you can forgive me.'

Vee thought for a moment. This new revelation had shaken her to the core. The trauma her aunt had gone through at such a young age with no support from the father of the child made her want to rage against the unfairness of it all. An idea came to her and she turned to face Yolanda, catching hold of her other hand.

'Why don't you come home with us tomorrow? We can get you put on our ferry ticket. Come and see Finn too. I'm sure he'd love it! And so would I,' she added, with honesty, knowing that having Yolanda with her would make the whole situation a lot less stressful.

Her aunt shook her head. 'I would love to, my pet, but my passport ran out years ago and I didn't renew it because I couldn't see when I'd ever need it again. I was angry with you for giving up your child so easily and livid with your mother and father for supporting you. I've made a new life here and I'm happy enough with it.'

'But could you get a new passport? Come and see me later? Would it be too much?' Vee asked. A longing for Yolanda to see what she'd done with her old home and to have a chance to really talk to her was intense.

'I... might. Yes, I think I might just do that. I could fly from Bergerac or Bordeaux.' Yolanda clapped her hands. 'I'll do it, so long as I can find someone to look after Ferdinand and the chickens. And the sooner the better. None of us are getting any younger. That's a foolish saying but true, unfortunately.'

They sat together quietly for a few more minutes until the end of a song and a louder than usual burst of applause signified the end of the first half of the entertainment.

'I must go and supervise the refreshments,' said Yolanda, getting to her feet rather stiffly. 'Come on, you must be ready for a drink by now, after all this soul-searching.'

Vee stood up too. She felt as exhausted as if she'd just finished a long run, but somehow more peaceful. The thought of the approaching meeting with Finn was still daunting and the prospect of a visit from her aunt wasn't nearly as cheering as it would have been before Yolanda's surprise revelation. Still, there was no knowing how many more chances there would be for family get-togethers, so she put her reservations firmly on one side for the time being.

'I'm sad to be leaving you and this lovely place,' Vee said, impulsively hugging Yolanda, who almost fell over but rallied and hugged Vee back. 'I'm really glad I didn't manage to drag the others home early.'

'I think you'd have had your work cut out there,' said Yolanda. She pointed to the square, where Maurice and Anthea were performing an impromptu tango to the piped music now coming from the speakers, and Winnie and Sid were doing something that looked between a Morris dance and an Irish jig. 'Your friends are party animals, that's for sure. And I think you'd be wise to detach that young man of yours from the clutches of the fearsome Simone before she eats him alive.'

'Rick's not my young man,' Vee protested, but as she walked

towards the hubbub of happy merrymakers and saw Simone snake an arm around Rick's waist to pull him into a passionate smooch of a dance, she felt a red mist descending. How dared the woman?

'Of course he isn't,' said Yolanda. 'Even so, off you pop and claim him back. He's turned out rather well, has Ricardo. I had my doubts about him at one time. And on that subject, I think you still have a few things to talk to him about, regarding... well, I'll leave that to you to find out.'

Yolanda had disappeared into the crowd before Vee had time to ask her to elaborate. She watched Simone drape herself more comfortably around Rick as they swayed together to the music. He had his back to her so Vee couldn't see his expression, but Simone looked like the cat who'd got the cream, to coin one of Yolanda's own phrases. As she made her way towards them, Vee seethed. From a brief period of calm, she was suddenly in a turmoil of unwanted jealousy. Not only that, there was now the unwelcome feeling that she would have to find out more about Rick's involvement in the events of 1985.

'Thanks, Yolanda,' Vee muttered to herself. 'You've really excelled yourself this time.'

36

The journey home felt very long but was uneventful, on the whole. After their wild night out, the older members of the party were noticeably bleary. They ate their breakfast quietly, and after an emotional goodbye, tearful on Simone's part, they were on their way. Yolanda came to wave them off but left abruptly. Vee could see her broad figure disappearing up the road even as they drove away.

Vee sat at the front with Rick, passing him humbugs or chewy sweets every now and again to keep him alert, but the others all dozed on and off, waking only for comfort stops and then nodding off again, propped against each other. Sid snored gently and Frank gave the odd snort, but otherwise all was peaceful in the back of the minibus. When they began to see signs for Chartres, Rick looked across at Vee.

'How are you feeling, energy-wise?' he said.

'I'm okay, why?'

He looked over his shoulder at the others. 'I'm guessing this lot are going to take some rousing if we stop here and they won't be up for sightseeing today. Do you reckon we could just carry on? Simone gave us packed lunches. We could have a picnic stop and you could take over the wheel if you want to press on home?'

Vee thought about this. The idea of being in her own bed a day sooner was enticing and there were plenty of jobs around the house she'd like to get done before... her stomach lurched... before Finn arrived. 'What about the ferry booking though?' she asked, playing for time.

'We can easily phone ahead and change it,' Rick said. 'I don't feel like having another hotel stop, do you? Rummaging in my dirty laundry for something presentable enough to wear for dinner isn't that tempting. Only if you're up for it though. Are you tired?'

Vee was surprised to find she wasn't. 'Let's do it. Should we rouse them to ask them what they think?' she said, turning round to observe her fellow passengers. Frank gave a loud snort at this point and almost woke himself up but nobody else stirred.

'On second thoughts, let's just go for it,' she said. 'We're all holidayed out. Calais, here we come!'

A couple of brief stops and many miles later saw the minibus rolling into the parking area of their homeward ferry. By now the others were awake and hungry. They all seemed delighted at the prospect of having a proper cup of tea in their own houses sooner rather than later and headed for the restaurant, happily discussing their favourite brands of teabags and biscuits.

The restaurant was busy and Vee and Rick had to sit at a table a short distance from the others. 'Phew,' said Rick, after they'd demolished their soup and rolls. 'It's nice to be on our own for a little while. I love them all, but I sometimes feel like a frazzled hen with a lot of chicks. Do you want to discuss teabags, or have you got something more pressing to say? I noticed you looking at me in a funny kind of way this morning. What's up?'

Vee swallowed hard. Was this the moment of truth?

'I was talking to Yolanda,' she said. 'Or rather, she was advising me to ask you a few more questions. I think she meant about the things that happened around the time of the fire and the school camping trip.'

'Really?' Rick busied himself with opening sugar sachets and stirring the contents into his coffee. 'I don't usually take sugar,' he said. 'But I think we need extra energy today.'

'Don't change the subject,' said Vee. 'Yolanda's worried about Beryl. Nobody was ever clear about who set the fire going in the churchyard and I think Beryl has spent years secretly worrying that it was Patrick. Or worse still, actually knowing it was him. I've been getting the feeling for a while that she imagines I was part of some sort of conspiracy to be cruel to him.'

'And were you?'

Vee hesitated. It was time to be completely honest. 'We were all irritated by him and we weren't always very patient, were we?' she said at last. 'Rhonda was the worst. I'm not trying to dodge the blame. I teased him too sometimes but he... wasn't a kind boy.'

'Patrick was a nasty piece of work, let's not mince words,' said Rick. 'He was the kind of kid who liked to get everyone else into trouble. He was mean to the younger ones at school, and he was rude to the teachers. Beryl must know that, surely?'

'She doesn't want to know it,' said Vee. 'Rick, did you dare Patrick to torch that old shed? I was there earlier in the evening, but I left before it started. I know you were there too. I saw you.'

Rick drank some coffee and pulled a face. 'Ah, *that's* why I don't take sugar,' he said. 'Okay, sorry, I'm prevaricating again. I get that you want answers but how is this going to help Beryl? If you must know, it was Rhonda who dared Patrick to start the fire, and she got him the paraffin and matches from her grandad's allotment. I tried to stop him, but he wasn't listening. He had a kind of wild look in his eyes. I saw him drop the match on the trail of paraffin and I ran to phone the fire brigade. I didn't give my name. Then I legged it home and climbed in the back window.'

Vee stared at Rick. 'You didn't go back to check everyone was out of the way of the fire? And you've never told anybody about this?'

'No. I'm not proud of myself, but we were fifteen. Our brains were wired up differently then. And I'm not about to tell Beryl that it was her son who lit the match. What good will it do?'

They sat in silence for a while, as the babble of conversation around them reached a higher level of decibels than ever. A small child began to kick the back of Rick's chair and another set up a loud wailing right next to Vee's ear but neither of them reacted.

'I could be wrong, but I've got a feeling there's something else you're not telling me,' Vee said, when the pause in the conversation began to seem much too long.

Rick shrugged and looked away. Vee pressed on. 'Come on, let's have it. What are you afraid of?'

He sighed. 'Okay, if you insist. I knew I'd have to tell you sometime. As for what I'm afraid of, that's easy. You'll think I'm a complete git.'

'That's a risk you're going to have to take,' said Vee. She mentally braced herself. How bad could this get?

'I know I am. Oh, well, here goes. On that night on the school trip, just before we went out in the rain again... you know when I mean. The day after Patrick had caused all that fuss by falling into the lake.'

'Falling... or jumping. Yes. Go on.'

'Well, I overheard Patrick telling one of his slimy mates that he was really annoyed with you. He said he'd already given you the best part of his brandy stash because you weren't well. He reckoned his mum always recommended it for colds and so on. He muttered something about you having it in for him and he was going to make you pay for it, but I didn't know what that was all about. And... later, I heard shouting, but by the time I got to your tent he was heading you off into the darkness with Shazzie after him and you were rolling around on the floor. I knew you were probably drunk and I was angry with you. I didn't even try to stop him running away or go after him. Rhonda told me to, but I didn't. She was there by that time and she was looking after you, in her own way.'

Vee stared at him. 'You already knew before he attacked me that I was going to be... in danger?'

'No!' Rick's denial came quickly and was so loud that even the wailing child turned to look. 'I didn't think you were in any danger at all, because Patrick was always shouting his mouth off about something or other. He was well-known for overreacting, wasn't he?'

'So why didn't you go after him, Rick? And why were you so angry with me? It wasn't my fault that Patrick flipped that night.'

He didn't meet her eyes as he said, 'Because I was jealous, okay? I know it was stupid but I'd always kind of suspected that you'd been encouraging him, even though you moaned about him so much. I always had a thing for you, Vee. I hated him at that moment, and I was furious with you. You never looked at me. You never even noticed me because I was fat and spotty, with greasy hair. I was invisible in those days.'

'You... you liked me?'

'Yes. That's one word for it. Anyway, Rhonda took you to the teachers and Patrick and Shazzie kept well away from the rest of us when they finally came back to the tents. I wanted to say sorry to you for being an idiot and not warning you about what he'd said earlier, but by then you were being whisked off by your aunt.

I tried to tell her to give you a message, but she was in a rush to take you home. I was crying, Vee. What a drip. She must have guessed how I felt about you because ever since we got to France, she's given me suspicious looks.'

They locked eyes across the table as Rick finished speaking. Vee's mind was in a whirl. This was too much to handle now, and she needed time to digest it. Eventually she said, 'Thank you for telling me. I... can we just concentrate on what's happening now?'

'Fine by me.'

'So, what we need to do... somehow... is to give Beryl the impression that Patrick was completely innocent of everything she suspects and that I had nothing to do with making him unhappy. He did that all by himself.'

'Yup.' Rick closed his eyes for a moment. He looked unutterably weary after his confession. Vee felt a pang of sympathy for him but forced herself to focus on their next steps. She carried on, her voice growing stronger as she remembered more about that troubled and troublesome boy.

'Patrick was horrible even in the reception class. He put powder paint in the goldfish bowl so that it died, and he used to sneak into the cloakroom and wee on the other kids' pump bags. He snitched on his classmates whenever he had the chance. Patrick stole all the nicest things out of our lunchboxes and then blamed his best friend, Floyd. That's just the tip of the iceberg. He got worse as he got older. Beryl doesn't need to know all that though.'

'Nice,' said Rick, with a shudder. 'I get the picture. Beryl must have a strong idea of what he was like but she's blocking it out, naturally enough. So, it's up to me to repaint the past in a rosy glow, give Patrick a clean slate and make you look angelic?'

'That's about it,' said Vee. 'Meanwhile, I've got a long-lost son to bond with. I think you actually have the easier job, don't you?'

37

The brief time leading up to Finn's visit seemed to drag at one moment and fly by the next. Rick finished a few odd jobs in the house for Vee but didn't try to bring up the emotive subject they'd been discussing on the ferry, to her relief. There would be time for that when the visit was over. As the hours ticked away, Vee swung between being madly excited and more frightened than she'd ever been in her life. A series of furious face-to-face calls with her sister didn't help.

'But you promised not to do this to us!' Cassie screamed from Vee's phone. FaceTime had its place, but it wasn't great for soothing tempers, Vee thought, as she tried to pacify the woman on the other end of the line, who had ditched her usual cool and was wading in with all guns blazing.

'I didn't do it,' repeated Vee for the fourth time. 'It was Aunt Yolanda, and she had her reasons.'

'Reasons for disrupting our beloved son's whole world?'

With a pang, Vee registered that the use of the word *our* didn't include her. Of course Cassie and Marissa were unhappy, but they were Finn's mums and they were running scared.

'I'm never going to try and take Finn away from you,' she said, struggling to keep calm. 'He's bound to want to talk to me, now this is out in the open, but it probably would have happened at some point in the future, wouldn't it? Wasn't he always going to be curious about his parentage one day?'

'I don't agree,' said Cassie, slightly less loudly. 'Finn might never have bothered to find out, and now he's furious with Marissa and me for keeping the truth from him.'

'Oh, come on, get real. Finn's known he was adopted for years but you spun him some ridiculous story about his birth. At some point he'd have realised it didn't add up. Anyway, this argument's silly. He's going to be here in a couple of days. Don't worry, I won't keep him hostage.'

The bitterness in her own voice brought Vee up short. The few times she'd met Finn face to face, obviously as his aunt and not his mother, she'd loved him unconditionally. He was kind, funny and talented, a credit to his adoptive parents and maybe... just maybe... to the genes of his natural mother. She'd made sure to keep in touch, sending gifts and then money on birthdays and at Christmas, but hadn't once overstepped the mark. It had been hard at times not to blurt out the truth, but she'd made a deal with her sister and Marissa and she would never have gone back on her promise. Yolanda had forced the issue, and now the shock waves had died down, Vee was longing to see what her new relationship with Finn would be like, even though the thought of the changes in store for them were daunting. It was so important to get it right this time.

A couple more of these traumatic calls followed but eventually, Cassie began to get used to the idea that Finn was coming to England, although she was still very unhappy about it. Vee knew there was nothing she could do to make things better between them but the rift with her sister stung. The age gap between them had meant that growing up, they were never in anything like the same peer group at school, but later they'd forged an easy-going friendship that spanned the miles and suited them both. Now, the distance between them was larger than any ocean.

The day of Finn's arrival brought with it a touch of frost and a new chill in the air. Vee hoped he'd had the sense to pack warm clothes. The Indian summer that they'd enjoyed in France seemed a long time ago, and she shivered as she dressed in her favourite cords and a red sweater, lacing up her flowered Dr Martens in an attempt to feel braver. She heard a horn toot outside and looked out of the window to see Rick in his van. He waved to her and Vee grabbed a coat before rushing out to join him.

'You didn't have to do this,' she said. 'I could have booked a taxi to go and meet Finn.'

'Moral support,' was all he said, as he turned up the radio and let the music fill the cab and they both sang along with Duran Duran at the top of their lungs as Rick drove towards the airport.

'There, isn't that better?' Rick asked. 'You can't beat a good old blast of "Hungry Like the Wolf". The good thing about this van being a bit on the elderly side is that it's got a CD player. Take your pick.'

He indicated a messy heap of CD cases stuffed into the door pocket. Vee rummaged through them and pulled one out. 'This is going to make me emotional,' she said. 'But maybe it's better to get it over with now rather than drip tears all over Finn as soon as he gets here. I can't believe how much I've cried since I came to Willowbrook. Nothing for years and then a tidal wave.'

'You've been bottling it all up. What's the song?'

Vee pushed the CD into the slot and clicked through the tracks. 'This was a hit the year Finn was born. I played it over and over again. The words summed up everything I was feeling after he'd gone with Cassie and Marissa. I tried to make out that it was easy to give him up but it was hell on earth.'

The Backstreet Boys and 'Incomplete' now rang out, overwhelming Vee with the emotive lyrics that perfectly captured the love and longing she'd felt for the tiny, beautiful scrap of humanity that was her newborn son. Tears flowed down her cheeks and through them, she saw Rick rubbing his eyes with one hand as he negotiated a complicated roundabout.

'That's enough of being maudlin,' Vee said, clicking the CD out as the song ended. 'You need to give your attention to the motorway, or this journey will be over before it's properly begun. Here, let's have something upbeat. This one's from our school disco days.'

It was a compilation this time, a collection of cheesy songs that took Vee right back to those heady, unpredictable days of flirting, trying to be popular and wanting so much to fit in that it hurt. She led the singing as the CD began with 'Wake Me Up Before You Go-Go', and Rick was soon outdoing her in volume. As they pulled off the motorway after countless hold-ups and headed towards the airport junction, Vee began to feel as if this thing was possible. She was going to meet her son as his birth mother for the first time, and she was going to give it her very best shot.

Rick parked as close to the terminal as he could and got out to open the door for Vee. He pulled her into a hug and for a moment she let herself be overwhelmed by the now-familiar scent of his shower gel and warm Rick-ness. He let her go and stepped back.

'Good luck,' he said, smiling down at her. 'You've got this.'

'Aren't you... I mean, I thought you'd come in with me?' Vee said, glancing at her watch. 'He should be coming out very soon, I'll need to run.'

'This one's for you to do on your own. Off you go. I'll be here waiting.'

Vee turned to walk away and just as she was almost out of earshot, thought she heard him say, as if to himself, 'I've always been waiting for you.'

Startled, Vee made herself keep going. There was no time to check if she'd heard right. She began to jog towards the arrivals entrance, dodging families with small children coping with tantrums and tiredness and arriving just as the passengers from Boston began to trickle out into the open area. Vee tidied her hair and tried to slow her breathing, but her heart was pounding so hard that she couldn't stand still. She moved from foot to foot as she watched the stream of bleary people wandering out. Some spotted their lifts or welcoming parties immediately, others looked around as if stunned that they'd finally made it. One or two marched off smartly in search of taxis and buses. None of them were Finn.

Just as Vee was about to give up hope and go to find a help desk to send out a message, a tall young man with tousled hair strolled out, as if he had all the time in the world. He looked around and saw Vee standing alone in the middle of the arrivals area. His expression was unreadable as he came towards her, dumping his huge backpack on the floor.

'Hi, Aunty Vee,' he said. 'I mean... I guess I mean... Mom?'

38

Driving home, Vee found herself sandwiched between a person with very little to say and an older one who looked very uncomfortable. She'd tried to make general conversation to get the ball rolling without success. Both seemed determined to be strong, silent types.

Vee reflected on the emails that had passed between herself and Finn over the last week. They had mainly been a list of arrangements to do with flights, transfers and the time Finn was allowed to have away from work. They hadn't really touched on the reason for his visit, apart from a brief comment from Finn that the two of them had a lot to talk about and her own final sign-off last night when she'd said how she couldn't wait to see him. Too much? But she'd so wanted Finn to know how welcome he was, even if this meeting was probably happening at a time in his life when he'd thought his world was stable.

They reached the outskirts of Willowbrook and Finn perked up, listening attentively as Vee pointed out places that were significant in her and Cassie's past.

'There's our old school,' she said. 'And that's the park where we used to play.'

'Cool church,' Finn said, peering up at the steeple. 'And look at all those graves. Creepy. Are any of our family buried there?'

'Oh, yes, both your great-grandparents on my side and... and friends.' Vee thought about Patrick, in a grave on the far side of the churchyard, ironically not far from the site of the doomed shed. She shivered.

'Are you cold?' Finn asked. 'It's freezing here. My moms told me to bring layers. It's warmer this week in Boston.'

This was the longest sentence he'd spoken so far, and Vee smiled at him in relief. 'You'll get used to it,' she said. 'I've put the heating on at home so the house will be snug.'

Rick pulled up outside Dragonfly Cottage and switched off the engine. He turned to Vee and Finn. 'I'll leave you here,' he said. 'I'm off to do a job in Meadowthorpe. Good to meet you, Finn.'

They reached over Vee and shook hands before Finn opened the door and jumped down, reaching out to help Vee from the cab. Her legs were stiff from being in the van for a while and she swayed as she stepped out. Finn put a steadying arm around her, but it was only a brief connection, and he was soon swinging his rucksack onto his shoulder and following Vee inside.

As she'd anticipated, the warmth from the radiators had turned the living room from the chilly place of that morning into a much cosier one. Vee's charity shop sofa was now covered in a colourful patchwork throw and although she'd argued with Rick about the wisdom of covering up the floorboards with carpet, she had to admit that the room would be chilly without it. He'd said that the old boards were too uneven and damaged to sand and stain successfully, and he'd been right.

'This is neat,' said Finn. 'A real country cottage, like on the shows the moms sometimes watch. Hercules somebody.'

'Hercule Poirot?'

'Yeah, that's the dude. I like it. Great pictures.'

They both looked round the walls, and Vee saw with fresh eyes the eclectic selection of paintings and old mirrors she'd gleaned from the local charity shops. Also, she'd relied on Maryam and Rashid's Treasure Trove table for additional bits and bobs to add colour and style. It was the place where villagers left their unwanted possessions and were free to take whatever they liked from the table in return. The previous guardian of the shop, Ingrid, had started the trend when she was divesting herself of a lifetime of unwanted belongings left to her by her husband and Maryam had loved the idea so much that she'd kept it going. Vee had collected a huge bottle-green plant pot only yesterday and it graced the coffee table that Rick had knocked up using old pallets found at the tip. The pot held a chrysanthemum plant, the glorious yellow one that had travelled all the way through France and back home with them. The others had donated it to Vee as a housewarming gift, saying that there would be no connotations of honouring the dead when it reached England. 'It'll remind you of the fun we had instead,' Sid said as he presented it to her.

'Did you do all this yourself?' Finn asked. 'My mom – Cassie, I mean – said this place was a wreck when you took it on and it would take years to put it right.'

'Rick did most of the hard graft,' said Vee. 'But I cleaned and scrubbed and decorated, so it's my work too. Let me show you your room.'

The stairs and banisters had now been painted white but a runner up the middle muffled their footsteps as they ascended. Vee opened the door into the guest bedroom that was now looking much more welcoming. An old brass bed took centre stage covered with another patchwork throw. This floor was sanded and stained but had a thick rug to warm the toes of anyone stepping out of bed on a cold morning. The walls were painted in a gentle shade of green and the only picture was a large black-and-white photograph in a gilt frame. Finn went straight over to it and looked intently at the figures grouped together. They stood on a grassy hill and had very solemn expressions.

'I found that one in the loft,' said Vee. 'The couple in the middle are my grandparents. They weren't miserable really. It was a serious business having your photo taken in those days. The others are my great-aunts. Now they *were* quite grumpy.'

Finn laughed, and the sound took Vee back to her childhood. He sounded just like Tallulah with her deep chuckle. 'You remind me of my mum,' she said.

Finn dumped his bag on the floor. 'That's cool. Come on, let's go downstairs. We need to talk before we go any further. This isn't as weird as I thought it was gonna be but it's still pretty strange. It's like I've been born all over again.'

'Yes, that's exactly how it feels to me too,' said Vee, leading the way back down to the living room. 'I don't suppose you want a cup of tea?'

He grimaced. 'I do *not*. Disgusting stuff. But you go ahead, I'll just have a water. Still, not sparkling. Unless... you might be making coffee?' he added hopefully.

Vee said that was perfectly possible. She went into the kitchen and put the kettle on, assembling a tray with mugs, a cafetiere and a plate of chocolate chip cookies which she'd bought to make him feel at home. They sat down together on the sofa and Vee wondered where to begin but Finn was already on the case. He went straight in for the kill.

'Right, before we go any further, I need to know why you

decided that it was a good idea to have a baby in the first place and more to the point, why you didn't want to bring me up yourself. I mean, you just gave me away like a parcel. Oh yeah, I get that you did it for your sister, and I guess that makes it a bit more okay, but even so... it stings, Mom. You must be able to see it from my point of view? And not only that, I also want you to explain why I wasn't told about you being my natural mother. I've said the same to the moms at home. They know... oh, boy, do they know... that I'm seriously unimpressed by all this but they haven't given me a satisfactory answer yet.'

Finn sat back and folded his arms, looking directly in front of him rather than at Vee. She bit her lip. 'Well, you don't mess about, do you?'

He shook his head. 'No point. Let's just get this out of the way, shall we? Then we can get on and eat cookies.'

The mention of the biscuits was less threatening than the first part of Finn's speech. Vee took heart.

'To cut a very long story short, I was in a strange place; at a crossroads in my life, I suppose you could say. My relationship had ended badly, I was thirty-five with no desire to find a new one, my sister was very much in love with the woman she'd met on a student exchange in America, and they were both longing for a child. Cassie was twenty-eight, still young but with a whole heap of medical problems that meant she'd never be able to conceive a baby of her own. Marissa had similar issues too. I wanted to help.'

'Yeah, that ties in with what they told me,' Finn said. 'But what I still don't get is how you could do it. Didn't you want to keep me... even a little bit?' His voice wavered on the last words and he suddenly sounded much younger than his twenty years.

Silence fell as Vee tried to think how to answer this question honestly. Eventually she cleared her throat. 'I did and I didn't,' she said. 'You've got to understand that it wasn't as if you were conceived in a relationship. The man who was the...' She paused, trying to think of a tactful way to put this.

'Sperm donor,' Finn said. 'Let's not make him anything but that.'

'Okay, the sperm donor. He was a friend of your parents, but he only did the job as a favour to them. He didn't want any involvement. He'd never wanted children, and he moved away soon after, with the proviso that he wasn't to be contacted again.'

'Yeah, that's also what they said. But you still haven't told me how *you* felt.'

Vee thought back to when the midwife had put her new baby in her arms. She'd been exhausted after a long and difficult labour but the sight of the tiny boy with his beautiful brown skin and big brown eyes had instantly melted her heart. In that moment, she had wanted desperately to keep him for herself. His fingers had closed around her thumb as she gazed down at him, wrapped in a snowy blanket provided by Cassie, who had learned to crochet just to produce her new son's first shawl.

'Yes, Finn,' Vee said huskily. 'I did want you. I wanted to keep you so badly that I didn't know how I was ever going to bear to give you up. But then Cassie and Marissa arrived, and I saw them fall in love with you the minute they held you. They were both crying, and so was I. Even the midwife had tears on her cheeks. She knew what I was about to do. I had to go through with it. I made a promise.'

'Have you regretted it? I really wanna know that.'

The question hung between them. It was time for the truth.

'Yes. Yes, I have. Many times. But a promise is a promise, and you've had a very happy life so far. I don't want to spoil it now by muddying the waters. I love you very much, Finn. I always will. But Cassie and Marissa are your parents, and they adore you.

They said they'd tell you about me one day, but I guess they were scared.'

'Of what?'

'Oh, that's simple. Scared you'd decide to come over here and make your life with me.'

'As if.'

The two short words pierced Vee's heart. Finn saw the look on her face and began to babble. 'I didn't... I mean, I... it's not that I wouldn't like it here... but... but...'

'I know what you meant. Your life's in Boston and that's how it should be,' Vee said, trying not to show the hurt inside. 'But you need to remember that you'll always have an extra home here with me, whenever you want to visit. It'll be different now, but we'll make a new kind of relationship, won't we?'

Vee waited, holding her breath. Had she got this right? There must be no pressure on her son to feel obliged to visit her. He reached out and took her hand.

'Sure we will,' he said. 'Now, why don't we get some good strong caffeine inside us and have a sugar rush. Hey, is that someone at the door?'

Vee got up to see who was there, wondering how quickly she could get rid of them, whoever it was. She opened the door and there stood Beryl on the step, smiling hopefully.

'I won't come in,' she said. 'I saw you get back and I don't want to get in the way while you're having your big reunion, but I'd like to invite you and your nephew to come around later. I've organised a fuddle at mine. I hope you haven't got other plans?'

Finn was now standing at Vee's side. He looked down at Beryl. 'What's a fuddle?' he asked. 'I bet I'll like it, whatever it is.'

'Oh, hello. Or should I say *hi*,' said Beryl, fluttering her eyelashes like a Victorian heroine. 'It's a party to welcome you to

England. We're having traditional British food. Winnie's even making a sherry trifle.'

'I don't know what that is, but I bet it's awesome.'

'See you later, Beryl,' said Vee. 'We'll bring a bottle.'

They watched Beryl go back into her own house. Finn turned to Vee. 'I should've asked you first before I accepted,' he said. 'But we can go, can't we... erm...'

'I think it's best if you just call me Vee. Drop the Aunty and forget Mom. There are two very important ladies who've earned that title, and I haven't done anything to deserve it,' said Vee, closing the front door. She made as if to go back to the sofa, but Finn put a hand on her arm to stop her.

'Wait up,' he said. 'That's not even a tiny bit true. Without you I wouldn't be here at all. It doesn't matter what I call you, though, does it? And we don't need to talk about it any more right now.'

'Fine by me,' said Vee.

The relief of getting this conversation over was intense and she was delighted when Finn yawned and rubbed his eyes, saying, 'I might have to take a nap if we're gonna be partying all night with the oldies. But after that...'

'After that, you'll see how Willowbrook paints the town red,' said Vee. 'Watch and learn, Finn. Watch and learn.'

39

Beryl had checked and rechecked her preparations for the guests and with nothing left to do, sat down with a loud 'ooof' in her comfiest chair. She'd just set aside half an hour to a complete rest and put her feet up on the tasselled velvet pouffe so loved by her late husband Eddie, when the doorbell rang.

'Who the heck is that?' she muttered as she hauled herself back into a standing position and headed for the hallway. 'Whoever it is, they're too blooming early. Or maybe it's one of those annoying men who are always wanting to clean out my guttering. Huh!'

She flung open the door, ready to give the person with the temerity to disturb her a piece of her mind, only to find Rick standing on the step, with a huge bunch of roses in one hand and a bottle of Prosecco in the other.

'I know I'm too early,' he said, as Beryl stepped aside to let him in. 'But I need to talk to you before all the others get here.'

'That sounds ominous,' said Beryl, leading the way into the living room. 'You'd better sit down. I'll put the Prosecco in the fridge, but what are the flowers in aid of? Not that I'm complaining,' she added. 'I hardly ever get a bouquet, and that one must have set you back a pretty penny.'

Rick handed both his gifts over but didn't answer immediately. He watched Beryl go through to the kitchen and deal with the bottle, putting the flowers in a jug of water on the windowsill.

'I'll find them a nice vase in a minute before the others come,' she said. 'If you want to say something in private, better hurry up, dear. You know how Winnie is for being bang on time for a party, and the rest won't be far behind her.'

Rick seemed suddenly lost for words. He perched on the edge of a chair and cleared his throat. 'I... erm... I...'

Beryl lost patience very quickly. 'Stop shilly-shallying and cut to the chase,' she said. 'You're worrying me now.'

'Right. Yes. Well, I wanted to talk to you about the past.'

'Any part of it in particular?' asked Beryl, checking her watch. 'The Tudors, maybe? Or the Romans? They were pretty interesting. I'm partial to a bit of Viking history, personally. All that pillaging... and so on.'

Rick smiled. 'Okay, I know I'm wasting your precious time. Nineteen eighty-five, to be precise. The year of all sorts of...' He paused.

'All sorts of trouble?' Beryl finished. She clutched the arms of her chair and faced him, swallowing hard. 'It's about my Patrick, isn't it?'

'Yes. I feel as if we've never mentioned him and we should. I do know what today is, and that's the reason for the flowers.'

'Patrick's birthday. How on earth did you know that?'

'Because it's mine next week,' said Rick. 'We used to go to the same birthday parties. Jelly, ice cream, cake. Mine was always the weekend after Patrick's. The flowers are because... well... I didn't get you any when he died. I should have. He was... one of us.'

Beryl felt her heart expanding. It was so good to hear her son's name. 'You liked him then?' she said slowly. 'I didn't think you and Patrick were particularly matey, Rick?'

'What I mean is, we shared a lot of memories,' Rick said. 'I know there was a lot of fuss about the fire, and I don't think we need to talk about that. As far as I'm concerned, it was just a joke that backfired. No harm was meant and nobody got the blame. It's in the past. But Vee and I were talking while we were away, and we both wanted you to know that we all cared about Patrick.'

'You did? Even Venetia? I always had the feeling that she mainly liked winding him up. He used to get upset. My Patrick was such a sensitive boy.'

Rick looked as if he was choosing his next words with care, and Beryl could hardly bear to listen. Was he going to say something terrible? She was going to have to live alongside Venetia in Fiddler's Row now, and Beryl found herself desperately wanting to think well both of her neighbour and to put to rest some very unpleasant memories of another member of the Prescott family. Their holiday together had been joyful and Vee had gone to a lot of trouble to make sure all the members of the party were well looked after and happy but there was still the other issue to deal with. Even now, Beryl couldn't think about Vee's father Ivan without a shudder, and she knew that eventually she ought to bring that subject out into the open. For now, though, this was all about Patrick.

'Vee was going through a weird time back in 1985,' said Rick. 'I think we all were. It wasn't much fun being a teenager, when I look back on that year. We were full of our own importance some of the time but totally lacking in confidence the rest of it. The school camping trip brought a lot of things to a head.'

Beryl wasn't at all clear where this was going. 'What are you trying to say?' she asked, watching the hands of the clock on the mantelpiece make their way much too quickly towards the moment when the other guests would descend on her.

Rick leaned across the small space dividing them and took both Beryl's hands in his. 'Just that we were all battling with our own demons and Patrick was no different. We might have done and said things that we regretted later but we were friends, and that will never change. Patrick was one of us and we miss him. I wish he was here to party with us, but we can still talk about him and remember the good times.'

Beryl squeezed Rick's hands. She was too full of emotion to speak. What a lovely gesture, to bring flowers and to take the time to make her muddled memories of Patrick's teenage years fall into a better, less painful shape.

'Anyway,' said Rick, letting go of Beryl and getting to his feet. 'That's the serious stuff out of the way. How about we open that bottle and have a toast to the future? Get the glasses and I'll open the fizz.'

Rick gave Beryl a hand to get up, which she was grateful for, because she suddenly felt rather shaky. Too much soul-searching was bad for the liver, as Winnie always said. 'A very good suggestion,' she said. 'And thank you, dear. I feel more peaceful about my boy, somehow. Oh, I know Patrick was no angel, I'm not totally blinkered.'

'None of us were angels,' said Rick. 'Let's not forget that. Teenagers are a law unto themselves. We'll drink to being safely over fifty, shall we?'

'A lot over fifty, in my case,' said Beryl, watching as Rick deftly popped the cork and poured chilled Prosecco into two champagne flutes. 'But still here and still ready to party.'

'Exactly.' Rick raised his glass. 'Here's to future fun and shenanigans. Age is no barrier to the Saga Louts and their friends. Cheers!'

Beryl raised her own glass in response and smiled at him fondly. She wondered what Rick had really wanted to say to her about Patrick. What had he left out, regarding his own and Venetia's opinion of her son? Best not to know, she told herself silently. Best to focus on the good times and remember Patrick with love. Anything else didn't bear thinking about.

The doorbell rang, mercifully putting an end to her pondering.

'Gird your loins,' Beryl said to Rick. 'It's showtime.'

40

At first, Vee thought she wasn't going to be able to enjoy Beryl's fuddle because she was so jittery about how everyone would react to Finn when he announced to them all that he was definitely not her nephew, as they'd previously thought. It was Finn's idea to lay their cards on the table. Vee hadn't understood why this was necessary, at least not yet, but her son was turning out to be one of the most straightforward characters she'd ever met.

Even as the first drinks were being distributed, Finn had made his way to a place in the room where everyone could see him and clapped his hands to get everyone's attention.

'Hey, guys,' he'd said, beaming around the room. 'We haven't been properly introduced, but I'm Finn Prescott-Barnes, and you may have heard of me as Vee's nephew. Well, it's a long story but she's actually my mom.'

There followed several loud gasps as everyone except Rick and Beryl digested this shocker. Vee's eyes were on her hostess. Beryl was clearly not surprised but she was smiling at Finn with the benevolence of one who fully approved of what he was saying. 'About time too,' Vee heard her murmur.

'So, this lady here, it turns out, is one of the most generous people you're likely to meet. She gave birth to me solely because her sister and her partner couldn't have a baby any other way. My two moms, Cassie and Marissa, have brought me up with all the kindness and love you can imagine, and I think they've done a swell job,' said Finn.

He did a twirl and a bow at this point, making everyone laugh. Vee felt as if her heart would burst with pride as she watched her son commanding the room. He had everyone eating out of his hand by now and began to briefly tell them about his life in the suburbs of Boston where he lived with Cassie and Marissa and was learning his trade, working alongside a carpenter who made much-sought-after furniture and the occasional wooden sculpture.

Vee opened her mouth to comment, but Finn held up a hand. 'I think Vee is going to tell you I got into a prestigious law school but dropped out?'

She nodded. 'That did take me by surprise at the time,' she admitted.

'I hated all that studying,' said Finn. 'I wanted to create beautiful things, not sit in a lecture theatre for hours hearing some boring dude in a suit drone on about dry-as-dust stuff. The moms weren't happy, but they came round when I made my first test piece. It was a bookcase for their study. Anyway, that's my story. Thought it was easier to tell it to you all at once. Looking forward to hearing all yours now. I'm gonna mingle, guys.'

After that, Vee didn't get chance to talk to Finn for quite a while. He was surrounded by all the others who were keen to chat endlessly about their own experiences of a variety of subjects, including woodwork (Sid and Frank), New England recipes (Winnie and Rick), current American fashion for men (Maurice and Beryl) and holiday destinations near Boston (Anthea). When

Sam arrived with Elsie, explaining that she'd had a party of her own to go to first, Finn was more than ready to sit on the floor and investigate the pack of cards she'd found in her goodie bag. He showed her how to play Strip-Jack-Naked, and she picked the rules up almost immediately. When the game palled, Finn began to regale Elsie with tales of all his visits to Disneyland over the years.

'You've been nine times? Really?' Elsie said breathlessly. 'Dad, when can we go? Could we visit Finn in America? I really want to see Disneyland.'

Vee was relaxing nearby at this point and was the only one to notice the sudden pause that followed Elsie's question. She looked up and caught the look that passed between Finn and Sam. It was over as soon as it began, but the moment was electric.

'Oh, you can come stay anytime you guys like,' said Finn. 'We've got spare bedrooms. We love guests.'

'Can we, Dad? Can we really go?'

Sam made a noncommittal reply and the moment passed, but Vee was watching him more closely now. When they were in the pub, he'd seemed dejected when he said his previous relationship was over. Now, Sam's eyes were shining as he helped Finn and Elsie to put the playing cards away, and Vee's newly honed motherly powers of observation noted the split second when Sam's hand brushed against Finn's and the two sprang apart as if, once again, electricity was involved.

So that was the lie of the land. She'd wondered why her sister had never reported Finn having more than a couple of dates with girls. Well, if Sam was going to strike up a relationship with someone from across the pond, he would have a lot to contend with. Vee realised that her mind had been foolishly thinking ahead to a closer relationship with her son, and then with his future wife, and possibly even with the babies they would produce. She let the vision slip away, replaced it with a somewhat different one, then inwardly berated herself for being so ridiculous. She'd witnessed a moment or two of intense attraction. It could come to nothing. But if it did develop... if Sam and Finn were to get together... Finn might even move to England.

'What are you thinking about?' Rick asked Vee, as he passed her chair and bent to top up her glass.

'Oh, nothing much. Just daydreaming,' she answered, blushing. How ridiculous to be acting like this. *But that's how regular mums sometimes think, I suppose,* a silent voice in her head said. *I'm starting to feel as if he's mine again after all these years. I mustn't let it happen. He'll be going home soon.*

The thought was depressing, and Vee forced herself to get up and go to the kitchen. It must be time to start helping Beryl to serve the puddings that she'd spied on the worktop earlier. But even as she passed round dishes and spoons, chatting on autopilot with the Saga Louts and the other guests, her gaze kept returning to where Finn and Sam were sitting on the sofa with Elsie between them. Finn was reading to Elsie from a book that Beryl had produced. With a pang, Vee realised that it must be an old one that had once belonged to Patrick. She hoped Rick had made time to speak to Beryl as he'd planned. The older woman certainly looked relaxed and cheerful as she listened to the story.

'This is a great book,' said Elsie, as Finn finished reading. 'Did you like it, Dad? The girls in it were a bit wet though, weren't they? They let the boys tell them what to do all the time. I don't do that, do I? I play football with the boys most break times and I'm always the captain.'

Sam didn't answer immediately, and Vee saw that he was having trouble focusing on his daughter's comments, having been watching Finn intently for the whole time he was reading. This hadn't gone unnoticed by her son, Vee observed. He was grinning at Sam over Elsie's head.

'Boys and girls are a bit different these days, I guess,' he told Elsie.

'Which do you like best, boys or girls?' Elsie asked, leaning on Finn as she leafed through the pages to get back to the beginning.

'That's a tricky one,' said Finn, his eyes still on Sam. 'I like you, Elsie, and you're a girl. And I like your dad, and he's definitely a boy. You're both very cool. So my view is that it doesn't matter whether you're one or the other, it's what kind of person you are that's the important bit. Same with the colour of your skin. We're all the same underneath.'

'We're not actually the same though, are we?' said Elsie, frowning. 'I mean, boys have willies and girls have—'

'I think we'll leave the biology lesson there, love,' said Sam. 'We've got the picture.'

Several of the others had stopped their conversations to listen in to the story and the following conversation. Frank was the first to comment.

'That's a very fine way of putting it, young man,' he said. 'I wish more people thought like you.'

'I couldn't agree more,' said Winnie. 'Girl or boy, black or white, rich or poor – we're all family if we want to be. And you lot are definitely my family now. Life's always better when you're with people you love.'

'Don't give Winnie any more Prosecco,' Beryl said rather gruffly. 'She sometimes gets soppy when she's had a few.'

'Cheeky mare,' said Winnie. 'I'm as sober as a... as a... well, anyway, I'm perfectly sober, thank you. I can't say the same for Anthea though. She's a bit squiffy, if you ask me. Oh, my goodness!'

This exclamation had been triggered by Anthea rummaging

in her handbag and then quickly putting on a pair of stylish diamanté-trimmed spectacles to have a look at the book Elsie was showing her. Anthea glanced up and grinned at them all. 'Well, I suppose you had to see them sometime. I had an eye test a couple of weeks ago and not only am I getting very short-sighted but apparently, I've got cataracts that need attention. So...'

'...so that's why you're not driving!' cried Beryl. 'We were all wondering. I must say you look the dog's b—' She glanced at Elsie. '...the dog's biscuits in them,' she finished.

'Thank you, Beryl. And for your information, Winnie, I'm not at all squiffy,' said Anthea. 'Mind you, I can't say the same for the rest of you.'

The party degenerated into a babble of good-natured arguments about who was and who wasn't squiffy, and Vee had just sat back in her chair to observe this entertaining spectacle when she realised that Rick was watching her intently. The look on his face was an unfamiliar one. It seemed like admiration mixed with a kind of puzzlement.

Vee raised her eyebrows at him in the hope that he'd explain the look. She was still trying to get her head around the fact that he'd liked her so much back in 1985, when she hadn't even known he existed, except as an unappealing person in the same year who didn't make any effort to talk to her group. Now, Rick had somehow morphed into the kind, generous man she'd come to rely on, but since the revelation about his version of what happened at the campsite and in the churchyard, they'd been avoiding any conversations that touched on those sensitive subjects.

'You've pulled it off, haven't you?' Rick said.

'Pulled what off?' Vee asked. 'I'm not a conjurer. I've not been doing tricks. What are you getting at?'

He smiled. 'I was paying you a compliment, actually. You've

already managed to integrate your son into Willowbrook society, or at least the part of it that matters to us, and I can see you've got a good relationship with him. The friendship must have been there before, but you've developed it really quickly without trying to smother him. It can't have been easy.'

'Thank you.' Vee wanted to say more but she was suddenly too emotional to think straight. She watched Finn and Sam organising a game of Consequences, asking Beryl for paper and pencils, sorting everyone out and explaining how the game worked to Elsie, who was hopping up and down on the spot.

'Those are two very good blokes, you know,' said Rick. 'You don't need to worry. Just let things happen. It'll either work out, or it won't. No harm done.'

'You saw it too,' said Vee. 'I thought it was just me.'

Rick shook his head but didn't expand on his previous advice. Vee let the soothing words sink into her mind as a strip of paper and a pencil was pushed into her hand by Elsie.

'It's a game about what happens,' Elsie explained. 'You write a boy's name and fold it over, then you pass it on.'

The little girl carried on with her commentary, but Vee was still watching Finn. He was making Beryl and Winnie laugh with a story about how Cassie had showed him how to play the game at one of their cocktail parties and he'd managed to work all the rude words he knew into it, thoroughly embarrassing Marissa in front of her very staid boss.

'Consequences,' she said to Rick. 'Everything we do has them.'

'But luckily, although it cost you a lot in heartache – yes, I know it did even though you haven't said as much to me – luckily, the results of what you did over twenty years ago are amazing.'

Vee didn't answer because, above the clamour, she'd just heard the doorbell. 'I'll get it,' she shouted to Beryl, when she saw that their hostess had heard it too. She wove her way through the group of friends who were settling down to write on their bits of paper. When she reached the door, she could see a shadowy figure through the frosted glass. She opened the door. There on the step stood a man of medium build, although he somehow gave the impression of strength. He was wearing a long black coat and a black fedora and had a short grey beard and moustache. Although his eyes were surrounded by fine wrinkles and laugh lines, they were the brightest blue Vee had ever seen.

'Hello,' the man said, politely doffing his hat. 'I know this is going to sound very peculiar for someone of my age, but my name's Benjamin Gale and I'm looking for my mother.'

41

TUESDAY, 6 JANUARY

Vee sat in front of glowing flames, toasting her toes and reflecting on what a brilliant investment the log burner had been. Finn had been determined there should be a real fire in Dragonfly Cottage, and the buying and installing of it was a very generous gift from Cassie and Marissa. In Vee's opinion, it was a present given in relief and gratitude that Finn was still living with them in Boston, although since his first visit to see Vee, he'd been in constant touch by email and the occasional long phone call.

'You must have known I'd never try to take your boy away from you,' Vee said, when she'd phoned to thank them for their generosity. Cassie hadn't given her a straight answer to that question, so Vee had to assume that her sister had been more than a little anxious when Finn had come back from his trip to Britain waxing lyrical about the cute village, the awesome people he'd met there and, of course, his amazing birth mother.

Christmas had been a subdued affair for Vee. Finn had elected to stay in Boston, whereas the Saga Louts, plus their trio of male attendants, had been in Tenerife, 'catching some winter rays', as Maurice put it. Rick decided he really should accept his ex's invitation to spend the festive period with his boys in Germany. Apparently, her latest relationship had gone pear-shaped, and she needed the support of the only man she could truly trust.

Vee seethed at this remark when Rick had reported it to her. 'Shame she didn't trust you enough to stay here then,' she said. Rick hadn't answered, and ever since he'd left, Vee had wished she'd never made that remark. Their friendship was still on slightly icy ground, it seemed. Neither of them wanted to discuss their joint past but equally, nor could they seem to move on without at least trying to clear the air. Matters hadn't been helped by Rick being offered a month's work in Cornwall, helping to make a friend's holiday cottage into a dream home by the sea. This had extended to an even longer period, in the nature of most such jobs. Rick had hardly been in Willowbrook since the day of Beryl's fuddle and Vee missed him more than she cared to admit. She was convinced that Stacey wanted to get her claws back into her ex and persuade him to relocate to Germany. The thought of this was unbelievably depressing.

Vee made her mind up when everyone departed for their various Christmases that she wouldn't let herself be gloomy but was nevertheless relieved to be invited to spend the day with Sam and Elsie. In the event, the two of them had come to Dragonfly Cottage early on Christmas morning and between them they'd created a day that suited them all.

'This has been brilliant,' Sam said as he persuaded Elsie that it was finally time to go home. 'I'm glad you talked us into having Christmas here instead of you spending the day at our flat, Vee. Having a roaring log fire's great at this time of year and Elsie's loved having a bit more space to play. Not to mention a TV that doesn't go on the blink every five minutes.'

'Yes, I promised you *The Grinch* was the best film ever, and I was right,' said Elsie. 'And I also told you that all that chocolate wouldn't make me sick. Actually, now I do feel a bit... um...'

'I think we'd better go,' said Sam hastily. 'Thanks so much, Vee. This was the best day ever. Keep me posted about what's going on with Benjamin Gale and the big reunion. Can't wait to find out how it all goes.'

Of course, even before Christmas had happened, easily the most dramatic event of recent times had been the arrival of Ben at Beryl's house. When Vee had brought him inside and given him a much-needed whisky, he'd told them all that he'd seen a small ad in the *Guardian*, asking if anyone knew the whereabouts of a baby boy who'd been adopted in the area of Meadowthorpe. It had given Ben's exact date of birth, and he knew he'd come from roughly that area.

'The timing was critical,' Ben said. 'My adoptive father died some time ago, but my mum only passed away last month. Until now I've had no desire to trace my birth mother because I was grateful for a good life, but the ad triggered something in me, and I couldn't get it out of my head.'

'But how did you end up at Beryl's house?' Vee asked, mystified. 'Yolanda – that's your real mum – never lived here and she was only next door at mine for part of her life.'

'Ah, now that was where I had a stroke of luck,' said Ben. 'Whoever it was who placed the appeal gave this address, so I came straight here before I could have a chance to talk myself out of it. So which one of you lovely ladies is my mother?'

'It's just like that film,' whispered Winnie. 'The one with Pierce Brosnan in it.'

'*GoldenEye*?' said Frank. 'I do love a good James Bond story.'

'No, not that one. The one with Julie Walters too.'

'*Educating Rita*?' suggested Anthea. 'An excellent movie.'

'No. *You* know; the Meryl Streep one.'

'*Kramer vs Kramer*?'

Vee's head was spinning by this time. 'I think Winnie means *Mamma Mia*,' she said. 'And I'm sorry to disappoint you, Ben, but your mother isn't any of the women here. Let me explain.'

It had taken a while for all the details to be revealed, but it finally transpired that Beryl was the one who'd contacted the *Guardian*. Tallulah had taken her neighbour into her confidence about the adoption of Yolanda's baby years ago, and once back from France, after having seen Yolanda and with her memory well and truly jogged, Beryl had decided to do her very best to get the estranged parties back together. If Finn and Vee could do it, so could Yolanda and her mystery son.

Vee got up from her comfortable fireside chair. It was time she had a final check around the house to make sure everything was ready for her visitors, because she was aiming to go out and leave Yolanda to her own devices as soon as she was settled. Vee planned to take Finn with her to the church this afternoon because today was the Feast of the Epiphany, a big moment in the church calendar, and Reverend Bev was insistent that her friends should help her to celebrate this important date in style with an extra midweek service and tea and cake afterwards.

At this very moment, Rick was at the airport collecting Yolanda, who had at last managed to organise enough neighbours to look after her hens and, of course, Ferdinand. Finn, who had requested a proper Christmas dinner during his visit, British-style, was arriving by taxi shortly too, having flown to a different airport. The plan was to provide the opportunity for Yolanda and Ben, who even now should be on his way to Willowbrook, to meet privately at Dragonfly Cottage while the rest of the group joined Rev Bev.

'But we wanted to see Yolanda and her son meet up,' protested Anthea, when Vee ran the plan past the Saga Louts. 'We haven't had this much action in Willowbrook for years. First young Finn and now not-so-young Benjamin. I must say, both of them are extremely handsome in their own right. Good job I'm taken.'

Maurice didn't look at all impressed by this train of thought but forbore to say anything. He was beginning to know his fiancée very well. 'I can't believe they've waited this long to meet,' he said. 'Ben and Yolanda, I mean. Why didn't they do this as soon as he turned up at Beryl's house?'

'Well, for one thing, Yolanda didn't have a passport so she couldn't just hop on a plane,' said Winnie. 'Simone's helped her to fill all the forms in and get herself sorted out to come over here, and then there was her brood of livestock to make provision for. Ben was intending to fly over to France in the meantime but then the poor soul got shingles and he's only just on the mend, apparently. Anyway, it's happening now, so fingers crossed it all goes well. Must be very strange to find your mother or son after so many years.'

Beryl opened her mouth as if to comment but apparently decided against it. Vee gave her a crafty hug when nobody was looking. To be able to see her son again was something her neighbour could only dream of. At least now she seemed to have reconciled herself to the fact that Patrick, though a troubled soul, should be remembered with love rather than vengeful thoughts about how he'd been treated by his peers. Those days were long gone, and it was time to focus on her son's happier moments. It was best that Beryl didn't know the full extent of Patrick's darker side. Sometimes ignorance really can be bliss.

As Vee waited for the new arrivals to land, she became more and more on edge. Finn's emails over December had been sparse, to say the least, and although they'd FaceTimed on Christmas Day, she'd felt as if there was something he wasn't telling her. And as for the Yolanda/Ben situation, the whole thing was going to be nerve-racking for them both. She heard a knock at the door and hurried to see if it was Finn or Yolanda, but there on the doorstep were Elsie and Sam.

'Hello, Vee,' said Elsie, flinging her arms around Vee's waist and hugging her tightly. 'We're just going along to the church because it's Piffinnee today. My teacher let me and Sophie and Cameron out five minutes early so we could get there on time cos we're carrying the magic men up to the front for Rev Bev.'

'Magic men?' Vee was bewildered. Her mind was full of her visitors, and she was puzzled to think that Bev was going to perform some sort of conjuring trick for them all.

'The Magi,' explained Sam. 'Elsie and her friends are going to take the statues of the Three Wise Men up to the altar. It's going to be a short service to celebrate the Epiphany on the actual day and then—'

'Cake!' shouted Elsie. 'Come on, Dad. We haven't got much time. We just came to see if we could borrow that fancy box you've got. Dad's going to be dressing up as a magic man and he's the one carrying the Frankenstein. He hasn't got anything to use for it.'

Vee remembered Elsie being enraptured by the *fancy box* as she explored the cottage on Christmas Day. It was a small casket Vee had inherited from her grandma. It contained a few pieces of costume jewellery and was studded with glass beads. In Elsie's eyes, it was a treasure chest, covered with dazzling gemstones that winked when they caught the light.

'Of course you can borrow it. It'll make a perfect container for the frankincense. You know where it is, don't you? Help yourself,' said Vee.

'I just looked up the word Epiphany to make sure Elsie knows what it means,' said Sam quietly, as his daughter rushed upstairs.

'The dictionary definition, apart from the Wise Men bit, is *a moment of great revelation or realisation.*'

Sam paused and Vee looked at him more closely. His cheeks were flushed and his eyes were very bright.

'I had one of those, just after Christmas Day,' he said. 'I'll tell you about it later. Oh, here she is, and she's found the box. Come on, sweetheart, we'll need to run. I'm going to have to fight Rick for the next-best Wise Man outfit from Bev's collection. Frank's already bagged the golden cloak. See you later, Vee.'

The two of them had gone before Vee had time to press Sam for more details. She stood at the door and watched them hurry away down Fiddler's Row. *A revelation or realisation,* eh? Hmmm.

42

Later, in the church hall, with the service over and the tea urn bubbling away merrily, Vee looked around at the assembled throng. It seemed incredible that only a short time ago she'd felt lost and vulnerable, adrift in this friendly place where everyone knew their neighbours and mostly liked them. Now, they were all familiar to her and she couldn't imagine living anywhere else, but there were still a few very important issues to address. She started with what seemed like the most straightforward, heading for Ben and Yolanda who had just arrived, all smiles and with Yolanda holding on to her son's arm with a proprietorial air.

'All okay?' she whispered, as Yolanda stopped to greet her niece.

'More than okay,' Yolanda replied, beaming. 'Benjamin is marvellous. We have so much to talk about, but I wanted to show him the village first. We're only staying for five minutes, and then we'll go for a tour. The turkey smells wonderful, and I saw you'd done all the preparation for dinner later, but I can help later when we get back, or failing that, do the washing up.'

Finn had joined them to hear the last part of this sentence. 'You mean we're really going to have a proper Christmas dinner?' he said, beaming. 'I can't believe you're doing all that again for me.'

'Mothers and sons,' said Yolanda, blinking away sudden tears. 'How many festive meals have we missed together? At least we can catch up on one of them tonight, thanks to Beryl, in my case.'

She waved to Beryl who was busy distributing cake to all and sundry. The other woman waved back, but appeared unsettled. She came over to stand by Vee and whispered in her ear, 'Could I have a word with you later? In private?'

'Of course. Is something wrong?' Vee felt a pang of alarm at the serious look on Beryl's usually cheerful face, but her neighbour only shook her head and carried on circulating with the cake.

As Yolanda and Ben moved away, Finn was joined by a tall, elegant lady and a rather gorgeous man. 'This is Ingrid and her partner, Joel,' Finn said. 'I don't think you've met them yet?'

'No, but I've heard a lot about you,' said Vee, shaking hands with the pair. 'You're the person behind the idea of exchanging treasures at the shop, aren't you, Ingrid?'

The other woman nodded. 'I am indeed. I loved having the shop and it's good that the swap's still going on, but I've come over to introduce you to Joel, really.'

Vee looked at her son, who was jigging from one foot to another. 'Joel's a carpenter,' he burst out, as soon as Ingrid had finished speaking. 'He's got a proposition for me. Tell her, Joel.'

The man, who was handsome, dark-haired and lean, and reminded Vee strongly of David Tennant in his *Doctor Who* era, said, 'I don't know if you've heard about the memorial benches on the country park, Vee, but I've designed and made most of them and I also produce bespoke furniture. To cut a long story short, thanks to Ingrid taking charge of my publicity – I was rubbish at that part, to be honest – the business has really taken off and I need to take on someone suitably qualified to share the load.'

There was a silence as all three gazed at Vee as if waiting for her to make some profound remark. She frowned. 'I... erm... that's great, but why are you telling me this?'

Finn took her by the shoulders. 'Because I'd already made the decision to try living on this side of the pond for a year and now Sam has put me in touch with Joel, and he's offered me a job. Isn't that fantastic?'

'*Sam* made this happen?' Vee's eyes searched the room and found that Sam was rooted to the spot, watching this conversation unfold.

'Yes, we've been emailing and speaking to each other whenever we could since I went back to Boston. After Christmas he realised... well, we both did, to be fair... that we might have a very good thing going if we were both in the same place for long enough to try. So here I am. Can I stay with you for a while... Mum?'

That last word finished Vee off completely, especially as he'd said it in the British way, and she began to cry, hugging first Finn and then Ingrid and Joel. Sam was by her side in no time for his own hug and the four of them stood together, unsure where to go from there.

'But what about Cassie and Marissa?' Vee said eventually. 'They'll be devastated.'

'No, they won't, they both said they'd seen this coming for a while,' said Finn. 'I've talked it through with them. They think it's a good opportunity for me to get experience in my trade. They're pretty sure I'll be back in Boston eventually, of course.'

He looked at Sam as he said this, and Vee smiled. 'Ah, the epiphany,' she said.

'Yes, and I'm not the only one who's had one of those,' Sam said, then stopped talking abruptly. His eyes slid over to where Rick was standing, arms folded, watching them all thoughtfully.

'Anyway, that's not for me to discuss. Why don't we all meet at the pub tomorrow night and celebrate my news?' Finn said. 'We can't do it tonight because there's turkey and what you Brits apparently call *all the trimmings* to eat later. I'm heading back to the cottage now. I'm in charge of roast potatoes. I've got my instructions.'

Ingrid said that a pub meeting sounded like an excellent plan and Vee left them to firm up their arrangements. Her mind was in turmoil with so many new developments to take in. Finn was coming to stay with her. They'd have time to really get to know each other, and not only that, it looked as if he was on the brink of a serious relationship with Sam. She'd heard from Cassie that Finn had only toyed with female flirtations as he grew older, but even now that the reason was clear she couldn't help worrying if her boy and Sam were heading for heartbreak if they let themselves get close and then decided they both wanted to live in different places, far apart. And there was Elsie to think about too. She should come first, whatever happened.

Telling herself sternly that there was no point in worrying and speculating at this point but not at all convinced that she could stick to this resolution, Vee turned to find Rick by her side, but remembered Beryl's words just as she was about to suggest that they made a move for home.

'There's something I need to do before we go,' Vee said, casting her eyes around the room to look for Beryl and finding that the older woman was already making her way towards her.

'Hopefully it won't take long, I'll be with you as soon as possible, okay?'

Vee took Beryl's arm as she reached her and they moved towards the kitchen, now empty of people but full of the debris from a successful party.

'Are you ready to tell me what the problem is?' Vee asked. 'You're worrying me. I thought you and me were on an even keel now?'

Beryl looked over her shoulder to check that nobody had followed them and closed the door between the kitchen and the church hall. 'I'll make it quick,' she said. 'There's something I need to get off my chest before I can... before *we* can be proper friends. It's about your father and the reason you all left Willowbrook so suddenly. It wasn't just because your folks were concerned about what new mischief you might get up to, was it? Or that he'd got a new job?'

Vee's stomach flipped. Where was this going? 'I... well...' she prevaricated, but Beryl was still talking.

'I think it was because Ivan... your dad... he wasn't safe around the ladies, and your mum wanted a fresh start for them. He could be very...'

'...inappropriate?' finished Vee, blinking away the tears that always threatened to fall when she let herself think about the way they'd left Willowbrook. 'Yes, he was, towards the time we left. I'm assuming he did something that offended you? Made a pass?'

Beryl nodded. Her cheeks were pink now and she was staring at the floor. 'Is that why you left?' she asked, huskily. 'For a long time I've just had the strangest feeling that I got it wrong somehow. He never seemed like that kind of man, in all the years I'd known your parents. I think I overreacted, but it was such a shock when he did what he did. In this very kitchen.'

'Yes, you got it wrong, Beryl, but you weren't to know,' said

Vee, swallowing hard. 'Dad had been showing all the signs of early-onset dementia and one of the things he did was to... to...'

'Come on to women? Try to touch them?' Beryl said. 'Oh, Vee, I'm so sorry. I should have trusted my instincts and spoken to your mum but I was just so horrified.'

'I wish you had,' said Vee. 'It might have helped Mum to deal with it. Anyway, we didn't leave because Dad had a new job. It was my mum that had been looking for work to support us all in a new place. Dad never worked again but we did eventually get a diagnosis and some help for him. It was a tough time.'

That was the understatement of the year, Vee thought, as she watched Beryl take in this new information. Watching her father deteriorate had been horrendous for them all but Tallulah had borne the brunt of the stress and it had eventually made her touchy and hard to live with. Now at last they were both at peace.

'It's okay, Beryl,' Vee said, reaching out to give her a hug. To begin with, Beryl felt rigid in her arms but after a moment she leaned in and put her arms around Vee's waist. They stood together until they heard voices approaching and broke apart just in time to look nonchalant as Winnie came in.

'What are you two doing in here?' she asked. 'My life, what a mess. I'm ready to start the washing up, but you should be on your way home, Vee. Young Rick is chomping at the bit out there.'

'Are you sure?' said Vee, but Winnie was giving her a little push towards the door to the hall and Beryl reached out again to kiss Vee on both cheeks.

'Off you go,' she said. 'If I had a handsome chap like that waiting for me, I'd not hang about.'

Still reeling after Beryl's revelation, Vee made her way to where Rick was standing, deep in conversation with Anthea. They both looked up and beamed when they saw her.

'Am I still invited for Christmas dinner, mark two?' Rick said hopefully. 'The German version was interesting, but I've been looking forward to this one so much more.'

'You are. Let's go, or we won't be eating until midnight,' said Vee.

They left the hall, after saying a quick goodbye to anyone within reach. The Saga Louts and their men were going to be following once the tidying up was done and would join Vee and her guests for a quick glass of fizz before dinner to toast Ben and Yolanda's reunion. Sam and Elsie were coming too. Vee and Rick walked in silence, their breath billowing out in clouds of mist in the chilly early-evening air. A strange kind of constraint had fallen upon them, and Vee was beginning to regret inviting Rick to eat at Dragonfly Cottage. It was a good job she'd asked Sam and Elsie to join them. That might make things less awkward.

'I've got something I want to tell you,' Rick said, as they reached home. 'It can wait though, I know Finn has... well, anyway, there's no rush.'

Vee, feeling as if she'd been told quite enough already tonight, was about to ask him what he was talking about when Finn came to meet them. He was wearing Vee's old apron; a flowered one of her mum's that had been locked away in the box room with a few other precious mementos.

'I'm glad you got here before the others. I need to give you something,' Finn said, taking Vee by the hand. He led her to the Christmas tree. Underneath it lay a large and beautifully wrapped parcel. 'I had to pay for extra luggage allowance to get this to England,' he said. 'But it's okay. I wanted to bring an extra case, as I'm staying.'

He reached down and picked up the parcel, presenting it to Vee with a flourish. 'For your new permanent home, and mine too. At least for now,' he added hastily when he saw her expression. 'I mean, I don't want to take advantage.'

'As if you ever could,' Vee said, taking the gift and tearing off the glossy paper. She gasped in delight when she saw what was inside, once she'd unwrapped the layers of bubble wrap and tissue paper. It was a beautiful wooden dragonfly, delicately carved. Underneath it was a sign, painted in subtle shades of green, blue and gold to match its wings.

'Dragonfly Cottage,' Vee read aloud. 'Oh, Finn, these are gorgeous. You made them for me? Thank you so, so much.'

Finn was pink in the face now as Vee kissed him on both cheeks. 'I loved doing them,' he said. 'And now Rick wants to talk to you about something else. Another present. I'm off to tend to my awesome potatoes.'

He made shooing motions to them, and Rick led the way to the back door. Vee followed, still stunned by the magnificent gift.

'Where are we going? It's freezing out there,' Vee protested as Rick headed down the garden. When they reached the bottom, he stopped.

'I had a quick chat to Finn before he went back to Boston last time,' he said. 'I told him that my dream was to build you a magnificent henhouse to replace your mum's old one.' He pointed to the wooden shed that was now leaning at a precarious angle. 'Finn said that he was intending to be here this year, at least for a while, so we're going to do it together and then I'll help you to find some chickens to live in it.'

Vee was so overwhelmed that she swayed slightly. Rick's arms went round her as if they were meant to be there.

'Why are you doing this?' she whispered. 'I thought you were getting back with Stacey and you'd be moving to Germany.'

'Are you kidding?' Rick leaned away to look Vee in the eye. 'Stacey already has another poor sod lined up to be her next husband and I couldn't be with her now if she was the last woman on earth.'

'You couldn't?'

'No, because I'm in love with someone else. I think I've loved this person since I was about fourteen years old, but she didn't notice me then, or if she did, she thought I was a complete prat. She's gorgeous; loving, caring and absolutely perfect. I've heard she even makes a banging Christmas dinner but the jury's out on that one at the moment. I'm going to tell her how amazing she is just as soon as I can stop myself burbling like a loon.'

Vee reached up a hand and placed it gently over his mouth until he was quiet. Then she put both arms around his neck and stood on tiptoe to kiss him.

For a while, there was no sound in the garden. The kiss that had been waiting to happen since 1985 took a long, long time. Eventually, they surfaced and clung together as if they were afraid to let go. In the distance, Vee could hear the sounds of a noisy crowd approaching down the road, but on reflection it was probably only Beryl and co.

'We'd better go inside,' she said. 'They'll get the wrong idea.'

'Or the right one,' said Rick, kissing her again.

When Rick and Vee finally made it into the cottage, they were greeted by cheers.

'What took you so long?' said Maurice. 'You young 'uns are very slow on the uptake. It's a good job some of us have a bit more go in us. You missed all the action. We've just been told that Beryl and Frank are engaged and Winnie and Sid are officially walking out.'

'Walking out where?' asked Finn. Beryl took him to one side to explain as Vee and Rick congratulated the other two couples.

'You might end up having a quadruple wedding at this rate,' said Finn, turning as Sam and Elsie came in, followed by Yolanda and Ben. 'Hey, guys, everyone's getting it together. I'm beginning to feel left out.'

Sam gave Finn a long, lingering look, as Vee held up a hand for silence.

'I just want to say that I have no intention of getting married, and neither has Rick,' she said firmly. Rick didn't comment, so Vee carried on. 'We're going to see how things go,' she said. 'I've only just moved back to this lovely place and my wonderful son has come to stay for what I'm hoping will be ages and ages. So, for now, let's just enjoy what's going on right at this moment. Having an epiphany's exhausting work.'

Ben had skirted around them into the kitchen and was now deftly removing the cork from the first of the bottles of champagne that Vee realised he must have brought with him earlier.

'Let's drink to that,' he said, as he filled the glasses already lined up on the table. 'A toast to *the good life*, and may we all continue to live it well.'

'Hold it one moment,' cried Beryl. 'I just want to say thank you to everyone for being such fantastic friends – and talking of weddings, let's add a toast to new beginnings, new partnerships and many more wonderful holidays. There's life in the old girls yet!'

Champagne flutes were raised, and the only sound was the fearsome shriek of the smoke alarm.

'My potatoes!' Finn cried, hurling himself towards the cooker, oven gloves in hand.

In the hubbub that followed, Rick turned to Vee. 'Did I mention that I love you?' he asked. 'But I'm hoping that in future, you let me take charge of the potatoes.'

Vee smiled at him. Suddenly, this new life of hers was looking very good. Very good indeed.

* * *

MORE FROM CELIA ANDERSON

Another feel-good story of fun and friendship from Celia
Anderson is available to order now here:
https://mybook.to/CeliaAnderson7

ACKNOWLEDGEMENTS

This was meant to be the fourth and final book in the Willowbrook series, but I already know it's going to be very hard to leave my characters behind so I'm sure we'll see at least some of them again soon. Huge thanks go to my fantastic editor Francesca Best for seeing the potential in the first one and encouraging me to carry on. Having the setting of Ferry Meadows Country Park near Peterborough firmly in my mind has provided a peaceful stimulus to create my imaginary village, although I've taken the liberty of altering the park and café a little to suit my stories. Recently, with my family, I revisited Ferry Meadows to see our own special memorial bench and was delighted to find that even more improvements had been made, although the Saga Louts still weren't to be seen in the café eating copious amounts of cake and scones.

Thanks also to the rest of the wonderful Boldwood team, copy editor Cecily Blench, proofreader Shirley Khan, cover designer Rachel Lawston, and to my amazing agent Laura Macdougall who always has my back. There are a few extra people to thank for this book – I spent a magical week in France on a writing course at Chez Castillon being inspired by Jo Thomas and the other writers there. We were royally entertained by our hosts Mickey and Janie with marvellous food and wine and sparkling company. After this, I moved on to stay with my good friends Jane and Tony, who continued the good work by giving me an extensive tour of the area around their home in The Lot, which generated the imaginary village where Yolanda and Simone live in the story. (The tree frog story was real though… honestly.) Also, credit goes to Jane and Tony's friend Debby in France who gave me lots of useful information about keeping chickens. This part of the story was also inspired by Matt and Lou Holman, who continue to successfully rescue many hens. It's my dream too, but I'm resisting because the foxes around my house would enjoy them even more than I would.

As always, I'm massively grateful to my lovely family, both in Brighton and in many other parts of the country. My cousin Matt Hancock in America took the time to advise me on what Finn's life growing up in the USA might have been like. New friends here and older (timewise, not agewise) friends from the Midlands never fail to be supportive, providing the love, the laughs and the incentive to keep going. And the grannying is my favourite thing ever. You're all brilliant!

ABOUT THE AUTHOR

Celia Anderson is a top ten bestselling author of women's fiction. She writes uplifting golden years fiction for Boldwood.

Download your exclusive bonus content from Celia Anderson here:

Follow Celia on social media:

facebook.com/CeliaAndersonAuthor
x.com/CeliaAnderson1
instagram.com/cejanderson
goodreads.com/CeliaAnderson

ALSO BY CELIA ANDERSON

Life Begins at 50!

A New Lease of Life

Dancing Under the Moon

Living the Good Life

Here Comes the Sun

Life in the Old Girls Yet

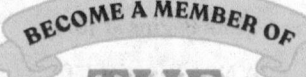

BECOME A MEMBER OF

THE SHELF CARE CLUB

The home of Boldwood's book club reads.

Find uplifting reads, sunny escapes, cosy romances, family dramas and more!

Sign up to the newsletter
https://bit.ly/theshelfcareclub